The Secret World
On The Other Side of Mind

Also by Sudhir Mittal

See You God

Life will Smile at You

Lead Like A Master

Invoking The Self

365 Gold Coins

The Life You Choose

Sud & Me

Life Again

Appetizers of The Secret World

Everyone has a parallel world which he doesn't know he has

Published by Sudhir Mittal
C/o Saraswati Book Depot, Near Marumal Sr. Sec. School,
Sadar Bazar, Gurgaon - 122001, India
smreadership@sudhirmittal.in
www.smreadership.com

THE SECRET WORLD ON THE OTHER SIDE OF MIND

Sudhir Mittal asserts the moral right to be identified as the author of this work.

ISBN: 9788192765099

Printed by CreateSpace, An Amazon.com Company
Available from Amazon.com, other online stores and book stores

Dedicated to my Gurus, ideals and fans

Introduction
of
The Secret World on the Other Side of Mind

Forget all that you know about your world; especially when the world was made round only to keep you wandering endlessly. Even though sometimes you might look racing up, but you end up merely in a loop. Without an exception, for winning the game of your apparent life in real sense, knowing its all secrets beforehand is indispensable.

Rubert, our protagonist, is a simple next door living guy. He doesn't see an iota of dark webs around his 'Apparent World', unless one day, he starts hearing some occult voices in his dreams. He gets intimidated by the voices which insist him to venture out and meet a white bearded master on the Himalayan peaks. The very following day he agrees to it, though in his dream only, lo! His employer happens to commission him on a new engineering project in the same mountains.

Midst the shivering cold, not many hours have passed after Rubert arrived in mountains, he encounters a strange old man in astounding circumstances. This chap turns out to be no ordinary man but the same advanced Himalayan mystic, who can perform any miracle of the world. He is such a master that he already knows Rubert's mind in entirety. After suspecting in the beginning, Rubert finally submits in and grows immense faith in his host. For four successive days the former visits the cave of master on the hilltop. During this time, master excites Rubert about the 'Secret World' and narrates to latter innumerable maxims, experiences, experiments, analogies and also the unheard before stories. Before the adieu, out of great love, the master bestows Rubert three things - (i) the capability of invoking a 'divine vision'; (ii) a miraculous wooden box which could produce enlightening text written on the green leaves; and (iii) the unfathomable knowledge of 'eternal truth' in the secret world.

Later on in the life of Rubert, everything keeps on happening strictly as per master's plan. After finishing the engineering project on mountains,

Rubert returns into his apparent world and continues living with his beautiful wife, cute daughter, loving mother, conspiring colleagues in his office and also a tyrant moody boss there. Although generally the life was supposed to be the same, but it is no longer that way for Rubert. Now he has got the mystical ability to watch out his 'Apparent world' and 'Secret world' both, that too simultaneously. Gradually he attains the capability of talking to and even seeing his master through the telepathy. Also through the miraculous wooden box which he possesses now, he can read his master's messages any time. And not only this, by way of invoking his divine vision, he enjoys another great advantage of watching eternal truth of the entire world around him. Given this all, his apparent world has never remained the same.

Running through the innumerable experiences, experiments and expounding by master, finally Rubert learns to conquer his 'Apparent World'. In his fulfillment, the mysterious mission of master also completes successfully.

'The Secret World.....' is lot more than a book for several reasons. Most figuratively it doesn't preach dogmas upon the reader; rather it sticks to the ground practicalities of modern life. This novel, which chiefly revolves around Rubert and Master, never imposes orthodoxy upon the readers. Sudhir Mittal's writing etiquette has never been in that way. After meeting master on the hills, when Rubert returns into his apparent world, the whole story takes a tantalizing turn. Written beautifully in 'Flashback' mode, this book puts up the intrinsic facets of householders' lives in superb clarity.

An important note at last! This book might reveal certain mystical experiments which the readers may tempt to try upon themselves, though it will be absolutely safe and easy for them. In this way, not only Rubert enjoys the 'Secret world', but you also do that greatly.

-Sudhir Mittal

Thanks

To the Divinity for making me an instrument behind this book. 'The Secret World' which the readers will find out in these pages, will light the lamp of bliss in the minds of millions.

To my family for tolerating a handsome corporate earner, now turned into a crazy moneyless author.

To young siblings Bhavya Bansal and Anshul Bansal for helping me in editing.

CONTENTS

RETURN

PART III - SEARCHING BOTH THE WORLDS IN ONE ANOTHER

PART IV - THE ELUCIDATING PILGRIMAGE CALLED LIFE

The Secret World
On The Other Side of Mind

PART I

TURNING BACK INTO THE APPARENT WORLD

ONE

Re-entering the Onrush

IT WAS SPECTACULAR, THOUGH slow and building. I had joined my apparent world's onrush again, that too in full bloom.

After those four miraculous days spent on the hilltop, I had been staying at the laboratory construction site for nearly two months now. In the position of chief designer amongst architects' team I was making out a terrific job here. After my employing company had won the tender of this prestigious state-owned project, I was playing a critical role in the construction of an astronomy laboratory. This enormous activity was taking place in the impassable mountainous regions. On the part of Government, to supervise the progress made under my spearhead, many directors and vice presidents were present. They had been immensely happy for the way the things were turning out one after another. Not long after the site had started taking shape.

I was leading the entire striving work force there in overcoming the obstacles of several kinds. In this course I had developed a nice rapport with all. Every evening after the work, we would all gather around the bonfire and share fun with each other. Such moments in hilly climates always become memorable. In the beginning our bonfire fun saw only few people, but shortly after, all site members joined in. One day while boiling corns on the fire, a couple of people began insisting me to sing. Finding me passing in shyness, even rest of the group joined the demand.

For the first time in life, I didn't feel as awkward about

singing. Though I knew I had only a duck's throat for that matter, yet I sang. I closed my eyes and focused on the tune alone. After I was done, people were generous in clapping more than I may have deserved. They never stopped asking me to sing in the following evenings as well. It began happening so, they would deliberately insist me to sing and soon after I would finish, they burst into laughter every time. Neither did I ever disappoint them by intentionally erring in the words or tunes. Sometimes occurred this also that I came first to laugh on myself. Though whenever I challenged others to sing the same tune any better, they would pretend laughing more but never sing at all.

It would be nearly forty people assembling around the bonfire every day. Here on the high altitudes each one was living far from his family and home. I could sense their bereavement. However a slight relief was that, we were developing an excellent companionship in each other. One day, while the construction work was going on full throttle, I suggested to my subordinate team leaders as to why shouldn't we all take our meals together?

One of the directors who was present on bonfire later in the evening, felt so excited for the idea that he went straight to his car and came back with a large pack of chocolates. Just when he was tearing the plastic wrappers irresistibly, he yelled in the air, "Voila! Here's the beginning." I can't forget the smiles on the faces of two watchmen who were also present there and were being bestowed with chocolates by their director. They were so humbled that they avoided matching eyes with the latter. Only next morning a local cook was hired and two tables were arranged in the backyard of our new kitchen. The first buffet was arranged. Nice delicacies were made and people relished those. Dinners and breakfasts also started taking place in the same way. Whenever anybody would ask whose wonderful idea it was, I felt slightly burdened with the honors. Actually it was the cook who was making wonderful food for all.

Around bonfire, the energy which all of us were creating every evening was showing up greatly in the day time. Here I realized one thing. When people are immensely happy, you can ask them doing the miracles and they will never fail you. Not only we were dining together but we were creating miracles on the site work as well. Soon progress of the project grew ahead of its schedule. The senior project coordinator was a lot astonished about it. Along with many others he also thought that it was I who was doing it. But only I knew that I was doing nothing as such. The great work was actually taking place because of the unity vesting in the happiness of all. Right from security guard to the senior director, everyone was just cheerful. And the one who did it all was basically out of question. After what I had seen and learnt in those four miraculous days on the hilltop, I knew it, the very moment I would have accepted the credit of doing magic on this project; I'd create many opponents. It was understandably better to refrain from taking credits and continue enjoying the happiness for whatever small piece of time we were to make together.

Godspeed, the first phase of our project completed successfully. Now it was the waiting time for the high range opticals which were to make the most important part of the gigantic telescopes on the top of this astronomy laboratory. One morning the project coordinator appeared with a breaking news that the needed optical glasses were still being manufactured in Russia, and were supposed to take two months more in getting delivered here. My own piece of work however, which was primarily related to the construction of site, had finished. It was now some other team of experts which was to take the reins from us.

For following two days I was busy in handing over the structure to the new team. Now I was free to return home. My bus passes towards Delhi and air tickets for Mumbai had been sent to me on email by my office people. With small luggage I had, I was ready to go away from this beautiful place and people.

My last day on the site was little emotional. The project director had brought a large box of sweet-cakes for me. I couldn't return him anything except a warm hug. Before finally leaving I made it a point to meet each and every member personally. I asked them to remain as happy as they had been during this matchless piece of time. They all obliged my request with moist eyes.

Quite a few people accompanied me to the small bus stop in the mountains. That local cook handed out me a small bag of rice pudding for my food in journey. Finally the bus started and I waved an adieu from the window. My friends sent their smiles along with me. I was humbled and grateful to them.

As the bus started moving down the hills I grew conscious of my master. I was leaving his place without knowing when I would be able to meet him again. This trip was unique only because of the master, for laboratory work was merely a pretext used by him for calling me to the hills. I thought about my four days of being at master's place. Instantly a wish grew in my mind to reach out there once again. But alas! He had already declared that he will leave that cave shortly after and move into the unknown higher altitudes. Sitting in the moving bus I looked out from my window. Indeed I had come far from this place. Now the crowded valleys were coming into my sight. In sweet reminiscences of my revered master I sat aloof. Then instantly, I rose from my seat and took out a smaller soft-bag out of my luggage. The miraculous 'wooden box' was inside it. I gently kept the bag on my lap and fished my fingers into it. I touched the mufflers and box for once and zipped-up the bag once again. During my stay on the laboratory site I had consciously protected it from others. As per master's advice, I had not discussed about the box and other things with anybody.

Now, instead of maneuvering on the swerved mountain tracks carefully, our bus was pacing up on the roads in plains. Still sitting aloof, I also began to wonder about the mantra which the master had given to me. All discourses which were made by him during those four days were still fresh in my memory. I hadn't missed even a single word spoken by him, for the reminiscence of his mystic smile had permanently fixed in my mind. Mile after mile I was approaching my apparent world, inside which I was to find out my secret world. Master had been repeatedly saying that the secret world existed nowhere else but only on the other side of my own mind. In order to reach there he had sufficiently armed me. This miraculous wooden box and the divine vision were part of the same only.

After the bus journey concluded in Delhi, I took a fight to my home – Mumbai. I already knew; the great astonishing life was waiting for me there.

And I was ready and awake.

TWO

Old Familiar World

ON FLIGHT TOWARDS MUMBAI, I was feeling drowsy. Since all mobile phones were switched off onboard, it was helping my secluded moments in a way. Peering through the window I saw a clear sky outside. Unlike my previous air travels, I was finding my view distinctively interesting. This time looking from above, the world was not looking chaotic, but it seemed only stilled. I noticed this small change in my outlook. I believed it was all because of my master.

On Mumbai airport my wife, Annie had come to pick me. In the lounge, while trawling my baggage, I saw her first. She was anxiously fidgeting to have a glimpse of me. I had no words to describe her joys when she saw me. While I was embarrassed about it in public, she was not ready to loosen her embrace at all.

In a second I submerged into her dancing eyes. Those had tears as well.

"You've grown fat", to change the topic I quipped on her. She fawned her eyes and saw me stern.

"No honey! I am just the same. But it's you who has changed", while still clasping my hands she retorted playfully.

"No, look again! My weight hasn't increased any", I didn't give in.

"I meant you have turned smarter than before", she rolled her eyes and charmed while pinching my hands harder.

"That's very right darling, but certainly you've become chubby in two months." I said in adamancy.

Now she gave in and dropped my hands. "But how does it

matter to you even if I've put on sixty pounds more? Shall we move now from here?"

I broke my laughter. As I began moving my luggage trawler, she offered her arm to pour into mine. Finding me hesitating, she flaunted her eye-lashes.

"You never feel shy", I whispered close to her ear.

"No! Never with you", she spoke rather loud. Here still finding me adamant to her offer, she finally crammed her arm into mine and started pulling me towards the parking area. I couldn't stop wondering about her deep love for me. While walking arm in arm on the floor, she pressed her temple into my shoulder.

"Oh! Annie I may fall!" I got scared. I knew her old mischief. I was struggling to draw my luggage trawler with only one hand.

"No you will not, I know", she said while clenching her teeth and pressing my arm harder.

I could smell the fragrance of her hair. "I love you sweetheart", I gave in.

For a second she stopped and looked about my face. I saw her pearl blue eyes when she said, "But not more than I do."

It would be seven in evening. In the parking area while approaching our car we two were alone. I saw her loving face again. I wanted to peck a kiss on her cheek but it was no good time and place. She always knew what ran in my head.

As we reached the car, I asked, "Shall I drive for you?"

She smiled and replied, "No, you must be very tired. Enjoy your beautiful lady chauffer today."

As she unlocked the car I started settling the luggage in the boot. She rushed in and helped me.

"Annie, give me that smaller bag. It has some delicate office stuff." I asked while trying to save that one soft-bag which had the wooden box inside it.

"How was your trip?" she asked while starting the car.

"Wonderful."

"That's your very typical answer I know, but anything special this time?" She asked.

Master's face came across my mind. I couldn't refrain from giving a sort of mystic smile.

For reversing the car she began looking into the rear view mirror. I could see that in past two months she had got lot better in maneuvering the car.

Before engaging a gear for moving ahead, she asked again, "You didn't tell what was special in your trip this time."

After a small pause I replied, "Yes a lot of special things have happened this time."

"Good, it always must be that", she said and turned a smile at me.

Now the car had picked up speed.

"Honey, fasten your belts ", she commanded.

I did.

After a silent moment I asked, "Didn't Maina come with you?"

"No, she was insisting but I asked her to wait for you at home. Only next week her term exams are falling due. Better she concentrate on her studies", she remarked.

"Sometimes, Annie, don't we push our seven years' child too much?"

While the car was talking to the winds, she quieted me very instantly, "Honey, are we going to have a fight over it again?"

I squirmed.

"Do not worry", Annie said, "she will be disciplined and have a happier life in this way."

I didn't say anything to the old sour subject. I reclined my seat a little more and stretched my legs.

"Shouldn't we change to a bigger car now?" To change the topic I asked her.

"But not before we've paid rest of the EMIs of this one. We must be careful about our finances, honey", she said.

"Hmm..." I sighed.

After a brief lull she asked, "What's there in this bag?"

Oh! It was just on my lap. "There are some important office papers and stuff", I lied.

"Why don't you put it on the back seat and sit more comfortably", she said.

I thought if the bag would remain in our talks for long, I could be in trouble. Immediately I turned back and put it gently on the rear seat.

Now our car was entering into the congested interior roads.

"So!" She asked again, "When are you supposed to join back the office?"

"Mark was glad with my performance. Yesterday itself he called me in the hills and advised to take rest for seven days before joining back."

"Wooow...! Is that really true?" Her mouth opened in awe. "Your boss Mark Dillasi doesn't generally get so nice on his people."

"Annie, it's Dallisi and not Dillasi", I interrupted.

She laughed, "It's the same thing."

I joined her laughter and said, "The very moment he will come to know how you have been toying with his name for past six years, he will fire me."

"Don't worry I will bring another job for you ", she laughed harder.

"But you already know it, I am no expert in cooking and mopping", I answered to her favorite taunt beforehand.

She didn't stop laughing and I looking at her face.

She touched my hand in love while braking at a red light.

I whispered, "You know Annie! You always move me."

She brought my hand to her mouth and kissed it.

Playfully I showed to her the red marks of her lipstick which had left on my hand.

She giggled and said, "And that is the proof."

Wondering what mother might say of it, I took out a cotton tissue and rubbed to make it disappear.

While the traffic signal turned green, she watched all this and said, "How come you are always more shy than me?"

"Because you always love me more than I do", I quipped.

"That's very very true", she jested and raced up the car.

Upon reaching our apartment as she knocked the door I began hiding behind the staircase. As my mother opened the door, seven years' Maina came out and started asking for her father curiously.

"Only in last minute, your papa decided to stay there for another month. He hasn't come with me Maina", Annie teased the child.

From behind I overheard my mother saying, "Why does he do that? What kind of his job is?"

"No grandma!" Maina interrupted at once, "Mama is fooling us. Do you want to see papa now?"

Probably my mother would be looking at her granddaughter animatingly. In no time Maina stomped behind the staircase and caught me there. At first she smiled looking at me but then turned stern.

"I won't talk to you", the sweet child said.

I rushed and swayed her in my arms. "Oh no my cute doll, don't do that. If you will not talk to me I will have to listen to alone your mom all the day."

"You never stop making fun of me. Shall we move in now?" Annie said.

I put Maina back on the floor and approached to touch the feet of my mother. She blessed and hugged me.

We all came inside when Maina started insisting me for a buggy ride on my back.

"Maina your father must be very tired now. Let him take rest", said Annie.

"But papa won't find time for us after his office starts", Maina replied.

I shared the good news, "Don't worry my baby. I will be at home for seven days now."

"That you did very good", said the mother.

Maina had already started dancing.

"Maina! Go to your grandma's room now and finish your work", Annie said.

Maina went in.

Annie rushed into kitchen to fetch me water and refreshments. Awhile this my mother continued talking to me. She was immensely happy about seeing his son after two months. When Annie had returned from the kitchen she put the tray on the table.

"Hmm... You've made my favorite delicacy, Annie", I said in joy of plate.

"Yes, but we love watching you eating more and speaking less", Annie said while smiling along with mother.

I laughed and busied myself with plate.

"Annie!" mother said, "Give me that basket of peas. Let me peel before those get stale."

"Yes Mother, I will also join you in that soon", said Annie as she hastened to pick the basket.

Here I picked some newspapers and went little deeper into the sofas.

Now Annie had started unpacking my luggage. Suddenly I became alert. Annie was just holding the smaller bag in her hands.

"Annie, I said it, inside this bag there are some important papers and stuff related to my office. Please keep it inside the bottom drawer of my study table. Please do remember to remind me of taking it back when I will join the office."

"Ok, I will", she said but put that bag over the table itself. Perhaps she was too busy.

She began unpacking my other larger bag. After a minute she stared at me frown.

"Where are your all mufflers?"

Perhaps I knew that she would ask about the three missing ones. "Oh! Aren't those all in the bag?" I pretended to be unaware.

"No, three mufflers are short!" She complained.

"May be I forgot somewhere", I lied.

"That you always do", she remarked to my old habit.

Sitting in sofas I pretended being engrossed in the newspapers.

"But hey! I think you've lost also the one which I gifted you on our first anniversary." Her voice was tinged in concern.

"Oops!" It just came out from my mouth.

By this time mother had gone to her room.

Annie stood in front of me expressing her sheer displeasure with me.

I looked up to her. I was blinking my eyes to make up for the error. At no cost I could tell her that it was right there in my smaller bag, which was resting over the table even to this moment. Had I, she would have certainly discovered the wooden box as well; and then I were to face her hundred questions. I remained silent. The smaller bag was still showing above the table. Escaping her line of gaze, I thought I must hide it inside the drawers as soon as she would move out of the room.

In no time I grasped a suitable opportunity and stashed the bag inside the bottom drawer of the study table.

Here Annie went busy in cooking our dinner. She asked what I wanted to eat. I preferred any light meals. She was surprised about my cold reaction. Maybe she was expecting me to ask for some spicy delicacy as per my usual habit.

"Would peas curry be fine?" she asked.

"Sure. But keep the spices low please."

"Are you alright Rube!" she touched my forehead.

"Yes I am perfect. I thought I must regulate my diet wisely", I replied.

"You look changed Rube", said Annie a bit seriously.

Looking straight into her eyes I changed the topic, "All for you honey."

She smiled and rushed into kitchen

Somehow, I was successful in settling down her curiosity.

THREE

But Where was My Secret World?

AFTER DINNER MAINA WENT to her grandmother's room for sleeping. Here finding me alone in the bedroom Annie tickled me in a playful mood. That night I came to know how desperate she was for me. And I also realized that more than her, it was me in that way under the quilt.

Soon after, while Annie was fast asleep, I couldn't help but remain awake. Instead of slumbering, a kind of dilemma had begun to take hold upon me. I began to wonder whether I had been trapped in my apparent world so much that the secret world would not occur to me at all. Annie's hand was still around my waist. The whole idea of being away from my master's presence for last two months had started baffling me.

Lying motionless in the bed I was now comparing between my two states of mind when I was spending four happening days with my master and thereafter up to now. After those miraculous meetings, the long period of two months at the construction site had given me a good hint of change which I visibly experienced in my socializing habits. But even as yet, I was away from the secret world. After I had returned home today, I feared as if I had returned to my old habits and temptations only. Once again, shockingly true as I believed, I was under the darkness of my warm quilts. Oh yes! It was the same 'darkness under the warm quilts' as was hinted by the master other day.

Gently I moved out my hand from the unaware clasp of Annie.

But, just as I was apprehending, Annie noticed it and said,

"Rube! Why don't you get sleep?"

"Hmm..." I sounded.

"Sleep now. It's quite late", she said in her drowsy voice and turned to the other side in the bed. In no time her faint snoring also resumed.

Here I had picked a quarrel with sleep. By passing of each day in my apparent world, had I started losing the edge of supreme knowledge discovered by me with the help of master? In past two months I haven't really had any dream about master. I hadn't approached my miraculous wooden box any time. I hadn't worked out the secret mantra and my division vision at all. I had made no serious contemplation about the 'eternal truth' either. Awhile this period nor had I meditated upon the knowledge of four illusions imparted by master. And here, alas once again! I was stuck in the darkness of 'warm quilts'.

A certain kind of guilt consciousness began to fill inside me. I didn't know how to comprehend my situation. I couldn't think about becoming an ascetic. Master had once said that it was not necessary at all. I wondered what could have he meant. In this moment I was raising fresh doubts to his admonition against my any possible wish for renunciation. If I were to remain a householder alone ever, wasn't I supposed to sleep in the darkness of warm quilts again and again? Will not Annie, Maina and mother, all drag me to the apparent world even more intensely every time? Now I knew why master had chosen to live amidst the solitudes of mountains. Perhaps he could live freer in this way; and maybe this was the reason that he had attained his metaphysical consciousness in the secret world. Without my master, I grieved, oh! How helpless I had been growing awhile this time.

I felt like getting up from the bed and check whether any new help had arrived for me in the wooden box. But I was afraid, lest Annie would become awake. Although she was fast asleep, but it was no wonder if she had later marveled my absence and caught me red handed with the wooden box. I had no choice but to stay in the bed.

In the faint light of night lamp I looked at Annie's face. She was entirely innocent of all this happening with me. It wasn't her mistake. Neither was it mine. In fact it was not a mistake at all. Then what was it? I delved into wonderments. Was it a privilege to have an inclination about secret world and eternal truth? Or was it merely a distinctive school of philosophy which was unsuitable for the householders like me?

Thankfully, not long after, the truthful realization occurred to me. It was actually the darkness under my quilts which was deluding my mind. I became cautious about it and recalled what the master had said to me. The memories of my initial talks made with him were still fresh. I had bluntly asked him, what if I do not heed him anyway. Why at all I was required to know about the secret world which he had been fancying me about for some time?"

Master's flat reply was printed on my mind. "That will be lamentable. You do not remember, but I do, that how many incarnations your sub-consciousness has taken to feel very this need. Don't you remember your recent mundane wonderings around your life and world? Don't you already see that, everywhere, the flocks of countless people have not yet felt this need? Perhaps, before they could, they will have to take many more incarnations again. In my view you must feel yourself rather privileged. However, if you find yourself adamantly unwilling, be at liberty to instantly ignore this opportunity once again."

No, I couldn't dare to ignore master's words. My eyes had witnessed the kind of freedom he had gained for himself. And he wanted me as well to attain the same. He said it didn't matter if my kind of path looked any different from the path of his kind. Our destination was only the same.

"Perhaps my kind of path can't help but start from the darkness of quilts only", Here I talked to myself in a pint of sarcasm.

I glanced upon Annie once again. She was partner of my life in the apparent world, though master had strangely said that the apparent world was nothing but merely a big collage of 'four illusions'. He had also remarked that it was alone the level of one's understanding about the secret world which scripted his or her way of happening in the apparent world. Given this, indeed, acquiring the sufficient good knowledge of secret world was necessary for me; else I was afraid that someday I would end up living amidst the fooling illusions only.

For a moment I broke my series of thoughts. I continued being in bed with closed eyes. A spirit of determination was growing inside me. It was alone the secret world which was important for my conquering over the apparent world. Master had repeatedly preached that secret world existed nowhere else but right within this apparent world; just that I was supposed to sincerely look about it on the other side of my mind.

In this moment, I desperately wanted to see on the other side. Moving out of the bed and reaching wooden box in the other room was certainly out of question. Annie would awake. Master had also strictly forbidden me from creating astonishment around the box, not even with Annie or mother. All his wisdom imparted to me was for my usage alone. He had stressed that every man's life was an individual journey, though it may look like living amongst many. Each of his words was fresh in my mentation. For my momentary helplessness, I felt baffled. But to my great luck, there was one more special advantage with me for seeing about the secret world. It was the divine vision to be invoked with the help of secret mantra which the master had given me on the hilltop.

Quite visibly, my erstwhile disconsolateness was giving way to the hope. While lying stilled in the bed, that too right here under the warm quilts, the entire turn of events began to picture back in my mind. This most startling episode of my life was merely two months old. The vivid images of my miraculous Himalayan journey had now begun to appear fresh in front of my eyes. In those days, master had passively started invading my thoughts. He was forming the background. He was preparing me for it. In the moments of starting my journey towards the mountains, all I knew in my apparent world was that, it was solely in relation to the laboratory construction project, which had been assigned to me by my company. Though I had been doubting my dreams from some time, but actually I was inadequately apprehensive about the upcoming turn of events. Lying awake in bed, now the entire Himalayan experience was picturing in front of my eyes.

FLASHBACK

PART II

GETTING DRAWN
INTO THE SECRET WORLD

FOUR

Mystical Pretext of the Big Journey

EARLIER TO THIS TIME, I had been to the foot of Himalayas only for twice. Both the tours, as expected, were accompanied by my family. Typical as it was for the vacationing spirit, all of us were desperate to absorb into our bodies, minds and souls the pseudo winters of the hills. On these two occasions, which were in Mussoorie and Nainital respectively, we witnessed countless tourists similar to us. I fear say sarcastically but I couldn't stop wondering about them and myself as well, that people never stop searching out for the adventurous ways of pleasing them; and also that, for most of the times they do it outside of their ordinary lives.

On both occasions it was invariably a family vacation; stretching a week or less. In the moments when our taxi would ascend the hills, everyone would look awed and happy. But on the contrary, when the tour was over, in the moments of descending towards the plains, we would look fatigued, perspiring and worn out. After returning to home, for many following weeks, again and again, we would watch our photography ventured in the hills; and in this way we would momentarily try to catch up the similar imaginary sensation as it was midst the actual hills then. We would all miss the winter-like climate. In the beginning I too had not been any different from others. It was however recently, that the very thought of Himalayas had started stirring my mind differently.

Onset of my third trip to Himalayas was unique and unprecedented. This time I was a loner. For the past few days, before setting out for journey, I had started anticipating very unusual things in my heart. I won't have wondered even if a miracle or two had taken place around me. Till that time I had no trace whether it was part of some divine plan, but other day in the office, my boss had summoned me to see him in his cabin. In next moment he was handing out to me the air tickets to Delhi and was advising about the road routes from there. In front of me he telephoned the accounts personnel and instructed them to provide me the necessary travel allowance beforehand. He elaborated that all this was being done for my newest assignment of supervising a new construction project of an astronomy laboratory. It was on the high altitudes of the Himalayan Mountains. This laboratory was supposed to be of national importance and its construction was sought after by the government ministry. It was for the first time that, ignoring my colleagues who had been aspiring for the same for some time, instead I had been chosen for such a prestigious project. I was supposed to be present amidst the chilling hills again; alone and without any familial presence this time.

On the threshold of December, even in the plains, severe winters had already made their way. After a flight from Mumbai to Delhi I travelled by road, reaching my destination, Ranikhet. Speaking geographically, Ranikhet is located at much higher altitudes than its nearest hill station - Nainital. Having reached this beautiful serene place, I intentionally checked into a smaller cottage this time. This spot was generously tranquil and surrounded by the picturesquely green hills all around.

And mentioning about my said inner strange anticipation, I admit that almost a day had passed here, but nothing unusual had happened around me.

The actual head-start of my official project was still a tentative matter. I was merely informed that it might start any day; but which day to be precise, it was still being worked out. My stay in the cottage was a nice chance to relax after the tiring journey.

Sick however I was to my persisting habit, I had carried

handful of books in my luggage. These books were supposed to fill my loneliness in the hills. In the moments of unpacking my luggage, almost in aloofness, I had chosen one particular book to start. It was about living in the company of Himalayan sages and seers. Though it was unusual to my general satirical preference in books, as I began reading it, the subject gripped me intensely. I did not know my first few hours with it. Steadily progressing in the read, I would often catch up the psychological sensation of being at thousands feet higher than I was already at. I felt as if some ineffable bliss was knocking at my spirit. I couldn't know whether it was because of this book or the mystic climate outside; or even completely because of those unknown divine voices in search of only which, as I was secretly once told, I had been called all the way over here.

Certain feelings in my heart, which were being constantly aroused by the book, were perhaps relating with my obfuscated purpose of being here. Even though I was desperate for hearing that divine voice again, but the book in my hands was acquiring my attention so busily, that I didn't mind the delay in voice's coming. I remembered that I had started calling this strange voice as 'divine voice' not only for my personal convenience but for two other reasons as well. Firstly, such a kind of affectionate sweet voice had never entered into my ears before. And secondly, I had never glimpsed the face of the man who was constantly telling me the mysterious words. As of this time I had experienced this mysterious voice only in my dreams. Almost every night, amidst dense sleeps, I would see a small cave somewhere in the hills and sitting outside this was a long bearded man. Every time in my dream visions it came about the time of dusk and a spectacular crimson sun would appear from the behind of this man's head. Perhaps, I had never seen such a beautiful sunset before. Or maybe, as I would always wonder later, things seen in the dreams were always more strange than those could be believed to be true. Nevertheless, the more I watched the sunset, the more reluctant I would grow to move my gaze elsewhere. Because of the darkness of dusk, and at the same time coupled with the momentarily flash in my eyes due to the crimson sun affront, I could never clearly see the face of this cave living man. Though, I was faintly able to figure out his smiling face in my direction.

And here in my outer physical world, I had been refraining to talk about my dream visions with anyone; not even with my dear ones in the family. My notion of maintaining secrecy was not without reasons, but actually, that divine voice had once forbidden me doing so. One night it said,

"May be it makes you wistful for a moment, but you must know that your life is alone your individual journey. No one else will ever be more interested in your journey than in the journey of his or her own. But remember yet, all these different individual journeys are invariably travelled by men together, for those are always interlinked. On one hand when you must not appear apathetic towards others' intersecting paths, on the other, you must also remain highly awake and ready for your own individual journey."

Another night, when I had just retired to bed with a heavy head over my myriad worldly perplexities, the same voice began asking,

"For how long will you be playing your part in the world so unskillfully? Must not you learn, at soonest, your finer competencies and then upon conquer this tricky sport of your worldly existence? When will you agree to this need?"

While still in the dreams, out of curiosity, whenever I asked more about him, his reply was ever the same,

"I will answer you only at my place. Under your warm quilt here, it's so much dark of the world."

Once I asked him that should I ignore his voice and such of my dream-visions. To this he felt compelled to reply. He said,

"Oh! It will be sad if you do so. You do not know but only I am apprised that how many incarnations, one after another, you have taken for becoming able to hear my voice. If you ignore it again, unknowingly, you will happen to choose waiting for it again. I will not force upon you. Feel yourself at liberty to not heed me anymore. The very moment you'll resolvedly say that you don't need me, I promise, I will not invade your visions again."

To his blunt offer, I couldn't dare say 'no'. I didn't know what was in store for me. But more than creating anxiety, my visions were wrapping around me an unknown old thread in assurance of my protection and supreme beneficence.

At one occasion, when I asked him, will people call me insane when they come to know about all this? He replied,

"But why at all do you need to demonstrate your ever existing divinity amongst the people? Remember that, to enjoy your worldly life, you are supposed to bring enjoyment to others; but to enjoy your inner entity which is much higher than your worldly life, you need literally nothing, not even the attention of people around you."

Whatever he spoke, was of mystical relevance. Sometimes finding him answering a question or two of mine, I assumed that I was perhaps able to make a sway on him. I would try asking him more, but he would sense my trick and forbid at once,

"Not at this place my son! It will be difficult for you to believe, if I reveal all in your visions alone."

And one night, in midway through a similar dream vision, when I was completely absorbed in the beauty of crimson sun shining from the behind of this man's head, he said,

"Why don't you come here yourself and see? Must not you start appreciating more the beauty seen in your real world than the beauty seen in your dream world?"

I said it; every word of his was of mystical relevance.
I was prompted in asking him, "Where exactly need I come?"
He surprised me by replying,

"Oh! If you are keen, soon it will be arranged."

And very next day in my boss' cabin when I was being handed over the boarding tickets and travel allowance money, I was secretly noticing the way in which the entire mysterious plan had started unfolding for me.

FIVE

Hearing Callouts from the Hilltop

AFTER CHECKING-IN THE cottage in morning, it was around four o'clock of evening now. I had forgotten to even bother for my lunch when I noticed that I had already finished more than a quarter part of the book. There are always the kinds of books which become so much talkative that they never let you drift away. In my case, I had just found one. Hitherto in life, I would generally keep my vanity satiated only in the awestruck expressions of people, when they came to know about the vast variety of books I could read. Always sunk in the motley of melodramas, thrillers, biographies, eroticism and many more, perhaps, I never saw what I had needed the most. This small ordinary cottage here, being very serene and secluded on the hill, was probably the best place where I could have found my 'most needed' genre in the books. In these secluded moments, it was nothing else but my own very self which was being reflected in big ways through this book. Reading page after page, as I was being introduced to my own self, I had not remembered my stomach for hours.

Shortly after, I moved out of the cottage. I felt it was necessary to take meals, whether or not the hunger panged as such. The nearest food place was at some distance, straight downhill from where my cottage was. As I locked the door from outside and turned around for walking down the footway, all of a sudden, I heard somebody saying, as if I was being called out.

"Rather why don't you climb uphill first and see how beautiful sun

is looking from here!"

Oh! Wasn't it the same affectionate voice talking to me in my dreams? Head whirling, but I sincerely felt as if the voice had come merely a couple of yards from me. I circled on my heel and looked around in daze, but saw no one. Thinking that it could possibly be some kind of hallucination caused by my past few hours of fasting, I started for the food once again.

I couldn't however stop being skeptical.

Unless I had returned to cottage after food, I didn't hear the voice again. One surprising difference, which I had newly noticed in myself after reading the book, was the kind of food that I had ordered today. Contrary to my usual habit of gorging up the hot spicy food, today I had taken only a simple plate. I didn't overeat either.

"O my dear son! After you've filled, climb upside here. Along with sun, I've been waiting for you."

All of a sudden, the same affectionate voice echoed again.

Unlike before, when I was hungry, this time I saw no possibility of hallucination. I turned around but the problem was same. I was trying to look in all possible directions.

I wondered why I was still not able to judge the particular direction from which the mysterious voice was coming. Generally I had known myself as quite an expert in judging the sounds. In this stupefying moment, although I was sure that the voice was coming from near about itself, but the continued invisibility of the speaker was dumbfounding me. I couldn't either guess the exact distance of the voice from me, for every time I was feeling it so close to my body.

Nevertheless, this riddle must not have remained unresolved. I began to look in my front more seriously now. It was the same cottage; but as I was particularly able to ascertain this time, there was perhaps something behind it; something which had skipped my attention since morning.

To confirm my ideas I had to fling across the barbs fence in the backdrop of the cottage. Yes, indeed there was something to be noted. It was a narrow footway going somewhere upwards in the hill. I didn't find it much wondering, for often around the hill-stations like here, one would see the similar tapering footways everywhere.

The voice had also stopped coming now. However feeling reluctant about reading the book further inside cottage, I found it better to venture about going up. Ambling in the Himalayan country always spells so magical on you, that you cannot contain the excitement of finding something more spectacular from your next spot. Even more suitable to my personal occasion, I also thought that a little uphill walk would help me digesting whatever little I had eaten.

Merrily, I started.

Besides being narrow, this steep ascending footway was undulated too. Especially when I couldn't foresee an easy end to my ordeal of climbing, it came upon me a lot more physical exercise. Nevertheless, the sight-scenes all around were keeping me entertained. On the way there were many twirls which I was not perfectly accustomed to walk on. Still I continued going up in the spree.

At last I reached the top, but quite stunned by what had come ahead of my sight.

Oh! Was I still in a dream?

"No, It's no dream", I remonstrated myself at once, "I am not such a fool who climbed an entire mountain merely in a dream."

I looked on to my amazement. Indeed, far atop here, it was the same humble crimson sun of the dusk. For the countless times in my dreams I had seen the same earlier. In reality from the high altitudes, it was looking just as indescribably beautiful. Floating in the wide horizon, the sun was preparing to pay a visit to the other side of the world as well. I checked more carefully, whether the sun, as looked from here, was any better than I had seen in my dreams. I couldn't make out a difference. This time too, I was growing as spellbound for the sight.

"Come close my son! This old man could be poor at his human eye-sight."

Oh Yes! The voice was again the same. I could clearly make it out. It was affectionate and sweet as ever.

I was compelled to drift my gaze down from the sun. As I looked far ahead, I traced the very same which I had been apprehending. Indeed there was a small cave-hole! Finding all this, as if insufficient yet, my eyes were still searching for the man who could be sitting outside the cave, well possibly.

And what a strange day down the heavens! All my guesses were coming true one after other. For the ground was not evenly plain here, I needed to go and check more about it. In the direction of cave-hole, as I advanced towards, lo! I had found the man as well.

"Welcome dear son", the man, who was sitting on a fairly large altar made of stones, said loud. As I looked on skeptically, I noticed that he was picturesquely smiling in my direction.

"Mmm..." Skewing my eyes, I grumbled. He was looking very old. Recounting my all acquaintances I tried matching his face, but no, I had not met or known this man before.

I came closer, but still maintained at least some distance from the strange old man.

"Say, how greatly you've enjoyed your alone individual journey up to this hill?" He asked while stressing upon the words - 'alone individual journey'.

Oh! *Alone individual journey!* He had repeated the same words of my dream visions. But I still couldn't stop being skeptical.

Finding me deliberately maintaining the distance, his spoke again, "You must be careful about using your time, son. See! For human beings, time often falls short. Nonetheless soon, your astronomy laboratory work will start. You must be diligent about the time you have before that."

Oh! Quite astonishing were his remarks! But even to this

moment, my fear of something unprecedented didn't allow me sparking any trust in him. In past I have had heard many stories about the strange 'Babas' (such as a white beard old men as here) who would easily read out what ran in people's minds in front of them.

Seeing me not melting yet, he spoke, "So finally you've walked all the way here in the curiosity of what I refused to answer in the darkness of your warm quilts. Ha ha ha ha..." He japed me like a child. While laughing, his eyes were examining my dumbness.

I just gave in now. I was left with no reason to disbelieve what was in front of my eyes. I looked in all directions once again. Indeed, it was the same sunset, same cave-hole and the same old man. Reminding myself of his continued promises which he had been making for my beneficence, I started growing confidence in him.

I came closer. This was the first moment when I saw his face clearly; the same face, which in the darkness of my dreams had remained so far only incomprehensible to me.

How radiant! He looked bright complexioned, with a long white beard, large matted manes on his head, and wearing alone a loincloth which was starkly unsuitable to the climate. Cross legged, he was sitting on a ragged blanket folded into many. He was smiling towards me, as if he had known me since very long.

But even to this moment, I was feeling more astonished than growing any reverent towards him.

My Cold Response to the Welcome

"SON! DO YOU FIND the way I look astonishing?"

This was the first question about his looks that he shot at my face. I didn't answer fearing how he might comprehend my unprepared response.

"Don't miss to sift my appearance." He japed and continued, "This is how the human body naturally grows when one keeps away from sundry cosmetic procedures of the world. Ha ha ha ha...! Since long I have stopped wondering about my looks. It's after all no use, you see."

With my hands still folded under the armpits, I stood dazzled.

"Son, why do you look dumbfounded? Is it because how dark are your impressions of the outwardly world, that you don't recognize me?"

As he remarked this, I tried figuring his face more carefully once again, but still, I was not able to relate it with any of my acquaintances so far. I had reasons to look dumbfounded, if I did.

"Ok!" asserted the old man again, "whether or not you show any kindness upon me today, but at least you must not miss out beholding the beauty of crimson sun there. After all, it won't come again in this day. Just look above and forget everything else in this precious short moment."

I craned my gaze in the west, as if I was too obedient of his command. That sight was really majestic.

Not a moment had passed, but sick as I was to my habit, I started arguing within myself. I wondered that the sun was looking amazing from here only because of the high altitudes of hills. In metropolis cities one can never see the same. Did I ever? My argumentative pondering didn't stop here yet. Very next moment another question struck me, "But living in a big city all these years, have I ever tried to see the evening sun as carefully?" On this very thought, a peculiar embarrassment shook me off.

Keeping my blush aside, I looked on again. I wanted to drench in the beauty. The sun was surrounded by the skimmed clouds and the entire horizon was colored only suitable to its taste. I had seldom seen a horizon in this way. I forgot, as lost I was, the old man, his cave, my downhill cottage and my unfinished book as well. And what to mention of the astronomy laboratory construction at all! After hearing about the delay in the commencement of work, it had already stopped grappling my attention since morning. Standing aloof, here on the hilltop, I was not minding to score as to for how long I had been like a statue. Although outwardly I was still hiding my hands under my armpits; but inwardly I had started surrendering to the mysterious man in my front.

In some time, the old man's sweet voice came again. "Son! Return to your cottage now! See, the darkness of the chilling night has started to spread. I would have loved your staying here but you are not yet accustomed to do without quilts. Return now and come back tomorrow once again. Come in the morning."

Hearing this, for a moment I felt as if I should release my hands from armpits and join palms in the grace of old man. But somehow, I couldn't stop being aloof and hesitating. Or maybe even to this moment I was thinking all this to be a dream and nothing else. Reading my quandary once again, the old man flashed a smile, and lo, to my utmost surprise, he had just joined his own palms in grace of mine. It turned upon me an awkward moment. Abruptly I reciprocated the gesture and bowed as well to him. He smiled wider and motioned his hands about my departure.

In mix of adamancy and reverence, I came down to my

cottage. Though in course of my descending down the hill, I was particularly careful about memorizing some way-marks and trees, which could be useful for my journey on the following day.

Before retiring to bed in the cottage, I replied to a few phone messages which had come from office and home.

SEVEN

Conquering My Reluctance

MY FOLLOWING NIGHT INSIDE the cottage started with anxiety. I was undoubtedly sure to visit the old man next morning. Merely half an hour before going to bed, somebody called on my phone and informed that the astronomy laboratory work might take a couple of days more to start. He added that I will be kept informed about the next status.

That book was still on my bedside, but there on the hilltop I had found things much more interesting. I began wondering about the coming day. I thought to open up in front of the old man. Why had he been telling me the strange things? What did he want from me? Was he trying to hypnotize? What had forced him to stay in the woods? What was his name and where did he belong to? Floating in my myriad psychological turbulences, I couldn't know when the sleep took on me. That night, I admit, no vision occurred to me. Perhaps neither it was needed. The splendid destination of my usual dreams was itself within my physical reach now.

Next morning, having nothing special to do in the cottage for the day, I was ready for the climb. Although the old man hadn't advised me the exact time of reaching him in the morning, I had started readying up since the dawn. After bath, and followed by a light breakfast, the first thing I did was to start my ascending on the hill.

Today, the climb-way seemed shorter than my yesterday's experience. I noted one more thing about my ascent. This footway had rarely been travelled. The moss was freshly green under my feet. I thought of saving it from my trampling, but there was no escape. Wondering about the killing of little lives under my feet, I moved on.

I reached the place. The old man was sitting on the same altar, in same posture and bearing the same mystic smile.

He had already laid down another blanket aside to his own. As he saw me coming, he came off the altar and hailed my grace. Abruptly, I also joined my palms and greeted him in the same way. Quite a broad smile, and perhaps freer too than that of yesterday, came across my face. He gently asked me to sit near him. I followed him and settled on the blanket.

"Son! Let us sit in silence for few moments and calm down our minds. Silence is the great stimuli for one's divine instincts. It also broadens the wings of the mind."

His voice was humbled as ever. Though I had many questions to ask, but gradually, as silently I wondered, all those were growing less important in his magical presence.

I tried following his command but didn't know in what posture I was supposed to sit or behave. Seeing me in quandary, he waved his hand and gestured, so as to ask me sitting comfortably in any which way.

I waited but sitting quiet like this didn't seem helping much. I had many things to ask and know from this man. True, he was powerful in mysterious ways, but what did he want from me? Here on this hilltop, had I already started falling in some kind of superstitious trap even outside the knowledge of my kin and kith? Was I safe? Why had this man been invading my mind? How doing so could become possible for him? How could he read any small or big thought of mine?

I continued sitting in silence but my mind couldn't become like one. I pointed my gaze to the face of old man. Unlike me, keeping his eyes closed he was absolutely free from the worries. He sat like a pillar, straight and unmoved. A faint smile would never go away from his face.

In some time, as I waited on, he broke his silence and spoke to me in unbroken posture, "There is no greater penance than observing silence for reclaiming one's hidden supremacy of mind. It's alone the functioning of mind which matters to both, the ones who live in world, and those who live in the caves."

I listened but couldn't add a word to his already wise assertion.

After another silent spell, his smile grew wider. With his gaze fixed on the horizon he began saying, "O see! How astonishing this all is. It's alone the mind and nothing else. Even this whole creation is all about mind. Never stop being grateful to the kindness of God, Who has bestowed each of us with such a powerful instrument."

It started occurring on me that his imaginations and thoughts were very different from the ordinary. Though getting moved, I had remained only silent.

EIGHT

Taking Aims upon Secret World

"SCRIPTURES SUGGEST THAT ALONE through the power of mind, the supreme force Almighty creates the entire universe. And only through that power, He also operates and annihilates the same", said the old man without moving his posture even little.

"However the other sublime secret", he added, "which scriptures do not reveal as expressively, is the fact that the potency of the mind is ever the same with all; be it of God or be it man's."

His words were creating great curiosity in my mind. Given the entire backdrop and context of myself being here, I was sure that this all was not without purpose. Infact, irrespective of how greatly I've understood the said things so far, very this purpose seemed sublime to me. Amidst my several inner wonderings, here I spoke my first ever words to him. I asked about my apprehension, "But, if the mind is same with all, why can't we perform such astonishing feats as does the God?"

"See!" making the talk interesting, old man replied, "This is the big point here. For so long as the man believes that performing such feats shall be up to the purpose of creating astonishments alone, they do not become able to do so. The very temptation of stirring astonishment unfailingly bears a sickly attribute to it. It dethrones even the true genuine miracles, as if those were merely the magical tricks. You see, even though you enjoy watching a magical show, you never believe it to be true or any substantial. The very moment you discover something to be magic and nothing more, the chasm of faith in your mind vanishes. And a mind, which is deprived of faith, instantly loses its all kinds of subtle powers and potencies."

One thing was sure - I was not wasting my time here. Although his assertions were esoteric, but if I was hearing with attention, I could really grasp those. I also realized that my faith was increasing in this man.

He looked about to check my face. Finding me keen and attentive he continued, "Having sincere faith in the subtle powers of mind, and to the contrary, fostering the temptations for creating astonishments, are two things which are poles-apart. Magicians, however big feats they may perform, yet remain insignificant. Neither their audience nor even they themselves keep any persisting faith in whatsoever act they perform. Son, understand this matter clearly. Without faith, any experience such as of magical tricks, will remain only momentary. These kinds of experiences always change. And also remember that whatever in this universe remains subject to change, does not amount to the eternal truth."

Oh! This was my first time to hear about 'Eternal Truth' from him. As of this moment, I had no idea at all as to what strong relevance this term was to play in my forthcoming life.

Lost in multitude thoughts, the old man turned silent. He was now absent-gazed. In a moment he looked in my eyes and asked,

"Do you want me to unfold the great mysteries of this creation, which you are also a part of?"

"Very much", I nodded.

"Creation starts from man's perception. Man's perception cannot take place without his mind. And his mind cannot exist without a human body. However overrun by this linked chain, man limits his understanding of creation only up to his understanding of the body."

I said it; I was not wasting time here.

He continued, "But actually it's not the human body or mind

which sustains and nourishes the whole creation, albeit it's the higher one - The Eternal Truth. Man's bodily existence, for instance, which man generally gives so much importance to, is not run alone by the five elements of nature, namely as - Earth, Water, Fire, Air and Ether. Had it been true, no human being would have ever died, because a dead body still contains all the five. Isn't it?"

I asked, "But doesn't a human body disintegrate after dying?"

"Deformation of a dead body", he replied, "takes place because of the *non-circulation* of five elements, and not because of the absence of those."

I was amazed. I said it. The matter was getting intense and interesting; and being in the company of this mysterious man was already a useful opportunity.

He continued, "More than the body, it's certainly something else which causes human beings to function in the creation. Shouldn't one be keen to know more about it?"

Although I was completely engrossed in his talk, I asked, "But why a simple person like me needs to know all this?"

Hearing this, a typical smile came across his face. He said, "Knowledge of eternal truth is indispensable. This knowledge is essential for the entire human race. Without this, they will live only unskillfully; life after life."

"But what if they don't concede at all that they are living unskillfully?" I asked again.

"If not now, it's later that they will realize", he replied plainly.

"And what if they don't realize it ever?" I added to my question.

Hearing this he smiled in pity. Only meekly he said, "I don't agree to this blame on the human race. If I had, we won't have met."

Once again he was sounding both, mystic and realistic. I remained positive about his intent upon me, and therefore I gestured accepting his insight.

He sensed my keenness again and continued, "I repeat,

knowledge of eternal truth is indispensable for man. It's alone this knowledge which runs him and everything else in the creation.

I was gradually forgetting my other questions which I had planned to ask him. Trying to scale the depth of his words, I asked, "But is this eternal truth, which scriptures claim to be only mystic, some kind of intangible phenomena or invisible force? Or is it merely a kind of theoretical fascination which is incomprehensible for the ordinary human minds, especially to the ones who are not living in the Himalayan caves?" I asked.

To my remark about Himalayan caves he laughed. He knew what I meant. He replied, "In a way what you've said has happened to be true."

I continued asking in the momentum. "In that case, do the people like me remain ever ignorant of the eternal truth?" This time my question was directed upon me.

He quickly remonstrated, "No! No one should assume the human perception faculties ever so frail."

I felt encouraged. "Then what's the way of knowing more about this mystical eternal truth?"

"See my son! That's the beauty of this creation. Here your question itself is showing the way to the answer. Having alone the sincere keenness about eternal truth is the way of knowing it."

I secretly kvetched in my heart, "Oh! Even his answers sound mystical." I looked to his face and asked humbly, "Please elaborate it; and also suggest how one should start."

He began laughing and looking into my eyes, as if he was melting in tenderness. He said, "In your present awareness, the best entity known to you is your own body. But unfortunately, since it changes, it is insignificant. In other words, since it is changing constantly, it never remains the same how you have known it previously. Apart from your body, what is that, which in your understanding, you've known sufficiently about?"

"Oh! In that case, can it be this all which I am seeing all

around through my eyes? Isn't it really this world which exists in all directions from my body?" While I asked this, I was witnessing my curiosity taking even bigger dimensions now.

"But see!" He replied, "What will you do when the world is subject to change even faster than your body? You say you see it through your eyes, but aren't your eyes already cultured and conditioned by your bodily experience? World also never remains the same, for it is changing rather too fast. Trust me, your experience of world through your eyes is merely but a part of your similar experience taken through your body. In this way, you can take it for granted, that your available knowledge of the world is more useless than the available knowledge of your own body."

"Hmm... Then how would I reach the eternal truth?"

Smilingly, he winked and asked, "Before I reveal more here, tell me, do you feel disappointed or dissuaded from your quest of knowing about the subtlest?"

"No I don't. Rather I am surprised, what is that which you are so proud of knowing and I am still clueless about?"

Once again, his voice became mysteriously encouraging. He replied, "That's why you have been chosen for this knowledge. From today you can think of yourself privileged, provided you enjoy this privilege only silently."

"Hmm... But see, I want to know certain other things as well. Must not I know first a little more about you?" I asked.

Hearing this, the old man replied flatly, "Such curiosity of yours is about my body, my physical existence alone. This question doesn't seem important to me."

"But I would still like to know. The way you've been controlling my dreams and thoughts for past some time, it has stormed me. Are you an angel?"

"No, I am not", he replied.

"Then, are you God?"

He stared straight into my eyes and laughed. "No; not at least in the way you have understood God so far."

Even as yet I couldn't completely refrain being skeptical about him. His feats of controlling my dreams and thoughts were still making me stupefied. Desperately, I tried asking again, "Ok, then are you the personified form of that eternal truth itself?"

I was tossing through every possible idea.

"In your existing awareness, I am not even that. You have not yet developed the ability to understand the human substance in that way", he continued taming down my all kinds of guesses.

"Then, are you some mystic sage or adept?"

"No. I do not need to become that for you. Infact if I claim being so, you will not trust me as much as you do now."

"Then who you are?" I just ran out of my wonderments.

"Listen with great attention!" Suddenly he had lowered his head in way of whispering, "I am your destined medium of knowing the eternal truth. This opportunity, which I am calling as destiny for that matter, is nothing but your own inclination in life. If at all you want to name me, merely for your personal convenience, you can think of me as your master. But I will allow you to assume so, only when you concentrate entirely upon the supreme knowledge imparted by me; and not in my bodily existence ever. My duty is to bestow you the subtlest knowledge of eternal truth, and along with that, to also take you forward in the secret world."

"Secret world!" I exclaimed.

He mesmerized me even greatly by saying, "Yes, the one on the other side of your mind!"

NINE

Divine Vision Bestowed by Master

"SECRET WORLD? DOESN'T IT sound very superficial? I may not believe any such thing which you speak of."

It just occurred to me that I was being taken on a ride.

He smiled in great humility and said, "Mere ignorance of a thing doesn't prove its non-existence."

"But what if I don't pay any heed to you? Why at all do I need to know about the secret world which you are fancying me about?" I asked.

"That will be lamentable", he continued replying in the same humility. "You do not remember, but I do, that how many incarnations your sub-consciousness has taken to feel very this need. Don't you remember your recent mundane wonderings around your life and world? Don't you already see that, everywhere, the flocks of countless people have not yet felt this need? Perhaps, before they could, they will have to take many more incarnations again. In my view you must feel yourself rather privileged. However, if you find yourself adamantly unwilling, be at liberty, to instantly ignore this opportunity once again."

"You are frightening me!"

"No, I am wishing your well."

"But still", I apprehended, "doesn't it sound fanatic talking about a secret world somewhere? See!" I continued, "Here is one kind of world which I've been witnessing every day. I live in it and experience it every moment. I can see it, feel it and touch it. I am ever taking part inside it. It's where I sit, stand and lie down.

It's where I can walk and sleep. But where could be the other one which you speak of as secret world?"

Not even slightly perturbed by my words, the old man replied, "It's right here in front of you. The secret world exists inside the very same world which you have just described. Even though you always continue taking place in the secret world as well, yet, out of your ignorance, you do not come to know about it. You remain unaware of it, because you lack the 'need' of knowing it."

Unappeased yet, I protested, "By alleging the ignorance upon me again and again, aren't you forcing upon me a kind of guilt-consciousness?"

"Oh! Certainly I must not dishearten you about the presented good opportunity. I assure you my humbler ways forward."

Instantly, I was taken aback by the sudden humility of my host.

"By the way, can I see this secret world right now?" I asked.

"By your ordinary human vision you won't be able to see that. To let you behold the secret world, I will have to enable you with the divine vision."

"Oh, Divine vision!" Suddenly I felt as if something miraculous was going to take place about me. Given my miraculous dream visions and also the strange way of meeting him here on the hilltop, I was sure that this was no ordinary man. For the first time now, feeling privileged was occurring to me. In front of him, I started prostrating and behaving suitable to the occasion.

"Oh, but why at all", he astoundingly asked, "have you started behaving strangely? Why have you tumbled on the ground and prostrating at my feet? And up to what now, you've formed even a lotus posture here?"

As he began wonderingly asking me, I imagined, perhaps he was unsure of my suddenly changed manners.

"Well, I thought", I tried reasoning, "that now some kind of white illumined rays would emanate from your eyes and will transverse into my eyes here. Nevertheless, your bestowing the divine vision upon me is such a unique endowment, that I must be prepared for it. Long ago, I heard about it somewhere."

He was utterly surprised. "That's not what I am talking about. Divine vision cannot be enabled by performing some mechanical exercises as demonstrated by you. I wonder what makes you believe that way."

"Then in what way you will give me the divine vision?" Blushed I was, I asked.

"But I am no one who can give you any divine vision? Don't you know that nobody can ever give that to the other?"

The old man's position was not still reconciling with mine.

"I didn't understand, Sir. If it's so, what was that you were to give me?" asked I.

To this he gagged. "I was merely to enable it, my son. You see! You've already been provided with the divine vision, the very same way everyone else on the earth has been. Most people no longer remember it. Nonetheless, the Supreme One Almighty has bestowed all kinds of people the all kinds of perception faculties. However, only few of these faculties, which are constantly used by men, remain active; while other ones, which are never put to use by them, become latent. No wonder, the ability of divine vision in your case is of the latter type.

"But how do I believe your words to be true? Had God been really bestowing all men the wonderful faculty such as the divine vision, weren't they all using it to the fullest? Why would have they agreed to let it remain latent?" I contested his point.

He replied, "They are mistaken over it."

"How can you say that?" I contested harder.

For a moment, he remained silent. He gaze was absent towards looking at the ground. Then all of a sudden, he laughing said, "Then let me narrate you, how it must have happened actually. Just like you they also might have heard about the divine vision; but have never experienced it any. Whenever they thought about needing this privilege, they would have surely squatted on the floor, in the lotus posture, and expecting some white illumined rays to transverse from somewhere outside. How foolish! They never tried or even thought about invoking their inner sense for the divine vision; instead, they propitiated it only in their external behavior. They couldn't have ever succeeded in that, and it was the reason, their natural inner faculty of divine vision developed only latent."

"I can only wonder if you may be correct. But in what procedure you are going to enable my divine vision, which, as per you, is already in me?" I asked flatly.

"I will remind you, of your good old ability", he said.

"Ability?" I could only wonder.

"Yes indeed, it's alone your ability to see the secret world on the other side of your mind. It's only you who can see that, because it's only your mind behind which it exists", he replied.

"Sir, I don't yet understand it fully", I said.

"My son!" he smiled in affection and explained, "Do not get dissuaded, even though it might take you little effort and time to understand this matter in completeness. Certain old locks are difficult to open for the first time, but once they've opened, they do not give trouble any more. Here in this moment, just remember that, regarding your entire existing life and world, the ways in which you see those from your physical human eyes, are merely the images reflected by the non-transparent mirror of your mind. Putting all these reflected images aside, when you've wiped the other side of the mirror, indeed your latent divine vision will set into working. Once you've wiped perfectly, it will restore its full transparency. And then this mirror will turn into a clean transparent sheet of glass. Starting from now, in this way, you will see across the sublime truths. Your vision will no longer be restrained by the untrue reflecting images. Instead, you will now become able to see much more about the same things. In such moments you will notice, that how stupendously, you had been ignorant of the new findings. But beware! Before you actually invoke your divine vision and start practicing it, remember one important thing, that all what has remained hidden from your ordinary vision so far, is the very secret world which you will be seeing now. At times, things may go unpleasant as well."

"But how different is this secret world from the apparent world?" I asked. My curiosity was growing manifolds.

"There is no similarity at all. If you are able to perfectly wipe behind the mirror of your mind, and thus make it fully transparent, you will get to see the secret world very clearly. In those matchless moments you will see the both – the reflective images and the real truth as well. Reflective images are what you get in the apparent world, whereas the real truths are in the secret world. At any point of time, you yourself can compare between the two. It's then you will come to the realization of what you'd been missing in your ordinary vision so far."

"Are the sights taken from secret world really so spectacular?" I asked in astonishment.

He laughed in a philosophical mood. He replied only briefly, "Not spectacular, those are only truthful."

Instead of floating on the spur of the moment, I felt disappointed. I asked, "You said I'll have to wash the other side of the mirror of my mind and make it fully transparent in this way. But I do not really know how to do that. It seems quite a fancy idea."

"In the beginning, as I said, it might go uneasy upon you. But soon, by way of practicing, it will start going easy upon you. It will become child's play. You will see the secret world at any time of your wish" He said as if trying to keep me encouraged.

I was still guessing.

He continued elaborating on his part, "And remember this also! You will have to experience your divine vision all alone. No one else can ever intrude into that. If needing enlightenment, you can although seek my help at any time, but you will have to be in your secret world all alone. It's the rule. In the beginning, should your experiences appear frightening, you must not dissuade yourself from the divine vision. Rest assured that soon you will invariably start enjoying the same experiences with the help of your elevated understanding."

"Hmm... But how will I at least start?"

"Oh! It's not difficult", he expressed sharing my concern and suggested, "I will help you. I will give you a mantra."

"Mantra!" Again, my surprise started floating.

"Yes. Whenever you feel like seeing on the other side of the mirror of your mind, just start repeating this mantra and continue unless your divine vision sets into working. Remember, more earnestly you repeat, the sooner you make it", thus instructed the old man emphasizing his each word.

"What's the mantra?" I asked on the height of curiosity.

He started uttering, "It's this – *Oh Lord! Make me see the truth. I am in search of it*".

"But sir", I apprehended again, "there hardly seems anything extraordinary in this mantra." I was perhaps expecting something complicated.

Looking about my face, he broke laughter again. He almost slighted me by saying, "That's what you have to learn and correct in yourself. I have said it before as well, it is only the faith that matters. The very moment you stop having faith in this mantra, your divine vision will also stop. At any time during your experience of the divine vision, you can yourself test by switching on and off your faithfulness in this mantra.

"Hmm..." I could utter only this.

"However", he quipped, "if you think that this mantra should be written in some complicated script or syllable, I will remake it for you. Say! Would you prefer it in Sanskrit, Arabic, Halmidi, Portuguese or any other inscription around the world? Rest assured, I will remake it for you right away. Nevertheless, its meaning still remains the same."

Perhaps I felt pulled. I tried replying humbly, "No, it's fine the way you have already given it to me. You see, it has already started striking something upon me."

As he looked to my face smilingly, I murmured and repeated the words, "*Oh Lord! Make me see the Truth. I am in search of it.*"

He continued examining my face, and filling my frame with his affectionate smiles.

TEN

Illusionary Tricks Played by My Mind

"YOU SAY YOU'RE MY master and will show me the way to the secret world. But why at all you will do that for me? Is there anything you will expect or want from me later in return?" I asked him. Wonderments about my mysterious host couldn't have become completely free from the doubts yet.

As opposed to my anticipation, he rather became more compassionate about me. "My son!" he said, "You've not yet earned a kind of thing which you can give me. Nevertheless, true masters never expect anything in return from their disciples. I do all this for only your beneficence. Only such is my work and I always do it dutifully."

"Oh! I regret for my ever doubting mind." Thus I expressed my apologies and started surrendering to him, "It's your grace. I trust your heavenly words and company. You've reminded me of my strange childhood reminiscences. True it is that since my childhood I've been witnessing countless strange curiosities inside me. I've never spoken with anyone about those, lest people may start ridiculing. Many such anxious wanderings of my mind were about nature, sky, creatures, behaviors, darkness, fear, and those were also about my clueless dreams, my extraterritorial possible existence, about my gliding in the air, about my previous incarnations, and a lot many others. But eventually as I grew up, amidst the hustling world, all these curiosities tended to become extinct, although I admit that I couldn't get rid of them completely. Sometimes I wonder wherefrom those all curiosities came? Why to me? Even though times I would think of same to be only pointless and shed off, yet those would return again. I've some bleak understanding made around these curiosities and I've read some books as well about the same, but largely I am bewildered. I submit all my ignorance at your feet. Enlighten me O Master, how will you initiate me and take me forward?"

Slowly he closed his eyes and became very tendering about my presence. When he opened the eyes again, he said, "Before your work on laboratory construction starts, you will spend here with me two more days ahead. I will narrate for your understanding the immense power of your mind. I will dispense one by one the knowledge of many supernatural principles around the tricky operation of mind, and also relate those with numerous analogies and stories."

"Oh! Analogies and stories! Certainly this unique revelation of esoteric principles by you is going to be very interesting", I said.

To my momentary excitement he merely smiled and said, "Yes, but you must be aware. A doctrine always remains more important than the legend or the story related to it. In our talk, at any point of time you must not get so overwhelmed by the story that you lose focus from the doctrine itself. Analogies and stories are merely for increasing your appetite for the doctrine. They are the body whereas the doctrine is the spirit. Merely spirit remains important and similarly the doctrine remains so. Take vow in front of me that you will not get overwhelmed by the analogies and stories that are employed by me merely for your eased understanding. Those are merely symbols and nothing more."

"Whatever you've said is truth", I humbly replied and added, "Here I tender myself at your disposal. Now when you are my master, only you bear my responsibility."

"True, but remember this also", he said, "A master helps only till the point you have attained enlightenment; then after you have to tread the path yourself. The supreme architect of your life will be alone you and not any master or God; though you can choose to take inspiration from both of them any time. What I am doing here is only helping you acquaint the potency of your own mind. Only through the power of mind, the Supreme Force Almighty generates, operates and annihilates the visible and invisible part of entire creation. And I have already said that the potencies of mind are same with all. Therefore, when God can become so much capable because of the power of His mind, why should you remain ever so frail?"

"Can I too create the world through the same power of mind?" I asked in surprise.

"Why you get marveled about it?" He replied, "You don't need to start creating the world afresh again, for you have already been doing that. Just that, as yourself has chosen out of your ignorance, you do not come to know about it."

I asked again, "But how it's possible that I have already been doing such a big feat and I do not even come to know about it?"

"That's no wonder actually", he said, "Countless people never come to know about it. You do not notice when every second your mind is playing illusionary tricks on you. You never get offended because it is the way you have trained it yourself. More un-masterly you train it, bigger illusions it creates around your perception senses. And this is the reason you never come to know the big feats you are already performing in your world."

"But still", I intercepted, "I do not fully understand what you say. How really a task, as big as creating a world, can constantly go unnoticed by me?"

He laughed. "I repeat it's no wonder actually. Let me help you in understanding all this. Let us first try to figure out what is your world. Are you ready to storm your brain a bit?

"Yes, very much", I said.

"Well, your visible world is what you can see through your eyes, is that correct?" He asked.

"Yes."

"But see!" he warned, "You anyway have only a limited reach of your sight, for your eye-sight traverses riding upon the rays of light. Now listen very carefully, light-rays have one peculiar attribute and it is their problem as well – that those always travel only in the straight lines. Do you understand and agree on this?"

"Hmm... You are correct." I was engrossing in his talk.

"First, your human vision is far sighted but only up to a limit; and making it worse, all you can see through your eyes is only in the straight lines. Such are the two limitations of the physical construction of your bodily vision capabilities. Do you contemplate this?"

I took a thoughtful pause before saying, "Yes, that's true."

"It's here and now your mind plays the illusionary trick. In your general capacity you think of your eyes, which are one of the instruments of your mind, to be your best available perception faculty. Going by this you further convince yourself by assuming the expansion of your world, but which is still limited to your restricted ability to see."

I tried challenging this problem and asked, "I understand what you mean, but can't I overcome this limitation by seeing in the different directions again and again, and also from different vicinities from the same viewed objects? I think in this way, perhaps, I can apprise myself better in and about the world."

"You talked about directions, but that may not hold enough still. Can you say how many directions there are?" Master began expanding his point.

"Oh! Even a child would know it. There are four – East, North, West and South", I replied.

"No, that will be the wrong way to answer my question", he smiled and glanced into my eyes as if giving more clues.

"Oh! I understand what you mean." Quickly I tried correcting it. "Actually I've heard about it. There are actually ten – the four which I already spoke, another four in between each two of them; and still the two more – upwards and downwards."

Hearing this, the old man smiled wider. He said in the same tone, "That would be still the wrong way to imagine. You said there are ten directions, but are you sure that there cannot be any more in between each two of them again?"

Great amazement swept me. "Oh! I never thought in this way. Indeed, it's possible. Infact that is what seems the truth."

Master remained only silent while I continued, "Even if, to the extent possible, we try counting the all number of directions at all, there will still remain a possibility of finding more directions in between each two of them newly found. How marvelous, there doesn't seem any end to it!"

"Now you get it better." He smiled and added, "The truth is that the directions in your ordinary physical world are myriad. Human beings name those and put numbers to them only for their personal convenience. Forget counting, the ordinary human perceptions cannot comprehend theirs vastness even remotely."

"Hmm..." In the awe of moment I could utter only this.

"In this way my son", my astonishing host continued, "When you say that you can overcome the limitations of your vision by seeing in different directions and from the different vicinities, actually it doesn't help for two reasons. One is, you can never count, that in how many directions you have already seen and in how many sufficiently more you will need to see again. And the second reason is that, since you can see only in one direction at a time, you never get to know what changes would have happened in the previous direction, which you've seen merely a moment before."

To this I completely agreed, yet I asked on the spur of my inner argumentative mind. "But can't I really see in the same direction again and again; and confirm in this way about the changes too?"

To this, the old man began laughing. He said "Do you believe that the changes are always in the physical properties of the things which can be perceived by your eyesight alone? Whatever is your ability to grasp from your eyes is still about the physical forms alone. Whereas on the contrary, the types of changes taking place in the world every moment are manifold and magnanimous. Isn't it really true?"

I slightly abated my position and said, "What you say seems correct, but I still think you have raised quite a big point. You have questioned the wholesome way in which people perceive things awhile their entire lives."

He mildly smiled and said, "You must not get carried away by this revelation. All I am trying to impart is about the *inherited insufficiency* of the ordinary human senses; to be more precise, it is about the faculty of vision, which people think to be the foremost amongst all five senses. My purpose is not to cause you disdain your own bodily construction or its different abilities, but certainly you must be perfectly apprised of the limitations as well. Knowing this all is indispensable for you, so that you can't be made fool by your own said limitations. For I have taken, in particular, the instance of human sight limitations, let me illustrate it with an analogy."

I already intuited something very interesting coming up. "Sure", I said.

"When you look at water, what do you find?" He asked.

"It's water only."

He smiled and asked again. "Correct, but merely by looking at it, can you say if the water is too hot or not?

"Hmm... Yes, I can do so. If there is vapor coming out of it, it would be hot", I replied.

"But don't you know that when the water is too cold, it still gives vapor?" He laughingly asked again.

"Oh! That's also true." I abated.

"Then son! With your vision faculty alone, how will you judge the constantly changing world when you can't even judge between the hot and cold water?"

"But wait", I objected to his suddenly made conclusion, "If the water is too cold, maybe I can sense it from the temperature of environment. See! If the vapor is cold, the water also would be cold; and contrarily if the vapor is hot, the water also would be hot. Doesn't it solve the problem?"

Before replying anything he merely watched me in pity. He

said, "I must remind you of your vow. It seems you have become overwhelmed by the analogy of water used by me."

I too caught my error. I tenderly submitted, "Oh, I apologize for not being careful this time."

"But still", he said, "when you have asked, I must reply for your satisfaction. You said that by sensing the temperature of vapor you can judge the water. But you forgot the rule of our analogy. Can you really sense the temperature of water through your eyes?"

"No", I replied, "I don't think anybody would be able to do that. Judging temperature with the help of eyes is not possible. May be I need to touch it."

"That is what I am trying to make you learn. Your understanding of the world which is arrived with the help of your vision faculty alone is incomplete and imperfect. Yet you always allow your mind, throughout life, to build perceptions and opinions on that basis."

"But master, tell me this", I asked in a new curiosity, "You emphasize upon the limitations of men's vision faculty but what about the other faculties of human senses?

He explained, "Besides vision, there are four more perception senses – hearing, smelling, tasting and touching."

"And now you will say that even those had limitations?" I predicted his answer.

"There is no doubt. For your understanding I can describe each of them at the exceptional length. But before I do that, I must tell you another big thing", he lowered his head and said to me.

"What?" I asked.

The old man continued, "See! I am your master and not the teacher. I enlighten you but don't constantly teach you. I have shown you the way of contemplating about this matter. The truth about limitation of human senses is eternally true and I do not need adding anything new to it. The images and perceptions, as received by all or any of the five human senses, are always incomplete and imperfect. To vouch this very fact if you choose to intuit this matter in your own secluded consciousness, you will learn it faster and firmer. Never forget that your best teacher is always your own intuition, and not me. What I am imparting you here on these hills, is only prescribing the ways in which you must teach yourself."

"Hmm..." I merely uttered. In my mind, I had already drifted towards my other senses.

"Do you still want me to describe in great detail about the rest of the four human perception senses?" He asked in tenderness.

"No", I replied, "I have very much begun to find this matter interesting. Maybe I am able to do myself. But at least tell me the right ways so that I do not get caught in some error." I didn't hesitate in revealing a naïve in me.

"Infact you have asked a very good question", the old man became happy. Merrily he continued saying, "Maybe you are not fully aware, but you have asked me the very method of meditating. See! Reflecting your own conscience in a completely unbiased manner is what is called meditation. For doing this you do not always need to specifically sit in a lotus or otherwise posture. You can sit in whatever way comfortable to you. To the extent it is possible, you must find out a secluded place for you. Remember, for about a secluded place you need not go in far every time, but you must search it around your daily life itself. More unfascinatingly you search, sooner you find it. Immediately before starting your meditation spell, you must not become agitated or anxious over something. Instead of hastening the meditation, it is better to wait and reclaim your equanimity first.

Expressing my valid apprehension I asked, "But I fear, lest I may conclude wrongly over these complicated matters."

The master negated it instantly, "No, it never happens so. Meditations never go wrong if you have been sincerely about those. This sincerity, which I talk about, is nothing but the honesty of your purpose. Going by that, you must constantly check and reaffirm your faith in your purpose that, you don't meditate in search of some *apparent world* exposed to your five senses, but instead you are the privileged one who is in search of the *secret world* on the other side of your mind. Whatever is discovered by you in the secret world is not complicated by its nature; albeit complication lies merely in your ways of finding; it is not in the found itself. The sublime truths may remain inaccessible to you only for so long as you see yourself far from them. The one powerful technique of reaching your secret world fastest is that, you must behold yourself very close to it; just nearby. You must see yourself at the door-bell point. Such a feeling of *self-assumed* proximity, although maybe seeming easy to you, but is actually most difficult to attain if your mind is tumultuous and not calm."

"Hmm... You say just and wise", I said.

Master now swapped his legs in the cross sitting position. He said, "So far, you must have very well understood that you cannot knock at the door of your secret world with the help of your human senses alone. Whenever you will perfectly convince yourself about such of your limitation, you will grow a serious inclination for experiencing the unknown yet. Exactly this will be the moment when you will enter your secret world. And once you've entered in, you will gradually develop a taste for it as well."

At this I asked, "For doing this, will I have to exit from the existing world, where I am living now?"

"Son! You must remember my words. I have already answered it. Though again I repeat. Your secret world doesn't exist somewhere very far; albeit it exists right here in the same world which you often designate as your existing one. You must start repeating the mantra, earnestly, which I have bestowed you. In those persisting moments as and when you have switched-on your faith in the mantra, you will enter the secret world at once; and in other moments when you've switched-off your faith, you will find yourself in the apparent world again. I mention it, physically you don't move anywhere, but mentally you are in two different worlds at the same point of time. For your convenience I can describe in an analogy, that in one case you are seeing through a transparent sheet of glass, whereas in the other, you are seeing in a mirror which is only reflective and not transparent at all."

"Whatever you say is the truth", I said, "But now I've got another curiosity. What kind of feelings I will be going through while comparing between the two worlds?"

Master said, "Son, listen with patience. Till this moment, your mind has not become completely free from the coils of past. For all years of your age, it has been conditioned by you in the accordance with your apparent world alone. Even if I explain the difference asked by you, you will not be able to perfectly absorb. I do not describe it for another reason as well. Actually experience of the secret world is best gained only when it is experienced, and not when merely explained, even by me. Do not worry; only shortly the secret world will start occurring to you. Till then give your necessary time and discipline for the mental preparation towards it. I warn, in the beginning of such experiences, things might go little hard on you. After all, those always conflict with the existing conditioning of a normal mind. But as you will continue experiencing the eternal truth with the help of your new world, you will soon graduate enjoying the given things. And this enjoyment, you will see my son, will be just matchless and permanent."

"Will I have to come back in the apparent world again?" I asked.

"You will be at liberty to live in either of two. I have said it, physically you do not move anywhere and you remain at the same place only. But mentally, since both the worlds will be lot different from each other, you can have choices. For you will experience the both as much as you wish, I will not force on you to stick to the one and ignore the other. Nevertheless, it's only you who is supposed to become the master of your life. My duty is alone to ensure that you are not left unaware of your secret world and the eternal truth on the top of it."

"Hmm... You see Master! I feel strange and anxious in this moment."

Master broke out laughter. "That's how it always starts", he said. "The great archer Arjuna had also became anxious before Lord Krishna imparted him the cosmic divine knowledge. But when he knew the eternal truth in full, you already know how big he attained. Similarly, your slight despondency in this moment, does not dissuade me from my duty."

In a very thoughtful moment, I said, "Yes, you are very correct. Arjuna conquered the world after that."

"No, he didn't conquer the world", master intercepted, "instead he conquered his own living in the world. And this he could do only because he had attained his secret world first."

ELEVEN

The Drivers of Human Attention

"SON, I AM VERY pleased with the way you have assimilated my imparting", master said. "Very shortly you will get busy in your laboratory construction work again. Therefore in these few days take from me whatever you want."

I felt humbled but didn't exactly get what he meant by saying 'whatever'. I was not feeling strange or anxious for being in his influence during this period. I asked, "I have complete faith in your words, though I do not yet perfectly know what should be wanted by me and what not."

To this he faintly smiled. He began saying, "You already keep the sufficient materials as are necessary for your worldly existence, and it is needless to mention that you will continue prospering in them too. The best thing here I can give you is the supreme knowledge of eternal truth, after attaining which your eternal happiness will be ensured for life. This knowledge, although being concise and succinct, still often needs manifold explanations to make one convinced. Isn't it?"

"You speak truth Master!" I replied, "My wonderment in hearing your words doesn't quench ever. Certainly I would've remained incomplete without knowing these hidden truths."

He smiled in empathy. He rose even straight in his sitting posture and said, "Certainly you have become keenly interested in knowing about the secret world. Remember, and never forget it, that this secret world is an ever existing reality and it cannot be created or destroyed by anyone, not even by the most powerful arsenals of physical outer world. If you are going to acquaint this secret world for the first time here, it doesn't mean you are creating it. You cannot create what is already existing, and nor can you destroy which has always existed. Sublime truths are primordial. Those are beyond the governance of the laws of creation and annihilation. Those do not require any human or otherwise intervention for their sustenance. Sublime truths sustain by themselves. Unfortunately though, in however big way I may try to narrate all these matters to you, in due course of time you might still run a tendency of forgetting and ignoring those."

"Oh! Why do you doubt so?" I asked in wonderment.

"It's none of your fault; it's nature; the very human nature. Here and now, let me conduct a small experiment on you. Do you allow?

For the sudden offer, it mounted my astonishment. "Oh, experiment! Master, since I have already established my faith in you, consider myself at your wish."

"Very well Son", said the master smilingly, "Now close your eyes and make a few rounds on your heal. Then at once open your eyes unprecedentedly and tell me upon which particular color has your sight settled first? Do not move your eyes from that one color unless I allow you doing so."

I followed his instructions. With closed eyes, I made a couple of rounds at the point I stood. As I opened my eyes again, I said, "Oh! My sight has accidently fallen on the small stone-pyre in my front, and the first color I've seen is a bright white one."

"Are there other colors as well in the stone-pyre that you behold in this moment?" He asked.

Still fixing my gaze there, I replied, "Yes, indeed there are other colors as well. It's some dark brown, violet and also shaded green.

"Now repeat the spinning on your heal and tell me which color is seen first by you." Master's voice was becoming playful.

"Can I drift a little for sake of spontaneity?" I asked.

"Yes, you can, but move a little only; lest you may fall with closed eyes", master laughed. He added, "You can do this small experiment the way you like."

I repeated the process and responded, "Ah! It's light green color this time. In far, I am seeing a small grove of trees."

"And what other colors do you see there?" He asked.

I replied, "Its dark color of tree skins, color of soil and the shadow of tree falling on the ground."

"Did you note something?" The master asked.

"What?"

"That in your apparent world, anytime and anywhere, your spontaneous perception of things, which influences your mind most, is actually never in your control."

"I didn't understand it, Master!" I said while looking to his face.

He began explaining, "For most people who live in the apparent world alone and haven't had any trace of the secret world yet, it's comes only natural that any person or object which is bright in color, will snatch their attention first. On the spur of the spontaneity, in first case you ignored the other colors but saw only the bright white. And in the second, you saw the light green and ignored the others. It's just a small example. Man often concentrates more on the people and objects which he has happened to only see first. This is a symbolic representation of what I am trying to impart you. You can repeat doing this experiment as many times as you want."

"But how do you relate this experiment with our previous talk, which was about my chance of forgetting the supreme knowledge imparted by you?" I asked irresistibly.

"Son, this experiment helps you in understanding very deeply as to why the human beings suffer form a tendency of forgetting the subtler knowledge of their own lives. In the first case you saw *and remembered* only the bright white, whereas you ignored dark brown, violet and shaded green. In second case again you saw *and remembered* only the light green color but ignored the others. Take a careful note here. You never remember the things which you've ignored once. But on the contrary, it is quite possible that the things you happened to ignore on the spur of spontaneity were actually more necessary for your understanding. Run over by your human nature, as being constantly established in the apparent world, your attention is largely snatched by the unimportant attributes of the objects and peoples. Color on the surface, is just one example of such unimportant attributes. Now, how does this infirmity affect you, is that, truth is ever free from the prejudices; and truth might come to you in any color whatsoever.

Oh! I was spellbound in the revelation made before me. I felt nicer being in the company of such an eloquent master.

Here, he continued expanding the doctrine, "Son, don't miss to see even this. What I've explained above, is the case about your sight-faculty alone. Your attention of hearing, touching, tasting and smelling is also snatched by the loudest, severest, tastiest and foulest respectively. You should now meditate within yourself and experience this entire stratagem further. Obstructed by your nature, as conditioned in the apparent world, you sparingly get your perception right. It is always swayed by the other factors which are but out of your control. Most people completely remain unaware of these magnanimous shortcomings throughout their lives. But those, who keenly sift the hollowness of their apparent world, soon start finding their secret world to be more rejoicing."

"Yes...that's very true", in deeply thoughtful mood, I nodded and uttered.

"And as I have said before, life's sublime truths on the other side are eternal in themselves and do not require any human intervention for their sustenance. They sustain by themselves. Once you've entered the secret world on the other side of your mind, you will find yourself highly enabled for watching, experiencing and even taking part in the operations taking place there. Can you imagine how distinctive this all journey is going to become?"

I was joyous, elated and beaming. I could merely voice, "Indeed, I can already feel that."

In the next moment, master closed his eyes. Sitting next to him I continued watching the surroundings absentmindedly. Perhaps I had begun wandering in some kind of other unknown world.

TWELVE

Delicious Lunch of Taproots

"OH SEE! THE BRIGHT sun has started coming in now from the big window of sky. It's the high noon arrived", master said gently. Only a while before he had broken his silence and was looking around now.

I barely nodded.

Then master began to look at me inquisitively. He said, "I think you must be hungry. And God says that a guest must be served well."

I responded to his smile but couldn't make out as to what in this dense forest he could have had to offer for my eating. In next moment he motioned his finger in the direction of a nearby tree and asked, "Son, go behind that tree and there you will find something to eat. Take as much as necessary for your appetite."

I hesitated slightly. I wasn't sure what he himself would be eating in the woods, but as I was really feeling hungry, it had bothered my host.

He read my mind like an open book and comforted me by saying, "Don't feel shy, for maybe you will see there something you never heard about. I understand that people living in cities easily get excited about the new things to relish." As he said this he broke mirth.

As I was approaching towards the tree, he called out from behind, "Bring your today's lunch here if you do not know how to operate it before eating."

That tree must have been about forty yards. While walking down, I was wondering about my new dish. No wonder, that after having climbed hilltop in the morning, the little breakfast I took, must have already digested. After master had mentioned of the food, my hunger became stronger. I felt I could eat anything which came by. Just about reaching, I saw that it was a big pine tree, of which the trunk was thick and steeply high. At nearby there was hardly any tree of its size. I also wondered why the old man had called out for bringing the food to him, in case I didn't know to operate. As I turned behind the tree, I was awed.

There were actually about half a dozen soft taproots. In daze, I looked on. No, those were not radish; for their color was somewhat pink and their thickness was almost double the size of the biggest radish I had seen in life. The peel of such of my new discovery was unusually stiff; and the green leaves atop had already been plucked off. I thought that although I had seen so many things in life but such a kind of eatable was quite a new experience. I couldn't either trace whether it belonged to the class of vegetables' or the 'fruits'.

I kneeled down to touch. Yes, those were fresh and clean. I picked up one and thought about starting; but alas! The stubborn peel of my food left me only wondering. I also thought that it would offend the courtesy if I eat alone and do not ask my host first. I believed that in any case four of the taproots were enough for both of us. I picked those and rushed back to the master.

As he saw me laden with four, he almost ridiculed me by saying, "Are you too hungry my son?"

Glancing again at the fruits in my hands, I blushed. But he comforted me.

"Bring to me. I will help in serving you." Master said.

I handed all four to him. He gently put those on the altar and picked one aside. He gripped it between his fists, and with a whack sound, broke it from the middle. He carefully started tearing off the skin from the broken edges. From bottom, he left a little part of it unpeeled. Only in a moment, half size of the fruit was ready for my lunch, well I hoped, to start with.

Momentarily I wondered, whether before eating, did I need

to rinse it with water? But he just handed out to me.

"Hold it from here and start", he pointed out to the bottom. He added, "How gracious mother nature has been upon us, that most of its fruits come with a skin to protect the hygiene from inside. Isn't it my son?"

I knew it. He was reading every thread of my mind. He was aware of my every wonderment.

"Start eating my son and tell me how do you find it?" Master pushed on me.

I took my first bite. It was softer than the radish; and it was sweeter too. It felt wonderful. On my second bite I found it to not be dry or coarse, albeit it was juicy. As I was about to take my third, I stopped realizing my error. It was none of my etiquettes to start eating myself and not ask the host first.

"Please allow me to peel off the rest half of it for you", I asked.

"No, no. It's all for you my son. I have already taken my share of the meal for the day. I kept those for you. Tell me how do you find it?" In asking, master's affectionate curiosity was coming obvious.

"Umm... I have never eaten such a delicious fruit before. Please tell me what is this called?" I asked being mouthful.

"It's called your food", he replied while examining my eyes.

"No, I mean what is it called by?" I asked again.

"I have actually refrained from naming it. I usually find it in the nearby forest. You see, it's the tastiest one out of the several other things which I usually bring for my food. Several other kinds of roots may not taste as good but are unfailingly beneficial for the upkeep of this body. Mind is very tricky my son! If I start identifying these particular roots, which are in your hands, by a unique name, I will start searching for the same every day, and in this way ignore the other ones which are more beneficial. If some day, I may not find this particular kind of roots to satisfy my taste buds, my mind will make me pensive. And in such state of mind, even if I am made to eat the more beneficial other kinds of roots; it won't feed my body for any good. That very moment my bodily sickness will take place. This is the reason I have refrained from naming it. Now every time I go to the downhill forest, I pick for me whatever comes in my sight first. Some day God is pleased on my tongue and some other day He is kind on my health. I've left it all alone to God." As master said this smilingly, I could imagine his control on himself.

As I finished the piece in my hand, I picked up the remaining half and peeled it myself. As I neared eating it all, I felt as if I had filled; though I couldn't yet stop wondering its taste. I gave an embarrassing look to the leftover taproots lying down in front of me. It was impossible to take more. Now I understood why master was laughing while asking me, if I was too hungry.

"In the evening when you go back downhill my son, take all with you. These roots can immune anyone from certain illnesses for a long time.

Naturally, I felt privileged to the offer.

"Let us move now for a walk!" He quickly stood up and said, "There are other kinds of foods also which are necessary for the human body. Those are the ones man can't take in through his mouth."

Saying this, master came down from the altar and waited for me. Already privileged about everything in his company, I hastened to follow him.

"Today before we assume our talk in the evening, I must introduce you with another of your own magical attribute", as we reached a new unknown footway, he said. This path was narrow, but reasonably comfortable in the company of master.

He continued speaking from ahead. "The magic I am talking about is your magic of silence. I can help you, to an extent, keeping your speech faculty silent by way of keeping my own one silent; but you see, for keeping your mind silent, it's alone you who can help it. A small pity in this moment is that, I have to name it for you as magic, but trust me that I have to do so only for so long as the power of silence remains unattained by you.

Magic of silence is actually no magic, albeit it's very natural; provided one has realized it."

I was all ears while he continued,

"Do this special exercise while you continue walking with me. Minister your speech faculty completely at rest and let only your mind do the talking with yourself; that too strictly as per my following instruction. Behold yourself very fortunate for having the opportunity of strolling in this wood. Look around for the trees, bushes, rocks, birds, streams, shrubs, grass and anything else that may fall in your way. Enjoy it. For these moments, forget your past world and allow your mind entering this altogether new world here. Forget even my presence. Immerse yourself in this divine scenic beauty. Do not perplex if you drift and do not find me nearby. You never go off my sight, not even in your dreams. Look in all directions and empathically feel in your heart about this very new kind of world; the very same which has been constantly felt in the heart of such trees, bushes, birds, etc. After all, haven't these all been living here since ages, just like the way you've been living in your kind of world there? Soak in this new kind of world here. Walk on; and just walk on."

Oh! What an experience it was; still vivid in my memories. Ever in life it was the first time when I realized that even the trees had great lives. Those flaunted flowers, fruits and sometimes their mighty numerous arms as well. Bushes were not merely the bushes. Those were rather notable landmarks, in bottom of which, several kinds of creatures had made their homes. Even the rocks were not purposeless; joined together those had worked enormously in the making of mountains. Those never melted from the sun, wind, snow or rains. Neither were the birds to be ignored. Those had homes, children, families and communities as well. Streams were also full of life. Those were many and were playing lifelines to many others around those. Tirelessly those streams had been nourishing all kinds of citizen of this world equally. Shrubs were like aged bent upon men who were always ready with the countless herbs to cure all.

Those had never felt bad if anyone plucked from their tips. And the evidence to this was that, those had never refused to give the herbs again and again to all. Looking at the greenest blades of grass I thought those were very new. But very next moment I reminded myself that perhaps the grass would be the oldest amongst all, and would be the great grandmother of all the vegetations seen around.

I was indeed lost in this world newly introduced by my master. I didn't know when my pace had slowed down so much that master was out of my sight. I didn't either know the time or place I was in. A profound realization grew in me, that the nature was most beautiful when it was unpredictable, spontaneous and untreated too. I could hear the sound of wind; smell around the water streams; touch the skin of trees; and overall, could capture the scenic beauty in my mind. I was indeed witnessing my joy of silence.

And as I came back to my normal senses, even before I could wonder of my lost master, I heard his voice from behind,

"Did you drink this nectar enough my son, which can make one behold the immortality?"

Only my smile answered him all.

"This forest is not as unique to all. Several adventurists and tourists keep coming in this dense wood, but they do not yet receive the same divine experience what you have gained today. Only those who have been sincerely curious about understanding the other kinds of existing worlds, are able to rejoice here."

I barely nodded in a blissful state.

"Don't miss to figure out for yourself my son, that today you have made two wonderful things, which you may call even *magic* for your convenience. Firstly you have learnt the power of compassion which is prerequisite for entering in to others' worlds. And secondly, it was your first hands-on experience with your divine vision. Without this you couldn't have ever been able to experience the tranquility here.

My eyes were wide open. I thought, wasn't it really easy?

Then why can't all people enjoy the tranquility in the same way?

Though I was still aloof, here my master commanded, "Let us go back to the cave. Your biggest lesson for the day is yet to come, my son!"

And I followed, just the way a child does to its mother.

THIRTEEN

How the Creation of World Takes Place

"SON! IN THE MORNING I said that as per scriptures, it's alone the power of mind, through which the supreme force Almighty creates, operates and annihilates this entire universe. Did you contemplate over this?" master asked. After returning to the cave-site I had sat down on the altar aside to him.

Though I had heard these words from him, I hadn't given any serious thought to it.

"I regret Sir, I have not been able to do this so far", I replied.

"But tell me one thing. Did you hear it from me for the first time or were you aware of it earlier as well?" he asked.

"I've read it somewhere else too my Master, though I do not remember where exactly. Also, in several Godly hymns and chants I have perhaps noticed the same hearsay. Though I have not studied the scriptures myself, but I can intuit, how greatly this idea would be extolled there."

Hearing this from me, laughter came on his face. "Well, I can understand this. Actually scriptures have two problems. One, those are written in a kind of language which the common people normally do not grasp. Their text is mystically structured in such a way that even their translation in suitable languages remains imperceptible. And the second reason is that, even a sincere reader may get bewildered by the vastness of their content."

I hadn't ever seen the scriptures myself, hence I couldn't add a word to master's.

After a silent pause, I barely looked at him. Master was

looking somewhere lost in his thoughts. In a moment he began saying, "Studying scriptures is not important but assimilating their real wealth is. The mystic text contained in those is merely a form of communication with the aspiring readers. But when only the text is extolled and not the core message itself, the entire hardship goes futile."

I was attentively silent.

He began to look about me and said, "You've been here to learn the sublime powers of your mind, but given the limited time here we have, I shall not expound the scriptures to you. Instead I shall take you through your own existing world. I've said that the supreme Almighty creates, operates and annihilates this entire universe through His mind's power alone; and I also said that in term of potencies, the human mind is also at par with God's. Now I will reveal another big secret. You see! God is not a person or object; yet His mind operates so wonderfully that He can perform such astonishing feats."

"True Master", I said, "But when you say human mind is at par with God's, then how God becomes so powerful and we mortals remain only frail?"

To this he laughed in his same typical style. He replied, "Listen carefully my son! Responsible for this are the strange attributes of knowledge. Without knowledge one cannot acquaint anything at all; and also this, the knowledge alone is useless. In your case, you already had the knowledge of God creating, operating and annihilating the universes through His mind, but still it was merely a piece of knowledge for you and nothing else. After coming to me, although you have known that power of your mind is at par with the power of God's mind; but again, this knowledge is merely a piece of information for you and nothing else. Do you know why this has happened?"

I shook my head expressing the total ignorance.

"It happens because when one doesn't experience his knowledge, it becomes merely an unutilized possession. Knowledge is no power, but it's merely a prospect power. Given the fact that human mind always has the tendency of forgetting those things which is no longer in its use, having unused knowledge is also prone to become extinct. Even as physical exercises are necessary to keep the muscles alive, mental practices are also necessary to keep the knowledge alive. This matter becomes even more important when the human societies never observe the custom of inheriting the dead things to their generations. A knowledge of any particular kind can be passed on from generations to generations only when such knowledge is alive; for dead knowledge is only to be forsaken by the mankind."

I was completely engrossed in master's words. I had already begun to contemplate that it was a great matter of worry that our modern mankind had already assumed the sublime knowledge about mind to be dead.

Only for a moment, master looked into my eyes and smilingly said, "Would you like to know how the universes are created, especially when you've already been creating one yourself?"

"Oh! Would I be really able to understand it?" I asked in boundless wonderment.

He laughed and said, "Even if you doubt yourself about this, it's my duty to take you through."

"It's all your grace, master", I humbly tendered.

"Now hear my son! I am starting your biggest lesson for the day. You are going to know the truest powers of human mind, including yours as well of course. Do not err by expecting some phenomena in progress of our talk. Phenomena only distracts from the core. What I am going to reveal here is the core of substance, so that you will stop wondering about the constant biggest phenomena which has been perpetually running in the conduct of universes. And be alert; there is another point of great significance. If I impart you only the plain truth around this matter, your understanding might get discomforted. In place of narrating the abstract truths, I am expounding hereby a great analogy, so that you will understand it easily."

I was all ears.

Master started, "Once upon a time in the primitive age, there was a small island on the earth which had constantly remained in the dark for very long time. Sun and moon, both had eloped from this place for the hemispherical reasons. On this island there lived only two people who were neither friends nor the foes. Their names were Shanuk and Kontal. They didn't live together. Neither did they ever use to help each other, nor did they wish any hurt. They knew each other but never talked; for they had no language at all. In the extreme darkness all around, they could recognize each other only by touching the thorny hairs on their heads. This entire place was so dark that they couldn't see anything at all. Whenever they would touch the water, they knew it was the ocean coast, and therefore would turn back instantly. They had no home to live, no particular food to eat and no compelling thought to work upon. They would often fill their hunger with the spontaneously hunted reptiles and roaches. They would catch them running and kill between their fists before eating up.

One day a great tsunami drowned the whole island. Out of storm, the great waves arrived. Both of these men were thrown into the big spates of water. They floated in unconsciousness for some time. Very soon the passing waves took them far from each other; and finally left them forlorn on the different sea shores of an unknown land. This side of the earth was under normal operation of the day-night sun. The two unconscious bodies, which remained like sandstones on the shore, were quite a few miles away from each other. Shanuk regained his consciousness first. It was night time in this land and moon was bright.

As Shanuk tried opening his eyes, the first thing he noticed was the strange light of the moon which he had never seen before. He couldn't bear it; for his eyes were completely unaccustomed to behold the light of any kind. Closing his eyes again, he continued lying on the beach sand. He began to roll his fingers in the sand and soon hit a small pebble. He clasped it.

The very next desire sprouted in his mind was to see what it was. But moonlight was too irritating. He opened his eyes only by half and brought the pebble underneath his chest. Now in his own shadow he could somehow see the pebble. It was a round piece of stone; and of a color which he had never known before. He began liking this pebble. He felt as if he had found a great company in it. He thought if he could see the pebble, the pebble would also be able to see him. He wanted to talk with, but soon realized that even the pebble would not know any language like him. Anyways, he had found a great company today. He began to open his eyes full from half. After some trials, he found that it was not as difficult as he had believed. Though, some inconvenience still remained when he tried to look into directions. Slowly he began to move upwards from the sea coast. In some time he was able to crawl up to a place where he could sit comfortably with his new friend, the pebble.

Miles away on the other hand, Kontal also gained consciousness. Similarly, for the first time, he also opened his eyes to the moonlight. But he could merely thought, "Aah! What hell!" And he closed his eyes again. Then in some time, he also began to roll his fingers in the sand and hit a pebble. He wanted to see it but didn't agree to the lightening offensiveness outside. He thought that his unaccustomed eyes would get pierced by the moonlight once again. But to this moment he was finding the touch of the pebble interesting. Kontal clasped it and began crawling towards some safer place. Keeping eyes only closed he didn't stop crawling for many hours. In due course he reached a cave hole. He crawled into it and stood up straight. Even with closed eyes, he could feel the perfect darkness suitable to him. He felt like chancing and slowly began to open the eyes. It was perfect, for keeping eyes closed or open, didn't make any difference at all. He was happy for his comforted eyesight and for the pebble as well.

Here Shanuk at his place, thought he was once again lonely in his new world. He felt hungry and started looking around with his skewed eyes. He stood up and began walking. Soon he found a low hanging fruit from a tree, which still couldn't be reached by his hands. He didn't know what it was; for he thought it to be only another pebble. While he was wondering about the same, a flying bird came and cut the peel of the fruit with its beak and few away. Drops of sweet juice of the fruit fell over the mouth of Shanuk. He was taken to surprise by the sweet taste and smell. He wanted to have that hanging fruit for him but didn't know how. His extreme hunger sprang an idea in his mind. Abruptly he threw his pebble in the air and hit the fruit. Pebble came down along with the fruit as well. He moved and picked up both. As he bit the fruit for the first time, he found it tastier than his hitherto food of reptiles and roaches on that silly dark island. He thought he had found a great companion in the pebble. He threw it on the tree again and again until some more fruits came down. Now he had filled himself good. He was happy; and then he noticed that throughout this time he had actually kept his eyes open only. The bright moonlight was not troubling him anymore. Rather he thought only because of the moonlight he could find the pebble and the fruits; and therefore moonlight and pebble were auspicious for him. He was immensely grateful to the both, as if he had met with God.

Kontal, on the other side, was also trying to settle in his new strange world. Amidst the dark of cave he had found his old familiar ambience. He also began feeling hungry. He tried biting the pebble, but it hurt him. He thought that he must find some reptile or big roach in the cave itself; for the moonlight outside won't let him live any comfortably. He began crawling inside the cave and soon found a hole in the wall. Familiar with his old hand-hunting practices, soon he felt as if there were many small roaches coming out of the hole. He had a great new idea now. Instead of killing the roaches between his fists, he repeatedly hammered the pebble on the mouth of the hole and killed a many of those. He ate in plenty to fill his hunger. Satisfied now, he was immensely happy. He thought only because of the cave and pebble he was able to feed himself and save him from dying. The taste of roaches was already familiar to his appetite. He thought that the hole in the wall will never be empty of his food. He thanked the cave and pebble, as if he had found God.

Only in next few hours the morning time arrived. The light of sun started very slow. Although Shanuk and Kontal had come from the same dark island, and here too they were living only a few miles away from each other, but their individual experiences with the 'morning' were starkly different. Even though Shanuk had accustomed his eyes to the moonlight, the brighter sunlight was proving quite piercing. He was not able to open his eyes at all. Much troubled by the sun all around, he thought, "But I must not stop trying. Old dim light (moonlight) found me the pebble and food, let us see what this new bright light (sunlight) makes me find now." Shanuk, as before, opened his eyes by half. It was difficult but he didn't lose heart. He walked towards the seashore. Here the coolness in the air was helping him little. As he reached the sand beach, lo, what he found! There were countless similar pebbles all around. Now he began to see more carefully. He jumped in joy. He picked many pebbles and brought all of those to his earlier place of staying. He played with those for the entire day. He put them one over another and he kept on doing the same. Soon he found that accidently he had started to learn making a wall. In the joy of finding more pebbles and also learning about the wall, his eyes were getting accustomed to the sunlight as well. Following day he made many rounds to the beach and collected a big heap of pebbles near his stay. Merely playfully in the next moment, he was busy about making a big wall there. When he had made one big wall, he sat down behind it. The next thing he realized was that, the heat waves had stopped troubling him now. Encouraged, he started having the ideas of creating more walls around him. Perhaps he had begun to learn erecting a walled home for safeguarding himself.

Miles away on the other side, Kontal was indescribably unpleasant with the sunlight. He wondered about doing something for shunning the sun. He threw his pebble upwards many times but it availed him no success at all. Only after a minute had passed in the sun, he had to rush into the cave and bring comfort to his eyes. He trusted that moonlight was at least some way better than now. He decided to stay put in the cave whenever it was sunlight outside. But again, a new kind of problem surfaced, for he didn't know what to do sitting idle there. Because of the sunlight, the interiors of the cave had already illuminated slightly; and because of this, Kontal grew became anxious about finding the darkest corner there. This cave also was no small place from inside, for it had numerous corners. Quickly he found out the darkest place for him. Trusting night to be the only suitable time for walking out of the cave, he slept for the whole day. He had found a readymade home here. When fell the night, he came out of the cave and walked in the direction of beach with only half opened eyes. His joy also knew no limit when he saw the countless pebbles around the beach. He picked a lot of those and came back to the cave. Encouraged about collecting more, for whole night, he continued ferrying between his place and the beach. Soon he collected a large heap inside. As he started playing with the collected pebbles, he put those one aside to another. In no time he figured out what he had actually made. Jostling about his very new idea again, he removed all the pebbles to the darkest corner for his sleep. He squatted down all in the same way and transformed the undulated floor of that corner into a plain surface to sleep on. He had actually made a good bed for him.

Kontal had started creating even the luxuries in his house, whereas Shanuk on the other hand, was still learning to build the walls and a roof above.

Very this moment master interrupted the story. He asked, "Son, do you understand what's going around in these two different stories?"

"Yeah, those are turning out to be very interesting", I replied.

He laughed and said, "Oh! Going by that standard the entire

life would be interesting."

He took a thoughtful pause and said again, "We must not move further in the story without analyzing some critical points met by us so far. As I've already said, you must enjoy the message factor more than the story factor."

Reminding myself about the same, I nodded.

"Tell me what made Shanuk appreciate the light more and conversely, Kontal appreciate the darkness more?" Master asked.

I tried replying, "Maybe Shanuk's way of thinking was better than Kontal's."

Master laughed again. He warned, "Son, you must not become judgmental right away. Judgment between good and bad is no easy business. Do not compare the standards of those two persons with the standards of your own. Mind's conditioning is always different from person to person. To my question, simply try to think only from their point of views, as to what made Shanuk appreciate the light more than Kontal?"

"I can't imagine this very perfectly, but perhaps both of them made their individual choices only", I replied.

"Yes", Master exclaimed, "It's now that you've started getting it right. Tell me, if they would have reached the new world and conditions two years later, could their choices about light be any different?"

This question forced me to think twice before replying. In a moment I said, "I think, yes, it was possible."

"Ok. Then tell me if it was only two months after instead of two years, will your answer be still the same?" Master was making his question trickier.

Again, I took a second in replying, "Well, why not!"

"And if I say it was only two days after instead of two months, then?" He asked again.

This time I wanted to take more time before replying. I began thinking about my personal life as to how I myself had been behaving differently in the similar situations but at different points of time. It was indeed difficult to figure out the founding reasons of all kinds of possibilities in life. Infact the possibilities themselves were endless.

Composedly, I replied, "Yes, even then their choices about light could be different. After all they both had come from the identical living conditions. There could be any possibility."

"Very well! Now will your answer change if instead of two days, I say only two hours or two minutes or two seconds or even less?" He asked on the same line.

"Master, I think I should not rule out any possibility. After all, how would I know what ran inside their minds in all kinds of possible scenarios?" I replied.

"Here you are", master became joyous about my answer. Now he elaborated the point, "The catch word here is the mind. In the very moment of finding first pebble on the beach, Shanuk's mind momentarily thought it was better to see in light; whereas Kontal thought it was not. Of course alternatively, they both could have thought differently, but you see, this 'would be' difference is never important in life. How those things which didn't take place, could be important? Here what remains important is what they had actually thought, and not what they could have alternatively thought. They both kept on moving and working in the directions of their individual thoughts. In each case, every successive thought of theirs was the consequence of the preceding thought; and they were also constantly turning their thoughts into some kind of action or the other. Now son, listen to this most carefully. In both scenarios, the two different individuals were actually making their own different new worlds; or weren't they? These individual new worlds were all about their new kinds of life. Their new kinds of life were gradually being constructed on the very basis of actions which they had been taking. Such of their actions were actually based upon their thoughts. And what more to say, all kinds of their thoughts were taking place nowhere else but in their minds. Of course their mind could have worked differently after an interval of two years, two months, two days, two hours, two minutes, two seconds or even less."

I had already begun to reflect as to how master was connecting the dots about mind.

He continued drawing more out of the story. He said, "Doesn't it seem very strange that it was merely a momentary functioning of mind which made Shanuk live his entire life in the light and Kontal in the dark? Isn't it such an uncomfortable idea that merely a spontaneous impulse of mind caused Shanuk roam about his entire life in the daytime and sleep at night, whereas Kontal roamed about his life in night and slept in the daytime?"

"Hmm..." Already lost in numerous kinds of thoughts, I could give only a humming reply.

"And imagine, had Shanuk's mind disliked the pebble at first sight, he could've never gotten to eat the fruit for satiating his hunger. Maybe he would have also started searching for the roaches again. And also imagine in this way. Had Kontal's mind also refused to carry a pebble along with him, he would have continued killing the roaches between his fists only. The possibilities are enormous if the things would have happened differently. But son, all these vague imaginations made by us are simply irrelevant, because things never happened that way. Only what had been taking place there actually, remains to be the most important part for our understanding. Now listen to the story further."

Oh! Once again I was all ears.

Master continued, "Shanuk started collecting more fruits in the daytime and fitfully sleeping at night. With numerous pebbles, he had now built many walls. One day he thought of having made a miracle by laying a hay roof above the pebble walls. Delightfully, he would collect many fruits everyday and put those inside his hut. He would eat as many as he could and threw away the remaining outside. Many of those thrown pieces of fruits decomposed, while a few of those got dried in the sun. Once he bit a sun-dried fruit and he liked its taste very much. In this way he kept on experimenting again and again. He was happy for the way his life had moved. He often thanked his mind which had tempted him other day for picking his first pebble in life."

"Here Kontal also was experimenting with his given and perceived life conditions. One night, when moon didn't appear at all, he was immensely happy. He began crawling here and there and soon found a big live bunch of hay. With some difficulty he uprooted it and dragged it near to his cave. He broke it several pieces and strewed above his pebble bed. Now his day time sleeping became more comfortable. Every night he ate the killed roaches and threw the leftover ones outside. One night when he was roaming outside of the cave, he occasionally picked a sundried roach. He smelt it and found good. He ate it and found even better. He collected all of those and put safely inside the cave. Now he could eat them even in the daytime. He was now thinking of using his pebble more skillfully for killing more roaches every time, and throw them outside for drying in the sun."

"One afternoon, no one knew from where, but two young ladies, who were aimlessly wandering until now, reached near about the Kontal's cave. Their names were Sheti and Keti. They both were surprised to look at the large heap of stomped roaches outside. Inquisitively they entered inside the cave. Kontal was in dark sleep at that time. The cave was almost dark from inside but they could sufficiently look about. Seeing a man sleeping on the pebble bed, which was nicely covered with hay husk, Keti also felt like sleeping. In no time she also laid down on the same bed with Kontal. Sheti, on the other hand, found the cave very uninspiring. Seeing her companion already slept on the bed, she came out of the cave and started wandering again. As the night began falling, she coincidently reached at the place of Shanuk. Outside the hut she found a heap of sundried fruits. In curiosity she picked one and ate. Her curiosity even increased. And when she gave a look at the hut, her excitement couldn't contain. As she entered inside, she found a man sleeping. She came out once again and finding nothing else to do, she began to eat the dried fruits more. She ate up to her fill. And when she also began drowsing, she came back once again inside the hut and slept with Shanuk."

Now, master interrupted the story once again. He said, "In sometime Shanuk and Kontal both raised families and began to live in their individual groups. They raised their own individual worlds and began to prosper as well. Now, what you think", he asked me, "how this all actually started? Would you say it was because of the pebbles, or because of the sunlight and moonlight, or the fruit and roaches, or was it because of Sheti and Keti?"

"I think it was because of the pebbles", I replied.

"You may be correct but tell me what role the pebbles played in getting Sheti and Keti near to the hut and cave respectively?" asked the master.

"Oh! I think that was none. Infact it was the hut and cave itself which had made the two ladies curious about."

"But tell me", master asked again, "what would the two ladies have done if Shanuk and Kontal would not have lived there at all?"

To this, I became slightly bewildered. I asked master, "Then what's the point of whole story?"

Instead of getting annoyed over my carelessly made comment, master began to laugh very loudly. In a moment when he came down, he asked, "Do you know how many people live in the world in which you live?"

"Quite a few billions I think", I replied.

"And see, each of them would have his or her own good story. But indeed, what's the point of billions of individual stories there?"

I was just silent. I was struggling to comprehend master's way of ending the story about Shanuk and Kontal. In the moments while I was missing a spectacular end to the story, master read my mind.

He said, "Son, I remind you once again. You must focus more

on the message and not in the story. Stories are more towards phenomena, so that those would easily astray you from their message part. Remember that the story of Shanuk and Kontal as narrated by me is merely symbolic. It's no account of real incidences, yet I emphasize that it represents the truth of worldly existence in the very accurate way."

Leaving me under the pangs of wonderment, master closed his eyes and slipped into trance.

After few moments, when he opened his eyes again, a mystic smile came across his face. He started speaking again, "Mind is indeed such powerful, my son! It's indeed that way."

In the meantime, I had started getting his point but not fully yet.

He asked me, "Even if we assume this story to be true, can you say who lived happier; Shanuk or Kontal?"

"It's Shanuk of course. He lived vegetarian. He worked in daytime and slept at night", I almost argued.

"But maybe even Kontal finds him happiest. Even Keti and their children may have embraced this happiness. You see they all lived in the dark cave and they all slept in day time; they may have enjoyed it. Together, they all may have enjoyed hitting pebbles on the roaches and drying those in the sun outside. Certainly they would have made many beds of pebbles and strewed the hay husk above those. What makes you think that they couldn't be the happiest?" Master asked.

I struggled in replying to this. I meekly said, "Perhaps you are correct. Indeed Kontal and his family might feel very happy about their own chosen way of life."

Master smiled and continued, "Similar may be the case with Shanuk as well. Man always chooses the standards for measuring others' lives as per the standards chosen by him for himself. You extol one and abhor the other, but you do these both in the ignorance of others' standards of measuring. Listen now very carefully! This is the big conundrum of mind, which I wish you to learn very perfectly. You always see what your mind impels you to see at; and you always miss what your mind impels you to miss. Alone this mind is the entity of your entire apparent world, and there is nothing else my son!"

"Hmm..." I nodded. I had begun to understand the point.

"Can't you see", master asked again, "that people inhibiting on the different side of the earth, actually live in quite opposite climates, cultures, habits and value systems? For example, the people living in Russia find a negative temperature of five degree much better than their worst seen in the winters; whereas you find a positive temperature of two degrees already the worst. Isn't this really because both of you are living in different kinds of worlds where you both are unaccustomed to the world of each other? Don't you see the mentioned differentiation of light and darkness between Shanuk and Kontal very similar to this? And there are many other factors as well, such as I said, cultures, habits, value systems and many more. Indeed the worlds are many and not one; infact those are countless. However the inherent cosmic unity in the core of all these different worlds is still one and the same. This oneness can be experienced by you only at the other side of your mind."

Speechlessness had occurred to me.

"This entire creation, which is scripturally called as 'matter'", master continued revealing, "is the gross product of mind alone. Can't you see that it were only the minds of Shanuk and Kontal, which built the entire worlds around them! Once they were living on the same island, and now they lived separately from each other. Even now, although they lived only a few miles away from each other, yet they could never get a chance of recognizing each other by touching the thorny hairs on their heads. They certainly would have forgotten each other. They both would have been highly busy in their two different worlds. For Kontal, there was no world without dark and for Shanuk there was no world without sunlight. You should never undermine this fact that being completely unaware to the world of each other, they both lived happily; and they never had to think about any other world outside of their own. In short period of time, they both would have forgotten their previous island as well, because now it was only their new world which mattered to them. Who can say who lived better than the other; it's impossible even for themselves, for they both have been unaware of the relativity."

Master quickly checked my gaze. Seeing me completely engrossed in the talk, he smiled and continued,

"Son! Foregoing the story right here, let us now move to your own real world. Can you say how many worlds are here on this planet called earth?"

I found this question amateur. Gladly I submitted the answer, "Sir, The world is one only. Isn't it?"

"No, it's not that", he said.

I looked on in daze.

He continued, "Actually worlds on this planet are many, infact quite beyond your imagination. Would you like to know about this matter?"

"Yes, very much", my curiosity was already on peak. I wanted to reconcile the difference.

"How many are members in your family?" He asked.

"Four", I said.

"Then in closest view, you live in four different worlds at least. I know all your life. You are a son, a husband and also a father there; therefore your world inside your home is limited to being a son, husband and father alone. With your unenlightened mind, you can never enter in the other world, to say, that of your wife, who herself lives in the world of being a wife, a mother and a daughter-in-law alone. Similarly different are the worlds of your child and mother, which you have never entered at all. On one hand you speak that the whole world is one; whereas inside of your small house alone, already you have four. Isn't it true?"

"Hmm..." I was sinking in an unfathomable sea of thoughts. Master sensed it.

"Son! You will find my words complicated only when you remain preoccupied with your previous unenlightened beliefs.

Otherwise, all matters in relation to the secret world are only simplest to acquaint. Eternal truth, which is the element of secret world, is not complicated; but it's the tendency of man which constantly fears complications around it. For assimilating the simple higher truths, merely keep your mind open for the sake of unprejudiced interpretations. What I am going to narrate now, is going to be the key for your advancement towards the secret world."

He just resurrected my concentration.

Master took up the conversation again, "In this world which you call as one, there are actually as many worlds as are the people in it. And again these worlds are manifold. For instance, at home your world is all about being a son, husband and father, but in your office where you work, you have yet other worlds of being a co-worker in different senior or junior positions. Alone for you at your work place, you have as many worlds as are your colleagues and the mentalities with whom you have to constantly or occasionally interact. And this all is again the same with your wife and children as well. Your wife lives in a different world when she is at her own workplace; and similarly is your mother and child in their own respective worlds when they are outside the home. Notice it sincerely, that whenever the position of yourself or that of others around you changes, the position of your world also changes. And the world which hasn't remained the same because of these changes, is invariably a new world every time. Such complex is the intertwined stratagem of the apparent worlds, that it undoubtedly brings only bewilderments to the human minds. And this the central reason behind so much anxiety, misgivings, prejudice and skepticism all around in the physical world."

I remained spellbound and only silent.

Master continued, "Can you believe this? Everyone on this planet is living in his or her own individual world and no one can enter into the world of each other because they all have merely an ordinary mind. Physically they all live together, but mentally they are apart. Even those who sleep together, who eat together, who enjoy the entertainments together, who worship together, who play or walk together, who praise or condemn together; cannot be said to be living in the same world. They all err by thinking that only the world in which they believe they live, is the only world to be believed. And this error has happened because no one has got the skill to see into the other secret world, which lies on the other side of mind."

Looking down and nodding, I was just speechless.

And master didn't stop yet. He said, "And this all I have talked is only about the human beings. Do you think even a fish, which lives deep down in the ocean, would also have a world of her own?"

"Oh, why not! Certainly it will also have one for itself." I took no time in contemplating and replying.

"And do you think a fish can also have a wife and children", asked the master again.

"Oh certainly, why not!" I just added.

"Now imagine how many fishes would live in the depths of ocean; and also this, how many creatures other than the fishes would live there. Do not miss to also include the creatures which never live inside water, for those live either on the earth or in the sky. There are also the tiniest creatures like bacteria and viruses which cannot be easily seen or noticed. There are creatures on earth which the mankind has not even discovered yet. Even the insentient stones can't be said to be lifeless, because those also change over the time. Do not also miss to include many planetary systems similar to ours in the big universe above. Can there ever be any man or machine which is capable of counting all these worlds? Compared to this, doesn't the job of counting the stars really seem easy?"

I just gave in. "Oh master! I can't comprehend it. I can't hold this view in my imagination. I feel too bewildered at this moment", even by saying these words, I couldn't vent my exasperation.

Looking at my position, master quickly comforted me. He empathically said, "Son, attain your peace now. What you have experienced in this moment is merely a flick of what Lord *Krishna* in his childhood had made his mother *Yasoda* experience by looking into his mouth. When you are beholding the magnanimity of creation, such bewilderment is natural. But if you are in the company of someone, who has already explored these secrets, you will regain your peace very quickly. Here too, as you are with me, you will regain yourself here and now. Just move your hands forward and hold them near your chest", he commanded.

Still in some kind of ineffable giddiness, I followed his command. As I held my both hands near the chest, master gripped those with his own hands and pinched those too hard. I didn't how it went about, but very instantly I returned to my normal senses.

Finding me at ease, master smiled in love. He said, "Son, what you've glimpsed today in your imagination is no ordinary sight. It's not possible for the ordinary minds to even go near to such vision. However few others, who have practiced the ability of seeing on the other side of mind, actually know how to comprehend these visions. Latent powers of mind, when invoked in the curiosity of eternal truth, can certainly make one as potent as manifesting the universes themselves."

Much soothed, I looked to his face.

He smiled in deep compassion, "Maybe in this moment, you are thinking of your mind being such a stupefying organ in your body."

I nodded.

"But that is not the complete truth my son. If you are constantly keen to acquaint the sublime truths about the eternity, you will find that actually your mind is the finest instrument you have." These of master's words were energizing me. He utterly surprised me by further saying, "You know what! I can perfectly count how many worlds are there."

"Oh! Is that really possible?" I was greatly awed.

"Yes", he smiled and added, "But I can do that only when I am seeing on the other side of my mind."

"Oh! Please tell me how many are there? I am curious to know what kind of a number it comes out," I couldn't hide my excitement. I already knew that here it was no ordinary man on the hilltop. He would always do the miracles and unusual things. As he began saying, my ears alerted more.

In a very thoughtful gesture he said, "Only one, my son! Only one."

My astonishment was on a new high. I couldn't do more than a whispering, "One?"

He now revealed the crux, "Only after I've become able to see on the other side of my mind, I am able to enter into the worlds of others. And once I've entered into the unified world of others, all kinds of distinctive worlds have vanished out, including my own apparent world as well. Indeed there has now remained only one world which is infinitely expanded and indescribably illumined. And once this unique secret world has occurred to me, unrestrainedly I can reach any time, any place, any object, any person, any mind and any life. As you have often wondered about me, know here, that this is the power through which I can travel into your life at my disposition."

My heart was pounding. I didn't know what to say in this moment.

Then master moved his chin upwards and closed his eyes. After muttering some formulae incomprehensible to me, he stood up and said, "Look there my son! It's dusk time now. You should go back to your cottage. You will be completely free from your laboratory construction work for two following days more. Make the most of your time available."

He gave me company for seeing off. While walking along he said, "Today you've learnt how the worlds are created. It is fundamentally no different from how Shanuk and Kontal did it. If you want you can imagine yourself and expand that story infinitely. World is not created for once and all, instead all kinds of creatures, including men, continue creating it forever. You too have been doing the same thing since long." As he said this, he broke a loud laughter.

I too laughed, all while coming down to the cottage alone.

FOURTEEN

First Night of Meditation

AFTER COMING DOWN I went straight to the same food point downhill. Quickly I took light meals and started back to the cottage. The chilling wind was getting strong by the fall of night, though I was aloof from everything around me. Having reached the cottage, I quietly unlocked the door and entered in. After a wash I tanked in my bed. My state was still lost in numerous thoughts. Probably it was the first time in my life when I was thinking more about the words than about the man himself who spoke those words. Whatever the master had said was truth; and as he always said, since it was truth, it was simple as well. I wondered why I couldn't understand the things in this way myself before. I thought perhaps it was now because I had started peering to the other side of my mind. Master too had said that on this other side there could be innumerable new discoveries for one. I thought about him reverently. Indeed I had found quite an indescribable man uphill.

Lying awake in the bed, I was constantly thinking about Shanuk and Kontal. Although master had remarked that the entire story was imaginary, yet it related with truth so easily. I thought about people living in merciless climates, such as in parts of Russia, and still living happily. Of course they would live in a different kind of world altogether. And this was the reason that whenever such people would escape the winters of their country and visited the easy winters of some other country like India, they would roam like in summers. How came it possible that roaming in the same climate conditions, someone felt like pleasant summers and other felt intolerable winters? And even this; climate temperatures are just one side of the matter. Even differences in the eating orders, cultural settings, basic human habits or physical appearances were not still sufficient to circumscribe this matter, for there could be innumerable other factors as well.

I thought this all was nothing but the hallucinating sport of mind alone. A person in his mind would feel about himself in one way and at the same time, would feel differently about others. He would always see himself distinctive from others; and others too would do the same. In this way would emerge the interminable differences amongst people, communities, religions, and amongst nations as well. Every moment this pervasive differentiation would gather the disturbances of several kinds. People live unhappily. They feel either threatened or bullying. In delusion of taming this differentiation by overcoming, they only enlarge the gulfs of several kinds. For overcoming their stature of being oppressed, they want to become the oppressors themselves. They always remain unsatisfied with their status quo, and it would compel them agitating, even violently. They would always grow unhappy over finding the others richer than themselves; but again they would foolishly maintain their unhappiness by ignoring the ones who were poorer.

Ah! My contemplation continued. I could see that this all was merely a sport of mind. Everyone, who thought he was unhappy, agitated or even outraged, could have actually felt differently through the power of his mind. Life of every one could have been otherwise; for it could have been soothed, happier and beatific. How everyone finds his life in the present moment and how he keeps wondering about it could be rather pleasant. Master had said it very righteously; indeed it's alone the mind and nothing else.

Lost in numerous extolling about master, I didn't know when the sleep took hold of me.

That night I had a dream. The pleasantness of its kind was

the first time for me. In the dream I saw that I was calmly sitting on a bench in the park which was nearby my home in Mumbai. The atmosphere was familiar to me. Amidst the green all around, the early morning climate was ineffably pleasant. Soon I started sensing that my weight had begun to reduce. I felt strange. Continuing sitting in the same way here, I closed my eyes and began to look about what I had freshly started noticing in my mind. It was some small round reflective disk which I was holding in my hands. Beyond that, I couldn't understand anything more about it. In the next moment, quite strangely, the disc spun in the air and disappeared. In wonderment behind closed eyes, I started noticing my weight again. It was still reducing moment after moment. My wonderment knew no bound when I saw that my body had become completely weightless. I was throbbing in awe. I didn't feel like opening my eyes and snapping the unique experience. I wanted it to go on. Only in a moment I felt as if my body was floating above the ground; indeed as if I was levitating. The very moment I grew up in the air, I started checking my position in curiosity. I could clearly see that I was nearly two feet above the ground. I wondered if I could go even higher. As this thought sprang in the mind, my body began moving even more upwards. I pushed even harder. Only in half a minute, ahead of the tips of nearby trees, I was floating like a stilled boat on the bank. I was in the air, with literally nothing below my feet. In excitement I didn't feel any wind or sun. I was alone at the top, smiling at whatever came in my sight. I was so greatly marveled with this experience that I hoped my all senses were alive and not merely sleeping. However doubtful as I was, I rechecked my sense. While still in dream I was fully convinced that it was all very real and not merely my imagination. But alas! The very moment I looked down in hope of finding someone in the park, who could be awestruck about my miracle, my dream slipped and I was awake.

This was the moment I realized that I hadn't covered myself with the quilt so far in the night. I smiled for this another trick which was already being played by my mind in the background. Although it was shivering chill inside the cottage, my mind hadn't yet reminded me of it. Perhaps for sake of illusion of dream, it had ignored the other illusion of weather existing in the outside physical world. I smiled about the instant feeling of the same shivering, which I had not even slightly realized until a minute before. Indeed, it was the mind alone and nothing else.

Covering myself well under the quilt, I waited for my next day with master. In no time, deep slumber had draped me.

FIFTEEN

Master Produces Rasagollas in the Jungle

NEXT MORNING AS I woke up, I felt happier and lighter. Reminiscences of previous night's dream were still afresh. I hoped, for master always knew my mind, he will certainly talk about my strange dream.

After replying to a few messages on the phone I gave a call to the deputy engineer at the laboratory construction site. He informed me that all kinds of prerequisites had started falling in place, and it was likely for me join him a day after tomorrow. I found master's prediction coming only true.

This morning I didn't plan any particular breakfast. I was already enjoying the lightness in my body and heart. Nevertheless I believed that these kinds of food joints rarely provide the breakfast which could be healthy in true way. Before starting out, I took only a glass of milk and nothing else. Immediately I started for my short pilgrimage.

Finding the innumerable shrubs all around, I chose and plucked off a handful flowers, and loosely kept those in the upper pocket of my jacket. I thought those would be for my master. While ascending, I was constantly wondering as to what great knowledge he would impart today.

Soon I reached his place and found everything quite familiar to the previous day. Master was sitting on the altar with his half closed eyes and straight erect spine. Without disturbing him in the meditation, I quietly sat down below the altar.

The cold wave was strong today. On the hilltop here, sun was playing hide and seek with the fog. I could hardly restrain from shivering while I wondered, how could the master, who was clad in only one cloth be able to sit in peace like this. I believed he must have perfected a habit for this; after all he had been at the places like this for quite some time.

As I looked to his face, he was smiling. I thought surely he was reading my mind.

After my prolonged moment of wait, master opened the eyes.

"Welcome my son", he said in an affectionate voice.

I prostrated and put the flowers at his feet. While looking on, he continued smiling as before.

He gestured with his right hand and asked me to sit next to him on the altar. I followed the command.

"No one should fight his body against the weather my son! Man's body is not his enemy, although man by his ungoverned habits can end up making it so."

I was not surprised at the new subject which he had randomly started today. Infact I knew it was not random, for he had been reading my mind only a minute before. He was answering the same.

"O my master! Do you keep reading my mind all the times?" I asked.

To my question, he passed a very affectionate smile. "You should not feel very stupendous about it. Son, it's not about reading your mind, it's about coming to know your needs. Everyone has been bestowed by nature with the fundamental right of keeping his imaginations secretive. Yet he is unable to stop others guessing about him. Such guesses may be right as well as wrong at different times. The probability of getting such guesses right increases when the invisible emotional bond between the two persons gets stronger. For example, a mother would always know the needs of her infant baby, even if the latter is too little to speak. In only the similar way I have known your needs and it helps me accomplish my duty towards you."

I couldn't add a word.

He added, "A divine preceptor does a great thing in the lives of his disciples. Let yourself acquaint this doctrine better so that you can comprehend how it works."

Already anticipating a great start of the day, I was all ears.

Master began elaborating, "Man always knows that God exists everywhere and He is omnipresent, yet he doesn't believe this fact as much. Had man truly believed it, he would have stopped sinning under the threat of constant watch by God. God knows all but He doesn't speak out right away in the language of man. This is the reason man never gets afraid of Him and rather continues indulging in sins. Imagine if the man was physically aware that God is limitlessly powerful to punish his wrong-doings, and He is also watching him all the time, he would have certainly made only the exquisite actions in life. Imagine how great life were! How great infact the world could have been! But you see, God hasn't chosen the way of power and threat. This is the reason that man has prompted to take only an undue advantage of it; such as the children take advantage of the excess love by their parents."

My nodding was coming naturally.

Here master revealed about my apprehension. "If you believe that I am constantly reading your mind, soon you will see your unmatched advantage to it. In the beginning, for feeling to be under constant watch, you will be afraid of indulging in sin. Remember! Goods fruits of your good actions, whether attained with self-inclination or under some threat, remain only the same. Trusting my constant presence in your thoughts, if ever out of your several bewilderments you will ask me the questions, my voice will take place in your mind and will answer. You will be able to establish a constant dialogue with me. It will be then occurring to you that you have stopped needing me in my physical body at all. Every time you need enlightenment, you will ask me the questions. I will answer, but for that I must read your mind to understand your curiosity well. You have the freedom to summon me any time, therefore it becomes necessary for me to read your mind all the time. However son, in due course of time you will see that you have learnt about the secret world quite enough that you can answer yourself. It will be then that your inner voice will become one with the inner voice of mine. Then you may call it telepathy or by some other name. Such will become the greatest day of your life when you will become so competent in yourself, that you will no longer require external assistances of any kind whatsoever."

I felt more revered towards him for this another great revelation made. One by one, he was unfolding all divine secrets before me.

Here master continued, "You must know the discrimination between a divinely appointed preceptor and a worldly appointed mentor. Primarily there are two differences. First, preceptor doesn't expect or even when forced doesn't take at all any worldly value from his disciple in return; whereas a mentor or teacher necessarily, and by custom too, has to take it. Secondly, contrary to your constant need of mentor or teacher, preceptor lives with you only for a limited short period of time. He merely initiates you by his words and self-realized actions; and in this way enables you towards invoking the supreme knowledge in yourself by yourself alone. I am not your mentor or teacher, but only your preceptor who will physically exist with you for a short period of time; though you will continue listening to my voice in your heart as long as you will want."

Master was giving a hint of sad news about my separation from him. I didn't know how to react. I sat only aloof. In following moments he sat quiet and still. Before closing his eyes in meditation, he spoke only this, "Let us observe silence till we go out for a walk again.

Now master was immersed in his own world. I wondered how he could sit still for such long spells. Doesn't he feel at least an itching or sensation? Doesn't this strong cold wind trouble him? Did he sleep while sitting, but if it was true, why doesn't he stumble in some time? Although looking in master's direction only sparingly, I was thinking about him alone. Then all of a sudden, another thought hit me; even he would know what was running in my mind in these moments. I remarked to myself that he was master and will remain the same. Instead of worrying about him, I must start worrying about myself. He had already previously said that I have still enough reasons to become conscious about in my life.

I tried sitting in the lotus posture similar to him. But it was difficult. Even if I could form that posture for once, I couldn't keep it for more than sixty seconds. Meekly, I sat in my normal crossed legs. However I could sit straight without much difficulty. In all possible manners, I was trying to emulate him.

I didn't know what formula he was muttering in his mind, but surely I didn't at all know any for myself. Sitting straight here on this fairly large altar, I began observing the nature and numerous birds roaming around. Few times I tried closing my eyes in short spells, but perhaps it asked for too much patience. Nevertheless yet, I was quite enjoying the company of my great master and the scenery around. Lost in two worlds in my inside and out, I was no longer getting troubled by the cold wind. The Sun was already bright and was taking necessary care of me. Numerous sports of birds were keeping me entertained. And the scenic mountains in far, as seen from here were already the best.

After about an hour master opened his eyes, and quite unprecedentedly, began laughing at me.

"What's wrong with you son! Don't you feel hungry today?" He asked.

Very moment he said this, the pangs of hunger began hitting me.

He commanded, "Once again go to that tree and bring whatever you find there. Bring some for me as well. Today I had delayed my meals in your wait." He laughed again.

As I started walking my appetite increased. In my mouth I could feel the taste of previous day's taproots once again. I thought I must not become careless this time and pick more than what two persons could eat. Else he will ridicule me again, saying, if I was too hungry.

As I turned to the other side of that pine tree, I didn't find any pinkish roots. Instead there was a large earthen pan which was covered with a leaf on its mouth. I didn't know what eatable could be inside it. Fearing to open it myself, I brought it to the master and placed before him.

"Come and sit down my son! Pour in your hand and take out whatever you find inside, he said.

But before my hand could reach the pan, he warned me, "Remember! You can pick from your hand only for once; although you will be free to pick as much as you can or want."

I knew it. Again he had started playing some trick with me. Already compelled by hunger and also by his dominating presence, I poured in my hand though the covering leaf. Perhaps there were some soft balls. Suddenly I felt as if those were Rasagollas, a kind of sweet dish. My appetite increased even more. Given the condition placed by master, I didn't know how many to take out. I wondered if there would still remain sufficient for the master. Nonetheless, I opened my paw inside and took out few.

"Eat my son!" said master lovingly.

Here to my steepest surprise, those were indeed the Rasagollas. I had no trace of idea as to how had those reached behind the pine tree.

"Start eating my son! I knew you liked these since childhood", master chuckled.

Apprehensive, I looked to his face in great deal of surprise. He was all smiling. As I started eating, I found those to be wonderful. It took me no time to finish the ones in my hand.

The sweets were too tasty to resist. Even though I remembered master's condition, I felt like taking more out of the pan. But master quickly warned, "Food to be eaten by man at one time is always sufficient what can comfortably settle in his single hand's clasp. If he is too hungry he can stretch his palm a little. But if he takes more than that, he only harms himself."

Then he looked in my eyes again. He merely said, "Those were enough for you my son."

In the following moment, he poured in his own hand into the pan, but brought out the same pink taproots of yesterday. I was taken by surprise. Why hadn't I touched those when my hand was inside the covered pan?

As he began to peel the roots, I asked, "Won't you take Rasagollas, master?"

"No, I don't feel like. For me rather this will be fine for rest of the day. Do you remember you had forgotten to take those with you yesterday? Few of those are still left in it my son." As he said this he took out four more taproots out of the pan and put them on the altar. Then he handed out the pan to me and said, "Please put it once again behind that tree."

I grew even more curious about the pan which was still covered with the big leaf. When I was holding it in my hands I felt it was empty. Quietly I moved on and while putting it down behind the tree, I removed the leaf slightly. But oh! It was indeed empty.

Having no way to the puzzle, I came back.

Seeing my bewildered eyes here, master asked, "Why you look dumbfounded about Rasagollas? Must not your host entertain you good? Tell me if you didn't like the taste of your food."

He broke laughter. Watching him still peeling the root, I also smiled. As he quickly ate it, he said, "Stop puzzling yourself unnecessarily. Let us go for our walk now."

As he came off the altar, he said, "And do not forget once again to take with you these taproots in the evening!"

My smile grew wider. I began following him in the dense forest once again.

SIXTEEN

Watching Master Communing with Nature

"LET US TAKE THE same path once again", he said before we turned to the familiar footway.

From behind I looked about more carefully. Master never walked unsteady. Even though his age would be some eighty or even more, I had never seen him frail in his frame. This time in the woods, he was walking slightly ahead of me and I never drifted away from him.

"Do you know my son, how mind can be perfected?" Master asked in his sweet voice.

After a thoughtful pause I replied, "But perhaps mind is actually the culprit; and it need not be perfected at all."

Hearing this, he laughed. "No son! Why blame the poor mind alone. Isn't anything in the world, if operated in ignorance, produces only the bad results?"

I listened on.

"Meditate in this way", master continued, "Whoever that can become your enemy in the world and whoever never, it's all because of the way you perceive the functioning of world, its people and its objects' inside your mind. I have said it that your individual world is always distinct from the countless worlds perceived by others, but still, as long as your mind does not understand this matter perfectly; it constantly relates itself with the pseudo of oneness of your apparent physical world. And consequently, very this pseudo perception continues administering each and every breath of one's ordinary life."

Here, the dense jungle had started on our way.

Master continued, "When I talk about making the mind perfect, I do not mean sprucing it or curbing it against man's ordinary will. Haven't you already seen, for example, that the bad addictions of men when forcefully curbed by them, often bounce back with a bang? Perfection is not in force; instead it's in the harmony with truth. Infact, the real need of mind about perfection is better described as the need for appreciating and accepting the truth in one's life. When sincere appreciation of truth takes place in mind, sincere acceptance also follows. You see, when man cannot ignore the need of food forever, how can he ignore the need of truth forever? Know here a secret, my son! Man's life is not run by the power of food but it is run by the power of truth. Somebody might be in habit of taking meals thrice in a day or even more, whereas some other one might take only twice. Yet someone else might take his meals only once in a day; and still there could be someone on fasting as well. Some person could starve yet not die; whereas many people die only because of the food. It's also possible that somebody might look in pink of health without even food for long periods. In the apparent physical world what is causing what, is quite a complex scenario to describe. It interests only those who are fond of ordinary riddles and discoveries alone. The biggest riddle and discovery however is nothing, but the human mind itself. Those, who become intensely curious about the operations of mind, actually make the biggest discoveries. Those are the people who harmonize with truth quickest and attain in this way the very perfection of mind."

"But master!" I asked, "Don't you think this 'truth', which you often extol, is still a theoretical concept? How do I know it as? How do I really define it? Must not it have some very cognizable dimension? Where would I search it?"

Hearing my desperate questions, master laughed. He spoke from ahead, "Knowing truth is the simplest task on earth. It's the thing which must happen to the man in the quickest way."

"Please elaborate this. Unless I know the rudiments, how

would I understand the almanac?" I said in a voice of desperation.

"My son! Providing answers to your all kinds of curiosities is my duty. Although I have described it earlier as well; but again I will repeat the same concept using a different insight, so that you would understand it perfectly. It's no bad if you are taking time to understand fully. Listen here the wholesome about truth. In this territory rudiments and almanac, are both the same. Once you've understood it, you will actually bridge kinds of these gaps."

I was all ears to his words again.

"I said that it is the simplest and quickest possible job on the earth, and this I've said on the very basis of fact, that knowing truth is knowing the world and its objects exclusively in the way in which those really exist; and not in the ways of how one's own conditioned mind perceives those. Say! To know a tree just to be a tree, what's so difficult in that?"

I counter asked, "But hasn't man already been knowing tree as a tree only? Where's the error?"

Master laughed loud. "You've again got swayed by the analogy. But still, when you've asked, I will return the answer in the same way. When you are looking at tree, you are only 'looking' at it as a tree, but not 'knowing' it as one. You come to acquaint a tree only after looking at its trunk, branches, leaves, flowers and fruits. If ever you do not get to see those first, you will never come to acquaint it as a tree. Isn't it?"

"But master", I asked, "If there are no trunk, branch, leaf, flower or fruit at all, how could there be any tree at all?"

Master had slowed down his pace. He looked back to my face and resumed speaking from ahead, "Why not! Just now I will tell you the second end of this analogy and you will contradict your own previous statement. Tell me how would you know those roots in the ground, which show no trunk, branch etc.?"

"But master, those are only roots and not the tree!" I contested his point again.

"Then what's wrong if I say", master asked, "that even above the ground are only the trunk, branches, leaves, flowers and fruits; but nowhere the tree at all?"

Once again he turned to check about my face. My brain was drumming inside.

"This analogy will help you greatly, son!" said the master. "Actually you've 'Known' only the trunk, branches etcetera, whereas calling those together as tree is merely your convenient choice speech. You have never 'Known' the tree. Had you, you would have never said those words about the roots."

I was already nodding.

Master continued enlightening on this matter, "Now listen how I look at the same. Even though I look at trunk, branches etcetera, but I 'Know' those all as nothing but the tree. I do not give more regards to the fruits than I give to the trunk; and I give no less regards to the roots either. Though my senses perceive the different parts of tree only differently, but I have perfected my mind to 'Know' all of those only in 'unity'. Truth, what I speak about often, is nothing but merely the cognizance of this unity. Trust me; attaining this cognizance is indeed simplest and quickest possible for man. It just takes appreciating and accepting the same on his part. Only this unity is what really exists; and whatever other things seem existing are only the creations of human conditioning of minds. For example, you might give higher regards to the fruits because you find those tastier; but at the same time termites might give higher regards to the roots, because those find that tastier. And why think only about the trees, all kinds of sentient and insentient existence in this universe invariably have the same unity which I have just mentioned about. When there is total unity, there can't any difference to be bridged."

While I was completely engrossed in his talk, master concluded, "Only 'Knowing' this unity is 'Knowing' the truth. It is of course simplest and quickest possible to attain for the man. When you appreciate and accept this eternal unity around you, you actually become united with it; you become a yogi. You become perfect. After all, the literal meaning of Yoga is 'to unite' only. Or isn't it?"

Although I had understood his expounding well, but there still remained some kind of apprehension inside me. I asked, "But master, still don't you agree that the layers of human life are imperceptibly magnanimous and those never stop hallucinating the people like me? Will it require me the astounding contemplations every time before I am made to judge about things in the perfection of mind? I am afraid, I would not be allowed enough time and opportunity for doing meditations first, and subsequently act upon the perfect judgments."

Master smiled again. He said, "Often when you are unprepared for a new job, it's not unnatural for you if your thoughts grow bewildering. But when such a job becomes indispensable, you will have to carry it out anyway. Most kinds of general duties amidst the worldly life generally become indispensable. Willy-nilly you'll have to carry out those. So when you have no alternate but to perform your worldly duties any which way, why not execute those highly skillfully?"

As anticipated, I was convinced of him.

"You see son!" master's voice turned very philosophical, "The truth of unity which is being talked about here is the same eternal truth which I had talked about on the first day. Here as I have emphasized on high skillfulness, know this too. The highest skill in the world is alone the skill which brings you closer to the eternal truth. Many adepts have brilliantly expounded the numerous theories around this matter. They say that truth is of two kinds; absolute and relative. They explain further that being absolute or relative are merely two different stages of the truth which are interchangeable; because in the end it's only the absolute truth which remains. For example, absolute truth is that harming or killing any living being in the creation is forbidden; but as per relative truth a tyrant oppressor of devil nature can be suitably punished or even killed. Whenever by the human beings, who lived in different times and ages, the absolute truth was brought into their practice, it only diluted its attributes, so as to only become the relative truth. Holding the 'absolute' in its absoluteness for long, that too through your faculties operating in the apparent world; is indescribably difficult. This is such a great matter for one's contemplation. I leave it to you as to how much interest you take in it and keep exploring further. If you read or listen to the various excellent commentaries by advanced adepts, your imagination will get exposed to many unforeseen lights."

In this moment of our walk we had reached the same beautiful scenic place of yesterday. Master wanted to sit here for some time. Finding it a suitable place to sit, I pointed towards a lowly dense tree nearby.

After two of us had sat down on the ground, master casually said, "Look around son! Isn't this all really so beautiful?"

I examined his face. Bearing divine smile behind his beard, master's eyes were drinking the nectar of scenic view. I too looked around again and again. It was just matchless.

"What you think I could have added to this beauty from my side?" asked the master.

I didn't understand his question.

"It's simply nothing my son! In my view I am nothing who would add anything from my side to the beauty of nature. Nature has become beautiful by its own. And it's the same way to the other question, as to what nature could've added to the inner beauty of my own. You can marvel my statement, but do you see the truth? Actually nature and I, are both the same. We are one. Nature never thinks of me to be different from it, nor do I think so. That is why cold waves do not perpetrate me on the hilltop. Infact there is no one who would perpetrate the other."

I agreed to this at once. I was very thoughtful in this moment.

Master looked and said again, "You are sitting here and admiring the beauty of nature. But do you know what would the nature be thinking about you in very this moment?"

I was surprised at his question. I moved my head in ignorance.

He continued, "At first the nature would be surprised at your uncommon ability to watch and appreciate it. And in the next moment it would be admiring the beauty of your own mind for developing such ability. Then also for sure, it would be congratulating you for having made your mind as beautiful as the nature itself. Nature also would be thinking that it had added nothing to your beauty on its part; infact it is you alone who made it. Nature appreciates you because you appreciate it; and nature accepts you because you accept it. Can you see another secret hidden in it? Actually life can be beautiful even before your total unity with eternal truth takes place; provided you're keeping your directions correct. Here my duty is only to keep your directions correct, for walking has to be made by yourself alone. And how wonderful! You have already started experiencing this beauty in merely a couple of days of our meeting. Look around and drink this nectar only silently. Once again I talk high about the potency of silence."

Indeed, I was feeling only the bliss all around me. I couldn't add a single word to the wisdom of master. Along with the nature I was also appreciating him; only silently.

But master was never unaware of my silence. He swiftly moved his gaze towards me. He had read my mind when he said, "Oh! Do you know what has happened in this very last moment?"

"No", I said.

"Just now, one new channel has appeared besides our erstwhile communion with nature. In the moments I was appreciating the nature and nature appreciating me, you also started appreciating my wisdom. And now, in the new channel, the nature has started appreciating you much more than before. Oh! Just look above in the tree. Greatly impressed by our invisible vibrations of love, even those birds have started now communing with the nature, which were hitherto anxious only about the usual strife of their lives. Can you experience this ever increasing chain of love, which was started by both of us only a few minutes before? Oh my son! Look around the great amount of happiness spread everywhere. Our silent invisible vibrations of love have already started reaching out beyond these mountains and even further."

I had become statue.

"Let me give you one more dimension of eternal truth. This happiness pervading all around is also eternal truth. The very original course of nature, which you cannot interfere or impede, is called the eternal truth. You cannot add anything to it because you yourself have emerged out of it. However erroneously if you still happen thinking otherwise, you will at once stop admiring the eternal truth and similarly the eternal truth will stop admiring you. Criticizing or rejection of nature's operations by man is his foolish denial of the eternal truth, which however makes no difference at all to this entire operation."

"And beware you." The master said with admonitory eyes, "Do not contract your definition of nature by limiting it to the kind of beautiful scenery what you are seeing about here. Instead, each and every sentient and insentient thread in and around this entire fabric of existence, which, whether in long or short period of time, remains subject to the course of change, is put together called nature."

I was spellbound. Both of us were sitting silent amidst the dense forest. I could easily comprehend that how wonderfully through his direct experience the master had demonstrated his philosophy. His decision of sitting for some time here was not without reasons. Awhile this he had exposed my imaginations to many unforeseen dimensions.

Master had now stood up and was prepared to walk back to the cave, "The duty of true preceptor is only to provide to his beloved disciples merely the key understanding of these big matters. In the expanded vibratory presence of master, the imaginary faculties of a disciple are appropriately conditioned to ponder upon further skillfully. Then soon the day comes when disciple becomes free from everything, even from the physical need of his preceptor. The preceptor and disciple become the same, infact there remains no individual to become any different from the other. And such is the most ideal state of relationship between each every sentient and insentient matter present in the creation. Only this unity is useful, otherwise my son, all else is illusion."

Having said this, master paced up his walk.

Now I knew the secret behind his typical way of laughing every time.

Like a child, I followed his footsteps till we'd reached his cave back.

SEVENTEEN

The First Illusion: Time

"MASTER, THERE IN THE forest you talked about illusions in the world, but I've not yet perfectly understood how to identify such illusions and steer myself clearly of those."

While coming back to the cave, many ideas were tossing in my mind. Whatever master had said was doubtlessly true, but another truth was that I was not as advanced as him. I could imagine that unless I'd learn how to deal with the illusions around my daily living, I won't gain much from his words. After reaching the cave and having sat upon altar with master, this was the first question I had asked him.

Hearing my never ending apprehensions again, a sweet smile crossed his face. He never discouraged me from asking the questions.

Master said, "Your question is wonderful my son! It shows your preparedness for receiving the subtlest knowledge of existence and elements. Let me start narrating to you four different stories in relation to four illusions."

For the prospect of stories, I was keen and alert.

"Listen carefully", master started, "Our spiritual mysticism popularly describes two kinds of illusions in the existence, and those are – 'Time' and 'Space'. Have you ever heard about those?" asked the master.

"No Master! At least not in way of illusion", I replied in surprise.

To my answer he laughed again. He asked, "Oh! You haven't? But again there are two more – 'Word' and 'Atom'."

For me, all four were new. Neither had I any trace of idea as to what kind of astonishing stories the master was going to relate. It was only later when I started sensing about things.

Master spoke, "As I've said that for your increased interest and understanding I would relate four symbolic legends about four kinds of ethereal illusions, therefore hear first about the Time."

As usual, I was all ears.

He began, "Once upon a time there lived a highly advanced yogi. In his outwards he was a simple and all loving person. His knowledge was supreme and he used to behold God in every particle of creation. Although this yogi had attained the capability of performing any miracle, yet he would never demonstrate those to others. He would melt by seeing the slight afflictions of others and would illumine them with supreme wisdom and reformed actions. His name was Aadisat.

Aadisat had a handful of disciples whom he was training in the advanced practices of yoga. He was preparing them for the service of mankind. One of his disciples was a young man, named Daarun, who was little obstinate and wayward. Whenever his guru would speak about the illusion of time, he would raise many questions and would remain adamant to the answers given his master.

One day Aadisat began to worry about his disciple. He wondered if Daarun will not assimilate the supreme wisdom of truth, his own duty as master will not finish. Quickly he summoned the young man and invited for a walk in the nearby forest. Daarun was happy for strolling outside the hermitage with his master.

As they began walking, master expressed his wish for walking in far this time. Daarun was even happier. Talking about various mystic subjects both continued walking and after some time they reached an unknown place in the forest. Soon, master felt thirsty and began to look around for a water pond etcetera. But unfortunately there was none around. He saw that Daarun was also thirsty.

"How can we find water in this jungle my son?" Aadisat asked his disciple. Now Daarun also turned anxious about his thirst. He climbed up a nearby tree and began to look around. He beheld a rising line of smoke somewhere in far. He came down and said to his master, "Gurudeva! For sure there is a village nearby as I can see the rising line of smoke. Please allow me to enter in the village and fetch water for you."

"Very well my son! I'll sit here and wait for you", said the master and sat down on a nearby rock. Here Daarun started towards the village.

In few moments, many thatched cottages began to appear in Daarun's sight. In expectancy of water he walked even faster. As he reached the first cottage, he knocked on the door.

"The door was opened by such a young beautiful girl, that Daarun was awestruck. He had only heard from his master about the celestial nymphs, but he thought, he was seeing one as well today. For a moment he forgot even about water. The very moment the girl smiled on her visitor's forgetfulness, Daarun fell in love with her. When she insisted what for he had come, he could utter 'water' only.

She went inside to fetch water. In the meantime the father of girl came out to see the visitor. Seeing a young handsome ascetic as his guest he bowed to Daarun and brought him inside. Daarun was made sufficiently comfortable by the host. As the girl came with water, the father noticed his guest's curiosity about the girl. He started making inquiries from his guest. In some time, finding the boy suitable, he proposed to marry his daughter to him.

Already lost in the unmatched beauty of girl, Daarun had now forgotten everything else after the proposal. He expressed his consent and made the father of girl happy and the girl herself shy.

On the following day both were married and the girl's father arranged a new cottage on the other side of village for the new couple. Bride and groom started living and enjoying together. In no time, in order to run the households, Daarun opened a small school for teaching the children of villagers. Villagers were already waiting for a knowledgeable person for their children. Soon the school began to generate enough money required for the households. Living in the starting bliss of household affairs, this couple was very happy for the way things had been turning out for them.

As passed the time, Daarun's wife gave birth to their first son. Many celebrations were held. As the little child grew and started going to the same school, Daarun's wife gave birth to another son. Once again many celebrations were conducted. In some time after that Daarun's wife gave birth to a daughter as well.

But unfortunately, soon after daughter's birth, there came tremendous floods in the village. Merciless waves of water didn't spare anything. The whole village was facing an unprecedented trouble. One after another the villagers' cottages were uprooting and following the waves. Daarun's school had already vanished in the water and now even his house was about to collapse. Traumatized, they had to leave the place at once. Daarun seated both his sons atop his shoulders and his wife clutched a bag of food and clothes in her one arm and infant daughter in the other. Amidst the unfathomable water everywhere, they both began to struggle finding the way ahead.

Very difficultly they could go only a few miles away, but any safer place was still out of their sight. They continued walking through the floods. In some time, unfortunately, feet of Daarun's wife stuck with a stone in the water and she began to stumble. While balancing herself, the bag of food and clothes fell down in the water. As quickly she leant to catch the bag, the infant daughter also fell down from her mother's lap and was taken away by the powerful waves. The lady tried much but couldn't catch her daughter. She knew swimming but she had no energy left in her body. Stuck with another stone once again, she finally stumbled and was also carried away by the mighty waves. This all happened so quickly that Daarun got no chance to act upon. He was now in terrible state. Seeing his wife drowning in the water he wanted to swim. But how could he, when both of his young sons were on his shoulders? Yet, as he started running in water to catch his beloved wife, water spates overpowered him and he also began to stumble down. In struggle of keeping himself straight, his elder son lost the grip and fell down from the shoulder. Before he could save his son from drowning in the water, his younger son was also in water. He couldn't brave the waves.

Now Daarun was alone in the water. What a grief! He exasperated. He closed his eyes and found no reason at all to live any longer. He cursed God for bringing these miseries to him and also submerged himself into the powerful waves. He drowned and didn't know what happened then after.

For several days he remained unconscious and flowed with water. In some time waves left him at a dry place. He remained lying there in unconscious state for further few days. When he began opening his eyes, the first thing he saw was the mud entering into his open mouth. He spit it out. He opened his eyes more and saw that he was lying unconscious on the brink of a muddy pond which had only little water in its center. He reminisced about his wife and children and began to moan heartily. He closed his eyes once again as if waiting for his own death.

Soon a familiar voice reached his ears – "Oh Daarun!".

"Surprised, he opened his eyes and turned his head. He found no one around. However surprisingly, even the muddy pond had disappeared. He thought that in the final moments of death, he had lost his senses. He closed his eyes once again.

"O Daarun! For what at all you are lying here like this", that familiar voice came again.

He looked about once again. To him the voice seemed really very familiar. As he turned his head this time, lo, what he saw! It was his master standing in front of him. Daarun was hugely dumbfounded and couldn't utter a word. He didn't know what was going on.

"O Daarun! I had sent you for fetching me the water half an hour before, but you are lying here like a drunkard. What's wrong with you? Are you hallucinated?" asked the master.

Daarun thought he was seeing a dream. But master sensed it. He said, "No, instead the one you had been living up to now was a dream."

Daarun stood up. Still aloof he touched the feet of his master. Aadisat asked, "Say! Aren't you really alright now, just like coming over a dreadful dream?"

Very quietly Daarun followed his master on their way back to the hermitage. Daarun noticed that even after reaching back, his gurudeva hadn't taken a pint of water to quench his thirst. He thought probably the master didn't need at all. For few days Daarun didn't talk to anyone and remained only dumbfounded.

After few days had passed, he asked, "Gurudeva! Then what was that which I had been living inside the village for many years?"

"That was a dream!" replied Aadisat.

"But what made it feel so real and authentic?" asked the bewildered disciple.

"Only because you strongly felt it to be real and authentic", replied master.

"But Gurudeva, I still don't believe and agree that it was merely a dream and nothing else."

To this Aadisat replied, "This is what is happening to all men in the world. They are living only a dream of life, but they never believe or agree about it. They find this dream so real and authentic that they never believe the truth."

"But Gurudeva, how can you say that", asked Daarun.

At this Aadisat looked straight into the eyes of his disciple who was greatly bewildered yet. He asked, "Tell me how many years did you live inside the village?"

Daarun replied, "Ten years, Gurudeva!"

"But wasn't it merely half an hour actually?" asked the master, "We started deep in forest in the morning and returned back in the noon. Only within few hours when we had returned to the hermitage, how did you live ten years." Aadisat laughed.

"But still I can't comprehend it my sir!" Daarun was too restless.

Now Aadisat resolved the matter to his disciple. He said, "This is what the illusion of time is all about. Earlier you had been finding this lesson difficult to understand, but now you can deal with it greatly. You live on earth and you measure your time as per the movement of your own planet. Do not forget that the movements of other planets are different from earth; and in this way the method of measuring time will also be different there. These all planets which you generally imagine about, are but within only one planetary system known to you. Up above in sky there would be many other suns and many other planets as well. Time measurements in each of such cases would be different from your one. So would you call the time measurements of others to be incorrect only because it differs from the method employed by you? And why to speak of living in different planetary systems; even you and I staying in the same hermitage, are not able to reconcile? You are saying ten years and I am saying merely half an hour?"

Daarun couldn't contend this.

Aadisat continued, "Very this unreconciled difference in the time related perceptions of different people is called the illusion of time. You believe only that most which you want to believe most. Broadly, it's your own unreconciled want which creates the illusions of all kinds; and illusion of time is just one of them."

~~~

Having narrated the whole story outside the cave here, master was playfully smiling at me. Looking to his face I also smiled. He began saying, "Oh son! Man thinks that he lives a life and sees dreams only at night, whereas the truth is that, this entire human life is a living dream. An unenlightened life remains engrossed only in the illusions. Therefore it's imperative for mankind to acquaint the truth and live only skillfully. Indeed from the viewpoint of man, human life is a dream; and from the viewpoint of God Himself, who commands over entire universe, this entire paraphernalia of planetary systems is like a dream. Or isn't it?"

"Hmm... Indeed what you say is correct, master", I replied.

Master continued very philosophically, "And the bitter truth for the mankind is that, illusions of all kinds bring only miseries in life and nothing else."

I nodded only silently. Ahead of what was coming up, secretly in my heart, I had already started wondering about the other kinds of illusions now. Master had said that there were three more – Space, Word; and Atom.

EIGHTEEN

The Second Illusion: Space

"WHAT A PITY THAT when any single illusion is capable of dragging the mankind into the misery of ignorance, man hasn't stopped clinging to the all four at a time!"

Such remarked the master after a short spell of his meditative silence. He continued, "And can you even believe this? Man has rather become skillful in enjoying his miseries! Foolishly he thinks that without having the challenge of unhappiness in life, his days would become charmless. Even if somebody gives him an astonishing dosage of bliss, he will find it only useless and uninspiring. It's no one's fault but. Indeed such powerful are the illusions around this entire cosmic dream, that man has started calling only these combined illusions as life."

For a moment I felt that master was abhorring the general worldly life too badly. However as he progressed in his expounding of rest three illusions, I could understand his reason.

He said, "Now hear from me about the illusion of space. Although the far reaching imagining powers of mind are certainly true, but also that, the very limitations of it start from the very point of physical medium of its existence. Nevertheless, mind lives in a human body, or isn't it? You see! However powerful mind may be viewed as by man, but actually mind remains nothing at all if it cannot be identified with a body in which it resides. Even as a wife can command dominion only upon his miserable husband and no one else, mind can also command dominion over the miserable body only. Listen how the illusion of space has been stupefying everybody's mind since eons."

I grew curious.

"Instead of telling a new story this time, let me experiment on you. Will that be fine?" He asked.

"Surely Sir", I replied.

"Very well", he smiled, "See! At any given point of time your body is either sitting, standing or lying at one place, is that true?"

"True Sir", I nodded.

He continued, "Human mind's biggest limitation is that it always identifies itself with the body, therefore the limitations of human body constantly constrain the mind. Every moment human body itself is identified with the geographical positions of its situation; hence the expansion of mind's imagination is also limited to the limited geographical dimension acquainted by the man. This very limitation of knowledge about the geographical situations actually becomes the mother of illusion of space. See how cleverly the illusion of space tricks the mind."

Master continued while my curiosity was increasing, "In one of our previous talks you have already understood the magnanimous enormity of directions which can be perceived by the human minds in relation to the place of their sitting, standing or lying; is that true?"

"Yes, indeed those are countless and incomprehensible", I replied.

"But this is not all what is to be known", he elaborated, "Even if you understand directions fully, you will still know them only in the relativity of your individual geographical position on the earth. You say that up above your head it's the upside direction; but ask the same question from the other man standing on exactly the opposite side's surface of the earth. He will also look upwards, natural to his individual position only, and will call just the opposite direction to be the upside direction. Both men are calling only the opposite directions to be the same, yet both are thinking their individual conceptions to be right. Even no one around these two people ever points out this inconsistency. You see, how poorly the human mind can give in to its limitations created by the illusion of space."

He continued, "And what I have told you here is merely a small piece of whole truth regarding this illusion. In your planetary system you have eight more planets orbiting around the sun in the center. Do you think that all these planets make rounds of the sun in a flat disk orientation? No, it's never that way. Infact each planet has its own orbiting path and none two of those ever fall in the flat disk orientation. Just imagine! Your self-perceived precise direction of north, for example, is never exactly the north for your fellow beings on the sides of earth; and neither can it be the same from the point of view of people's position on the other planets. Even an inch away from your position, the directions are changed for others. For our earth is spinning constantly, even a minute after from your present, your own position gets changed. Every inch and every minute, the people, here on the earth or elsewhere, are living in the different directions and positions, yet they are giving common names. For instance, they all call it north, whereas actually there is no north existing anywhere."

Saying this, master took a pause with closed eyes.

"Son, do you know why the mankind so far has failed to discover the living substance on the other planets besides earth?" Master suddenly asked.

Oh! I was stunned for the revelation that master was going to make. I moved my head in ignorance.

He replied, "Unfortunately every time our human science commences and concludes its advents about discovering the life substances on the other planets merely from its own viewpoint about the directions and positions. What is space? Actually space is nothing but one's own position identified with as many directions as possible up to his cognizance. One's cognizance of his own position is his knowledge, but his unawareness about others' position is his ignorance. Further, even his adamancy towards recognizing others' position is his illusion. Trust me my son! Alone this illusion hasn't let the mankind discover the substances of life on the other planets so far. Once they will have enough curiosity about the possibilities of life in altogether different kinds of positions and directions, they will develop the true understanding towards the phenomena of life, which could be starkly different from their own set of beliefs."

"Modern men say", master continued, "that there is no life on the other planets, but how false such statements are! They say that all planets spin and orbit around sun, but they do not understand the crux. When there is already so much activity, how can the life be absent? When on each of such planet, there is wind creating the dust storms, how would remain the life non-existent? Even though all men take a millennia to recognize and witness life there, but for now they cannot proclaim that life doesn't exist unless they are able to personally vouch that. Amidst the stupendous planetary activities there, even the activities of life would be stupendous."

"Man's capacity for perception through his sensory faculties would always be finite. However to understand beyond the finite, first the understanding of infinite must be developed by him. People living in the modern age of science do not believe the ideas of telepathy or transmutation; but the advanced yogis have been performing such phenomena easily. They have been able to do so because they are free from the illusion of space. They've trained their minds to get freedom from the limitations of their physical identification with positions and directions. Instead, they're able to cognize altogether different kinds of places and directions as well. They can easily commune with those living in far and they can also instantly reach the places in far. I repeat, they can do so only because they've liberated from the illusion of space."

Having said this, suddenly master stood up and asked me to follow him to a nearby shrub. He began to show me a tiny caterpillar on the edge of a green leaf. Pointing towards it he filled with enormous joy and asked me, "Ask yourself my son! Can you really commune with the positions and directions which are relevant to this small creature? In terms of your own relativities you give those names like north, east, west, south etcetera, but can you imagine how differently this caterpillar would be knowing and remembering its own positions and directions? Look! Even this worm would be teaching a lot of things about the directions to its children. Even these would have a complete school of knowledge and education, which these are transferring from generations to generations. Why do you need to go up there to the other planets for understanding more about their situations when there has left still so much for man's understanding right on this earth?"

I was trying to immerse into the life of this caterpillar when the master spoke wonderfully, "Listen son! The illusions of all kinds are created right here and those are also broken right here alone. No one needs to go anywhere in far, but man's very own mind is enough capable of breaking the illusions of all kinds."

And after this, master said even more wonderfully, "You see! You do not always live in the world where your body lives, but you actually live in the world where lives your mind. What bigger evidence I can give you when I have sufficiently made you understand that you live in a world which is alone a product of your mind and nothing else."

I was only spellbound. The small caterpillar on the leaf had now crawled to the other side invisible to me. I was kneeling down to look for it again. In this moment, one thing was surprising, that gravity was nothing to this worm. No matter which side of the leaf it was resting upon, but it never fell down. Even if it was gripping the leaf with its numerous legs, but its own weigh was not bothering it at all. Quite strongly, in this moment, I could intuit that how different would be the perceptions of positions and directions to this worm; how different would be those from the ones in my own mind.

And here master was smiling at me as ever.

NINETEEN

The Third Illusion: Word

MASTER HAD NOW RETURNED to his altar. He said, "Son! Now hear from me about the third illusion called word."

"Word is the sound which you listen from the hearing faculties installed in your body. Your mind always listens to certain types of sounds and identifies your world according to the same. Although human capability of listening sounds is limited in numerous ways, yet ordinary people hardly wonder about the same. Lately even the modern science has started acknowledging these facts."

"Let us start from the extent to which modern science has known the facts so far. It is pleasant to see that scientific developments are heading in the right direction. Science has confirmed that man can listen only to the kinds of sounds which fall between a specific range of frequency. Although this range is only a part of total spectrum, yet the existing variety of sounds which are possible in the given range is already tremendous. Mankind has never stopped inventing the new kinds of sounds and neither will they stop doing so ever. The world of sounds is so phenomenal that people never find sufficiency in their discoveries. They've been always filling their worlds with the new types of sounds, even before the sounds of old types haven't stopped resonating. Mankind's journey of adding new sounds to the previous sounds is ceaseless. Given this, however, if you sarcastically think that such a huge and ever increasing collection of sounds will someday produce in the world another kind of unbearable blasting noise, then know that it won't happen; for all kinds of sounds, after reaching in the ether, finally submerge in it. The bigger trouble on the other side, is the persisting one, that by passing of each day of progress by the mankind, people will have to live amidst the more volumes of sounds than before; and this very problem will reflect upon their increasing loss of concentration and equanimity."

Continued making even greater revelations, master asked, "Have you ever wondered that what kind of truth it would be, when the ancient scriptures suggest that, the entire existence was generated by Lord Brahma merely by chanting the sacred word 'Aum' from His holy mouth once? Have you ever contemplated how this could have been possible? And when I've already said that you also can create a world by the power of your mind, what is its relation with that?"

In great awe, I expressed my unknowingness.

"Let me now reveal this another secret to you", said the master affectionately. "This planet called earth where we all live is already full of countless kinds of sounds. One cannot hear simultaneously all these kinds of sounds primarily for two reasons. One is that, travel of sound from far depends upon its loudness and also on the atmosphere through which it passes. Human mind thinks that certain kinds of sounds never reach it, but it's untrue. In reality sounds of all kinds never cease or die; and neither do they stop travelling ever. It's just their audibility which weakens gradually in the atmosphere of their travel. Secondly, even if human ears are constantly listening to this mix of many sounds, they cannot isolate them from one another. They cannot perceive different sounds perfectly at a time; therefore they begin to ignore many of those. Constantly ignoring many kinds of sounds, gradually their mind develops dumbness and it starts believing that the sounds unheard by it never existed at all. Although they are constantly hearing these extinct sounds, but they never agree upon."

Then master raised his head and added, "And given that, what to speak of the other kinds of sounds which fall beyond the human audibility range of between twenty and twenty thousand hertz? Certain insects and birds are able to hear those. Even the variety those would be phenomenally enormous. And who can deny the existence of further kinds of sounds which are beyond the capabilities of those insects and birds even?"

Now master laughed and looked into my eyes. He asked, "Doesn't your mind find all this very hallucinating?"

Smilingly I nodded.

"Indeed it is", replied he, "But listen, there is one common attribute of the sounds of all kinds; and that is, those are all vibratory. Whether or not you can listen to those, the vibrations created by those nevertheless reach you. The persisting ignorance of human mind about the countless phenomenal sounds has actually made the human bodies immunized from their vibrations as well. Although these vibrations continue touching the human bodies every second, yet the mind has developed a successful numbness towards those. In this very way, the human mind has skillfully added to its existing illusion that it denies the existence of what has existed; and it accepts the existence of what has never."

"Do you know", asked the master, "what will you hear if you go a hundred miles above in the space and try to listen the sound coming out from the entire ball of the earth?"

Once again, I moved my head in awe.

"There you will not be able to isolate the ocean of unfathomable sounds from each other, but what you will hear will be the grand humming sound, resembling with the sacred Hindu word '*Aum*', and also the holy Christian word '*Amen*', and many more similar words in other religions as propounded by the awaken sages who have already had this subtle experience."

"And now coming back to the point, I impart you the secret behind creation of the world by sound. Think and tell me that what it is, which takes away your sudden attention first always?"

I was guessing many answers but scaring to say any in front of master. I only expressed ignorance.

"It's nothing but the sound only, son!" He answered. "No matter how busy is your mind elsewhere, but it suddenly starts following the directions of sounds. It's the sound of 'word' which takes away your sudden attention first. Presently your mind could be busy in some kind of psychological world, but a sudden outburst of sound would drive you off to another kind of psychological world. And do not miss to notice the prowess of the illusion of word, that even before the light could drift away your vision, even before the taste could drift away your tongue, even before the smells could drift away your olfactory, and even before the touch could drift away your sensation; actually it is the sound which drifts away your attention altogether. For example, just when somebody shouted upon you a word from far, forsaking everything else you automatically turn your head into his direction. Merely a second before you were busy in producing one kind world through your mind; and only in the following second, after hearing and responding to the shout, you get busy in producing a world of another kind." As master said this, he began laughing.

Then in a moment he became serious and asked me, "Now hear another small secret. Would you like to experience right here and now as to what you will hear from the entire ball of earth from one hundred miles up above?"

I was ever astonished about his feats. I thought another one was just coming up.

"Move your both index fingers upwards and then slightly press over each of your ear-holes. With help of your index fingers' tips try creating a slight of vacuum inside. Adjust the pressure of your fingers unless you start listening to the sound which is actually coming from your own body. It would feel like a gentle humming. Once you start hearing that, you will find it interesting. Concentrate more. This humming sound is actually the great admixture of many countless sounds which the human mind has already stopped listening since ages. The sound you would hear in this way is the collection of inaudible yet subtle vibrations which your body has continued absorbing every moment, even without letting your ears know about it. And son, this is the same, what you will hear from the ball of earth. This is the same great sound which is most closely represented by the sound of '*Aum*' and '*Amen*' as well."

I did this experiment on myself; and yes, it was true. Ever in life, I had never known this sound existing in me before. I never knew such a kind of great vibration always existing in me. I listened again and again to what was emanating from my own body. I wondered how could have I remained fooled by this ignorance. What would I be able to know about the world, when I hadn't known my own mind and body sufficiently? Hmm... There was indeed something great about this man. He would be no ordinary mortal, I see!

Much awestruck, I asked him, "O Master, tell me who really are you?"

"What a foolish question? How does it matter here?" He remonstrated me at once.

I couldn't argue him but he increased my anxiety by adding "Am not I just like you?" He just broke laughter.

Now he came off the altar and began saying, "Look there, son! Sun is going down fast but my imparting of fourth illusion is still remaining. Illusion of atom is a great deal to understand. It will be only better if we start it tomorrow. Now you must also be feeling tired. Why not return to your cottage and come again tomorrow. You see! Your laboratory construction work is about to set on any day from now. You must be careful about your time."

Once again, he accompanied me till some distance before seeing me off.

And here, while coming down from the hilltop, another idea gripped my mind, "But master didn't talk about my levitating in the dream. Maybe he would not know my every dream." Thinking this I chuckled and hastened towards the food corner ahead of my cottage.

TWENTY

Glimpse of Magical Box in My Dream

THAT NIGHT I HAD another dream. I didn't know from where but a strange box had reached me. Perhaps I had never seen earlier a box as beautiful as this. It was particularly made in the shape of a large book and was beautifully adorned with fine wooden craftworks from all over. I was rolling it in my hands and was unaware of what was inside it. I was going apprehensive about the unknown purpose of the box. Even if sometimes I became too curious about opening it, I didn't know how to. It tried to find out its seam to open from, but it seemed intact and all made in one piece alone. I pulled it hard but no use. I shook it near my ears. It sounded empty as if containing nothing inside. Helplessly I continued watching its outer shell alone. Being exactly in the shape of large book, from upside and down and also at the spine part of it, it was the finest work of engraving on a thin veneer of wood. Varied kinds of flowers and creepers had been carved on its surface. Time and again I looked at the front and back covers of this book-shaped box. It was marvelous and a master piece of craft. On the other three sides opposite to the spine, it was a straight smooth while-pale surface as if showing the paper thickness of book.

I couldn't make out any from the object in my hands. I had carefully checked the entire engraving on both the surfaces, but had found nothing to read about. However, even as I started noticing on the spine, I was awestruck. Smartly hidden in the cumbersome engraving, a few words were written there. Since I was in dream I do not remember whether I had put on my spectacle or not, but I could read even the smallest fonts perfectly. I guessed it was the title of this book-shaped box. It read:

"It Opens Only When Your Mind is Open"

Just as I read the line, my dream broke. I woke up empty handed and sad. I wondered what kind of a dream it was. Why couldn't I open the box in the moments of holding it in my hands. Was my mind not open? Or was it merely one more in the strange series of my past dreams? I was lying down in my bed and quickly caught a fitful sleep again.

Next morning was foggier than usual. Atmosphere around the hill stations usually remains unpredictable. Here, although the fog was not literally adding to the already chilling temperature, but glancing outside at the floating clouds of mists had begun to shiver my bones. I looked at watch. I still had approximately two hours to leave for the cave. I sank in my quilt a little more and felt like going nowhere today. The very moment I closed the eyes, another painful thought banged in my skull.

"But how would be the master doing on the uphill? In this moment, will he be inside or outside his cave? But oh! Even if he is inside, would he have enough quilts as well there?"

The unpleasant answers came easily upon me. Within the same minute I decided to brave the fog and was now preparing for the bath. Thankfully, the cottage organizers had made a nice arrangement for the hot water tap inside.

Instantly after bath my hunger pangs began striking me. I rushed to the same food-joint. Today the crowd of people was much less here. Perhaps many would have decided to skip the bath and this had delayed their hunger. Lost in various thoughts about master I started taking tea and toasts. Today I ate one extra, thinking that all would digest on my way of climbing up to the hill. Having paid the bill, I rushed out.

As I continued trotting upwards I noticed that gradually the fog was getting scantier. I couldn't know whether it was because of the progress of the day or otherwise. I kept on scaling the narrow undulated path steadily. Instantly I had reached my destination of the day.

But oh! Master was absent from his altar this time. For few moments I stood waiting for him but indeed he was not around. I wondered what the things could have been up to. Then all of sudden my gaze fell upon the cave. I thought he must be inside. As I began advancing towards the cave, my heart started pounding. It was my first time of getting close to the hill-house of the master.

As I put my first step inside the cave, my fear started going away. True to my willy-nilly anticipation, master was not inside. I began to look about the cave more carefully now. Perhaps it would be a little larger than my cottage, though there were no straight walls or any cross roof above. I glanced all over. Actually this cave was a drifting gap between two very large stones blocks which were rising from the ground and were touching each other on their tips. There were numerous stone-pieces which were forming a kind of wall to cover the backside of the cave. In the backdrop there was also a large mound of sand rocks. It would save the smaller stones from falling down by the crazy winds.

And that was the all worth mentioning about inside and outside of the cave. It was awkward and uneven on the floor, except a small stretch nearly of human height which had been filled with soft sand to make bed for master's sleeping or sitting. On the other side of this sand filled bed, I could also see two blankets which were put one above another. I tried looking for more articles inside the cave, but in the name of human possessions, except these two ragged blankets there was nothing at all.

"Oh, you have come, my son!" All of a sudden master's affectionate voice came from my behind.

I turned. Just about the cave master was standing holding a bunch of green leaves in his hands. I felt as if he was smiling at my inquisitiveness about the cave. I however felt blushing for entering the cave without his permission.

"Tell me how you have liked this cave?" he asked while putting the green leaves outside of entrance.

I didn't know what to answer. Rather I had begun feeling bad, for such an advanced master was living here like this. I didn't answer him, albeit I directly asked, "Why do you live here in the woods?"

He counter asked, "Oh! Even I can ask you the same question, why at all do you live in the chaos there?"

Again I couldn't answer him. He broke into laughter.

Finding me getting embarrassed over the question, master said, "Actually it doesn't matter where we live, but what matters is how we live. Perfection of living is not in the place but it's in our ways of living there."

"But still", I contested his point, "Don't you think you can benefit more people by living nearer to them?"

"Benefit!" He looked surprised to the word. He repeated, "What benefit? People rather think that the good advices put them at loss."

"Please, come on! Not at least you can become so sarcastic", I almost provoked him.

He resumed silence and didn't answer.

I also felt bad for my harsh words spoken on him.

He meekly began saying, "God doesn't ask me to become teacher. He says I must ever remain a student. This human life remains beautiful only when one remains a student."

"But master", I carefully sweetened my voice, "I think people will be able to see more light if they will get close to it source."

At this point master laughed. He said, "Your analogy is almost correct my son! But when people get too close to the source of light, they begin focusing more upon the source than the light itself. To do away the darkness, the amount of light is not important. Be it less or more, but light is always light. Similar is the wisdom in God; be it less or more, its amount is not what is important. However faint the light be; it always shows you the way."

His answer couldn't fully satisfy me.

Finding me unrelenting yet, master asked, "Tell me what new I can have to tell the people. Aren't these truths which I am imparting you here as old as the sun and stars? Haven't those existed since eons? And aren't these truths already written everywhere; in the books, on the stone slabs inside the shrines and everywhere else too. If people do not heed them, do you think they will heed me, repeating the same things again and again?"

I didn't know how to argue the master, but still I had not completely fallen in line with his choice of living in these conditions here.

"Then what made you choose me alone?" I looked on his face and asked.

He went very humble in replying, "No! It's you who have chosen me."

"But you had been appearing in my dreams since long!" I asked.

He smiled in affection and asked, "It is true, but do you think it was alone me who made you start taking interest in such dreams? Wasn't it yourself in fact?"

"You are again trapping me in your words", I complained.

"I never do that. What I have been talking about here are the bigger theories of mind's operations. See my son!" he squirmed, "You can go through as many theories till lasts your life, but unless you start taking deep interest in the end purpose of such theoretical knowledge, you do not really gain. But on the other hand, once you've understood the end purpose very well, only scantier theoretical endurance will suffice you."

I was still thinking about his invasion in my dreams. I didn't reply.

Master instantly read my mind and said, "Very well, I will tell you this matter in short. The reason behind your dreams, in which you had been seeing me since long, was not created by me, though I was fully aware of such happening. I wield no extraordinary powers to appear in your dreams, but it's alone your own intuition which makes you taking interest in those. Ordinarily, the dreams come in spontaneity. It's only the intuitive interest taken by man in his earlier dreams which guides the turn of events to take place in the following ones. This is how the series of dreams develops. Dreams always come in plenty and in varied kinds, but man forgets the one kind thereof and remembers the others. Even out of the remembered dreams, he takes particular interest in the dreams which he thinks that those were about him. Therefore a series of similar dreams, amidst the many other already going on, holds up in his conscience. And now, as believed by your mind, you think that your dreams have been coming true on this hilltop?"

Oh my goodness! Just having revealed another big secret, master was looking as easy as always. Once again, I was filled with many questions.

"But tell me", I asked in bewilderment, "how has it happened that this place is exactly the same which I used to witness in my vision?"

Hearing this master laughed in such a way, as if he already knew my question. Instead of answering, he began telling me, "You still do not get it right. Now tell me one thing; of what shade your dreams usually are? Are those colored or merely black and white?"

For once I thought dreams were just always colored. But before putting up a reply, I stopped to imagine it once again. I knew master would never ask me the easy questions. I took me a little while before replying. I was imagining of what color was that wooden box which I had seen in my dream previous night?

"No! Dreams are always colored I am sure", I replied to master's question.

Master smiled at me as if I was merely a child. He said, "Then tell me, the exact color of that wooden box?"

I have no words to describe my startling state. My Goodness! It was hardly a moment before the wooden box had come to my mind, and he knew it. I compellingly asked him, "Just tell me master, how at all you come to know what runs in others' minds?"

"This we will discuss later. Again you have more questions than I can physically answer in this last day of our meeting", the master slightly remonstrated me.

In following moment, master turned only silent. Certainly he was aware of the great tumult inside me. He consoled me by saying, "But when you have asked, I will answer it in short. You often wonder that how can I read others' minds. But you are not 'others', you are mine. I can read your mind just the way a mother successfully reads the mind of her baby child every time. Love can make anything possible in the world, and only the compassionate love is the kind of food which a human mind relishes the most. Understanding this love between a mother and her child is the first step and the first example for you. You can increase your dimension of love and move upwards to the next steps in order to have more examples to be experienced. The beginning shall always be small and narrow; and it will require you to have patience and faith. It's nothing but only my selfless love towards you which makes me aware of all your needs; either those are physical, psychological or spiritual."

By now I had followed the master towards the platform. We both had sat down when he said, "let us now talk about your dreams. This discussion was erstwhile lost in your quandaries."

I felt embarrassed for having thrown upon him too many questions today.

Master said, "It's no wonder that when I can remain conscious of your mind in the aforesaid way, I can remain conscious of your dreams as well. You see these are just higher stages of love between you and me. Since I have been through these stages, I have grown aware of not only your mind, but of your dreams and even more as well. I have already said, it's my ordained duty to enlighten you. This duty is specific and I am trying to fulfill it in my all capacity. My son! You insist me for living in far from this cave, but there is no real need of it. If I move from my place out of dissatisfaction, instantly, my long penance will be lost."

I remained only silent.

Again master asked, "Now stop wondering unnecessarily, just tell me of what color was the wooden box last night?"

I gazed in the eyes of master and said, "Perhaps it was of wooden color only."

"Was it oak polished?" he figuratively asked.

I was more surprised. "Yes", I said.

Once again he broke into laughter and said, "But your both answers are wrong. The variety in colors is indentified by you through your physical eyes only. But when you're sleeping and dreaming, your physical eyes no longer remain at work. Those are infact closed. Isn't it true?"

I nodded.

"Have you ever wondered that when your physical eyes are closed, through which other eyes you see your dream?" Master asked.

Oh! I was blown by the question.

"It's true that you do see the colors in your dreams but those are never in the same way how you've been seeing through your open physical eyes." He had just started making another revelation.

He continued, "Dreams are always seen by your subconscious mind, although those are greatly cultured by the combined learning of your conscious and subconscious minds. In the beginning of your previous night's dream, you couldn't make out whether what was in your hands was actually a book or a box; but still you were thinking about it more as a box than as a book. And that was the reason you'd understood it to be a box only. No wonder that this kind of illusion always takes place in the dreams. Only because you thought of it to be a box, and more particularly as a wooden box, you're telling me now confidently that it was of wooden color. Quite were the chances that box could have been made of steel instead of wood, but again you were helpless to judge; for you never feel the weight of things seen in the dreams."

After a thoughtful pause, master said again, "I have already elaborated to you the key of analyzing the illusion of dreams. What you had been seeing in your earlier dreams were not my cave and altar, infact it was only your mind which made you believe that those were cave and altar. Even now, it's alone your mind which convinces you that these cave and altar are the same which you had been seeing in your dreams. For you, your meeting with me is a sweet consequence of your dreams, but for me it is merely an incidence known to me beforehand. I do not marvel it, for I have cultured my mind beyond marveling. For a mind which has been cultured only towards truth, you see, nothing remains impossible."

As master said this, a state of high bliss occurred on him. I knew that only his body had now remained with me; for he himself was somewhere else. The supreme wisdom imparted on me by him was incomparable. In great reverence, I was extolling my master in the heart. After few moments master returned to his outward consciousness and began saying, "It is also true that your dreams seen at night also get influenced by what you experience in the day time. My son! Your earlier dream of levitating was not without reasons. That night you were feeling very light in your body and in your mind as well. You were feeling delighted about the source of knowledge which had newly sprouted in your heart. Through the assurances found in me, you were gradually freeing yourself from many unnecessary psychological entanglements in your mind. Also your subconscious mind had been constantly wondering about those levitating saints, about whom you had read in the book on our bedside. Combined all these reasons you dreamt as if you had become as light as air. You felt like becoming weightless. Wasn't it all really so good? Aren't these beginning omens in the process of knowing the true powers of your mind, really satiating?"

Master was in bliss once again. Straightening his spine he had closed his eyes now. Sitting on the altar he didn't seem to me any smaller than God Himself. What a great fortune of mine had brought me here! I was feeling even the vibrations of his bliss.

He sat like this for about fifteen minutes. During this time I had a number of things to think about. Without deliberately creating any fanaticism or fantasy, he had been taking me to the secret world on the other side of mind. And yes, he was right. This secret world existed nowhere else, but right here in this same world only.

Once again I was feeling much lighter than in my usual frame. Looking at the master in trance, I would not have wondered if the master had really started levitating in front of my eyes. But I knew this too, even when in trance, he was fully conscious of all kinds of worlds, secret ones and the apparent ones as well. And never in any case whatsoever he could grow interested about demonstrating his great feats to the people. After all, as he said, this was the very reason he had chosen to live in the woods only.

When he opened the eyes, he pointed towards the green leaves which he had brought in the morning. So far those leaves had been lying outside the cave only. He asked me to take them to a nearby narrow stream of water, wash them well and come back.

However before I came off the altar, I didn't know what had made him say this, "For the skilled life workers it's necessary to conquer the two – Appetites and the Slumbers. In one case I will help you and in the other you will have to work yourself."

Aloof to his new words, I merely followed his command and rushed for taking the leaves to the stream.

TWENTY ONE

Master Makes Me Conquer the Appetites

"INSTEAD OF EATING ANYTHING else this noon, you must eat only these leaves", as I had returned from the stream, master said affectionately.

He continued, "Skilled life workers are called as Yogis in the Hindu scriptures. These yogis still may be of two kinds. Those skilled in knowledge and wisdom are called 'Jnana-yogis' and the other ones who are skilled in awakened actions of life are called 'Karma-yogis'. When a yogi becomes highly perfected in any of the two schools, his distance from the yogi of other school vanishes. For him, both become one. Here giving reference to Hindu scriptures is not important; but what is important is the understanding of becoming yogi of either type. Becoming yogi is highly pertinent because as long as you will remain unskilled in living your life, you will not meet the perfection; and therefore you will remain unhappy. The adopted method of becoming yogi, that is skilled working in life, may be any as suggested by one's own religion and endorsed by his conscience. But in any case whatsoever, for living a contented and satiated life, these yogic skills must develop in the man. If someone offends to the name of 'yoga' for being it related to Hinduism, it's no harm to change the name itself. After all it's only the skill which is important and not the name given to it. Yoga of either kind intends to discipline one's thoughts in the mind; and once the mind gets disciplined, man's actions through his body also get automatically disciplined. You already know, it's alone the mind and nothing else which matters. Only yogis live the skilled life, for the rest ones live only ordinarily."

In the following moment master took the green leaves from my hands and began to chant some mantra while keeping his eyes closed. After opening the eyes in a while he smiled at me and returned all the leaves in my hands. He said in deep love, "As I've earlier said that a skilled worker of life must conquer the two – appetites and slumbers, I am going to help you in case of appetite. For slumber you will have to work yourself. I particularly wish you to experiment the control on slumber yourself because in this way you will experience the constantly increasing power of your mind. I will myself help you in developing an understanding about it. However for now, let us work on your appetite.

I was looking at the leaves in my hands. I asked, "Master, what mantras were you chanting on these leaves a moment before?"

He laughed. "No no. You mistook the way of it. Mantras are not miracles; albeit those are merely the powerful expressions of mind in a disciplined language and syllable. More disciplined and conscious becomes the chanting, more powerfully expressions of mind work. These leaves have great medicinal powers but these powers may not work upon you unless your mind keeps unconditional faith in them. In the secret world since you are too new to have perfect faith of your own, through making mantra's chanting I have done the job for you. As of this moment, you have more faith in me than in these leaves. But now, because I have chanted the powerful expressions of my mind on your behalf, which too coupled with your persisted faith in me, you will now have an unconditional faith in these leaves as well. This is very old technique often used by masters for the beneficence of their disciples."

Then after master repeated the mantra once again and handed over leaves to me in great affection. He became silent and motioned his hand to command me for eating.

Although it seemed to me little awkward to graze up the

untreated green leaves, yet prompted by master, I started. Yes, those were not great in taste, but at the same time, were not intolerable either. Those were quite handful and I thought I will take time in finishing. Maybe master intuited my state. He said, "Chew those well and do not swallow in hurry."

After I ate all, master smiled on my alacrity and out of affection, put his hand on my shoulder. This was first time for such of his gesture. Then he spoke up to my slight surprise, "From now onwards you will be free from the pangs of hunger. Your appetite will kick in only when your food will be in front of your eyes; not even when you might look at others' food. You can view it as my wish, my blessing or my boon, either way as you like."

I felt greatly bestowed. I bowed to his feet in reverence and he blessed.

"Let us move now for a walk. After we come back I will narrate you the fourth and last illusion as well. As you've learnt only three so far, your last day with me must not fall short before I impart you the complete knowledge of secret world."

I started following him in the woods once again. Master's knowledge was unfathomable. Even during the walks he continued telling me many facets which were completely unknown to me. By this time, I had also started relishing the after-taste of the herbs which I had chewed only moments before. It was a kind of unique fragrance in my breath.

TWENTY TWO

Imparting the Precious Lessons

"DO YOU KNOW WHO'S your best friend and the worst enemy as well at the same time?"

Master was walking ahead of me in the midst the dense forest. He had never stopped asking me the strange questions.

I only tried guessing but didn't speak.

"It's only you my son!" answered he. "Other than yourself alone, who can it be at all? Only man himself is his own best friend and the worst enemy as well at the same time. If he does not comprehend the vile tricky mind and allows it to overrun him, he becomes his enemy. In your coming days, you also must regularly test the stature of your correspondence with your mind, so as to know - who is playing upon whom? This exercise will be immensely helpful to you at any place or time of your wish."

I nodded instantly.

"Also tell me this, when are you in the pink of your bodily health?" Master had asked me another question.

Once again I had no precise answer up to the thought plane of master.

He said, "It's just when your mind thinks so. It's alone your mind which can choose to ignore a pain and focus on the work, or alternatively to focus on the pain and ignore the work. Can you see! Even a lame might feel in very pink of health sometimes. Or isn't it? Bodily capabilities actually have little to do with your feelings regarding the health. Strongest muscles in a man, who never aspires to become, for example, a wrestler or puller, are actually burden on him. Such a man will either misuse his muscles to overpower the innocents or he will simply find those unutilized and therefore become violent. Muscles are never the real signs of healthy body. Now hear the greatest cure of body my son! Whenever you are suffering with any minor or major bodily illness, consistently engage your mind assuring yourself that all this has been in the tune of God's wish; and your own wish too cannot be different from His wish. Holding this very thought, stop minding your illness and compel yourself in carrying out your possible duties. Those who meditate on the duties in this way, get instantly relieved from pangs of pain. Busy your mind away from the pain and relief both, and overcome the pain instantly in this way."

"Hmm...", I had taken another great lesson in master's company.

"Now tell me this, do you know which attribute of mind makes it the most unpredictable? He asked me another.

While walking down the woods, I had now begun to realize that master was not asking me the questions; rather he was providing me the solutions to the most pervasive challenges around my worldly life. Again, towards his asked question, I didn't know the perfect answer.

He elaborated, "It's the childish nature of mind which makes it most unpredictable. Like a child it thinks that it knows more than it actually understands. Although children have the privilege of parents who understand more also, but ungoverned minds have no parents for that matter. Those are orphans, that too, wayward ones."

I nodded silently.

"Now tell me this, do you know which desire of man makes his life as worse as hell?" master asked again.

I sensed that the master was rushing his lessons due to lack of time. He wanted to give me all. To his question, once again, I didn't know the precise answer.

He replied, "It's the desire for sense-pleasures which makes his life hellish. You must never forget or undermine the indomitable powers of your five perception senses, that are vision through eyes, sounds through ears, olfactory through nose, tastes through tongue and pleasures through touch; and neither about your five action senses, that are locomotion with legs, actions with hands, speaking with mouth, and two others related to reproducing and excretion. What an irony that although these ten sense horses are only servants to the man's existence, yet without the mind having sufficient control on the reins of such horses creates all kinds of troubles in life. Mind must be the king of all ten; but if the mind itself becomes corrupt, it puts all ten into the corruption only. Beware, behind a misdirected life, it is not the senses to blame, but it's the mind. Indeed it's no one else but alone an ungoverned mind which craves sense-pleasures and therefore engages its ten servants in the unscrupulous activities of life. And what bigger irony may become than this, that all ten corrupt senses become so much ungrateful to the body that those damage and eventually perish also the very place of their own dwelling. Indeed, the senses destroy the same body in which those live. This however doesn't affect the mind yet, for it never physically existed already. Son, even if you undergo all kinds of possible medical tests, still you won't find a trace of physical mind at all. In generality, you might think of your heart or brain to be your mind, but actually none of the two is more than a physical operational apparatus. If you search your mind inside your physical body, you're on an altogether wrong course. Mind is your subtler force, much beyond your body. Only when it is cultured unwisely, it kills the body, kills the senses and eventually kills itself too. What a grief, that nobody takes the appropriate lessons out of the examples of others!"

"Hmm..." I uttered. Whatever master was saying, was truth only!

"And do you know who sustains above your body, mind and soul?" Master asked me afresh.

I weighed my answer for a second and replied, "Yes, it's God."

"No, let us become more precise about this," corrected the master, "it's actually You! In no scenario or situation God can be a different identity than that of yours. For so long as you will think of God living somewhere far from you, His goodness will also live far from you; but the very moment you will grow faith about God living nowhere else but only inside you, you will discover His entire goodness just within you. To become like God there is no other way than becoming God Himself. God doesn't exist in degrees or levels, but He is that absolute one. You can't have Him in small or big quantities; instead you can either have Him all or not at all. Son, if you may find this definition difficult to interpret and practice, there is simpler one too. Becoming God is all about becoming His goodness. Tell me what is the great deal in doing this? Can't man practice goodness enough?"

"Yes that's very true", thoughtfully I asserted.

"You see my son! The supreme knowledge which I have been imparting you for last three days may appear manifold and vast, but it will seem so in only the beginning. In the starting of practicing this knowledge, maybe you have to remind yourself the doctrines again and again, lest you may forget and err. But soon you will start enjoying such of your practices very naturally. This will be the point of time when the supreme knowledge and wisdom theoretically attained by you will dissolve in your life days just as sugar dissolves in the milk. You cannot separate the two; infact you never need to. You will no longer be required for putting in any extra effort to carry out the awakened activity around your days, for only the higher ways of living will become your natural ways of living."

"And this is another way of putting it", continued the master, "You can truly enjoy your world but only through knowing its reality in full. Possessing the supreme wisdom must not cause you offending or ridiculing the worldly manners or its people. Being yourself a householder for life, you must live for the world but not become of the world. You must play your dutiful part in your world, and you must do this through your awaken conscience only."

My thirst for his nectar words never quenched.

"Do you know which place is best for you to live?" He asked.

"Wherever I am happy", instantly I replied.

"Very well my son. You are just close", said the master joyously, "There remains only one catch. At any such place once chosen by you, you will not however remain happy for long if you do not add to the happiness of others. Your happiness and that of others must become complimentary to each other. Mathematically put, happiness gets multiplied when it is added with others'."

I simply nodded to this universal acclamation.

Master continued elaborating, "Also know about the importance of your activity. Operation of five primordial elements of nature, which have formed your body, has essentially nothing to do with the operation of your spark of life. Identification of your liveliness is invariably annexed to the activity undertaken by you. Five elements of nature are actually as inert as is your body; although those may be a necessary carrier, but it is alone your chosen activity of life which defines your sustenance."

Sitting like a child, every lesson was precious for me.

Master added, "Mind is very clever and formidable my son; though it is only man who makes it so in either right or wrong direction. Conquering the unruly tendencies and the unscrupulous impulses of one's mind is his significant progress in his way towards the Godly tendencies and impulses."

Master then looked to my face and said, "On the path of realizing your secret world, in beginning you might undergo varied kinds of anxieties. You will have many strange questions, of which the answers also would feel imperceptible. But as you will explore that world more, you will find the answers as well. You won't need to be taught by someone from outside; instead you will become best preceptor of your own. In this moment I reminisce one of such questions which I had myself faced in the beginning of my path in good old days."

I was more than eager to listen. Master was revealing a thread of his one studentship.

He said, "Once I wondered in my own secret world that whether a sovereign appointed executioner earns a sin in the moments, when he hangs a heinous criminal person to death after receiving the judicial orders? I wondered, would such of his act of killing earn a discredit to his spiritual beneficence earned so far, if any? My question even expanded further, that, will a contract killer earn the similar amount of sin when he assassinates an innocent man after being ordered and paid by his client? And then I wondered about this also, will an ordinary civilian incur the same sin when he kills another man in fit of rage? My questions were really subtle?"

I began looking straight to master's face when he just said, "No, I will not give you the answers. In process of becoming in yourself the best teacher, you will have to find the answers yourself only. My method of finding out the answers in the secret world can be different from the methods employed by you; this is the reason I do not disclose my own course undertaken then. Though you can remain assured that whatever is the method employed, destination of everybody's secret world always reaches the same place. Doubtlessly you will reach the same answer to this question, as did I, but I wish you to experience and assimilate your own course fully."

After a pragmatic pause, master said, "In this moment I am reminisced of another question as well which is of similar depth. Take it from me for your meditation some time. How becomes it possible that even the ordinary earthly people, who ever keep busy in the lower temptations and tendencies of life, still look happy? Do they have to suffer in the end? Even if they have to, what's wrong if they've chosen the happiness, of whatever kind, at least in beginning of an already uncertain life?"

I began sinking in search of the answers but master

interrupted me with another revelation.

"Son, I have also observed that you easily get fascinated about the miracles, but do you know what actually the miracles are?

Oh! Once again I was too engrossed in his talk.

"When somebody else does something awful, we become astounded and call it miracle. However in due course of time, when we ourselves acquire the knowledge and potency of performing the similar awe on our own, we start valuing it less. We primarily do so in our aspiration for the otherwise higher things. Trust me my son, there is no miracle on the earth which can be performed by one and not by the other. It's just about your choice of the kind of miracles that you want to perform in life. Throughout your entire time on the surface of this planet, you never live a single moment without a possibility of performing miracles of one or the other kind. Human life itself is a miracle, isn't it?"

I simply nodded up.

By this time we had reached back the cave. In my forgetfulness during the illuminating talks made by master, I couldn't know when we had turned back from the forest.

TWENTY THREE

The Last Illusion: Atom

MASTER HAD NOW SAT on the altar and became silent. With closed eyes, he was intensely busy in meditation. I saw that he was intermittently smiling. I was able to guess what lessons he was going to impart me now. Three had already been elaborated and now the time had arrived for the fourth and last illusion. So far only in couple of days spent with master my imagination had been exposed to the myriad territories of mind. His each talk had made an indelible print in my memory. And why not, such an opportunity was most rare and privileged.

Enjoying the ineffable vibration emanating from master's silence, I was waiting for his words. As only foretold, today was my last day with him and only few hours had left for the last illusion to be explained by master.

As he opened his eyes, he looked immensely enraptured. He said, "As you know son, that this is your last day near this cave, take from me the enablement of your mind so that you will perfectly understand the illusion of atom as well. Oh, just feel around once again! How astonishing is the entire sport of magnanimous creation, that, it originates and blooms only in the little miniscule and invisible human mind. Son, very this viewpoint of perceiving the strange compatibility between the magnanimous creation and miniscule mind is the enablement which I am talking about. Now take from me the supreme knowledge about the illusion of atom as well."

"Do you know what atom is?" he asked.

I couldn't think of any precise answer suitable to master's

expectation.

He answered, "In literary sense atom should be referred as unit. However the limitation of perceiving the size of unit creates illusion in human minds. Man cannot measure the unit beyond his own unit of perception. Have you ever imagined son, what unit your body is made of?"

"It's the human cells master!" I replied.

"And what unit the human cells are made of?" he asked again?

Oh! Had I remembered my school biology books to this day, I would have answered him perfectly. Still I somehow tried replying, "Sir, I do not remember greatly, but I have read that inside a human body cell there are again some smaller particles. One of them is perhaps called mitrocandria."

He laughed and said again, "No! It's mitochondrion. Would you know what this mitochondrion would be made of?"

Oh! Perhaps master in his old times had read the biology books better. I guised my limit by saying, "I think scientists would still be researching that. Or even if they have discovered it, I may not be aware."

"Let us assume that they have already known it, would they be able to describe what that matter would be made of again?" he asked.

I became perplexed on this. "But won't this all be a foolish way of thinking?" I asked.

Now master gave a mystic smile. He said, "Indeed this is the very point. This all has been insensible. Ordinary human mind had perpetually erred to measure the things in their physical dimensions only. Notable scientists look upon the things only in their physical unit. This error has led up to the great amount of illusion which has been persistently believed by them. And on the other side, common people have developed a habit that the ideas which remain uncontested for a long period of time are believed by them to be true and correct. Measuring things in their physical dimensions alone is basically of less use. Let me narrate for you this matter in a way so that you will become able to grasp the illusion of atom in great detail. Let me ask you the same question again but in different context this time. Do you know what the smallest unit in the existence of element is?"

"Yeah, we all call it atom only", I replied.

"True, but do you know what remains inside of an atom? Don't worry I will not start this time asking you about inside of it again and again." He laughed.

I gathered my school reminiscences once again. I carefully began saying, "In the center of atom, to my knowledge, there is a central nucleus around which protons and neutrons, which are even smaller particles than atom, revolve."

"Let me add a little to complete your reply. Such protons and neutrons revolve around the central nucleus in such fast motion that this all activity appears to human eyes as one round atom. Is that right?" asked the Master.

"Yes, it is true", I said.

"But remember, man cannot see one atom in isolation through his bare eyes." Master continued, "Infact countless atoms are so stupendously annexed with each other, that those form the things by taking different shapes, densities and attributes. Ordinary human knowledge has so far understood the existence of atom in this way only. They believe that their entire planet is made of zillions of zillions atoms of different kinds of condensations charged up. But they do not yet comprehend the otherwise truth which is even bigger than the physical existence."

"Oh, what can be the bigger truth, master?" I asked.

"Son, as of your present perception capabilities, this matter may go difficult on your assimilating", master said, "therefore, let me first help you to understand the higher element of physical existence. This will need a small demonstration. Let us go inside the cave and check there something." He came off the altar and asked me to follow him towards the cave.

When we'd reached inside, he pointed towards a small hole which was made in the roof of cave. It was just above our heads.

While it was a bright afternoon outside, sunlight was pouring in through this hole and was radiating inside the dark of cave. It was a small beautiful line of sun starting from the roof hole and landing on the floor near our feet.

Master said, "The beauty which you are beholding in this moment is nothing but merely the physical dimension of this ray of sunlight. Men always marvel those things more which meet less often with their eyes. People do not mesmerize the opulent sunlight outside as much as they do in case of a rarely seen ray of sunlight like this. Anyway, let me speak about the illusion now. Son, if you are seeing carefully, you will find many dust particles roaming in this virtual pipe of sunray. Do you see that?"

I nodded in affirmation.

"Although these dust particles exist everywhere in the atmosphere, yet we are able to see those only in this pipe of sunray. Now, try to fix your gaze at any one of these particles and tell me what you think that particle would be made of?" asked the master.

I did the same and after an intriguing moment I replied, "It would be made of atoms only, Sir!"

"Yes, that's very true," said the master. He further added, "Observe now the playful activity amongst all these dust particles. So beautifully and freely those are roaming about, even without concerning any surface or foundation. Look on! Sometimes those collide with each other and some other time those escape. Although we cannot see with our bare human eyes, but while colliding with each other they would certainly defect into many new smaller dust particles, so that, the new ones would again start taking part in this eternal activity of roaming. Then, in some time again, a few smaller dust particles would congregate with each other and make a bigger one together. This chain would never end. Isn't it really such a playful sport?"

I nodded but without having fully understood what the master had meant.

"Now will you think of me to be fool", master astonished me

by asking, "if I say that each of these dust particles is a wholesome universe in itself?"

"I didn't get it master!" Great surprise was spilling in my voice.

Master explained, "I mean does it seem incredible to you if I say that each of these dust particles contains a whole universe within it?"

I couldn't be at ease. I asked, "But how come that is possible, sir! Aren't these really very small?"

To my amazement master broke a loud laughter. He said, "This is what the illusion of atom is! Start understanding now the finer threads in this relation. Forget these miniscule dust particles for a moment and imagine about seeing your own planetary system from above. Imagine as if somehow you have reached up above in the space and now can view the sun and its planets in great detail. Imagine that you are able to see the stilled Sun and also the planets in motion. Imagine that you are also seeing many satellites which are orbiting the planets. Try to observe such an interestingly playful activity there. Can you imagine that my son? Close your eyes for doing that if you need to."

As I closed my eyes and concentrated, indeed I was able to imagine it all. Imagining in this way was not really a big deal. My childhood mesmerizing around the geography books in my school days was helping me greatly in this moment. With closed eyes as commanded by master, I was able to see the Sun in the centre. It was bright and didn't move. Orbiting the Sun were many planets which I didn't mind to count. Those all were of different colors and sizes. One of them was indescribably beautiful, for it had big blue rings around it. Ahead of it was the biggest one. I started looking in far. There was lot of darkness there. Even though I tried to count all the planets but I found them in too far. I thought, surely they would be lot more in numbers than our modern science had known about so far. Then I had begun to see the different satellites as well. Those were also making no small businesses there. Quite surprisingly few planets had multiple satellites.

"Keep your eyes closed. Don't open." All of a sudden master commanded me. He added, "Do not drift your vision. Be right there. Now look towards your upside. What do you see there?"

"It's a strange kind of darkness all over. Here it is light yet here is dark. I can see about all but it's not in the usual way, master", I replied.

"Above your head do you see any other star there?" asked he.

Still marveling my vision, I replied, "Yes, here are many. Infact all around it's nothing but the stars."

"Choose any of them and move towards it", commanded the master.

I followed.

"Keep on moving unless you reach adequately near to it. Remember, to reach it very fast, all you have to do is to increase the speed of your mind", said he.

"Hmm...". I uttered only this. So astoundingly I was witnessing that increasing the speed of my mind was no big feat. It was coming easy upon me.

"Yes master, I am here", I exclaimed.

"Do you see that star just as a sun in the center?" Master asked.

"Yes, I do."

"And do you also see a few planets orbiting around?"

I replied, "Yes I do."

"Do you see few satellites as well orbiting the planets?" asked the master.

"Yes I do even that master", I replied.

"Would you like to count all of those?" Master asked.

Still keeping my eyes closed, I asked, "Master, do you think it will make any point at all?"

I heard master laughing. He said, "Look again now in your other directions. You will see many more stars in far. Would you like to visit a few of them and look about?"

"Oh! I can try but I think those all would be the same only", I replied.

"Well, in that case, would you be interested in counting them all?" Master asked.

My eyes still closed, I felt puzzled. I apprehended, "But master, will it be any possible? I think even if I try it will be a pointless job only."

Then, suddenly, master voiced, "Open your eyes now."

I opened. My mind had returned to the cave at once. Indeed, its speed was incredible.

"Look in this virtual pipe of sunrays once again. Look at the dust particles. Would you like to count those?"

"But master, won't this also be a pointless job?" wonderingly I said.

He looked into my eyes with ease and said, "Yes, now you are here. Look more carefully now. Don't all these dust particles just look the same?"

I started catching his point. "Yes, they do", I replied.

"Now will you think of me a fool", master repeated his old point again, "if I say that each of these dust particles is an wholesome universe in itself?"

Good he tried, but I was not fully convinced yet. I asked, "Master, but can we really prove this matter in this way?"

"Truth doesn't need to be proven; for it can be only discovered," master began revealing more, "The crux in what I have demonstrated here is that, human beings actually err by differentiating between two atoms because of their physical sizes etc., whereas they do not comprehend the multitudes of dimensions about the atoms in their bodies in form of cells. Your eyes say that these dust particles are too small to contain universes in them, but only a minute before your mind conceded the eternal similarity amongst the celestial stars visited by you."

In a moment master sat down on the floor and observed silence in the cave. I also sat down. Then he asked, "Do you know about the five elements of creation?"

I replied, "I've heard about but do not know those in detail."

"Let me relate this briefly, so that you can expand this doctrine perfectly in your mind later. These five elements are Earth, Fire, Air, Water and Ether. The entire sentient and insentient creation is the product of the combined energy of these five elements. This energy includes your and my body, the leaves you ate few hours before, the altar on which we sat, the tree from behind of which you brought the Rasagollas yesterday, Rasagollas too, and anything else you can think of. Now, give a look to these dust particles once again. Select any one of these. The element of dust, which is soil, is infact the element of earth residing in it. The energy through which it roams and revolves is the element of fire in it. Its responsiveness to flurry of activity is the element of air in it. The portion of moisture is its element of water. And the scattered gaps of hollowness inside this dust particle, is its element of ether. You find this dust particle irrelevant and you do so merely because of its being small in size. But see, when moments before you were in the proximity of other celestial stars, of what size you were finding your own planetary system containing your earth inside it? Didn't you notice that all individual planetary systems merely look of miniscule size for being far away from each other? Even if you compare the distance amongst stars and the distance amongst these dust particles, stop fooling yourself now; for such differentiation is only a kind of hallucination caused by the illusion of space."

But still I couldn't get fully convinced. Logically master could be correct but my mind hadn't fallen in line.

Here master had instantly sensed my state. He began smiling and saying, "Do you know how this subtle truth which I have explained to you, matters to us?

Yes! I intuited. It was now master was going to make the big revelation. I meekly expressed my ignorance.

"It is that we must live in harmony with all kinds of atoms as perceived by us. Either those be up above in the space or be right here in this cave; we must not disregard the existence of atoms. One atom lives in the other; and that other atom lives in another one. In this way, goes on the entire physical chain of different sizes of atoms. In this cave each of these dust particles is a collection of atoms. Our own planetary system itself is an operation of Atom. Our whole galaxy with many stars similar to our Sun, is a collection of many atoms similar to our individual planetary system. Even our grand universe comprising the countless galaxies is again a big collection of atoms similar to that of our galaxy. And who knows even how many universes could exist up above there?"

Then on the spur of the moment master stood up in the cave and moved his hands upwards. He quickly began to plug out the wooden pieces from many similar holes in the roof. I was amazed to see so many holes in the roof which had remained unnoticed by me so far. Master stepped up and down, here and there on the uneven floor of the cave. In no time he had plugged out all the holes. Cave was lit bright, for many new virtual pipes of sunrays had opened now. Each one was showing a different cluster of dust particles. This sight, still vivid in my memory, was such a spectacular.

"Can you see that?" asked master in wonder making voice, "Aren't here really many galaxies in each of the sunrays? And aren't here really many universes in the form of many sunray pipes? And also do not miss to notice that in between the universes of different sunray pipes here, it's the darkness of black holes. Son, feel the great celebratory vibration created by the atomic energies of galaxies and universes right here inside this cave. Isn't it showing the great harmony amongst all of them? This harmony is not created by us, the human beings, but they can merely feel that. True, in superiority to wilds, human beings have been empowered by nature to sync or unsync themselves with this grand harmony of atomic energies; but unfortunately run over by the illusions in effect of disregarding this harmony, people have actually fallen about treating these different atoms distinctively. Very this anomaly has been creating the atomic imbalance in the operation of nature. Uncalled for diseases, mental imbalances, disharmony and wars, disproportionate distribution of resources are merely a few examples. Even calamities, cyclones, climate disorders and other natural disasters do not come without long persisting reasons."

"Oh! But can we help it?" I asked with some hope.

Master smiled and said, "It's only you who can help it and no one else. Each effort is individual always; in unit per se. In the beginning you can help it by harmonizing your individual existence with the existence of all kinds of atomic operations in the nature. Put more exactly, you can do this by sincerely assuming yourself being no different from the five elements of nature, which I have already mentioned to you. Doing so is such a simple task that you might not believe. Only remaining staunch to your constitutional operation of life will do entire suffice. Your constitution regarding operations of life is all about your 'willingly' observing the righteous course of your living as sanctified by your very surrounding nature. If going by this, you do not offend any person or object around you. You never fail to enjoy your life in this unique way. And soon a kind of stage comes when you attain the supreme oneness with the atoms of all kinds. Amidst that stage, the atoms present in these dust particles remain no different from the atoms present in the universes. Only such harmony can bring about the ultimate peace in your life. You become free from the vibratory perturbations taking place in these particles as well as in those universes. You attain in this way the ultimate state of bliss and complacency. This very stage is the state of getting rid of the illusion of atoms."

I had no words to describe my satiation. Now each and every point was clear to my mentation. I had already started enjoying the playful activity amongst the dust particles. Master was smiling at me; and I was smiling at the multitudes of universes, right here in the cave.

TWENTY FOUR

Bestowing Me the Wooden Box
Before Adieu

"WE STILL HAVE FEW hours left before the dusk falls, therefore let us move to the altar now", master said while coming out of the cave.

I followed and sat quietly aside to him. I looked around and thought about my home and workplace. It was the same world and the same things in it, but merely in three days master had changed my outlook miraculously.

For many moments on the altar master sat only silent and with closed eyes. Truly, I was enjoying his company in all manners. So far in the day I had not been consciously reminding myself that it was my last day with him. Probably my mind was busier about his presence than to worry on account of his imminent bereavement.

In some time master opened his eyes and began to look at me very affectionately. He said, "Son! Now I have imparted you the best education in the school of mind. But I also must warn you. Just the way without adequate practice the normal school education does not fructify into one's growth, you should also not behold this supreme education received here concluded only. Without sincere and awaken practice, any knowledge would become redundant."

"Hmm...", I nodded.

"You have learnt enough about the illusions of time, space, word and atom. It's only such plethora of illusions which clouds the mind of man with untrue apprehensions and vanities. Because of the constant presence of these illusionary clouds, man's mind becomes habitual to those and stops taking a diligent notice of the truth. Mind overlooks the foolish tricks played by these clouds as those obstruct the way of wisdom-sunlight from reaching the conscience of man. Man without sufficient light, acts upon in dark and tumbles down again and again. Unfortunately, still choosing to remain aloof of the sunlight of wisdom, he wants to develop the better skills in tumbling down. He mistakes of the act of tumbling as the act of adventure and he further mistakes that without the thrill of tumbling, his life would become charmless. In the same way have passed many ages, that the man has never stopped tumbling down in the darkness of ignorance. Overrun by the constant appetite for sensory pleasures and also by the following apathy, he becomes slave of his own mind. He never endeavors to regain his mastership on his mind, for every moment he is undermining himself to be so weak and frail. Trust my son! It's not the man himself but it is only his mind which indulges in every small or big sin during his life. And to make it worse, since mind is merely an intangible entity and nothing more, it turns out to be only that poor man who has to receive the punishments from the nature or sovereign. Just see, how wondrous and astonishing this fact is! Literally mind is nothing and no one to be tried against sins."

In amazement I asked, "Is mind really nothing and no one, master?"

"Yes, that's the only truth", he replied and now began asking me inquisitively, "Tell me where is mind? Can you see or touch it? Can you locate it inside or outside your body? The one thing what you call as heart, is just a blood pump made of flesh. It has no properties the mind is known for. Another thing which you call as brain inside your skull is again somewhat similar. Often your mind wanders away from your body; or isn't it? For example when it reaches your friend's place in the other city, it is certainly away from you but is yet unknown to your friend as well. For ordinary people, mind is always incomprehensible. Finding the man bewildered by its every motion, mind masters upon him quickly. And soon after, man starts chasing his own mind just as a donkey chases the carrot hanged ahead of its head. Isn't this all so ridiculous?"

I was in all agreement with master.

He added, "But still, when you've established a dominion over your mind, you also get to see its miracles. You come to the realization that it's nobody else but you who is the master of your life."

I asked a question then, "But master, unless one attains and practices this supreme education imparted by you, should he consider his mind as his enemy?"

"No!" remonstrated the master instantly, "Mind is never your enemy, albeit it's merely your spoilt wayward child. You never think of your children, however big wayward they become, as your enemies. But you constantly try to endure them and even reform them at the same time. It's only your children who are supposed to take care of you in your old age. However if you continue spoiling them by providing wrong knowledge and means, you not only harm them but you harm yourself as well. Similar is your mind. Once you have trained it with your sincere and awakened supreme knowledge, the mind becomes finest instrument of your very same body. It brings you all kinds of happiness and satiations in both; in this life and after life. Therefore make your mind your best friend by awakening it to the supreme truth and wisdom; and not foolishly make it your worst foe by feeding it with sense pleasures and keeping it in the dark of ignorance of illusions. Always play with mind, and don't get played by it."

One thing was very certain to me. It was only my mind which mattered. I had to master it and make it my best friend as well at the same time. It was the finest instrument I had in my body and I had to culture it in reformed ways.

Master then said, "Son! Here completes the education which I could impart you in this short period of time. I have given you my all. Oh son! I am very happy with you. You have got a curious mind and by way of assimilating my lessons well, you have proved my choice in you correct. After this day maybe we never meet again. Tell me, what pleasing to you I can do about in this moment?"

As soon as he said this, I sensitized my upcoming bereavement from him. At once I was filled with the pangs of sorrow. In merely three days he had changed my life. Had he kept me for long, imagine what could have happened.

"Don't feel sad over it, my son!" said the master sensing my state of mind, "More than me you need my words. More than the person who preaches righteous thoughts, it's the righteous thoughts which must be worshipped. I have imparted you all knowledge I had. By doing so, see, I do not become empty, but you become filled. You must meditate for years about the education received here in three days. Meditation is necessary, for without it this knowledge can't become useful. More you meditate, sooner you establish the enlightened friendship with your mind."

"But still, why can't I see you again, master?" I asked in deep love.

"No cave has been my permanent home. I usually come down to the lower altitudes only in a particular kind of season; else I roam ever alone in very high altitudes of the Himalayas. Those places may be very uncomfortable to your unaccustomed body. And neither staying there with me is necessary for you. Now when already you have acquired the supreme knowledge, only meditation remains to be your course ahead. It's alone the mediation which matters after the supreme knowledge. It's the same what I practice in the mountains here. Remember for yourself, whatever stupendous I am doing about here in solitude, you can make right here amidst the world. Trust me it doesn't make any difference where you live, but it is only how you live."

"Master, you are going very hard on me in this way," I said with a heavy heart. "You always call me your son but you do not let me have you company often?"

Awkward to my sobbing state, he laughed very loud and said, "But why at all I must get attached to your body or presence? I have practiced the supreme knowledge for long and now my mind has enabled me reach you whenever I want. You must also practice in the same way and therefore become able to reach me any time at your wish. After having realized the subtle powers of mind, we must not need human bodies to commune with each other", said the master.

"Whatever you say, my master, is law for me", I said, "but please also consider this. It's going to take me some time in fully assimilating your education into my practice. I fear who will help me if I begin getting lost amidst the stupefying worldly chaos. I do not want to wrong your choice in me and neither fail myself. Nothing is impossible for you, master! Help me in this most important ordeal of my life. You must continue being excessively kind on me."

Master flashed a faint smile at me and resumed his ever poignant silence. After a moment he motioned his finger and commanded me to go to the same pine tree once again.

"Bring from there whatever you find", he said only this.

Following his wish I hastened to reach behind the tree. I was wondering as to what new kind of food master had planned out for me now; though I was not feeling hungry at all.

However as I reached the spot, I was stunned with the finding. Indeed, master could make anything out of his mind's power. While returning to him, I was holding in my hands the most astonishing object of my life.

Finding me dumbfounded he began laughing and telling, "Say, isn't it the very same beautiful wooden box which you had seen in your dream previous night? I knew you had liked its design too much. Why don't you take it from me?"

In total aloofness, I couldn't say anything except, "How can you perform such astonishing feats, master?"

"You are mistaking it again. It's not my mind; but it's your mind at work in this feat." He replied and added. "Do not grow bewilderment. I promise that you will solve this riddle as you will advance in your meditation."

I was holding in my hands the same large book sized box. It was beautifully adorned with wooden craftsmanship from all over. Reminding myself of the dream I feared about tapping it and open. I began to roll it in my hands and noticed the same unmatched beauty around the spine and elsewhere too. Just then, on the spur of the moment, I was reminded of something secretly engraved on the spine. Too much curiously I brought it near to my eyes. Yes, it was there and it read:

"It Opens Only When Your Mind is Open"

I smiled in amazement. I felt encouraged but not yet enough to tap and try the box. I didn't exactly knew whether my mind was open or not in this moment.

Master knew my perplexing. He suggested, "In any moment you want to open this box, imagine what it will take you to open your mind first? Once you are sincerely sure about the 'need' of opening your mind, the box will open. For now, since you are with me, simply tap it in the opposite side of the spine and it will open up in the way typically a book does."

I did the same. And lo! It opened. Before looking inside the box I barely looked at master's face.

"What?" Master flaunted his eyebrows in a playful mood and said, "Look into the box and find there every time in this way what is needed by your mind most."

I looked down. It was hollow from inside with merely a large green leaf cut into the suitable size of inside chamber. Something was inscribed on the leaf. Although the sun had started going down in the horizon but I was able to read the inscription perfectly.

It read,

"Welcome to the Secret World on the Other Side of Mind."

I smiled.

Master also smiled and said, "Remember to let only your mind know about this box and the messages inside. Also remember that it is not you who opens this box, but it's your open mind which does it. Every time this box opens, you will find a new leaf with a new message on it. The previous leaf will vanish. Do not take away any leaf outside with you, for even if you do that, the leaf will gradually dry up and soon will break into pieces. You have wanted me to remain with you. I will grant your wish in form of this box. At a time, only one of my messages will be sufficient for your meditation. I wish that the day must come soon when you will stop requiring any external assistance like this. This box will vanish when you won't require it any longer. While possessing it, you must never grow fantasized about it. Remember, only the message is important and not the box itself. Neither do you ever need to demonstrate or boast about it in public. The very moment you err, although the physical box may remain with you, the messages will stop coming for your help. I repeat, it's only the messages which are valuable and never the box. I hope you are able to regard more the substance than the phenomena."

I nodded my head to the warning.

"Now you must leave for the day, my son! I will also move upwards from here. My purpose of staying here this time is over. You must now become highly prepared about your worldly duties ahead", said the master looking in my eyes in this ineffable moment.

I bowed to his feet. He touched my head in blessing and said, "Go my son! And win both of the worlds on either side of your mind."

Once again he came with me to see off and bade me adieu in

an uncontained affection.

Feeling mixed about bereavement from master and holding the miraculous box in hands, I came down to my cottage.

That whole night, I couldn't find words to thank my master.

TWENTY FIVE

My First Day without Master

"THE FIRST THING I must go careful about is this precious wooden box", I thought.

As I woke up in the following morning inside cottage, the wooden box came across my sight. It was lying next to my pillow. After a completely dreamless and relaxing sleep, the morning was fresher than usual. For a moment I sat on the bed and didn't move. I picked the box and began to roll it in my hands.

Indeed, what an outstanding possession had been bestowed by the master to me. More I looked at the box, more astonished I felt. My mind was swinging in excitement. After all not everyone could have become as privileged as I was.

Suddenly, a thought about opening the box flashed in my mind. But I hesitated. I didn't know what could have I expected from the box in this moment. Master had already forbidden me against toying with it anytime. He had warned that the box would not open to any curious instinct of mine. For few moments I struggled with my willy-nilly state, but when I couldn't restrain my mind, I just tapped it.

The box didn't open. I tapped hard, but it still didn't. I sifted around its seam of opening and near about as well. I tried opening the lid from the seam, but it didn't open. I employed my muscles too, but in vain. Even I used all my entire strength, but the box was simply adamant.

Sheepishness fell on me. In past two minutes, not only I had disregarded the words of my master but I had offended it too. I intuited that master would certainly know about my folly. What he would be thinking of me? I was able to imagine his rebuke upon me. I had made a shameful act.

I rid of my impulse and meekly put back the box near the pillow. I began wondering what exactly I had brought with me from the master's place in past few days. Besides the immense knowledge about illusions and wisdom, it was two. The first was the Mantra to bestow me the efficacy of divine vision, and second was this box. I had tried none of the two in my present world yet, or probably I was foolish enough in getting too much excited about those. It was merely my first morning without the master; and I had not even risen up from my bed properly.

Along with the supreme knowledge and wisdom imparted by master, the mantra was also in safe custody of my heart. But only this book shaped box was something tangible and needed special care from me. It was precious and I was supposed to safeguard it from the unnecessary curiosity of other people. Although I hoped that even if somebody finds it, he would understand it to be merely a wooden box and nothing more. He would never believe my story even if I tell. Yet precaution was the best safety measure; why at all I was supposed to advertise about this to the people? Even master had warned me against this.

In this moment I found it my duty to protect the box. It was not mine; rather it was merely lent to me. I recalled that I was carrying handful of mufflers in my luggage. I came off the bed and opened one of my bags. I fished in and took out three woolen mufflers. In following moment, carefully and quickly, I had wrapped the box in mufflers and had put the new bundle safe in the bag.

Now I came about the window and looked through the glass. Sun had started doing its daily feat. Fog was nowhere. I guessed it would be a bright noon today. Glancing the dewdrops everywhere outside I felt wonderful. I came back and picked my mobile phone from a small table. As I pressed a button to check the time, I noticed that one of the messages was unread. It was from the onsite deputy engineer. I opened and read his long message:

"Sir, site plan of the construction work is now finally ready from our side. Could you please reach the guesthouse at 11 a.m.? I will send the car if you confirm. Certain government officials will also be there to discuss about."

As it read the message, I smiled about reminiscing the master's prediction. In his last words said to me he had asked that I must be highly prepared towards my worldly duties now. Immediately I replied the phone message with a 'Sure please' followed by my address. Instantly after, I turned highly active and busy about readying myself for my first day on the project site. After ablutions and bath I walked out for food and then returned to the cottage. I started repacking my bags.

To this moment I still had more than one hour to go before the car would arrive. Without any pretext, but I wondered that master had told me everything in detail but not the method of worshipping God in particular. In this spare hour I was strongly feeling to please God in some way. Standing beside the bed and busily active in repacking my luggage, I picked up the wooden box wrapped in mufflers. Out of deep love for master, I felt like seeing it once again. Before I would immerse in the site work ahead, I wanted to glance my master's present once again.

I began to unwrap. As the box came in my hands, oh! I felt as if it was just about to slip down on the floor. I quickly swerved my hands and saved it from dropping. However awhile this act, my fingers accidently tapped the box, and lo! It just opened.

I was amazed.

Certainly there should have been a message inside for me, I wondered. I looked in. The earlier green leaf of welcome message had no longer been inside it. Instead there was now a fresh leaf with some words inscribed on it.

I began reading:

"Only your awaken activity around received life is your best

worship to God. Never forget to intuit Him sitting next to you while you are busy in discharging your enlightened Karma of life. You can always please Him through your body, mind and spirit as equally."

Oh! Once again he knew what I was wondering about. Could have I ever had a master kinder than him? He knew all my needs. Only a moment before I had been complaining that he had not taught me the way of worshipping God; and just now he sent the answer! I read the message once again.

Now I knew I couldn't keep the leaf with me; I had to place it again inside the box. And I also knew that I would not be able to read the message ever again.

Immediately I took out from the bag my pen and diary. I copied the entire message on a page of it. Once I was done, I put back the leaf inside and closed the box before wrapping it in the mufflers again.

After a brief up down inside the room, I looked out from the window. I still had more than half an hour. I opened my diary and read the message once again. Now I was sure about how to spend this spare time before the arrival of car. I started flipping the previous pages in the diary. While in Mumbai, I had already written down in it many intricacies involved in the process of laboratory construction ahead. More I was reading my scribbles, more I was feeling like being on the site.

Only in few moments I had submerged in the best worship of God; that was nothing but my awaken activity in the 'received life'. I continued reading in the diary the figures, illustrations and hand drawn graphs meticulously. As of then I had no trace of idea as to what more this diary was going to record in the following times.

Infact I had no trace of what the life was planning around me.

RETURN

PART III

SEARCHING BOTH THE WORLDS
IN ONE ANOTHER

TWENTY SIX

My First Experience with Divine Vision

NOW MY CONSCIOUSNESS WAS returning to the bedroom. I looked on. Annie had tumbled to the other side of bed. She was grossly unconscious in her sleep. I didn't check time, but I could guess it was nearing the dawn.

Lying awake in the bed and bearing a pint of smile on my face, I began to take my divine stock in the mind. I thought about the things which I had brought with me from master's place. In this moment I still had no chance to go and seek help from the wooden box. I couldn't take risk of Annie; for however fast she was asleep, but I knew she would get up on a pin drop sound. Only the other way of divine vision seemed easy to me. Therefore I closed my eyes and began to engross my mind on the mantra.

It was, "*Oh Lord! Make me see the truth. I am in search of it.*"

Although I was constantly repeating it in my mind, yet I didn't find it making any difference at all. I grew uneasy. Despite repeating the mantra almost ruthlessly, I couldn't have any vision as foretold by the master.

"Oh! Perhaps master forgot to instruct me about the exact method of invoking this mantra." Quickly I had begun unfolding in my mind his conversation made on the other day. He had asked, more earnestly I repeat the mantra, sooner the vision will occur to me.

I wondered, haven't I been doing it earnestly already? Then why it didn't happen? I thought about chancing once again and closed my eyes. This time instead of getting discouraged by my initial failure, I continued repeating the mantra more pressingly. But still, as I believed, under the warmness of quilt, it proved to be no good place at all for the mantra. I strongly felt like moving elsewhere. But the idea didn't come easy because of Annie.

I started growing restless. But luckily, I found a way. Master had been claiming that worlds are created only through the power of mind, therefore now I had also inclined to make one for myself. I began to picture the same undulated footway towards the cave on the hilltop. Behind the darkness of my closed eyes, the green painted rocks came alive. In no time I had reached the cave of master but he was not there. I sat upon his altar and began to feel as if he was just watching over me. In no time the imaginary climate of hilltop took a complete hold upon me. The same serenity of master's days grew. Once again, afresh, I focused upon the mantra. This time I didn't repeat it mechanically, but I rested and meditated upon each word of it. It was:

"Oh Lord! Make me see the truth. I am in search of it."

No matter how slow I became in muttering the mantra, but I did not move to the next word of it unless I had submitted my whole contemplation to the preceding one. Oh, what a bliss! Now I was getting the meaning of it. I didn't score when I had fallen into the joyous trance of this mantra. My eyes were closed and my consciousness was floating in joy. Soon I had begun to see something strange in the darkness.

Perhaps it was a kind of shining object in far. It was reflecting a thin beam of light. Apart from it I couldn't see anything else. I began to move in that direction.

I didn't mind whether I was walking, floating or flying. I had no consciousness about my physical position, but whichever way I was doing about, it was an ineffable experience. Promptly I had reached the shining object. Oh! As I had been anticipating, it was a small round mirror. I was surprised to see that it was hanging freely in the air. I also noticed that this darkness everywhere was not frighteningly black; albeit it was strangely appearing to be washed in hazy blue fluorescent. It was same in all directions. I didn't know my whereabouts, for I had left the cave and altar far behind. I brought my hands in front of my eyes, but I couldn't see those. Shocked, I began to look downwards, but I couldn't find my feet or rest of the body. It was alone the dark blue haze everywhere. I didn't know where I stood. Whether I was on ground or in the air, I couldn't ascertain. Aghast, I glanced upon the mirror once again. This was the only visible object here. The shining beam of light which was coming out of the mirror was so feeble that it could show about only the mirror itself and nothing else there. I waved my hands against this light, but still I couldn't see those.

In curiosity I clasped the mirror in both hands. I began to see what it showed. Oh! It was showing my face, quite clearly. I found nothing new in it. I looked in more carefully, but the mirror was showing me in the usual way only. In order to see elsewhere through the mirror I slanted it a little. Oh my goodness! It was showing the familiar walls of my bedroom! Heavily surprised, I looked down; and covered all over in quilt, it was Annie fast asleep on the bed. I felt like checking her face but the quilt was coming in between.

I was on the height of anxiety. I turned myself and the mirror in all directions. It showed me the entire room. I could see the door, windows, frames on the wall, cupboards, ceiling fan and everything else too. What I was seeing in the mirror was no different from the things as those had been actually in the room. Even though my spell of viewing in the mirror was quite magical, but I couldn't make out any particular message or meaning of it. It was all similar to how it had existed in real.

"As was described by master, indeed the divine vision has occurred to me, but I do not yet know what to do of it." I had started talking to myself. "What the master could have asked me to do in this moment?"

The mirror was in my hands but I didn't know what to do about it. I badly feared the imminent loss of my divine visioning privilege for my ignorance. Only master could have saved it in this moment, I wondered.

I clasped the mirror even more tightly, lest I may lose it. I began to recall master's words again. Only he could save me.

It was pleasantly surprising that my habitual forgetfulness was not swaying me this time. I was able to recall each and every word said by master, as if a motion picture was being rewound. I could see his affectionate smile, just as before, in front of me. His words began ringing in my ears.

"My son! Do not get dissuaded, even though it might take you a little effort and time to understand this matter in completeness. Certain old locks are difficult to open for the first time, but once they've opened, they do not trouble any more. Here in this moment, just remember that, regarding your entire existing life and world, the ways in which you see those from your physical human eyes, are merely the images reflected by the non-transparent mirror of your mind. Putting all these reflected images aside, when you've wiped the other side of the mirror, indeed your latent divine vision will set into working. Once you've wiped perfectly, it will restore its full transparency. And then this mirror will turn into a clean transparent sheet of glass. Starting from now, in this way, you will see across the sublime truths. Your vision will be no longer restrained by the untrue reflecting images. Instead, you will now be able to see much more about the same things. In such moments you will notice, that how stupendously, you had been ignorant of the new findings. But beware! Before you actually invoke your divine vision and start practicing it, remember one important thing, that all what has remained hidden from your ordinary vision so far, is the very secret world which you will be seeing now. At times, things may go unpleasant as well."

Perhaps I knew what I was supposed to do with the mirror now. I left it once again hanging in the air and moved my both hands behind it. From the other side I began to rub and wipe it with my gentle fingertips.

It started working. The mirror was losing its dross on the other side.

I hastened the wiping. Soon the mirror lost its reflectivity and had become now as transparent as a plain sheet of glass. My divine vision was progressing simply as per the master's words.

I clasped the hanging mirror once again. Now instead of seeing the reflective images in it, I was able to see through on the other side. Picturesquely I was looking into the mirror as if I was peeping across it. Casually I slanted it to the bedside once again.

Slightly uncovered from the quilt I was lying on the bed. Annie's hand was once again showing around my waist. I wanted to check her face, but the quilt didn't let me.

As if all of this was insufficient yet, my astonishment began to see a new height. Now the quilt was dissolved in the air. Annie was asleep while clinging to my back. I checked myself too. I was motionless, perhaps pretending to sleep for that moment. Seeing across the mirror I saw Annie's face once again. She was beautiful as ever.

Now I turned the mirror upside and looked about the room. On the other side of wall Maina and my mother were sleeping in the next room. I felt like seeing them as well. Instantly, nearly to my frightful surprise, the wall also dissolved in the air. Here, mother was momentarily awaken and was covering Maina with her own quilt. Mother would always do that for the child. Wondering that children never feel the chilling winters the way grownups do, I smiled.

I began to look back into my room. My gaze fell upon Annie. Her clasp had now loosened on my waist. Nobody counted as to how many times this had been repeating every night. My body shook a little and was lying straight with my chest upside now. Maybe Annie felt something. She brought her nose close, kissed on my cheek, pressed my waist tight and was asleep once again. I could feel her breath warming my shoulder.

"How could she love me like this?" I asked myself while seeing across the mirror. "When master says it's all illusion, in what way I should comprehend this?"

Mirror was still in my hands. Just casually I brought it near to Annie's head and began wondering, "Who is she actually that loves me so intensely?"

The very moment this thought sprang in my mind, Annie's body started dissolving in the air. First her flesh went away and I was seeing a skeleton there. As I looked on in great amount of stupor, even the skeleton began dissolving. Now merely an oval shaped lobe which was made of emanating lights and nothing else, had had remained there.

I was in bloodshot state. Out of fear, I cast off the mirror aside and closed my eyes. But my curiosity couldn't be over yet. I began to feel like chancing to see without the mirror as well. Quite apprehensively I reopened my eyes. Mirror was still in my hands, but was away from my face. Barely, I looked down to the bedside once again. Quilt was still covering her and I was not able to see the body, skeleton or lobe either. I glanced at the mirror once again. Though it was astonishing, I couldn't help but hating the very idea of seeing the skeleton of Annie once again.

However yet, I couldn't curb my curiosity completely. Irresistibly I brought back the mirror in front of my eyes and began to see myself this time. Once again the scene started to develop in the same way. Flesh of my body began to dissolve. And when only my skeleton had left there, even that started disappearing. Only in a moment there remained nothing but the same oval shaped lobe, which was made of the emanating lights.

Now there were two light-lobes on the bed. I tried comparing but couldn't make out any difference between the two. Except the light, there was nothing. There was no sign of even gender differentiation. These light-lobes had nothing to be described. I was more shocked than astonished. Appallingly, I moved the mirror to see across the wall. Here too, in the next room two other light-lobes were sleeping on the bed. This time, at least for the age gap, I was particularly trying to figure out any possible difference between my mother and daughter, but there was none.

The light-lobe of my daughter was just the same as was of my mother. I looked back to my bedroom. None of the light-lobes was any smaller or bigger. None of these showed to be of a male or female body. None was younger or elder than the other. None was looking sleeping or awake.

I couldn't make out any of it. I started dwindling in great perturbation. I wanted to see the master. I wanted to ask him questions. Surely he must be smiling from miles away in this moment. Any why not! He always knew all the answers.

Although the mirror in my hands was no less miraculous in a way, but it was not giving me answers. Through it I had seen something very strange and couldn't compass its meaning. Burdened by the bafflement I brought the mirror upwards once again and looked for Annie.

There was no Annie but only a light-lobe like the other one of mine. I closed my eyes and didn't want to open.

In this very moment, I felt as if the mirror was gone out of my grip. I opened my eyes but didn't see anything except the dense darkness in all directions. I closed the eyes but it was still the same. It made really no difference at all whether my eyes were open or closed. I couldn't see either the cave or the master himself.

I sensed that my divine vision was gone. Once again I was conscious in my body lying on the bed. Annie was there, just as beautiful as ever. In that moment, I didn't know what happened to her, but she moved a bit, kissed my cheek and slept again.

I turned my face to her. A pillow stirred.

She shook a bit and uttered in her drowsing voice, "Rube! Why don't you get sleep?"

"Hmm..." I replied just the same. Annie loosened my waist and tapped on my chest. "Sleep now Rube. It's very late." She just turned her back towards me and in no time, she resumed her snoring once again.

Here, wondering how at all I could connect with master, I didn't know when I too had fallen asleep.

TWENTY SEVEN

Needing My Master Again

NEXT MORNING, I GOT up early. It was my first holiday out of the seven granted by Mark. Generally on holidays I had liked to remain in bed for long, but this day I didn't know what occurred to me. Maybe it was my previous night's experience. I remembered each and every detail of it.

As I got up from the bed, Annie didn't know my move. She always said that she enjoyed her morning slumbers the most. After getting fresh, I came in the drawing room and began to look out from the window. Winter mornings were always reluctant. I looked at wall clock. It was 5:10 in the morning and dawn had not yet fully surfaced.

I turned back to the study and checked my mental stature. Previous night, although I had been overrun by great hallucinations but I was feeling precisely composed. I figured out that it was my similar psychological state which I used to feel during my mornings spent with the master. All I had in my mind was curiosity and not the fear at all. Yes, I had questions but those were not bewildering. In one of his talks master had already forewarned me that on the path of truth, the protection of mind and body is undertaken by soul. Indeed, only he could impart such gems of wisdom. I have had never seen anyone like him.

Sitting aloof in my chair I began to feel like meeting him very much. He was hard upon me when in our last meeting he had said that we won't meet in each other's body once again. But here I had really needed him, rather badly.

Bearing a sweet smile on my face I began to wonder about the ways of master. Though across the entire time I was on the hills, I had my camera with me, but it never occurred to me to click a picture of master. Believe or not, only he must have made my mind forgot about it. After all, he could work out any feat through his mystic powers.

I sighed. Had I had his photo with me here, I would have felt a little better.

Just casually I picked a book from the table and began to roll it in my hands. Ooooh! As if a lightening bolted on my head, I gasped, "But also didn't have I the best book in the world with me?" Before doing or saying anything else, I jumped from the chair and peeped into the bedroom door. Annie was still asleep. I moved to the next room. Even mother and Maina were same.

Great chance for me! I came back and opened the bottom drawer in the table. I unzipped the chain of small bag and it showed me the mufflers. I gently took it out and unwrapped. The wooden box was in my hands now. I slightly doubted whether my mind was open or not in this moment. After all, the opening of wooden box depended on that alone. I laid my left hand on my chest. It was a racing heartbeat. My doubt was confirmed. I didn't try tapping the box; rather I had put it on the table. Fixing my gaze on the box I stretched my chair. I began complaining to the master in my mind, "Why do you keep me anxious?"

I felt as if he had just replied. There was no voice coming from outside this time, but the answer which I had heard, was so authentic that I couldn't disregard it. I felt as if master had just rebuked me by saying, "Oh! What makes you think that it's me?"

Reverent smile crossed my face. For a minute or so I imagined nothing else but the mystic countenance of my master. He was wonderful; knowing all kinds of wonderments, yet keeping from all of those.

I put hand on my chest again. The racing had stopped. In deep love I picked the box and tapped it.

Lo! It opened. A fresh leaf was here with master's message

inscribed on it. I picked it out and started reading:

"Son! What you've seen previous night was neither a dream nor hallucination. It was your first experience with Divine Vision. Your mind was remarkable in comprehending it. You have seen a part of secret world of souls. Seeing souls in the way of individualized fragments of cosmic light is only one of the ways. I am glad for the way you have been constantly culturing your mind towards the eternal truth. Your continued good practices will take you far. And I remind you, your overwhelming experiences in the secret world must not make you lout about your dutiful part in the apparent world. Keep realizing the subtle powers of your mind. My wishes are with you."

I sat motionless for moments. Wooden box was on the table and leaf was in my hands. I was feeling blessed and with more energy in my frame. I unzipped another pocket of the small bag and took out my pen and diary. Without wasting a second I copied the entire message in the diary and placed back the leaf into the box. Having closed the box gently I wrapped it in the mufflers and put back in the bag. Now the bag was safe-put in the bottom drawer again.

I looked at wall clock. It was 5:40 now. I went straight to the bedroom and shook about Annie.

"Annie... Annie! Are you getting up? It's morning."

She shook her head. "Rube! Why don't you get sleep?"

I laughed. "Annie! It's morning", I spoke loud.

Without opening her eyes she peered out from the quilt. She made a face and said, "No, it's not. My alarm hasn't rung."

I laughed louder and looked her face. It was covered in her long black hair.

"Annie, listen! I am going out for a walk; will come in an hour."

She opened her eyes slightly. "Oh... Are you sure? It must be great cold outside."

"Yes, I will return in one hour", I said.

"Put on enough woolens. Also do not forget to take the duplicate key and lock the main door from outside." Just having said this, she hid her face behind the quilt once again.

I smiled at her usual habit. I drank some water and moved out.

Indeed, it was big fog outside. While entering the park, which was merely at walking distance from our apartment, I saw a lot of people already working out there. I felt surprised and pleasant as well. Perhaps it was my first time that I had been so early here.

I started walking slowly. As of this moment I had a mind of talking more with master. But here amidst people, neither could I have the wooden box and nor a chance for divine vision.

Walking on the concrete track of the park I found a crowd. Solitude was impossible. I stood still and looked around. It was strange to see flocks of people on the jogging track but almost no one in the central orchard of park. I left the track at once and walked towards the center. It was faint fog all around. Grass was wet and frozen cold. Quickly I reached the orchard and entered under the dense of it. Although braving the fog in this orchard was first time for me, but I had been familiar to such climates previously as well. I had spent similar moments with master in the hillside forests. I marveled being here. Indeed there seemed no difference between the hills and orchard here. It was the same fog all over.

I felt tranquil and ambled around. Here were countless high-rise trees which had lined up so close to each other that it made a dense green roof above. Below at the ground there was no trace of grass.

"Oh, how beautiful it is! Wish, master could also come here with me", I wondered.

"Master says", I continued wondering in myself, "that it's alone the mind which can create universes. And today in the wooden box he has said that he is happy about my ways of culturing the mind. Oh! Can I do this wonder here?"

The plan had set in my mind. Though I knew it was impossible in the physical world, yet I began to insist in my mind that the master must walk here next to me. I had filled with deep love and reverence for him. It enabled me to demand like a child. My silence sought him that I didn't want to create any astonishment but I sincerely wanted to meet him again. I couldn't go to the hills again and again. And even if I go, I was sure to not find him near the cave. Although I had been bestowed with the divine vision and wooden box, but why should I remain deprived of his divinely presence? I was assuring my mind of his presence with great force. I had compelled myself to believe that it wasn't possible that he was away from me.

Quite instantly, I felt as if his smiling posture was walking behind me. I turned back but there was no one. I restarted walking. I didn't lose heart. Oh! Just then I felt him again. I turned back. But no! He was not there. I intuited that master always disliked my slightest fancy for the miracles. Now I stopped expecting any. I thought I would not turn back at all. But I did not stop supposing him walking behind me. He was smiling, I knew it. I could see that even without turning my back. He was right here, for I could feel his vibration of love flowing towards me. He didn't speak a word, because he knew that as I would turn my head to his voice, he will have to disappear.

But here my wit played good. Instead of turning back I began seeing downwards. I saw master's holy feet clearly. It was enough for my satisfaction. He walked with me for some time. We didn't exchange a word but it was all love in the air. I saw his feet again and again. He was walking barefoot in his familiar style. I didn't ask him questions. Neither had the questions remained of any use here. Only love was in the air. He had already been answering me through the wooden box. Here under the dense trees I was enjoying his company in the same way as I did in the hillside forests. Whatever be the place, he was kind and affectionate upon me.

This was the moment I realized that in order to feel my

master's presence I never needed to go in the hills or somewhere else. He was right here, wherever I could attain the peace and tranquility. It had been quite some time now. As I took out my phone to check about the time, I lost his presence.

Thinking that Annie would be worried, I paced up in the direction of home.

However before exiting the park, I turned and looked back to the orchard. I smiled and thanked my master unstoppingly.

TWENTY EIGHT

Relishing the Apparent World

"SHALL I MAKE TEA for you?" Annie asked.

Just as I had reached home, I found everyone in action. Annie had woken up, most likely by her ringing alarm. Maina was dressing up for her school. And mother was preparing for bath.

"Rube! Tea?" Annie asked again.

"Yeah, sure", I said.

I went straight to the balcony and picked the newspapers from there. As I came back and began reading the headlines, Annie brought me the tea. In usual morning rush she would never give me a company. She was busiest. Over the years she had become so skilled in the household chores that she worked like a magician. I would often wonder of her dexterity.

Sipping hot tea and reading newspaper had always been my favorite moments. Though today, turning page after page was not helping any interest of mine. I felt as if newspapers were bringing only the same news every day. It had been my long standing realization that the newspaper companies would merely change the names of people and locations, and publish the similar kinds of news again and again. The kinds of happenings in the world, at least in the way how presented by newspapers, were only repeating. I looked the papers more carefully. Just as every day, even today the newspaper was at its best. Besides the boring political front pages, there were pages about business and commerce, sports, editorial section, local news, national and international news too. And in the supplementary section there were also many colorful pages which were story-telling about the 'colorful' lives of many Bollywood, Hollywood and struggling celebrities.

My tea cup had finished; and so had the newspaper. I stood up and checked into bedroom. Quickly I returned with a blanket and bedded on the sofa.

"What happened Rube? Today you finished the newspaper too fast!" Annie passed a comment from kitchen.

"There was nothing new in it", I said,

"That's the same I have been telling you for years", she taunted while settling some utensils in the cupboard.

"Yes Ma'am. But it's now I could realize it", I spoke animatingly.

"That's better", she laughed.

I closed my eyes and began to think about the master.

But just then, "Papa! Aren't you going office today?" Maina came up in her school dress and was surprised to find me lazy.

I smiled, "No Sweety, for me it's an off today."

"An off? Then I will also not go to school", Maina screamed.

"What do you say girl!" Annie intercepted, "Papa will be at home for seven days. Will you also not go to school till then?"

"What, Seven days!" Maina screamed. "O mama, let me be at home at least for today please!" She began insisting.

"No! You must go. You've already dressed", Annie reasoned.

In the meantime mother had also come from bathroom. Hearing Maina's screams, she came about and looked on.

"Grandma! I want to be with papa today. Do you know he is at home for seven days?" Maina had suddenly drifted to plea her grandmother.

"But that's not the way Maina", Annie warned stern.

Mother shook the chin of the child and smiled. She gestured to Annie for keeping the wish. Annie looked to my face but I was already smiling.

Maina at once knew what was going on. Without wasting a second she rushed and banged into my blanket.

"Hey! But at least change your dress!" Annie called out.

"Later, later, mom!"

Everyone laughed; and I did the loudest. Mother and Annie went inside again.

"Papa! What special we are going to make today?" Maina asked. In excitement she had hit her head on my chin. She was clinging to me while looking my face.

"You tell, my Chichi", I teased her name.

"Papa how many times I have to say that I am not Chichi", she admonished.

"But today I will call you Chichi only", I mocked.

"Then I will call you...Hmm... Hmm... Yes, Chuchu", she laughed at my face.

"Chuchu?"

"Yes, it's Chuchu", she repeated.

"Ok! But don't tell my new name to your mother. Else we will have to give a new name to her as well", I quipped.

"And grandma?" Maina asked with the double smile.

"You naughty girl", I squeezed her cheek, "you will get me a beating today."

Maina burst into laughs.

Only in a minute Maina asked again, "Chuchu tell me, what special fun are we going to make today?"

"Umm... We will only sleep like this for the entire day", I replied while keeping my eyes closed.

"Oh! That's the best Chhuchhu", she began tickling me.

"Aye! But you said it was Chuchu", I pretended complaining.

She tickled my arm once again, "But Chhuchhu is more cute."

"Chhuchhu! What you say? If so, I will also call you with other name, and that is...that is..., yes, Chhichhi", I winked.

"No... no papa. That is cheating. I am ok with Chuchu only", she said innocently.

We both laughed in chorus. Just then Annie came about rolling her eyes and carrying the laundry load in her hands. She asked, "What's the Chuchu doing here with Chichi?"

"Mom! How did you know our new names? Did you hear it

too? But you were in the kitchen", Maina wondered.

"I know everything", Annie flaunted her eyebrows and passed.

"Hmm... That's very right, that's very right", I joined Maina in chorus.

In a moment, mother came about strapping her wrist-watch and said, "Rubert! I am going out to hear a sermon nearby; will come be back in two hours."

"Shall I drop you there mother?" I asked.

"No. There are more ladies coming from this society. Walking in group, the distance will not be far."

She went. Here I continued telling funny jokes to Chichi. I asked about her school and she had many tales to relate. She was happy for being with me today; after all I had returned after two months. Once again Annie asked Maina to change her school dress. She went in with her mother and came back in a new dress. She thronged herself into my blanket again and our funny chatting continued.

In some time Maina fell asleep and I carefully came out from the blanket. Annie had already taken her bath and it was my turn now. Being alone in the bathroom, today it pressed me with a different feeling. I found this was actually the only place in the entire home where I was completely alone. After master had entered in my life, many changes had started taking place in my mentation. Now I would feel about the same things differently. While bathing as I poured the water on my body, my ears were shut. In the sound of falling water around my body, I wasn't able to hear any other kind of sound at all. I was with myself alone. Although these moments were small but I felt quite good. Reminiscences of the light-lobes witnessed by me at previous night and also the following wooden box message from master began to rush in my mind. Though it was an awkward place, but amidst the splashes I had caught my solitude. Without interrupting the process of bathing, I was comparing between the two kinds of worlds which were starkly different from each other. I remembered what the master had responded upon my asking on the other day, "But how different is this secret world from this apparent world?" He had only increased my anxiety by saying, "There is no similarity at all."

I imagined about four identical light-lobes witnessed by me in this house previous night. And I also thought about the four different persons living here. Yes, it was the very same house wherein the both kinds of worlds were existing – Apparent world and Secret world. And indeed, there was no similarity between the two.

All of a sudden, I heard a knock on the door. "Are you going to take more time Rube?"

Breaking my series of thoughts here I replied, "No, I am just coming Honey."

"Come soon. Your food is waiting for you", she spoke loud and went away.

I hastened up and readied after coming out. As I arrived on the dining table I saw that Annie had prepared some special spicy delicacies for me. She was sitting there and waiting for my compliments. At the very sight of spicy food I felt reluctant but didn't show up. I started eating and Annie continued reading my face. I just withheld and asked, "Won't you take for yourself Annie?"

"Yeah, I am starting after you", she said inquisitively.

As I ate on, perhaps her patient ran thinner. She chipped in a smile and said, "Today I made your favorite rolls darling!"

"Yeah!" I also smiled but escaped her line of gaze.

"Couldn't those be tasty today?" She asked in somber voice.

"No no. Those are very tasty Annie!" I tried filling in.

"But today you are looking uninterested Rube!"

"No, it's not that way. You always make those great." I smiled into her eyes and was somehow able to please her.

However unusual to my habit of gobbling up many, today I took only two. I sipped hot milk and smiled at Annie's long face.

"Why haven't you started Annie! Are you looking sad", I

asked her.

She didn't reply and just began to move.

I took her hand and made her seated again. "Annie", I said in honeyed voice, "I know what makes you sad. But I was thinking that I must regulate my few habits. It's not because my trouble of stomach, but otherwise too, I must regulate my diet only as needed by my body. You always make wonderful food and it's only you who can help me about this."

She glanced upon my spared rolls once again. "You look very changed Rube! But what you've said is good." She forced in a smile.

"It's all for you Honey!" I smiled also.

"Where did you get this dialog? Since yesterday I am seeing that you are muttering this on me", she quipped while returning to her joyful mood.

I smiled but didn't answer. I picked one more roll and broke it into half. She was watching me surprised. I kept one part in my plate and offered the other to her. I brought it close to her mouth when she took her first bite. I winked in love and pushed the entire casserole near to her plate. I japed again, "It's all for you Honey!"

She laughed and blushed at the same time. She also took only two rolls and closed the casserole. At this I felt surprised. Watching her finishing the half roll in her hands, I added, "I love you Annie."

But she was smarter. In one hand she clenched up her plate with only two rolls and with other she made a 'V' mark from her fingers. She rolled her eyes and reciprocated to me, "Me TWO."

Thankfully, it was lightness in the air. See her face, I chipped in, "You know Annie! You always look more beautiful when you laugh."

"No, I look as beautiful always", she began flaunting her eyelashes.

After eating her rolls, Annie turned busy in her household chores. Maina was still sleeping in the sofa when mother also returned from outside. She came and sat next to me on the dining table. In few minutes Annie brought tea and rolls for her. I inquired about her health and medicines in detail. Her response was as cold as always. In such matters she would always close her answer by saying, but what can one do with the old age?

While taking her rolls, mother offered to me one from her plate. Annie was watching this. Mother always had this loving habit of offering food from her supper to the children. Since Maina was sleeping, it was my turn. Even though wondering what Annie would think of it, I didn't resist to mother. As I took and began eating, Annie also spread her hands before the mother and said, "And my one?" Mother laughed and gave to her as well.

My beautiful holidays were passing like this. Sometimes I felt that everyone was taking notice of my changed tendencies and behaviors, but categorically they never insisted asking me. Master also had strictly admonished me that it will be useless to tell people about my miraculous meetings with him, or about the divine vision, or the wooden box as well. He had forewarned that not everybody was ripe enough to assimilate this understanding and knowledge. As per master's instructions, I was supposed to live in this apparent world while having a complete consciousness towards the secret world existing in parallel.

The smaller bag which contained the wooden box was safe in the bottom drawer of my table, whereas my divine vision was safe in the mantra. And what to mention of the words spoken by master himself, for those were ever vivid in my memory.

During those seven days spent at home, I had few more divine visions as well. Even in further days those didn't stop coming on me. Occurring of those depended upon my faith in the mantra, which kept on varying from time to time as per my mental tranquility. Not every time I was able to invoke the divine vision at my will alone. Wooden box also never disappointed me whenever I needed its help. Yes, sometimes it refused to open whenever my mind was not prepared for the truth. In form of these two blessings, master had bestowed me his divine protection. Such of his constant assurances never failed to come for my rescue. In my heart I would always fall short of words to thank my master's kindness upon me.

I didn't stop taking the morning walks either. I had begun liking to be alone in the park and would always search for a secluded corner there. While walking under the dense trees of central orchard, my mind would become still and unruffled. I would start feeling master's presence consciously. In the beginning days he never talked to me. Perhaps he had senses that I would ask him only the endless questions. In other times than being inside the park, whenever I became too eager about meeting him, only his smiling face would come across my eyes. One similar day, when I thought that I had badly needed him over something, he had turned kind upon me and allowed the wooden box to open even though my mind was not any serene. This time he had left a very small note in the box, which read:

"O Son! More than me or divine vision or even this box, what you need is your constant awareness of the secret world. It's the only thing that you must look for."

Every time I read master's messages, I understood those only for my betterment. But contrarily at the same time, neither my desire for meeting him could be terminated. I often became glad that though master had never affiliated my insistence for meeting, he hadn't heavily protested either. Such of his generosity raised my hope time and again.

After seven days' enjoyment, fun and rest at home I joined back in office. Several rounds of discussions were held about the laboratory project. Everyone was happy with the progress. Boss, in particular, had now started including me in the key decisions around other projects. There were some colleagues who had started raising the eyebrows over my new proximity with the boss. In all, I was having varied kinds of experiences. There came several occasions and instances, where without the new consciousness about secret world, I would have terribly erred. But master saved me every time. The supreme knowledge imparted by him was highly useful in my apparent world. Only because of this knowledge's consciousness I was able to identify my dutifulness in the tricky moments. I was able to steer away from many blunders which I could have incurred otherwise. Master was protecting me in all walks of life, though he would never take any credit for himself. He was generous.

I had other experiences at well. Besides at home and in office, those mostly occurred when I was alone at some place. As the time passed on, I started intuiting master's feet behind me more often. For this, even being in the park or under the dense shadow of trees was no longer necessary. Out of my deep love for master, I could do it anytime, anywhere.

I had never felt my apparent world in this way before. Though I was new and imperfect in the secret world, I realized that I had not been any perfect in my apparent world either. With wooden box and divine vision, a lot of things had started happening around. These revelations were precious. I continued recording those in my diary. The remaining part of this book brings you the account of same only.

PART IV

THE ELUCIDATING PILGRIMAGE CALLED LIFE

TWENTY NINE

My Birthday

"ISN'T IT STRANGE THAT you look so cold about your birthday this time?"

Annie was surprised. Once again she had strained the sour string with me. And not without reasons too; for less than in a month after joining office, my birthday was falling due. For past few days Annie had been trying to drag me in a discussion about celebratory plans, but somehow those were failing to interest me any. Today at breakfast table she had tossed up the matter once again. Though mother was also sitting with us, but she was merely a spectator.

"Don't you remember the great fun we made last year? It was such a wonderful get-together with all friends and relatives. People have cherished it till date. Or haven't they?" Annie insisted on.

"Hmm...", I rather pretended to be busy in newspaper.

"Mother!" Annie quickly turned and complained, "Look, Rube has been avoiding talking on this for a week."

Mother began looking my face. Maybe she found me pensive. "What happened Rubert?"

Fearing the boiling temperature around, I said, "Annie! Why perplex mother for it?"

Sensing a household war about to strike out, mother quickly intercepted, "Maybe Annie is right Rubert! But what's in your mind? If you don't tell, how do we know?"

Now both the faces were staring at me. "Mother!" I began revealing my dilemma, "I think I have grown up now to celebrate my birthdays. We must rather do it for Maina."

Annie put it quickly, "But that also we do every year, or don't we?"

Mother quieted Annie for a moment. She asked me, "But when Annie wants to celebrate your birthdays also, shouldn't you let it happen?"

I felt mother favoring Annie. She would always do that because she loved me more, I knew. Getting mother's support now, Annie began to roll her eyes upon me. For a moment I found myself in minority vote. I didn't exactly know what to answer to the point, but the very idea of celebrating my birthday in older ways of cutting cakes and cheering wines with kith and kin was completely failing to inspire me.

I kept only quiet, with my head down in embarrassment.

"Shall we interpret your silence in Yes?" Annie held her spoon straight and pretended to break laughter as nearly getting my nod.

I looked about her face. Her visage was of victory after a cold war of one week. I looked at mother's face too. I felt as if she was satisfied about averting a household war at least.

"Shall we take it as Yes?" Annie flaunted again.

I knew it was my last chance. I gave up in stern and said, "I wish to celebrate my birthday my way this time."

"Yes, yes. You have been leaving me guessing about the same for past seven days", said Annie, "but can we know how exactly it would go this time?"

"Annie", I drifted in edginess, "are we about to start a war on it? All I am saying is that in case of my birthdays, I find no sense in gathering people and toasting wine in the house."

"Then alternatively what shall we do?" Annie held her chin in the cup of her palms. She looked ready for the options.

"I wish to remain alone", finally I submitted my mind.

"Will you at least invite us?" She taunted in distaste.

"Annie! Don't do that. How can I go without you, mother and Maina?" As I said this, she looked a little pacified.

Now mother interrupted, "Rubert! Why don't you tell Annie your plan in detail?" I knew it; mother secretly loved me more.

"Mother, I have no plan as such. Maybe I will take a leave from office and remain at home in peace. Perhaps in the evening we will go to the church or some other place as I feel.

"Annie!" Mother turned to her and requested with a smile, "You may consider this."

"I don't know what's going to happen if we have no plan at all", Annie grew a long face. She stood up and began collecting the empty plates from the table. However before entering the kitchen, she said, "But if you are happy this way, I shall also be."

I looked to mother. She blinked and assured me of Annie's better mood later. I checked time on the wall clock and found myself getting late to the office. I hastened upon dressing and shoes; and left quickly.

Although busying all day in the office chores I tried calling Annie's phone a couple of times, but she didn't respond. I sent a few messages as well, but I suspected she never read her SMSs in time. As evening approached, I started getting pensive about getting back to home.

I tried to engage my mind more into the office work than into my internal perturbation. Just then, all of a sudden, a bright idea flashed in my mind. Years before, even before my marriage, some of my senior colleagues had remarked beautifully about women. He said that flowers and bouquets had some kind of miraculous powers in those. He kept on telling how he would make her wife happy by bestowing a small bouquet in the evening. Funnily, he had also said that it was not only the most economical way of pleasing an annoyed wife, but also was the only option when nothing else worked.

Instantly, the glow of smile returned to my face. I was decided about testing the prophecy today. I hoped it to work. Else, it was a deep pain to see the grim faces at home.

While driving back to home in the evening, I turned to the marketplace and bought a beautiful bouquet of flowers. From a nearby store, I also bought two chocolates. While roaming ahead in the market I shopped a woolen shawl as well.

Enchanting about surprising everyone at home, I restarted. In less than half an hour, I was knocking the door with an overflowing heart. I wanted to see Annie's reaction. I was quite hopeful.

As the gate opened, it was Maina. Ignoring my smiles, she stared at me while planting her both hands on the hips. As she glanced upon the bouquet she rushed back in the bedroom. Holding my office bag, bouquet, shawl and chocolates, I found nobody welcoming me.

I put off my shoes and kept the bag and things on the table. As I moved towards the room, I overheard Maina saying, "Mama, Papa is coming to bribe you."

I imagined Annie's face getting even longer since morning. But right then, I also overheard Annie saying in sweet voice, "Oh really! We will take the bribe and will still keep adamant."

As the both broke laughter inside the room, I felt encouraged and relaxed. Playfully, I turned to mother's room instead. As usual she was reading her sacred book. I bent to her feet and presented the shawl. She smiled and gestured as if there was no particular need of it. I smiled and came back in the other room where Maina was whispering in her mother's ears.

"Look what have I brought for you!" I announced in a poetic way.

"And this is for my big darling", I waved the bouquet in the air and put it in Annie's arms. Curiously I watched her reaction.

And yes, the prediction of my ex-colleague was right. It worked wonder. Annie was surprised. "How come you remember doing me favors?"

I chipped in, "I always do that for you sweetheart!"

"Yes, yes, why not!" She cocked while fawning her eyes. I felt at ease. All this while I also knew that Maina was waiting for me.

"And this one is for my small darling", I started waving the two chocolates and turned to Maina. She raised her hands wanted to snatch those from me, but I made her wait.

"Chuchu! Give me those", Maina screamed.

"Yes ma'am Chichi!" Obediently I lowered my hands and gave the chocolates to her.

She snatched both and rushed to show to her grandmother. Within a minute, the entire house had turned lively.

Maina came back and said, "What will you do Chuchu if I give one of those to you?" She was flashing her chocolates to lure me.

"Oh really!" I sounded imitating the voice of her favorite cartoon character, "is that really possible Ma'am! I will give you a horse ride."

"Hmm... You are the only useful soldier!" She continued playing the cartoons. "Take it and become the horse now."

I bended on my knees and put palms on the floor. I clasped the offered chocolate in my jaw and motioned Maina to ride on my back. Quickly, she jumped on me and I began to neigh and roam like horse.

Maina couldn't stop her laughter when her mother also started pleading in the cartoon voice, "O ma'am Chichi! I am too tired to cross this mountain here. Will you also allow me to sit on the horse please?"

"Oh no!" Even before Annie could come close to the horse, I was flat on the floor. I pretended my tongue out.

Mother was smiling and watching our fun from the door. Hearing the shrieks of Maina she had come out.

"Look Annie! What a beautiful shawl Rubert has brought me", mother said gleefully.

"Hmm... I see, mother. This evening Rube is extra kind on all of us."

"Let's bring the dinner. He would be hungry." Mother said.

"Yes mother, dinner is ready. Please arrange the table. I am coming in two minutes", Annie replied and rushed to the kitchen.

After wash and towel, I mounted waiting for the dinner. As

the food arrived on the table, I was surprised. Annie had prepared my favorite salad and spices-free yellow lentil. She had already guessed my surprise when she said, "I know your food habits have changed Rube! I thought to please you by making your food as per your new preference."

"Mama, why is papa taking only tasteless food nowadays", Maina asked.

But before Annie could reply, I jumped in, "No! It's as tasty as your fried cakes. Will you taste?"

"Ok", Maina said. As I extended a spoonful curry to her mouth, she apprehensively took it.

"No! It's just tasteless", she gave the expected feedback.

We all laughed when mother suggested to the child, "Child, but this is of course healthier than anything. Your father has started taking more interest in the vegetables than the spices going into those."

"Hmm... Papa goes tummy conscious nowadays", as Maina said this, I pinched her cheek.

In this way continued our chatting and dining till late. In some time we all started preparing our beds.

Few days after, finally, my birthday arrived. As yet none of us had discussed the precise ways of celebrating. In my personal outlook, there was nothing called for such as celebration. Just that, I was thinking about making it special by spending some time with master. Already having taken a leave from office, I was relaxed from the previous night itself. I went to bed little early than usual, for I had plans for taking a longer morning walk on the following day.

In contrast to my persisting habit for years, this time I started my day of birth in wee hours. After wash, I had a straight walk to the park. The morning was cold but not errand. As I reached the central orchard, I felt very serene. Out of my deep reverence for master I was longing to meet him. After I had made two circulatory rounds of the orchard, I began to intuit master's feet next to my own. As it happened by itself, I grew conscious about him walking with me. I didn't wish bothering him to disappear because of my act of turning back. I was glad for his walking with me and I wanted this moment to prolong.

Silently I was no less thankful to the master for his continued presence all this while. I wanted to talk to him; inquire about his well being; and also immensely thank him for whatever he had bestowed upon me.

In deep love and tenderness, I asked him in my heart, "O Master! Why don't you talk to me?"

In a dash, I felt as if I had seen his smiling face in front of my eyes. I stared, but there was nothing except the trees in the far. I looked down again. His feet were still with me.

I submitted in my heart again, "O Master! I am not yet fully prepared. I need your active presence more."

"But when did I go away from you, son!"

Yes, that was the voice I wanted to hear. Astounded by master's gentle voice, accidently I turned back. But alas! There was no one. Thinking that perhaps it was my own imagination, I felt disheartened.

No longer after I had resumed walking, his cautioning words came again. "Son! You must not insist for my physical presence. If I grant you that, you will start responding to me and forget your apparent world. You might create unnecessary chaos around you in this way. You cannot make others see me as per your wish; and nor it is possible as per my wish. It's alone one's intuitive want which enables him to behold the materialized forms of his wishes. Isn't it true?"

"Can others listen to you the way I am doing in this moment?" I asked

"It's again up to their deep intuition only", he replied.

I closed my eyes and sighed. "O master! Do you know how much I miss you?"

"Yes I know it all. But more than that I am pleased with your progress made in the secret world", he said in an affirmative voice.

"Maybe you are saying this only to keep my morale. Else, I cannot hide from you the fact that intermittently I've skipped being to the secret world several times. Somehow, whether knowingly or unknowingly every time, I fall in the shackles of the apparent world. Often I regret it too."

Master laughed. He said, "You never need to search about the secret world all the times. It is not something about amusement or astonishment; but it's about the permanence of truth, whether or not felt by someone consistently. Truth will always stay with you. You must not become so desperate for it that you grow restless."

"But master, I am afraid that the continued throngs of apparent world will eventually take me away from the truth contained in the secret world. Do you know, I often get lost with people at home and at office? They all continue swaying me with myriad of impulses. How will I fight that?"

"No, you need not to fight those, albeit you need to learn living with. Apparent and Secret worlds, understand, do not have physical clashes anytime; whereas the inherent contrast between the two is eternal. In any scenario or time, you cannot stop taking place in the apparent world. You cannot escape it; it's impossible."

I turned speechless. Master was hard in his lessons; or probably he had no other way than speak of eternal truth only plainly.

"But master!" I continued walking and forcing questions in my heart, "I am finding my progress on the path of secret world very insignificant. You would already know I haven't been to the divine vision or the wooden box for more than twenty days now."

"Those two things and even my presence or words included, never forget that, are merely your means and not the ends. Infact, insignificant are these ones and not your progress, however small it may be. Whatever you gain on your path, is immensely precious. Don't you remember what I've said, that someday you will no longer require these articles or imaginations for getting into the secret world. You will very much live in that. Infact you will behold the two as one."

"Yes master. I remember that." I submitted to his slight reproof. But in my heart I was unsettled yet. My guilt consciousness was not going away. I knew that my progress had slowed down over past one month. The apparent world was going stronger on my head than I had appreciated.

I admit that master would have read my mind as always. But he didn't say any. Silently I also kept walking in the orchard.

In a moment he said from behind, "Son, you must learn how to deal with your momentary disappointments occurring every now and then. Contemplating failure is not bad, but you should be careful about noticing, whether you've been building out of it an atmosphere of hopelessness or of the hopefulness? Not meeting the expectations is the strongest driver behind the myriad movements of human life. And very these movements can be either of two opposite types – backward and forward."

"But master, what take should I have on my progress if I am continuing to stand in the middle and not moving anywhere at all?" I asked.

"Firstly, if your mental state is perturbed, you are not the appropriate person to assess your own spiritual progress. You can rather trust me in this moment. Secondly, in your journey so far, only your developing discernment towards the dichotomy of hopelessness and hopefulness; and also of backward and forward, has been your privileged advancement. Remember that, the ability to identify one's own truthful stature, however lacking it is, is no small deal. As long as you can at least watch for you a conscious choice between these kinds of dichotomies, you will not fall in the middle."

Master's words were always pragmatic. I couldn't confront him further.

But perhaps he felt compassionate about my peril. He said, "Forget anything else and take my words. Immediately release yourself from this despondency. Such of your state is sham. Your mind is playing evil with you by sticking to this grimness unnecessarily. A child being reluctant for going about school is nevertheless forced upon by its parents. The same thing I am doing for you. See! If you really want to behold your progress made so far, by way of a short spell of meditation, I will make it evident to you. Can you see that lonely bench in far ahead of you?" asked the master.

Suddenly alert to his command, I said, "Yes master, I can very much see that."

"Go there and sit calmly. Start meditating about what and how you have learned and earned in the secret world so far. Sit in your comfortable posture and try to keep your spine and head straight. Do not look in the other directions. To save yourself from distractions, you can also choose to concentrate between your eyebrows. Sit there for as long as you conveniently will. Dispel your mind from the busily activities of the apparent world. Onlookers in this park will think that you are doing the physical yoga only. Start meditating by comparing yourself now and as you were a few months before. Take an account of what you have actually gained with the help of divine vision, wooden box and my company. Also meditate how it matters to you if you keep away from the supreme knowledge for several weeks or months. Does it seem blocking your progress? If honestly yes, increase your frequency of visiting the secret world. Secret world is also as vast as is this apparent world. You never find an end of roaming in either of both. You yourself have to stop at some point, where you think you have had enough of it. Just go there to the bench and liven up your precious moments of solitude."

To his command, as I began moving in the direction of bench, he said again, "And I will not be around you during that time. You must learn to develop yourself without me."

"Master, I am completely at your command. But before you go, I wish to ask you of my curiosity about this particular day."

"Yes", master was ready to answer.

"This day is my birthday. What should I do of it?" I asked.

Master laughed loud. "Why are you getting a long face over it? If you want to celebrate it, then celebrate it?"

"But here my wish matters only little. The apparent world demands from me doing something which I find meaningless." I made my sullen apprehension obvious to him.

"That's hardly a thing to bother about in this moment. Do not fool your mind, or else it will later fool you bigger. In this moment, only your inclination about meditation, which has been incited by me, is important. Forget everything else and concentrate sitting on that bench. Mediate your actual progress made in the secret world. Real you are not your birthday or forced celebrations, but it is how you are about to happen here. More skilled you become in the secret world, more skillfully you will be able to tackle your apparent world as well."

I reached the bench quickly and sat over it in the advised way. It was a perfect solitude here. As I started concentrating upon and recollecting my journey in the secret world so far, my outer apprehensions gave away. Indeed I had made a considerable progress which was not common for all mortals. The only reason which was disheartening me was that, I was not treading this path frequently. Primarily this lacking had occurred because I was not fully able to control my temptations about wonderings and wanderings in the apparent world. It was true that I could not ignore the apparent world all together, but neither giving it my entire mind-space was called for.

Awhile this beautiful mentation, I asked myself, "What will I need to grow disciplined on this path?" Then the answer sprouted from within myself alone. It was - 'The Daily Inspirations'.

As a matter of fact, it was nothing but the lack of daily inspirations which was displacing me in the apparent world. More frequent recalibration of my thoughts was required and it could be done by the factor of daily inspiration alone.

I had now many anxieties resolved. On my way back home, I was taking stock of my possible resources of 'daily inspirations'.

No wonder, the right kind of books came in the first place. There were certain other sources as well. I was constantly making the plans and beaming in my frame.

This day was unique for not only master had spoken to me, but he had also enlightened me greatly. I was ever thankful to him. And what to mention of my birthday later in the day! Later in the morning, both mother and Annie had agreed to my idea of distributing meals and woolens to the alms-seekers outside our nearby church and temple. By the time noon had arrived, all of us were busy in executing the plan. Afternoon, when Maina had returned from her school, she began insisting to go about a picnic. I submitted to it happily. Mother chose to remain at home whereas we three ventured out to a spot. Few hours later, while returning, I took Annie's suggestion to take dinner at some restaurant. She phoned mother at home as to what the latter would like to have in dinner. After the phone call, without any pretext as such, Annie began suggesting that instead of eating inside the restaurant, we also must get our food packed and take dinner together at home. I was humbled upon seeing Annie's care towards mother. On way back at a traffic signal, when Maina asked for balloons from a peddler, Annie got her those in plenty.

After parking the car outside the home, we all went in while jostling the balloon at each other and chanting the birthday carols loud.

After a joyous dinner at home, I spent some time at my study table. I penned down in my diary the all which I had thought upon 'daily inspiration' during the day. In some time, when all were fitfully asleep, I brought out the wooden box from the drawer and smiled at it in tenderness. I hoped, master would have written something for me. As I tapped, it opened. Once again inside it there was a new leaf, which read:

"Happiness must be responded whenever it comes by spontaneity and not merely by attaching it to some particular day in the calendar. But also, when it is the calendar which is bringing the occasions of

happiness in others' life, you must not rule out or separate. The end purpose of life is only the timeless happiness. It knocks your door often, but before letting it in, the door has to be opened by you. Always move towards the timeless happiness and nothing else. And also remember one thing. Never cast yourself down. Divinity has bestowed each mind the immense powers for turning about the reasons of ordinary happiness into the reasons of timeless happiness."

In this moment I noticed that how wonderful gifts master had bestowed upon me today. Not only this leaf, but he had also started talking to me in the central orchard. I had now even stronger reasons to spend my mornings there. And yes, this was also an invariable part of the 'daily inspirations' only.

THIRTY

Only Human Reactions Construct the Life

MY USUAL CHORES AMIDST the apparent world, which majorly comprised spending my days and nights at office and at home respectively, never remained a paradise for granted. Those continued throwing upon me the new challenges every time.

To start in terms of physical health, I had an old problem of infectious tonsillitis which occasionally made me feverish every now and then round the year. Maina's teeth had developed certain cavities, for which we had to see a dentist at least twice every month. Her another trouble of growing adenoids was the newest worry at home. Mother's old problem of arthritis used to become worse in every winter and spring seasons. Annie, however fortunately, was comparably healthier in the family.

And that was only little mention of physical problems. Psychological problems were in myriad. Every now and then, breaking out of cold wars between me and Annie was not rare. Over a matter or other, it often occurred that we couldn't come on the same page. In a way it was good also; for it showed the healthy democratic administration at home. But still, the gloomy days looming at every short interval couldn't be averted at all. Annie was growing a persistent complaint against me, that I had been developing an unnecessary kind of coldness towards many worldly joys. I wanted to help it, but couldn't meet the expectations beyond one extent. Although inwardly advancing consistently in my secret world, whenever I would come across any hollowness about the apparent world, I couldn't help but look uncomfortable. Annie viewed it as my great apathy. She still believed, for instance, that it would necessarily make great sense for us to dance together in the parties and show everyone that what a great couple we were. She had other countless of kvetches also. Very clever and smart as she was, I couldn't ever win a single logical argument from her. Whenever it came upon the rationale behind the worldly manners, she would easily silence me. I'd also find it better to refrain from magnifying the domestic differences. Fortunately, none of our cold war lasted for more than a couple of days anytime. Mother would always resolve it on the meals.

Office life too was no less challenging. I am ashamed to admit that there were occasions when I felt like running away from house to the office and also from office to the house in very next hour. My boss, Mark Dallisi, who was chief director and prime investor in the company where I worked, was extremely happy with my work during my initial years after the laboratory project. In those times, he had almost rained me with the promotions and pay-hikes. But lately, things were not going well. My one or two jealous colleagues had been somehow successful, to certain extent, in concocting a bad name of mine in his eyes. I couldn't protest or retort their jeopardy anytime; for I never felt like spoiling the things further. Casually, in my mind, I had begun to criticize Mark as well. I wondered how he had grossly failed to see and appreciate the truth. I never confronted him face to face on the matter. I found it better to switch my job than to argue with a man who was already impaired of vision. More often, I was getting bad tastes with Mark and these cunning colleagues. Whimsical allegations, when remained partly uncontested by me, began to make their stronghold as well. Even if I tried to struggle it sometime, Mark started showing his true colors. His love for whims was a new discovery for me. Soon I realized that I had no way but to set apart our ways.

But alas! In the newspapers, everyday's growing stories of gloom in the national economy had been keeping my edgy for some time. Even if desperately I was hunting for a new job, the response was meager. Month after month, it changed nothing. Frustration of my office life had begun to take hold on me. I would often land up venting the same at home. I was creating unnecessary stress with Annie and others. Although Annie understood my trouble in the backdrop, even then she would break out on my inconsistencies sometimes. Things were not going on fine. I was under tremendous pressure of finding a new job; and possibly a happier life too. I was living in fear of Mark. I even feared being completely out of job, if I couldn't tolerate his anarchy at all.

One evening, while driving back to home, I was particularly distressed over something. I started wondering what kind of life it was. On one side, the master had bestowed me the invaluable capabilities and on the other side I was striking miseries. Just then another realization occurred on me that more I was getting engrossed into the worldly troubles and fears, farther I was being tossed from my inner wisdom of secret world. Indeed, it had been long time now that I had forgotten my promise made with master. I had committed him to visit my secret world more frequently, only so as to know the truth of my apparent world better. But in the spate of circumstances, I had allowed myself being carried away in the wrong tide.

Without any obvious reason, I felt like stopping the car at once. Heeding my strange intuition, I maneuvered the car to an isolated spot downside the road and jammed the brakes. Switching off the engine I had rolled up the windows. It was all silence inside. Infact I was feeling here more peace than I could ever imagine at home or office or anywhere else. The small cabin of the car had made an insulated island for me. I could hardly listen to any sound from outside, although the sound of my own breathing was now quite audible to me. For several minutes I didn't move at all. Sitting inside a stationary car was coming about a pleasant experience.

I reclined the seat and stretched my legs as much I could. I had never imagined that a car could give so much serenity. I was pleasantly surprised about my newest discovery. I was successful in putting off my mental perturbation for few moments. Soon I intuited that the same old spirit had started filling in my body.

Now I had rested my head and closed the eyes. Master's smiling gestures began to float in front of me. Momentarily I wondered, would he know about my miserable situation? In the same moment my own instinct answered me. There couldn't be anything ever hidden from him in the eternity.

I began guessing how badly I had lacked in tackling my life in past some time. The piling adversities were consequences of the same only. I wanted to figure out whose fault it actually was, but only within a minute my mind was invaded by a series of allegations and counter-allegations. I badly needed help in this moment. I knew if my master was here, he would have labeled my all troubles only as untruth. He would have certainly condemned my own allowance into the sufferings. I too, just wanted to hear from master that it was all untrue.

But master couldn't come in the car here. Nor had I been carrying the wooden box with me any time. If the box was here, it would have certainly showed me the way. Both of my remedies were away from me. Master was in the hills and the wooden box was at home. But still I wondered, would master like the idea of appearing in the car at all.

And just then, a different idea charged me. Divine vision was the help which I could approach in this moment. Though I doubted whether it would occur to me in the closed car, but I chose to keep faith.

Soon with closed eyes and an open heart, I began to repeat and engross my attention upon the mantra. While doing so I was emphasizing upon each word of it and also the meaning of same.

"Oh Lord! Make me see the truth. I am in search of it."

"Oh Lord! Make me see the truth. I am in search of it."

I repeated on and on, but nothing happened. I didn't see anything except the darkness ahead of my closed eyes. I even searched for the shining object as it was in my previous experience, but I couldn't find at all.

In dimness of hope I opened eyes. I noticed that it was the similar disappointment which I once felt only minutes before my previous attempt at home had succeeded. I tried to recall what difference I had made that time. Instantly it came to me.

Now after closing my eyes once again I had drifted my mind back to the mountains. I continued the mantra - *"Oh Lord! Make me see the truth. I am in search of it."*

Instantly, in my imagination, I saw the cottage where I had temporarily stayed, then after I reached at the hilltop; and finally to the empty cave as well. I was beholding the familiar surroundings, the marvelous sunrise, the big pine tree and the deserted altar as well. I bowed to the invisible presence of my master and sat on the altar. Quickly, the same old serenity took hold upon me. Sitting with closed eyes, I felt as if master was sitting only next to me. Instantly now the difference occurred. As if by speed of light, the much awaited shining object came in my view. Merely in first glance, even from far, I knew it was the same mirror.

I couldn't know if I was walking on the ground or flying. Although I was rushing very fast, but stunningly I was not feeling any wind hitting my face. Was here no air at all? I couldn't be sure. I just wanted check my own breathing and blew harder from nostrils. But oh! It didn't make any difference either. Drifting my gaze from the mirror, I looked around. It was the same hazy blue fluorescent light in all directions. I looked down to check my body, but didn't see that. Similar to a feather, I was floating effortlessly. As I reached the mirror I found that it was hanging freely in the air as before. I satiated for clasping it in my hands once again. Even this time it was reflecting a feeble beam of light. This beam was barely enough to show the mirror itself and nothing else in front of it.

Now I had brought the mirror close to my face. I was seemingly sleeping in a chair, though there was no chair visible at all. I slanted the mirror and began to see in the other directions. It showed me the back seat of my car. I turned more and saw the dashboard and steering wheel too. As I turned even more, it showed me sleeping in the seat once again.

Instantly I recalled what the master had said. I brought my hands on the rear side of mirror and started rubbing it gently. Soon it began to lose its dross. For I continued rubbing, it became more transparent. Now it was as clear as a plain sheet of glass. In curiosity, while I was peeping through, it showed me something which I could have never imagined.

First, it showed me Mark Dallisi, my boss. As usual he was sitting in his plush chair and was crowded by papers, phone calls and his laptop. Sitting alone, this late in the office, he would occasionally press his forehead by his palm and pass a weird look. This scene was not new to me, for I had witness the same about him earlier as well. Just now he broke a fist on the table and came off his chair. He had started up-downing the cabin. Then suddenly, biting his lips, he returned to the chair. In this moment he was typing something on the keyboard of his laptop. Although the mirror could easily let me see in all directions, I didn't feel like invading in to his screen. I couldn't guess why he was overstaying in the office and looking uncanny. Was he thinking about me; or about the unpleasant impasse occurred between me and him during the day? I didn't know how I could've read his mind even with the help of mirror. I wasn't sure whether my divine vision was capable of doing that. I wondered what my master would have answered, had I inquired him about the same.

While I was absent mindedly looking at Mark, he just stood up and barged into his fellow director's cabin. They were both worried about something. Mark had picked up a pen and begun to draw some graphs on the white board. He wrote two lines; one upon another – 'Top Line' and 'Bottom Line' and the fellow director began to answer about those nervously.

Interrupting the fellow director in the middle, Mark took out some pills from his pocket and phoned the pantry boy for water.

While he was waiting for water, the fellow director continued searching something restlessly in his laptop. In a minute, the pantry boy came and went back. Mark popped in two pills in one shot and restarted his heated exchange about the two terms written on the board.

I didn't understand what they were exactly worried about, but surely the center of discussion was not me. And further surely, even they had not very easy life. They were also worried, anxious and restless over something. They both were not minding the late hours, for their minds had been too busy about the arguments and contentions between them.

Now I slanted the mirror rather heavily so that I would look about into the other places as well. I wanted to check my cunning fellows, and the mirror didn't disappoint me. In next moment my view had settled on the fellows, whom I believed to have devastated my rapport with Mark. They were both drunk in a roadside wine parlor. Their eyes never blinked and their hands were boating in the air. Badly intoxicated, they were violently boasting about something and trying to pacify each other whenever either of them would stand atop his chair and start making a scene in front of all. What they were talking or planning, I couldn't hear. The noise of music was too much in the parlor. I continued watching their show for few minutes more when they both stood up and came outside in the car parking. One of the fellows, almost spinning, just saw something and barged in while kneeling down ahead of the bonnet. He was yelling an abuse and pointing angrily towards the broken bumper of his car. Perhaps some other car had damaged it moments before. The other fellow was trying to pacify again. In next minute they somehow settled in the car and fled away. I didn't feel like checking what they had done afterwards. I thought it won't be any different yet. In this very moment, I also noticed my pity on them, rather than enjoying to watch their regular wrench as this.

Holding the mirror straight, I turned around on my heels to

see in other directions. I wanted to see about my house. And instantly I was there. Maina was on my table and doing her home-work. Mother, in the other room, was busy in reading her usual holy book. Annie was in kitchen and was milling something in the grinder. She was looking busy and sweating too. Frivolously, she glanced at the wall clock and completed the milling quick. She rushed to the bathroom and washed her face. In a minute when she had wiped with towel, she stood up in front of dressing glass and squeezed a cream tube for rubbing on her face. I was watching all this animatingly. She was doing all this as if hastening upon something else. Even quickly, she opened a box and unscrewed the cap of a lipstick. She made some red on the lips and watched herself smilingly in the glass. While turning back she looked to wall and glanced at our marriage photo hanging there since years. She watched it as if staring in my eyes. In only next moment she came around the kitchen and stared the wall clock again.

In a tizzy, she had picked her phone and pressed a button or two.

Just in moment my divine vision broke. I had lost any hold on the mirror and my imaginary presence around the cave of master was gone. I was back inside the car and my phone was ringing tirelessly.

I flicked a bit and picked the phone from the dashboard. Oh! It was Annie.

For a second, I was too astonished. The phone call cut. As I was about to start the car, it rang again. It was she again. Quickly I picked the call,

"Hello"

"Are you getting late honey?" Her voice came from other side.

"No, I'm just on the way. Around half an hour more."

"Rube! Are you driving this moment?" she asked.

"No, I am parked in the mid and starting again just now."

"Oh!."

"Shall I bring something from the market, if needed?" I asked.

"No. Nothing. Just come."

"Well, bye, bye."

"Hey, listen, listen. By the way, what would you like to eat today?" She quickly asked.

"I think you have just milled something in the grinder."

"Oh! How do you know that?" She asked in surprise.

Oops moment for me! "Well.... Don't you do that always this time?" I pretended laughing and added, "Haven't you prepared my favorite peas curry today?"

"Yooh Rube! Your nose is getting longer every day. You can smell it even from half an hour away."

"Just half an hour honey! Keep the curry hot." I chuckled.

"Umm... come with care my life."

"Sure, bye bye."

"Bye."

As the phone cut, I found my mental state booming. Perhaps this was how familial life meant to everyone. I started back to home. I wondered what had actually turned my mood beaming. Was it divine vision? No, it was the master himself and no one else. Today he was kind on me.

As I reached and knocked the door, Annie rushed and opened it. She was looking gorgeous today.

"Your curry is hot", she said while rolling her eyes.

I smiled and said, "Yes, I know, I know."

We had a wonderful dinner that night. Maina and mother were also looking extraordinarily happy. Or maybe it was their happiness seen by me through my own happiness itself. Whatever it was, but it was just amazing and happening after many weeks in the house. Every minute of it I was noticing the difference that my own happiness had been making to that of others.

Later in night, before retiring to bed, I spent around an hour at my study. When got a chance of being alone, I took out the wooden box and tapped it. Responding to my easy composure, it responded and opened.

Wooden box was showing me another leaf this time. It said:

"Most of your life is ordained by the ways you react to things, events and people. Happening of those around you is not important, but how you let yourself happen around those is. Things, events and people together are what make your destiny in the apparent world. Change your destiny by changing your way of letting yourself affected by them. And see! Maybe in some time your wife will find out this wooden box despite of your hiding so far. Let me see how smartly you react and handle it."

Oh! Master had set a difficult test for me. Rather it was too difficult. If Annie would catch the box, what will happen?

After holding the leaf and box in my hands for a minute, I thought, should I go by the words of this message, Annie's finding out the box is not important; albeit important is my reaction to it. Let us see how smartly I am really able to handle it.

I took no time in copying the message in the diary. I safe-put the box in mufflers and kept the bottom drawer. Feeling mixed, I entered into the bedroom. Annie was already asleep. I smiled at her face and caught my own slumber as well.

The following morning, while ambling in the central orchard of park, I asked master how did he know that Annie will find the wooden box? Will he himself cause Annie find it? Master replied that he was no body to change the future events. Those were always as spontaneous as was the direction of wind itself. Just that, through the power of his mind, he had the ability of intuiting those in advance. In course of this discussion, he also gave me a key about it. He said that I also could use the great powers of my mind by making it least expressive towards any stimuli taking place in the world.

Nearing the time of my returning to home, I asked him why I couldn't come to know what ran in the minds of other people who were being seen by me during the divine vision. I also asked why I couldn't hear their voices and sounds as perfectly.

He clarified that my divine vision was concerned only about my own position towards others in the secret world; and not at all about others' positions towards me. He reiterated that my secret world was alone about myself. Therein all I could see was the truth of myself towards others; and not vice-versa. He also warned that if I would become aware of others' position towards me, I will lose my entire peace forthwith. He concluded his talk by repeating once again that I must focus exclusively upon my own position in the secret world and nothing else.

Each word asserted by master was soaked in divinity. I returned to home in the ecstasy of my privilege with him.

THIRTY ONE

Truth of Reincarnation and Salvation

"REINCARNATION IS THE CONSEQUENCE of your unfulfilled desperations from the past, which are however possible to become satiated in your present forthwith."

I was particularly captivated by this line in a book which I had started reading lately. The matter of reincarnation was taking my great attention in those days. In progress of my resolve for the daily inspirations, books had started becoming my most favorite company. Entreatingly, almost daily, I would spend late hours at my study. I had made a small collection of religious and spiritual books. Around my table, it was growing a small library. There were both kinds of books – ancient scriptures as well as modern spiritual philosophies. The ones of latter kind was easy to understand whereas the former required deep interpretation and expounding. However there was one thing which was common between the two. Actually both advocated that the purpose of human life was to not take birth in whatsoever form again. The purpose was salvation. All kinds of related philosophies were gathering an opinion that the future occurrence of reincarnation was actually a result of unfulfilled desperations in man's present living. Reincarnation, as per these, meant living up the human-age-long sufferings as cyclically caused by disregarding the opportunity of enlightenment again and again. This state was suggested to be the greatest misery. The pages soaked in wisdom strongly expounded that alone the salvation was the end purpose of human quest. Coming back on the earth was almost abhorred.

Steadily I had been developing great interest in these kind of talks. Although I had read and understood the literary text of such books, but the certain kinds of their advocacies were largely running over my head. The conundrum of 'Reincarnation' was a conundrum yet. Even after trying a lot, I couldn't understand why the reincarnation was abhorred, especially when nobody was able to connect the dots between one life and the next life of himself or of somebody else.

I also wondered about salvation. Literary meaning of salvation was much varied, hardly giving me anything specific to understand. But whether or not I could've understood the same in suffice, I couldn't overlook its significance altogether.

One Sunday morning, when all were fitfully asleep enjoying the weekend, I started setting out for the park. As I was putting on my boots, I overheard heavy downpour outside. I peered across the window and found my apprehension correct. Although my mind was reeling in curiosity and I wished to know what master had to say about it, I had to cancel the trip. I paced up-down in the house, and checked about Annie and others. All were asleep.

Good chance for me. I opened the bottom drawer and took out the mufflers' bundle. While unwrapping, my gaze fell upon the beautiful wooden box. I began wondering that when Annie will find it, will it disappear or stop showing me a new leaf every time?

But maybe master had only wanted to check my reaction in that horrible moment of being caught. I continued trying to assure myself that he did not want to take back this divine help from me; instead he had wanted to check the strength that my mind had developed so far. Master had been emphasizing that by my way of reacting towards the things, events and people, I could change the fate between me and those. And the discovery of wooden box by Annie was only a part of this test.

Still apprehensive, I hastened to the other rooms for checking again. All were in deep slumbers. Resting assured, I came back to the study and sat down in the chair. I picked up the beautiful box and started rolling it in my hands. In a sort of absentmindedness, the wonderings about reincarnation and salvation had begun to cloud my mind again.

I hoped wooden box to answer. I also hoped that my mind was not too anxious to let the box not respond to my tapping. I tried to test whether my thoughts were frivolous or the substantiated ones. My inner voice said that my curiosity was subtle and was guiding me, in this way, only towards the truth.

Bearing a smile in assurance I tapped the box for help. It gently opened to my glee. I took out the new leaf from it. But it had only a short note inscribed.

It said,

"Why don't you test your arrived understanding on yourself first?"

Oh goodness! Perhaps it was my first time with the box that I was not able to make out anything of its message. To test my gathered understanding about reincarnation and salvation, that too on myself, was I supposed to first die? What could have the master really meant? He would not ever write, I knew, a single redundant word. I reread the message and noticed one new thing. Master had suggested about trying and not dying. I mourned again, for the conundrum was still the same. I wanted to hear more on the matter but there was no help available except the small awkward note on the leaf. I looked out. Still it was raining as heavily.

Sitting alone in the house, I tried imagining master's feet next to mine, but no success. He never worked at my terms. I desperately wanted to make talks with him, but my deep perplexity over his message was not letting me have any kind of success. The leaf was in my hands and the box was empty. I wished if I could have found more leaves inside. But alas, it had not been a case with me so far.

In this moment, a slight childish mischief occurred to me.

Although anticipating a rebuke from master, but I wished to take the chance. I turned the leaf upside down and wrote this on it:

"But master, I must have at least the fundamental knowledge of precepts before trying those in my life."

I placed leaf back into the box and closed it. I waited a little; tapped it in fear that it might not respond to my newest mischief. But wronging my apprehension, lo! The box had opened.

The previous leaf was gone and a new one had arrived. It said:

"You are very clever my son! But still, I will not let you fall short of my responses. Not only in case of reincarnation and salvation, but also about many other similar mystical precepts, you cannot experience them in full unless you experience those in yourself. The two terms you are wondering about in this moment have nothing to do with your birth or death; but these are what matter to you when you're very much alive. While living every moment, whether consciously or not, you are already running through a choice between living and dying. You can't escape exercising this choice. Son, never forget that living and dying have nothing to do with your body; instead it's with your mind. Before birth and after death, you experience neither of two. Reincarnating is already your mind's ongoing process; and so is salvation. There is nothing above the clouds or deep down in earth. You have to exercise your choices here on the earth only. In relation to eternal truth, reincarnation is your constant endurance for your elevation; and salvation is your ultimate reward in freedom from the bondage. Realize your process of elevation and reward in freedom, nowhere else, but in your daily experience alone."

This time, thanks to his grace, master was comprehensive for my understanding. I quickly took out my diary and copied the message. Reverently joyous, I put back the leaf and closed the box before wrapping it in the mufflers. Just when I had closed the drawer I overheard Annie's footsteps coming towards the kitchen. I was safe; and well in time.

"Rube! Why don't you get sleep?" Annie had suddenly drifted towards me and asked while rubbing her eyes.

"No, certainly I do! But little less than you honey!" As I teased her, she mocked a face and entered the washroom.

Diary, though closed, was still on the table. But it was no worry. I glanced down for double checking the bottom drawer. It was alright and safe. I wondered about the day when Annie will be able to catch the box. Master hadn't talked about it precisely.

I stood up and peered from the window once again. It was still raining. In faint light which was coming from window panes, I opened the diary and began to read the message again.

In the beginning of message, master hadn't rebuked me for my mischief. Instead he had welcomed my playfulness with him. I admired him for his generosity.

As I read the message once again, I started perceiving its true parlance. Just in the moment I was slipping in the bliss of master's grace, Annie approached me and seized my attention,

"What food shall I make for you?"

"Aaa... Annie, I was thinking to observe fasting today", I said fearing her reaction.

"Fasting! And You?" Still rubbing her eyes, she laughed.

"Yes, why not?" I almost offended to her surprise.

"Rube, you have already started taking scantier food, and now, why take complete fast?" She asked perplexingly.

"It's good to keep your body-machine on rest for a day. Or isn't it?" I tried making a story for my plea.

"I don't know what happens to you sometimes. Are you sure?" She asked.

"Yes", I tried comforting her with a smile, "I will take some fruits or milk in the evening."

"And what will mother say of it?" Annie hadn't stopped protesting.

"She herself does it often." I contended.

"Ok. I was thinking to make some delicacies for all," She tried tempting me.

"No. Please don't stop for Maina, mother and yourself. I will enjoy seeing you enjoying."

Suddenly Annie kvetched, "But all of a sudden, what has happened to you?"

"Annie, please. I sincerely wish to make it. If you cooperate, it will be easy."

"But for what benefit at all?" She argued again.

I tried making it light. I pinched a finger into my growing stomach and said, "It's all for you honey."

"Umm...all for you honey!" She mockingly repeated my words and made a face before hastening to the kitchen.

When alone again, I looked for another book on my table which was about diet regulation and fasting. I had read it only little, but certainly to make some great discoveries. For past some time, indeed I had been undergoing some changes. The kinds of books, the kinds of foods and also the kinds of thoughts were all about revolutionary changes. I didn't exactly score my progress made so far, but I was considerably satiated for whatever amount of it had been fetched by me.

Speaking further about the day, mother was little surprised about my idea. When I told her that I wanted to feel the same way as she would do often, she agreed; though she insisted that I must take milk twice instead of once. For slight solace of Annie as well, I agreed to it. In the day, while all were enjoying the delicacies, I remained alone in the bedroom with my books. After taking bath, I had already shifted for the day.

Without engaging my body digesting the food I would have otherwise taken, I was in better position to comprehend what I was reading. This effect was coming evident upon me. In place of picking any new book this time, I had picked an old one which I had already read and appreciated few months before. Reading it again was quite an experience. I noticed that not only I was able to recall each and every paragraph printed in these pages, but I was also grasping the written thoughts more intensely. The book continued gravitating me.

Intermittently, Maina came and checked whether I was any free for her. I wanted to comfort her and therefore had agreed to play carom with her. As we started, Annie and mother also joined. Hitherto Annie was little upset over my ways; but as she won a match by her old habit, she turned jubilant. After another match or two, she looked to the clock and hurried up for something. Now she was phoning the housemaid to check why latter was getting late today. In an almost sullen face, Annie put down the receiver and informed that maid would be on leave today.

In next moment, she had herself picked up the brush and started cleaning the furniture. While I was still busy in playing carom with Maina and mother, I didn't know when Annie had reached my table for cleaning it.

Just when Annie pushed back the first drawer of table with a whacking sound, I sensed the big trouble on my head. The slight creaking sound of drawers had been familiar to me. I could recognize those even from the bedroom here. I peered through the window. Quite unaware, she was about to find the miraculous box. My heart started pounding.

In a minute she had cleaned the second drawer as well and had pushed it with another whacking sound.

And just when she opened the bottom drawer,

"My goodness! See, all the mufflers have been hiding here!" She exasperated.

Now she turned to the bedroom. She came and stared in my eyes. I showed no surprise still.

"Rube! You said mufflers were lost in the hills, but see, those had been hiding in your drawers."

"Oh are those?" This time I pretended marveling. "May be I forgot", I tried chipping in.

"But what's this inside there", She wondered while pinching the bundle.

I saw her unfolding the mufflers and checking out some hard object felt inside. I knew that master's prediction was just coming true.

"O Wow! What a nice box." She was astonished while rolling it in her hands and showing it over to me.

"Rube! You never told me that you had such a beautiful box."

"Oh, this one! Maybe I forgot Annie." I carefully spoke while keeping my voice unexcited. I was still trying to look more at the carom than up to her visage.

Now she had brought the box to me and handed it over. "Rube! Wherefrom did you get it?"

"Well....This box! Yes, one of my friends gave it to me when I was in hills."

"In hills! Which friend?"Annie was always like a police inspector whenever I tried to hide something from her.

"You won't know him. We became friends in hills only", I replied in an unconcerned tone. I was showing no attention to the box.

"Hmm... Anyways! But you must have gifted this to me earlier."

Annie had surprised me by saying that. I had now given up the carom striker and was looking to her face.

I witnessed the dancing eyes of Annie but couldn't speak a word. She had grabbed the box from me and was completely lost in its beauty. She was rolling it again and again. In the meanwhile, finding me already given up the carom game, Maina had started insisting her grandmother to join. Now mother was with Maina and I was with Annie.

"But how does it open rube! Do you know that?" Annie asked while trying harder on it.

Right in front of my eyes, she shook the box twice or thrice but didn't hear any sound inside it. She was carefully sifting its edges, but was unable to find the crease from where the box would have opened. She didn't give up.

Deep in my heart, as per master's directions it was best to

not add anything to Annie's curiosity, lest there could be a chance of foregoing the miraculous box forever. Showing my complete apathy to her anxiety, I moved out from the bedroom and settled on the sofa outside. I had picked up a newspaper and was pretending to read. Still shaking the box in her hands, she also followed in.

"Do you know Rube how it opens?" Failing again and again, she asked.

"Umm... I don't think it opens", still staring at the newspaper, I replied.

"Then what use of it?" She sounded dejected.

"It's beautiful; just that", my answer was cold and blatant; though I feared, lest she might throw it in garbage.

Annie was still trying to open it. But to her sheer disappointment, she failed and finally said, "Your friend has fooled you."

My eyebrows raised.

"Else how come", she tried reasoning her harsh words, "that something which has been carved so beautifully, doesn't open at all? A box which can't contain anything inside is no use anyway."

Annie was particularly revenging the box.

"But still, gift from a beloved friend must not be disregarded", I said in hope of saving it from the imminent threat.

"Then only you keep it. It's anyways your old habit to collect the junk", Annie spoke harshly and unkind upon me; though unknowingly she was going kind on the box.

I got up from the sofa and walked to my table. I took the box from Annie's hands and smiled. Looking in deep affection at the box, I merely said, "He was indeed a big man."

"Rube!" Annie made it clear, "You have nobody here to listen your stories on the hills."

I felt she was unnecessarily rebuking me. Actually I had never been trying to tell my stories on the hills to anyone at home. I gave her only a tasteless smile and put the box back into the drawer. She gave me a look as if she already knew that I will keep the junk.

I felt bad but didn't cut an argument with Annie. She also moved to the other furniture now. I returned to the sofa and put newspaper in front of my eyes; though reading was my last intention. Today not only the wooden box had been safeguarded, but also the anticipated anxiety of Annie was extinguished. Perhaps I had passed the test set out by the master.

"Well... Annie! Can I have those mufflers please?" Before she moved, I asked.

"Yes, yes. Why not! It's anyways the summers. Mufflers won't be needed. They can serve the junk."

I just wanted to shot a tantrum. Why at all she was raging today? But I stopped. Perhaps I knew the reasons, for my test couldn't have completed yet.

I picked the mufflers meekly and turned around to the bottom drawer again. I opened it and took out the box on the table. Aside to it, I spread the mufflers and bundled the box into those. Now the bundle was made as good as it was in the morning. I gently placed it into the drawer and closed.

Once again I was hiding my face behind the pretence of reading the newspaper. I wondered why Annie was behaving that way. Ah! Instantly I realized that she had made great delicacies this morning which I had not tasted or appreciated yet. I looked over to the wall clock. It was four in the evening.

Making sure that Annie would overhear it, I turned to mother and said loud, "Mother I think I can't hold it for long."

"What?" Mother asked.

"The big hungry cat in my stomach!" I replied.

Annie intercepted at once, "No, why Mr. Saint? Weren't you on fast?"

I didn't retort. Folding the news papers, I ushered into the dining chair and waited.

Obviously, great food was about to be served. Annie was pacing up things in the kitchen. I thought about my fast. During my several hours spent in the bedroom with books, I had already been to great enlightenment. It was no sense to keep Annie dissenting.

As she brought my plate, I knew my duty. As I took my first bite, I shouted, "Oh wonderful, wonderful! Who has made such a tasty food, mother?"

Annie jumped in to say, "Who else at home cooks the food?"

"Oh...", in the cartoon voice I replied, "Certainly seems it's you my lord. You've made it outstanding. Shall I get two more than usual?"

"It's all for you honey", Annie mocked me in the same tune. I laughed gaily.

Awhile this, Maina rushed in and sat on the chair next to me. Mother also came in and made a plate for child. Only few minutes later, Annie came with full bowls and pushed those on the table.

"No, no," I screamed, "I won't take so much."

"It's for Annie as well, Rubert. She also hasn't taken any yet." Mother informed.

"Oops!" Now I understood why she had been boiling since morning.

I didn't pick my spoon until Annie also arrived and started. For several minutes, only silence ruled our table. But then Maina started talking about her school and friends.

It turned into a nice evening. Later while retiring in bed, I humbly asked Annie to not protest my similar occasional requests. Although she was not visibly happy about my stories on diet regulation and fasting, yet I hoped for her cooperation next time.

Before slumbers took over me, I reviewed the gone day. It was wonderful overall. I had passed the test set out by my master, and I was not feeling any less reincarnated for that matter.

THIRTY TWO

Why Divine Veil on the Human Minds?

"WHETHER OR NOT YOU take any conscious note of it, but your mind is already dwelling in the higher experiences every moment."

Such were the words once master had left for me in the wooden box.

Actually I could have never stopped wondering about the great feats performed by him. He always knew the things which were inaccessible for my imagination. Though he would never extol his awareness, but he revealed to me a part of it whenever I had necessarily deserved to know about. If any time, I rode upon the horses of curiosity and sought master's help in resolving my wonderments, he was careful in checking first the foundation of my need. If he'd find my questions undue, he wore only silence.

One day during the morning walk, I asked him, "Why should one's knowledge know any bound at all? Why should there be a limitation?"

He smiled to the perspective of my question and merely said, "Knowledge itself is as unlimited as are the dimensions of creation. Limit of knowledge, if there be any, is only in the human mind."

"But master, when mind craves knowing more, especially about what is running in others' minds, why doesn't it succeed?" I asked.

Already sensing my intentions he laughed. "It's because of the divine discipline in place."

"Master, please elaborate this matter for me", I pleaded.

"Son, sometimes I find you hunting in a circle. But still, when you have asked, let me describe this matter with an analogy."

I was all ears.

Master started, "This divine discipline, which I am talking about, can be understood by you as motherly care for her child. She always protects it from getting harmed."

But I needed more to understand.

He continued, "For example, let us assume that you go and meet your fast friend in some time. You stay with him for two hours and make affectionate talks. You both let each other know your secret matters also and feel like building great confidence between you. In the moments of taking leave, you shake hands with your friend in great warmth and come back to your place. Later in the day, you start feeling apprehensive about your disclosures made to your friend. You wonder, what would he be thinking of you in terms of your secrets revealed?"

I knew it; some great precept had started taking place in his words. I listened on.

"Now son, let us assume that there exists no divine discipline over the operations of human minds; will not your mind find success in knowing the mind of your friend even from miles away? It would instantly know if your friend is thinking favorable or adverse about your revealed secrets. If it's favorable on one hand, it will hardly make a difference to you, for he is already your good friend. But on the contrary, if such friend is thinking adverse about your secrets, certainly your friendship will be ruined at once. Not only that, the very moment you will come to know your friend's mind, your own mind will also start thinking adverse about his own secrets revealed to you. Instantly your friendship will become worse. And what to mention of another problem, which is that, if your own mind is able to read your friend's mind from far, will not your friend's mind also be able to do the same? Will not the erstwhile friendship be turned into animosity? This is the reason that divine discipline, such as of keeping a veil over the operation of human minds, is inevitably necessary."

I understood his point but had a new question now. "But master, don't some people anyways have the skills of reading others' mind? For instance, you are able to do that in my case always. Doesn't the divine discipline work here?"

"I have said it my son. It works like a motherly care on her child. You say that I always know your mind, but tell me do you always know what runs in my mind?"

"No, I don't, master", I replied.

He continued, "A mother would always know the need of her child, but child would never know about its mother in the same manner. Do you know why it happens so?"

"Maybe child is too small to do that", I tried replying.

He laughed and said, "Add ten years to the age of child. Now check again and tell me, do you still think the same?"

I couldn't make it out.

"It's in this way because mother's mind is far mature in the goodness towards child than mature is the child's mind in the goodness towards mother. The divine discipline, which I have been talking about repeatedly, is actually a wonderful veil to protect one mind from the other. This veil makes the vibrations of minds oblivious to each other. Exceptionally however, this veil goes away when a mother wishes to know about child's mind. She unfailingly knows because her love and care for the child is unconditional. You can imagine the height of purity in this love, that whenever her infant baby falls sick, it's she who takes the medicine herself. Baby gets it through breast-feeding only. Forget a single thought of harming or uncaring the child, but this mother puts herself at stake. Only such height of love makes the mother knowing all about her infant."

"Hmm... ", my utterance came.

Master continued, "However, as the child starts growing up and having its own mind, gradually the veil of divine discipline intervenes and mother starts believing that the child no longer needs her love and care as much. She remains no longer connected to the child's mind in the previous way."

"But master! How will it go if mother gets to know her child's mind forever?" I asked.

"Son, understand this precept well. Functioning of mind is never subject to the names given to objects; instead it is concerned with the nature of objects alone. It's a complicated study my son! Do you think a child ever remains a child? Or a mother ever remains a mother? Child and mother, both are merely appellations and nothing else. Whether or not the names change, but the nature always changes. There is no escape. And do not also forget this, the example used by me of mother and child was only one of the numerous possible connections amongst the several minds. Can you really scale the myriad of diversities of a single mind when a mother is also playing, at the same time, the mind of a beautiful wife, an obedient daughter, a daughter-in-law and of many other kinds. Perfection of her one kind of mind with all other kinds may be starkly different from each other. It is indeed very difficult if you wish to scale the diversities of a single human mind."

"Hmm..." I uttered again. I was feeling tiresome over the complicated matter expounded by master at my own request. I couldn't know how to comprehend it in a nutshell.

Perhaps master had guessed my perturbation when he said, "But on the other side in the secret world, it is extremely easy to understand this all."

I looked down to his feet once again. He was still walking behind me, making only his feet visible to my sight.

Master said, "If you can eliminate all kinds of differentiations and can view all minds as one, you can certainly comprehend this matter far easily."

"Is that really possible master?" I asked in a somber voice.

He began laughing. "You are looking tired, son. Will you really understand if I elaborate this complex subject any further?"

I thought I couldn't take any more. It was very awkward that master was willing to impart more knowledge but I was not able to grasp.

"You reminded me another great thing, son!" He burst into laughter again and said, "Sometimes self-study becomes more effective than the way of teaching by a preceptor."

Ashamed, I alerted towards his words.

"Tonight", master said, "regarding this matter, you will find my message in the wooden box. You should meditate on it and evolve your own answers. Soon, the things which you are finding complicated in this moment, will unfold for you easily."

As I turned back to apologize my dumbness, his feet disappeared. I looked my wristwatch. It was time to go back and get readied for the office. Feeling embarrassed for not keeping up with master today, in a sort of melancholy, I started for home.

Later at night, I was anxious for the wooden box. I no longer feared as much, if anyone at home had seen the box. But I had to be careful, lest one could see it open. Secretly, I opened the drawer but didn't take the box out on the table. I tapped it therein only. It just opened. I took out the leaf and closed the box before wrapping it in the mufflers again.

Under the shine of table lamp, I began reading master's message:

"Feeling great unity amongst all minds is the only way to subside the perceived diversities around those. Reject the very idea of discrimination based upon the forms. Forms may be different and subject to change constantly. For seeing the truth, one has to look beyond the forms. It's alone the substance which is true; and it's true only because it is one and not diverse. When your mind will stop discriminating amidst the world and would start unifying itself with the presiding sole substance of God, you will overcome the veil of divine discipline that I talked about in the morning."

Since morning I had been trying to calm myself. After reading master's message, I found that I had lot many ideas to ponder upon. I took out my diary and copied the message quickly. I thought about putting the leaf back into the box, but I had already packed the latter in the bottom drawer. I didn't want to open it again, lest even littlest noise would have disturbed the sleeping people. In anxiety, I folded the leaf into four and kept it between the pages of my diary itself. I had not tried this anytime before.

I reopened the diary from the page of copied message. I read it again. It could be said to be mystic but not beyond one's grasp. I could comprehend it.

I wondered about what I had been thinking in the day about my sorry meeting with master. I had made certain observations. Just below master's message copied in the diary, I wrote a few of such observations as I could have remembered.

"Generally mind is unruly. Unfortunately it takes its secretiveness for granted and assumes no harm in imagining bad about others."

"Mouth's watering merely at the sight of favorite food is also a kind of higher experience for the mind, though disdainful. Everyone is already equipped with the higher consciousness, though he must direct it in the righteous directions."

"Mind is intangible but at the same time is also most physical in terms of guiding man's outwardly behaviors. I must be careful about the tricks it constantly plays upon me."

"Never should I assume that I have conquered my mind and senses. The very moment I do so, my defeat sets into making. I must be constantly watchful about the conniving between senses and mind.

"I should be quick in tracing the malice of my mind. If I delay, I worsen my living. Quick I diagnose, quick I recuperate."

In this moment, I was feeling satiated. I hoped that my written thoughts were only the echoes of master's message.

Gleaming in master's continued trust in me; I switched off the table lamp and moved into bedroom. Whatever way this day had started, but it had ended well.

THIRTY THREE

Talk between God and Allah

"IF GOD IS ONE, O master! Why people have to understand and worship Him differently at all?"

My sudden desperation for knowing the real fabric of God was not without reasons. As per newspapers and media reports, recently great commotions had broken out between two religious communities in the country. This matter couldn't have made the news big, but when the handful of extremist vandals had started killing people on the other side, the great national ruckus had set in. For past one week, the riots had been worsening beyond imagination. Although the city wherein I lived was relatively safer from such turbulences, but the chief-priests of the local religious fitments had started giving provoking speeches in the public. Whenever in newspapers or on TV I would see the pictures of dead bodies lying one on another on the roads, I'd feel indescribably pained. I never knew which religion those dead bodies belonged to. Those all looked same.

One morning, amidst such perturbations in my mind I was in the central orchard. Master, for his kindness, was with me. I asked him why at all this utter nuisance was taking place.

"You must not get carried away by this." Master began replying, "Once your mind has known the eternity of the secret world, such tumults occurring in the apparent world must not shatter your peace."

I was surprised to his apathy shown towards the brutal killings of people. "But master, when people are insanely killing each other, how can one remain totally unaffected?"

"Son!" he began saying in compassionate voice, "Merely remaining worried for that matter won't help; or will it?"

He was correct in a way and was hinting towards something which could form my actionable in the presented crisis.

"O master! I am greatly pained over the killings made in the names of religions. Is there really anything possible which I can do about?"

Hearing this master started laughing. My tumult got even increased. I hadn't imagined him taking this matter so lightly.

"Don't you get pained over such things, master?" I asked.

To this he asked, "Does my laughing make a difference to the situation?"

My reply was no.

"Then, does your mourning over the similar news make a difference?" He asked again.

My reply was again no.

"Then shouldn't both of us do something which makes the difference?" He asked.

Instantly my eyebrows rose up. "That's what master! Is there anything possible about it?" I asked him.

"Possibilities never end, son! With an industrious human mind, those work infinitely", he replied.

"So, what exactly can I do in this grim situation?" I guessed he was about to suggest or do a miracle.

"First of all you should reacquaint the eternal truth and resettle yourself in the same. Unless you have done that, you can't be able to perceive this matter in way you should", said the master.

It was not the first time I was finding his words procrastinating. I was seething in pain and was expecting a quick solution from him. But master was delaying it in his talk. I had no choice but to keep up with him.

"What eternal truth must be known in this moment, master?" I asked.

Now he started imparting the supreme understanding. "More

than about anybody else you must be conscious about your own Self. Do not misinterpret my words for being selfish. What I mean is that, you should be awake in the truth."

I had not understood his perspective fully.

He continued, "Imagine what would be the God Himself thinking about this? Wouldn't He be lamenting over the foolishness of attacking people at either side?"

"But then why doesn't God stop all this at once?" I asked impatiently.

Master appeared to be surprised by my question. He asked, "What you say, my son! How can God stop it?"

"Why? Doesn't God make miracles?" I contested master's point.

"Oh! That's the deep pain in the bosom of God since ages. People do not understand the true meaning of Him but they always want their own anarchies and disorders to be fine tuned by some kind of miracle." Agitation came obvious in the voice of master.

After master's rebuke I remained only silent.

But he eased and said, "Son! Before expecting God's miracles, one should understand God's true meaning."

"Hmm...." I uttered and nodded.

"Do you think God is a person who was born and died millennia ago? These foolish people who are fighting and killing each other, actually have no ability to imagine God beyond that. God is not that way. He cannot be God who is subject to taking birth and dying. And particularly the one, in whose name people are being killed, cannot become God at all."

I was carefully listening to his revelation.

Master continued enlightening, "For so long as people will think of themselves to be different from God, they will have the ungodly troubles around them. They believe God to be superior and themselves inferior; and in this way they find it rationale doing the inferior acts around. Son! Do you want to know who the real God is? And would you like to meet Him now?"

Now I was reeling in boundless astonishment. I knew it, master could do anything. Lo! He had invited me to meet God only a second before.

He revealed, "Real God is your own Self and nothing else, son. When had you been away from Him, that you could meet only rarely? In fact, every moment you are with your Self and there is no question of meeting God somewhere else. This alone is the truth and is same with everyone. Only few realize this Self and are called Self-realized, whereas the others, who do not realize Self, call called only Self-ignorant. Can you imagine this, son! There is no God living in far and visible only rarely, but every moment that Omnipresent is marking His availability in the very fabric of creation. I repeat, only your Self is God."

"What you've said master, is true", I apprehended, "But how can this shameful violence be stopped?"

"You cannot stop it the way you want, for it can be stopped only by them who have started and flamed it. You are feeling pain for this one instance of violence, but are you sure that there would be no similar or even worse instances in the apparent world?"

"Oh! Certainly there could be many", I replied.

"Then why you want to fix the one and leave the rest? Shouldn't you work similarly for all?" He asked.

"Oh! Indeed I should, master. But how can I help all when I am not able to help even this one?" I asked.

"If you have realized the power of your Self, you can do lot many things beyond your outwardly imagination. This planet called earth has not been empty of such people in the past. There have been people who were Self-realized and have worked beyond ordinary men's imagination. Self is the only God and it's the only powerful entity around. Self is equally potent in everyone; however it may remain dormant unless invoked. Very realization of this Self is the realization of God. And never forget that realizing God is not about becoming something else, but it's about becoming God Himself. Can you ever imagine God killing the people like this?"

I replied, "Never master."

"And can you ever imagine God being killed by people like this?"

"Oh! It's never again."

"So! The most perfect understanding already exists there; merely the people wish and choose to remain ignorant sometimes."

I asked, "Master, certainly these people are attacking and killing each other because of their ignorance about Self. In the given state, shouldn't these be overpowered and punished, so that they will stop the nuisance and calm down?"

"That is no great method but", master replied. "The sovereign laws of each country have been doing that since centuries, but did they ever succeed?"

"Then what's the solution, master?" I asked.

"Solution is the same which I have narrated", replied he.

"But I fear, neither those who are killing and nor those who are being killed will have patience to listen about Self." I expressed my apprehension.

Hearing this master laughed. He said, "This is just how the spinning of apparent world continues. You cannot make it perfect. The only thing you can do about is perfecting your living in the apparent world by way of perfecting your living in the secret world. You may have remembered when I said on the hills that secret world is not some other distinct world at some different place; but it exists right in this apparent world. When you grow your perfection in the secret world, you grow the same in the other as well."

Master had been emphasizing only on the Self, and he had a long term vision instead of suggesting to the current fiasco. I also thought that short term fixes were not any good.

He said further, "You must not grief for those who are being killed and neither should you rage against those who are killing. Instead of doing this, you should ascertain your duty towards both of them and execute it with compassion. Remember, hating those who kill, will not fix the problem, for killers would be on the both sides. Instead curing the hate itself will do the wonders. In this troubled moment, to the extent possible, not only that you should turn in the service of afflicted ones, but you must also try your best to spread the knowledge of truth and Self. Message of Self will invariably touch all, provided you deliver that in the suitable languages to the people. When you will insist upon both attacking communities that Self is ever the same and identical for all, gradually they will develop curiosity for it. It will be then they will get introduced to the real God. Can you imagine their uncontained happiness there after? Haven't you also been an example?" Master's voice was beaming in joy.

"What you've said is auspicious, master. I feeling contained. You have shown me the path. In my every bit, I will act upon in the same direction. My life must not pass ordinarily; rather it must become an opportunity to serve many who haven't yet realized their Self and God. I am grateful to you for showing me the way of service."

"You are my loving son, Rubert!" Master smiled for taking my name for the first time.

I also smiled looking to his feet.

"Go and get busy in your apparent world while never removing your aim from the secret world."

I glanced at my wrist watch. Indeed the time had arrived to go back home.

Before I took leave, master told me, "Son! Whenever you are feeling very contented and blissful in your mind, you can assume yourself blooming in the secret world. Those will be your precious moments of life and you must spend those creatively. Service to mankind is the best expression of creativity. Start your work. Once you will start making positive differences to others' lives, your own happiness will become boundless. Go now and live your duties in both worlds together."

After this I returned to home and started readying for the

office. In the day, while talking to my close friends about riots, a very new idea sprang in my mind. I suggested them that we should collect some money get an advertisement published in the newspaper. We will appeal all for the restoration of communal harmony. One of my junior colleagues informed that he had a personal contact in the newspaper office and we could have a chance of getting big discounts in the advertising costs. After all, our cause was social and in public interest. The whole lot of us felt encouraged with the news. Only within half an hour this junior colleague informed that the newspaper office had agreed to become kind upon us with half of the price slashed.

In excitement of newspaper publication, our group collected the funds from their kin and kith. In merely two days sufficient amount was ready with us. Secretly I knew that it was master's grace; though he would have easily disowned the credit. In the meantime, I had prepared the content matter of the newspaper publication. When I showed it to all, they were pleasantly surprised. They never knew that I could be creative in writing too. So far I had been popular only about civil engineering.

Only two days after our advertisement got published in the national daily. It had slightly long but a meaningful story. It purported a talk between two kinds of Gods, in two different religions. Showing up two different kinds of God was necessary so that each attacking group would feel compelled to read the story. The text of advertisement went as per following:

Vishnu (The Hindu God): Look! Why are fumes coming out from earth today?

Allah (The Moslem God): It's because I am sad. Your people are burning my people alive.

Vishnu: But aren't your people also burning my people alive?

Allah: Yes, I am sad for that too. This is the reason that

fumes are getting worse.

Vishnu: Hmm... I am also very sad for this. I gave them the scriptures and divine knowledge so that they would realize the truth and become kind upon each other. But foolishly they have misinterpreted all my text and have become vehement on impulse.

Allah: It's same here. I also gave them the holy books. But they never understand the true motives of my words.

Vishnu: What will we do now? This massacre must stop anyway.

Allah: Don't ask me that. Days and nights I've been thinking about it but have found no solution at all.

Vishnu: Ah! It's only the same here.

Allah: You know what! Whenever I see a body of child or grown up being charred or cut into pieces; I fail to identify whether it is of my people or your people.

Vishnu: Oh! It's again the same here. When at all they will stop? Sometimes when I get too angry on it, I feel like annihilating everything. But then I stop in pity. If I destroy them at all, it will no longer make any difference to them; for it's only when they are alive that they can make the difference.

Allah: Even the very same thought stops me from devastating the entire creation. If there will be left no one, what difference at all it will make?

Vishnu: What do we do now?

Allah: What else! Let us do the same thing which we did when the similar massacre occurred last time. Let us wait.

Vishnu: (Smiles in sarcasm) True... Let us only wait about the smoke, what else! Let us wait till these people get tired and stop by themselves. From my side, I have made sure that man never becomes so powerful that he doesn't get ever tired.

Allah: Oh excellent! Even the same thing I've done with my people. However mighty they grow, they can never annihilate the entire mankind. Long before that, they will also get tired.

Vishnu: And also let us hope that they will learn to interpret our messages correctly. But tell me, how do you feel in your heart when you see them fighting like this?

Allah: I feel like being a big father here and watching my children bickering over the petty issues on the earth.

Vishnu: But they are even killing each other!

Allah: Yes, they are doing that. But after dying when they come back to me, I find them imperfect in my lessons and therefore send them back to the earth for learning the lessons again.

Vishnu: Oh, that's very well. Even I have been doing the same for past many ages.

Allah: And I also tell them clearly that unless they will learn my lessons well, I will not allow them graduating from earth to my home.

Vishnu: Oh I wonder! How alike we are. Even I have been doing the same.

Allah: Yes, we are very much alike.

Vishnu: I am feeling delighted in this moment. But what shall we exactly do while waiting for the people getting tired down there?

Allah: Let us stop worrying about those foolish creatures.

Vishnu: True. What you say about going for a walk in far?

Allah: Yes, that will be a relief from this painful sight of fumes. Let us move along the sun and see the other parts of world as well.

Vishnu: For doing that, I think moon will be better.

Allah: Oh yes! You are correct. Moon will be better.

And then both the Gods moved away from the site of fumes. After some time when then had returned to the same place, the fumes were gone and it was only coolness in the air.

Vishnu: Oh See! Didn't I say it will be alright?

Allah: What's new in that? It always happens in the same way.

Vishnu: Yes, indeed it does.

Allah: So, what shall we do now?

Vishnu: Let us go for the walk once again. I always enjoy your company. Every time you have new great stories to tell.

Allah: Yes, it's pleasure for me also. Neither have you ever fallen short of your stories.

And since that time, both Gods never stopped ambling hand in hand.

~~~

I didn't know how much influence this newspaper publication had on the matter, but in matter of few days the riots were over. It was quite a relief to see the print and electronic media getting busy over the Hollywood and political news as usual.

THIRTY FOUR

Master Makes Me See the Real God

"HAVEN'T I TOLD YOU many times that it's wrong to limit your perception of God merely in forms?"

Every now and then, whenever my wish of having a direct sight of God caught spree, I rushed to master. And every time it turned that he answered me the same. I would listen to his enlightening words and agree; but later some time again, I would be captivated by the same wish.

Master however, never got spited with my repeated insistence. In fact I had never seen him frown.

One morning in the central orchard of the park, when I had expressed my old wish again, he began laughing.

"You want to know when you will see God and you've never stopped wanting that", he said in hilarity.

In these moments I was appearing like an obstinate child in front of my master. In token of insisting my wish even more intensely on him, I remained only quite. I thought he will do anything for me.

"Tell me what kind of God you think you will become satisfied after seeing?" He asked.

I asked in astonishment, "Are there many kinds of Him, master! But don't you always say that He is only one."

"The One I talk about has never been far from your sight", he grew serious now. "Don't you know you cannot see from your eyes anything that is not God? This is big obvious truth if you can understand it well. God is not someone who lives in every atom of the creation, but every atom of creation is God."

"But master! Yesterday I met with an old man in my neighborhood. He was kind enough to reveal to me that few years ago, after a cardiac arrest, when he was fighting between life and death in a big hospital's ICU, he saw something very unusual. He told me that he had been lying unconscious for past many days and doctors had no hope for his surviving. Many medical instruments were attached to his body and bed; and every kin and kith was prepared to get the sad news of his demise any moment. But just then, as he was narrating to me, he had the direct vision of God who was approaching towards him. He said that in such of his vision, God came very near to him. Former was smiling and tossing the sweet-cake balls for latter's eating. As he took a sweet-ball and ate, he opened the eyes on the hospital bed here. Quite surprisingly, he recuperated very fast. Not only in matter of few days he was discharged from the hospital, and he has been living astonishingly healthy since then."

Master was listening to me with all due care.

I asked him, "Is such a response by God a miracle?"

Hearing this, he burst into mirth. "Son, will you ever stop having deep interest in the miracles?"

I also smiled and waited for his revelatory talk further.

"Such experience or vision may have greater considerations for the old man you are talking about; but for you, isn't it merely a very nice story?" He asked.

"But master, do you say that the incidence of his seeing God was fake and merely a product of his subconscious imaginary?" I asked fervently.

"Son, seeing God by that man is not important, but the degree to which he believes that what he saw was God, is important. I am sure that he has complete faith in his experience, that's why he cherishes the same as God till date. As long as he will have faith, the matter of his seeing God will be true and not fake. Now for a moment think about you, did you feel the same when this of your neighbor was narrating the story in front of you? Did you feel that he was not faking it?"

"I believed whatever he was telling me was truth only", I replied.

"That's wonderful. It means that you had shared not only his experience but his faith as well. Do you know what reward you will get from him?" Master asked.

"Oh, reward? I never imagined about it. I didn't even adequately express my joy in front of him", I informed master.

"Your expression in this matter doesn't count. Human vibrations do not require physical expression. Whether or not you've spoken your joy, he would know. Just the way you knew his joy while he was narrating his experience, he would also know. Faith has tremendous power."

"But master", I asked, "How do I relate this to my own want of seeing God?"

A mystic smile beamed on his face. He said, "Know the higher truth, my son! Experience of God is not in seeing Him but it's in the experiencing itself. Even when God is standing in front of you, but you don't agree upon experiencing Him as God, you won't gain anything. You are mesmerizing about your old neighbor having seen the God, whereas that man is mesmerizing about having experienced the God. Difference is in between seeing and experiencing. It's similar to two different persons; one who watches the floating boat from the shore of river; and the other one being in the boat itself. Latter can only extol his experience to the former, but he cannot make the former really experience it. It depends upon the former, for if he himself is too fond of riding the boats, he will find the extolling by latter very authentic; else he will think of all merely fake. Similar is the case with you, O son! Only because you too aspire for the same, that story has seemed authentic to you."

"But master! Could such vision of God be really possible for him? I mean, would have God really appeared only in a form aspired or known by him?" I asked.

"Son, we are nobody to decide or judge that!" Master replied in a humble voice. "Even if we do that rightly or wrongly, it will not matter to that man. Experience of God to everybody is only individual."

"But is seeing God in this way possible for others as well?" I asked impatiently.

"I have already said that seeing is not important; only experiencing is", master replied. "Experience does not necessarily crave seeing. And especially in terms of Godly experiences, your normal sensory organs like eyes, ears etc. are no use."

"But didn't that old man really see the God!" I contested.

"Son, you've said his eyes were closed while lying on the hospital bed", master crossed my point.

"But maybe he saw God in very authentic dream", I asked in non-submission.

"But you said he had been unconscious for many days and was fighting between life and death. In such a state how can one have authentic dreams?" Master crossed my contention once again.

"Hmm..." I had to submit finally.

Master didn't speak for a moment. It came good that I was able to concentrate and gather my scattered thoughts.

Suddenly master chuckled. He said, "Son, I have felt that you never feel satisfied of hearing or watching the miracles. To make you understand this point better, let me perform a small miracle here."

Oh! I grew most attentive now, though I had no idea of his plan.

"So far now in this orchard, you have been able to see only my feet. Now whenever you will turn back, you will see my body as well. I will not disappear. But to this, I have a condition. Whenever I will appear on your turning back, I will become deaf and dumb. This is necessary because if I start talking to you in normal way, you will create ruckus in the park. Finding you talking to an invisible man, people will start making fun of you", as he said this he laughed gaily.

Oblivious to the strange condition, I became rather glad for getting to see my master once again. It was my first time after meeting him on the hills. Enraptured, I looked down. I felt as if I was able see more than his feet now. My heartbeat went pulsating. I knew he was right there, in his full body. In reeling sensation, I turned back.

Lo! It was indeed my revered master standing here. I was leaping in joy for his sight. As I began to prostrate at his holy feet, he held me by arm and stopped me. I saw his eyes; he was full of love for me. He gestured me to turn forward again and continue walking in the orchard. I sensed the reason of his admonition and followed the command.

As I resumed walking I couldn't contain my joy. The scenes of my meetings with him on the hills were coming refreshed. While walking ahead, I looked down once again. I could see only his feet this time. I knew it was all child's play for him.

"But why did you behave that way, son?" Master asked from behind.

I didn't get him.

"Wasn't I already with you? Then why you started prostrating at my feet all of a sudden?" He asked.

Well, now I knew what he meant. I said, "But master, I couldn't contain my joy of having you in my sight once again."

"Do you want to have me in the same way always?" He asked deridingly.

"Is that really possible, master?" My curiosity was touching new height.

"But what use you will make of me when I am only deaf and dumb", he asked funnily.

Yes, he had a point, I thought. "But master! You should be kind upon me by removing your strange conditions."

He continued saying from behind, "What difference at all it will make to you if I am speaking from behind or from the front?"

Oh! He had a greater point now. I couldn't answer it.

He continued walking behind me in silence.

"Even if you want me to become visible to the other people as well", he said again, "I can do that. But the matter is – will it make any difference again? Even if people see me, they will believe or disbelieve me based upon their individual experience only. It is alone the experience which matters and not the sight."

I was listening to his words spellbound.

"And even if you wish me to perform miracles in front of all, it hardly makes any difference again. People, based upon their individual experiences only, will think of me either as a yogi or as some treacherous magician."

Perhaps I was appearing riddled.

"You need not lose your composure on this, my son! For so long as you will wonder about the experiences of others, you will not discover your own bliss in God. Your bliss resides in your own experience and not in that of others", master said.

Although I had understood master's point but largely the concept of God had remained only imperceptible in my heart. Master sensed my melancholy when he said, "There is no other way, son; for God can be tasted only by experiencing Him. When you feel He exists, He does; otherwise not. When you feel He exists for you, indeed He does for you; otherwise not. When you feel that you are protected and cared by Him, then indeed you are protected and cared. And remember all this is not any superficial tale, for there cannot be anything more evident than the omnipresence of God. Man usually wonders unconvincingly only till he hasn't experienced God himself. Once he has, the wonderments of all kinds vanish away."

Hearing his words I felt encouraged. I asked, "Please tell me master, what can be the way of experiencing God by a person like me?"

"It's one and the same for everyone. Only engrossing on the other side of your mind is your discovery of Self; and discovering the Self is the only way of experiencing the God. Say, where God lives? Doesn't He live in your own existence? The Almighty cannot be a different entity from you. He is you, provided there has remained no egoistic you in your thoughts. This state of oneness with God arrives only when your self-realized entity is persisting in you. Such a high state of consciousness can be achieved by everyone, rather instantly. What to speak of men, lower creatures and animals; even the insentient fragments of this creation can attain this bliss of consciousness easily."

"But master, does a person living in the said bliss of consciousness start looking or behaving like a madman?" I asked.

"Certainly not!" master remonstrated me quickly, "A truly self-realized person, in his outwards, need not look differently from others. He discharges his usual worldly duties as efficiently as any other skillful person would."

Maybe my face was still looking astounded. He sensed it and said, "Son, can you notice this great change which has already started taking place in your life?"

"What master?" I asked in anxiety.

"You have already started experiencing the supreme knowledge of God. Only this knowledge is the path towards God. Without this knowledge, even God Himself standing in front of you will appear naught but a stranger. And on the contrary, if you're having this knowledge, at once God will become authentic and very dear to you even when He is invisible."

Now I started getting the bliss.

Master continued further, "Vesting in the supreme knowledge of God is the rudimentary stage of vesting in God Himself. I am glad for the way you have been able to assimilate this knowledge so far. And understand this as well; only because of this merit you have been able to behold the secret world during your divine visions; and only because of the same, the wooden box has also worked for you. If you can see my feet or body, or even listen to my voice; that also is the result of your vesting in the supreme knowledge of God. Else who else in this entire big orchard can even trace my presence! You are on the path, that's why you can do it. I wish you greatness. Soon, when you will have had enough experience of the secret world on the other side of mind, you will start vesting in God Himself. You will live your worldly duties greatly, now and even then."

Today master was very kind on me. In great love I said, "It's all because of your grace on me, master."

"No, it's because of the choices that you have made for yourself. Your life in the apparent world and secret world is nothing but all about your own choices made. It's not that those, who do not get any trace of their secret worlds in their lifetime, do not live secret world. Such oblivious people of course live their secret worlds, but they remain only unaware, ignorant and susceptible about it. Ignorance of the secret world leads to imperfections in the apparent world only."

I couldn't ever become satisfied with his enlightening words.

After a silent ambling for a while, he advised, "Till the time you roam around here and reach back your home, observe silence to the extent possible. There is no powerful perseverance for mind than observing a meditational silence. Just now I will reveal the answer to your curiosity. You are worrying about seeing God with your eyes, whereas you've been seeing God many times before in life. You couldn't have known this because you didn't experience it. Do one thing now. In the day, when you're running through your busyness as usual, prepare a small list of people and coincidences which, on numerous occasions, had saved you from dreadful mistakes, threats and fallouts out of your control. Wasn't that also God which has protected you? And why should only protection be the reason of experiencing God; why not love, compassion and service also. Believe more in experiencing than seeing God; and never stop doing that. I am sure you will discover the deeper pearls more easily. The education imparted by me upon you is ripe now."

Suddenly, as I turned back to thank him for his divine kindness, he was gone.

I looked at my wrist watch. It was just the time. While leaving for home I followed master's instructions about silence. I was trying calming my mind as well. I realized that bearing an intentional aloofness over the mind is rather helpful sometimes. I was feeling very serene. Whatever my eyes were falling on, I intuited for the first time, that it was fragment of God's creation and therefore no different from God Himself. The view of world was changing for me and I was smiling in great ecstasy. Perhaps this was the 'experience' master was talking about. In this moment I had also started understanding the great myth behind the esoteric smile of master himself. It was the same smile which had started coming on my face as well.

As my day progressed, I had taken a piece of paper and folded it in four before putting in my pocket. Whole day, whenever any name of person or event, which had made Godly differences to my life, came into my mind, I took out the paper and jotted down.

Before retiring to bed at night, I unfolded the paper gave a look to my collection. It was astonishing. Merely in a day I had written about more people and events than I had imagined in the morning. I glanced through the list again, and on the top of it I wrote – 'My Loving Master'. Just then, I put this paper near to the wooden box bundle in the bottom drawer. I touched the mufflers in reverence and closed.

This night I had a wonderful sleep. After all I had experienced God lot many times in the list.

Indeed I had been 'experiencing' God for the entire day.

THIRTY FIVE

Abhorring the Past
or Extolling the Future?

"OH! HOW GREAT WERE the old times! Weren't those really better than what I see now?"

Actually whether or not the very idea of democracy could have made the countries in the world perfect, but in the individual lives, particularly in context of expressing one's opinions, it was the perfect pretext. If democracy meant freedom, being opinionated was its most misused form. I had recently happened to observe that the world of opinions and my findings was astonishing. Generally, whenever people had a chance of comparing their lives with others', their findings were either biased or were driven by the kinds of considerations away from truth. Least must be spoken about this; or else the tales would never end.

However in cases where people compared between the gone times and the present times of their own lives, their finding was so astonishing that it couldn't escape one's attention. During my days with master and his miraculous presence continued around me, I had started experiencing this matter quite intensely. In the tricky moments of my own usual life, when I were alone and being overrun by the constant treacheries of my apparent world, I would often fall about comparing my present times with the past times. And in this way misusing my psychological democracy about forming opinions, I would incur the same error again and again.

Precisely, the error was this.

After a worthwhile of aforementioned psychological tussle every time, I would invariably end up concluding that the past times of my life were lot better than my present times. I would compare my present days with the times when I was younger; especially when I was merely a bachelor and having lesser responsibilities. It happened that this kind of psychological patch in my life stretched into nearly a month. During this time, I was feeling the exceptional pain. Or maybe the pain was same but only my negative experience was exaggerating.

In the center of it, the matter was that, my differences with Mark Dallisi, my employer and director of the company, were growing. He had something wrong in his mind; and I knew it very well, that once Dallisi had made a mind, nothing could have ever changed it. On few occasions even if I tried talking to him on this matter, he gave only diplomatic answers. Given the anarchical atmosphere around, I was growing convinced that the rubbish of provoking Mark by my cunning jealous fellows were actually invincible. More than feeling agitated over these fellows, I was surprised for the blind faith Mark had in his flatterers. My disrupted dialogue with these fellows and my hesitation in ironing out the differences with Mark, were actually making me helpless. For past few months I had been trying hard to either get a new job or please Mark with my work, but I was failing in both. Occasionally I would feel comfortable in blaming it on the prevailing gloom in the world economies, but the ground reality was that, things were not happening up to my desire. Few of my acquaintances had lately been successful in getting their employment renewed or replaced, whereas this couldn't become the case with me. Day after day frustration was becoming more difficult to hide from my visage. Too much worried as I was, I had begun appearing visibly less composed and contained.

And as if this alone wasn't enough; my troubles at home were also flooding. On and off, Annie would start arguing that Maina must go to the best school in the town. Here 'best' meant, of best repute and the bills. For her it was a matter of education of our child; but secretly I was interpreting her idea to be a matter of taking pride with the most expensive school in the town. Had it been the last decision to be taken in life, I would have easily given in; but the life, in terms of monetary needs, seemed only endless. In my already humbled stature, every such decision was involving only the finances and invariably the pain attached to it. Annie and I had not planned our second child so far. She was almost against it, whereas I was in favor. Having lived in this city for more than five years now, we had not been able to plan our own house yet. Although living in rented house was not as such a painful experience, but future never looked secure if continuing in this way. Also in terms of prestige amongst my kin and kith, this matter of house had been a humiliating truth for me. The household expenses couldn't be ever tamed from increasing month after month. Although I had made reasonable savings in the past, but those were not able to make up for the insecurity complex looming on my head. Often I wondered, for how long life would go like this? For how long I would remain able to pay the ever increasing rents of the house wherein we lived? Would a life hugely burdened by EMIs, in case I had alternatively chosen for hire-purchasing a new house, remain any easy? What really had I been up to all these years? What really at all?

And then I would try repressing my negativity of one kind by the other. I would wonder, oh! How great were the old times! Weren't those really better than now? Believing this, I would feel the pangs of pain of one kind being comforted by those of other kind. The reminiscences of times which had gone and couldn't be reversed, only later I realized that, were also a kind of pain and not my salve.

I was taking notice of the present times and gone times in plenty, but the other thing which I had been missing out on was that, how greatly I was being fooled by my own mind! This had been going on for a month now. Though by grace of master, I had the divine helps in form of divine vision and wooden box with me; but going about completely lost in my apparent world, I didn't trust those helping me out. It was not the first time I was running through such woes. Those were the days of monsoon and every time it happened that slight drizzling or heavy rains would restrain me from going out for the morning walks. I had been away from the holy sight of master's feet for weeks now. I was spending my mornings with only newspaper, which was full of tidings and interviews about the economic depression all around. More I would read those, more I was able to reason my personal psychological gloom. Away from my master here at home, I had been cooking my own lurch; well, too imperfectly.

Even if somehow I could think of the wooden box or the divine vision anytime, I comfortably escaped by wondering – What would but the master know about the national economy? Or even this – What would master do of the cunning side of Mark or my reprehensible colleagues. Perhaps I was secretly enjoying my stuck position as if it was alone my battle of life. I thought it was my individual quest and I was not supposed to expose or discuss it with Annie or mother, and not even with my master.

One night, in desperation, I ended up writing my woes at length in the diary. I wrote a lot about myself. It was perhaps the first time I had written so much in one spell. Sleep was already displaced from my eyes and I was enjoying the sarcastic silence at home. After everyone had retired to bed, there was nobody to witness me awake. In diary I wrote about my past life of college days. I found I had more freedom and less worries in those days. I was bachelor and free from the kinds of worries which had been haunting me off late. In diary I felt like successfully revenging by way of abhorring my present scenarios of life. When I had finished criticizing my present in comparison to past, at least for once, I felt like validating my findings. Perhaps I wanted to root-out my doubt, if left any, about my newest opinion. I said to myself, "Indeed the gone days were better. I do not live greater life than I did before." And confirming the same, neither the hopes for future were any bright. I had succumbed even further in the process of said validation by assuming that even as per ancient scriptures, the older age was better than the new age. *Dwapar Yuga* was of course better than the concurrent *Kali Yuga*. Even the predecessor *Treta Yuga* was better than *Dwapar*. So if I was finding the smaller unit of time from my past days to be better than my present days, it was indeed in line with what had been endorsed by the scriptures themselves.

Oh! Who can argue a point against the scriptures, even when that is misplaced?

Having confirmed my horrible state of mind in scriptures, I stood up and moved to the bedroom. Till this moment I had not realized the severity of my error. I sank in the bed.

As I caught sleep, I felt as if I had seen a minute of mirage. It was the smiling face of master coming across me. He merely said, "Tell my son! Who is fooling whom? Is that the scriptures fooling you or is it you fooling the scriptures?" As he spoke this he giggled like a child and disappeared. He had left me alone midst the darkness of my closed eyes.

Distressed, I shook in bed. It was similar to an electric shock. Though awake now, instead of opening my eyes in astonishment, I tried to search master's talking face once again. But I didn't succeed.

Now the sleep was miles away from me. I turned my head to see Annie. She was asleep and her nostrils were making slight sound of snoring. I thought about master's face again. Quite many days had passed but I had not been in his company; I meant his company of any kind. Perhaps master was wishing me to seek his help in solving this conundrum. That's why he had appeared in my closed eyes and remarked a taunt.

Lying in bed, I picked my phone from the side table and checked time. It was half an hour past twelve at night. I felt reluctant to go about the table and check wooden box. Perhaps I was too tired to do that, or maybe I had been sinking in pessimism. Divine vision could be the only option left for me.

However I was feeling uninspired even about that.

I continued tossing and turning in my bed and so remained my dilemma also unsettled. As I began catching the sleep again, another dream occurred to me. This time it was long and strange. I was holding a brown wooden shaft in my hands and was knocking at an unknown door. I knocked it twice but no response came from inside. I pushed it. The door gave in and opened. As I put my first step inside, the scene came very astounding upon me. Similar to the one I was holding in my hands, countless other shafts were hanging from the lowly ceiling inside a room. Those were so many that I could barely walk amidst them. Wanting to check more about room, as I put in another step, the door had closed from behind with a thudding noise. Frightened, I turned back and tried to open the door for running away. But as I had already suspected, it didn't open at all. Helplessly, I turned to the hanging shafts once again.

Those were of varied colors. The hanging height of each shaft was also different from the other. Some of those came touching my shoulders whereas others were even low. Few ones would touch my head while some other ones were even higher. I looked down to the floor. It was all deserted and comfortable for my walk. I looked about the walls too, but even those were deserted for my any kind of guess. I didn't at all know what to do with the hanging shafts and also the one which I was holding in my hands.

For once I thought to not touch or quiver any single of them, else who knew what kind of new magical trouble could set in by my act. I turned back to the door and tried opening it; but it was still merciless upon me.

Not knowing what to understand or do about the things, I turned to the hanging shafts. However this time I noticed a new thing about those. There was something written on the bottom edge of each. Though it was a dimly lit room, but I could somehow read it. It was a word 'Future' written on it. I checked another shaft carefully. It also wrote 'Future' on its bottom.

Standing on the brink of room I checked about a few more shafts which were easy in my approach. All of them were showing the same word only.

Till this moment I had remained only scared about touching or quivering those. Quite carefully I narrowed my shoulders and took forward a step amidst the hanging shafts. As I looked ahead, the bottom of even forthcoming shafts were written with the same word – 'Future'.

Annoyed as to why I was here in the room, I took a step or two more. All shafts hanging in my front were showing only the same and nothing else. Assuming that all would show only the same word till the other corner of room, I thought about returning and try to open the door once again. It seemed totally a pointless job to read the same thing again and again; though the erstwhile adamancy of door was keeping me worried.

As I turned back, the one shaft which was hanging right in front of my eyes, astonished me. Merely a second before, if I remembered right, it was showing 'Future' written on it, but now when I had turned back it was showing a new word - 'Past'. I doubted myself; maybe I had not remembered this one shaft perfectly well.

I began looking to the other shafts. Greatly amazed as I was, I clasped the one shaft already in my hand even tighter. But lo! How could it happen that all those which were showing only 'Future' written on them, were now showing 'Past'? I checked and double checked all again and again.

Carefully narrowing my shoulders again, I came back to the door and began to look at the first row of the shafts. Now those were showing 'Future' only. Feeling badly perplexed over this, I had forgotten about the door. Instead I ventured into the opposite side of room and began to look back.

My wonderment was still unresolved! All shafts were showing only 'Past' written on those and nothing else at all. Carefully, I circled on my heels to check whether those had two different writings visible from the opposite sides. But no! Each one had only one writing on it at one time. I trudged in all directions and noticed that the changes happening to the shafts' writings were actually taking place in accordance of the changes in my own position towards those. Whichever of those was appearing ahead of me, it showed "Future"; but any one behind my back was showing only 'Past' written on it. All by themselves, the writings were changing.

Except understanding that whatever was in front of me was the future and whatever was behind was the past, I couldn't grasp beyond. Till this moment, very carefully, I had not shaken or quivered any hanging shaft. But now I wanted to take chance.

I clasped my own shaft bit tightly. I coined the idea of hitting one with it and see what happens. In mix of fear and anxiety, I hit one of those as gently as I could. That hanging shaft, which was near to my head and showing 'Future', swung only a little and in few seconds stilled back to its previous position. Besides the slight swinging I didn't see any other difference developing out there. Feeling encouraged with the harmlessness, I hit back the same shaft somewhat harder this time. It swung with increased velocity and took longer in returning to its original position. Again, I did not witness any difference made by that.

Thinking of it as meaningless as harmless it was, I gripped the one in my hand toughest and came about hitting the same hanging shaft once again. I wanted to do it hardest. As I hit it, it accidently hit the next one, and then the latter hit another one; and it just started the chain. In a fraction of second, as if by some domino effect, there was great commotion in the room. All shafts had started swinging and hitting each other again and again.

While swinging, few of those hit my head also. But more than a gentle tap, those didn't do anything. I rushed to the corner of room and watched the entire din created by shafts. While the swinging movement was on, I couldn't really read what those were now written with – 'Future' or 'Past'. But I felt those all were playing with each other; sometimes hitting and sometimes escaping.

I continued watching unless those had slowed down and returned to their original position once again. I disdained about hitting again. There was no point in repeating the whole commotion. Already it had made no difference to the room, nor to themselves, and nor even to me.

Now when all the hanging shafts had completely stilled, I tried reading those. Again those were showing the both – 'Future' and 'Past'; changing automatically as per my own position towards those. The way it seemed to me in that moment, it was all nonsense and insanity. The whole room was useless. I felt like running away from it; though the stubbornness of the door was still unresolved.

In aloofness I began to look at the shaft in my own hands. My fist was still clasping it tight. Suddenly, my curiosity increased as to what could have been written on this one, if it was also of the same kind.

I brought its upper tip near to my eyes.

Oh! It showed nothing there but simply one letter written on it – 'I'. I glanced again but couldn't make out anything. I tried comparing the 'I' written on my shaft with the 'Future' and 'Past' written on the hanging ones. But still, couldn't make out any.

On a musing, holding that 'I' in front of my eyes, I made a half circle on my heel. But disappointingly, even when I had changed my position to the shaft, it made no difference to the 'I' written on it.

Maybe I was failing to grasp the whole matter, but I was certain that there was something meaningful behind this all. Casually I moved this shaft from my one hand to the other.

Oh my goodness! Just then the secret started unfolding. As the shaft changed my hand, it showed me what was written on its opposite tip, which until now, was hiding in my tight fist. It was the new word – 'Present'.

I was awed. I was advancing in the right connotation of my surroundings. In my hands I had two things – 'Present' and 'I'.

Now the meaning was clear. It was all in my hands. I looked

at the hanging shafts once again. Those were 'Past' and 'Future'; and were capable of making merely the commotions and nothing more. Hanging from the ceiling, those were utterly useless.

Bedazzled by this insight, I tried checking whether there was written something on the upper tips of the hanging shafts as well.

Oh yes! Indeed something was written which had previously escaped my sight. It was all the same everywhere, on all shafts, even unaffected by the change in between 'Past' and 'Present' corresponding to my own position. It was just a small sign – '!'; here, there and everywhere. I sifted again. Yes it was '!' only.

The meaning was even clearer now. 'Past' and 'Future' had only anxieties on their other ends; whereas it was only 'I' on the other end 'Present'.

I looked around the room once again. Now it seemed even more meaningless, for the most meaningful thing was already in my hands. I wanted to come out instantly; but how?

I rolled the shaft in my hands and saw the 'I' and 'Present' once again. This closed room was not the place for me; no, it couldn't be ever. For me, it was outside. I felt my heart was redeeming from the heaviness. I just came about the door, and as if I already knew it, I hit the shaft hard on it. The door opened with a thud.

Here, as the door opened, my dream broke and I was awake in the bed.

In front of my eyes, which were blindingly looking for the shafts even to this moment, master's face came across. He said, "Tell my son! Who will fool whom now?" As he said this, he just laughed and disappeared.

Master had indescribable powers indeed. Even though I had remained reluctant about the wooden box and divine vision tonight, he had worked through my dream.

I had a better sleep now. And by no reason known to me, I woke up one hour earlier than anybody else in the house. I found it a great chance to check wooden box in this moment. As I came around table and brought out the bundle of mufflers, I already knew that master had great words for me.

I held the wooden box in great reverence and tapped it gently. Quite surely, it opened with a new leaf which said:

"Apparent world will always be full of exclamation signs; however with enhanced knowledge of secret world, it will come easier upon you getting rid of these signs. Exclamations about 'Past' and 'Present' are not themselves bad, but man's ignorance about 'I' and 'Present' amidst the commotion of formers, is bad. You must remain careful about this trick which your mind will constantly play with you. Son, understand well; past can never be better than present. Not even future can become that way. The demonic, destructive and evil tendencies of mind did exist even in SataYuga, TretaYuga and DwaparaYuga. Or didn't those? Scriptures are there for empowering your 'I' and 'Present'. You must not misquote or misinterpret the text for creating the walls of exclamatory signs around you. And finally, why perturb yourself so much about the small regular challenges in your apparent world? I have already taught you enough. Whenever you happen forgetting my lessons; start kindling your secret world more frequently."

Relieved, I lifted up my chin. He knew my every single thought, in all days and times. I couldn't wait for seeing his holy feet again. I repacked the wooden box and placed into the drawer. I came to the window and looked outside. Great luck, it was a clear sky today.

What a wonderful morning it had to be. In only few minutes, I was ambling in the central orchard of the park.

THIRTY SIX

Finding the Real Victory of Life

"WHY DON'T YOU REALLY set me free? The worldly responsibilities are dragging me into the deeper pit every next time."

It happened that despite master's repeated warnings, more knowledge I was gaining in the secret world, more useless I was finding myself in the apparent world. Greatly perturbed over the similar things again, one day I had asked this from master during the morning walk.

"You always ask me the same questions", master quipped laughingly.

"Master, my life doesn't ever stop going treacherous upon me. Don't you think that being a householder is endlessly difficult?" I asked him while looking at his feet following me from behind.

He replied, "It's just the way you think about it. If we go by your standards, do you think that life of ascetics dwelling on the hills would be any easy?"

It was no point arguing with him. He could make me speechless any time. But still, I didn't run dry of hope about getting resolves through him. Infact it was only him, in refuge of whom I could rest assured for my deliverance.

I tried reasoning my discontenting thoughts. I replied, "But master, I have not yet grown as skillful as you have."

To this he laughed again, "It's again just the way you think of it. Else, haven't I already given you whatever I had? If you do not become satiated by the knowledge imparted by me, you must continue knowing the same precepts in different ways again and again. I will not stop being with you unless you yourself agree to it."

I took a pause. "You speak true master", just uttering it submissively I turned silent and continued my walking and wondering. This morning I didn't know what had happened to me, but I was not perfectly able to cope within myself. Actually the matter which had been perplexing me constantly was again the same. It was about my financial security in the apparent world. I was facing many competing questions in my mind. As I would start trying answering one question, some other one would sneak in and bewilder me. This entire chain of questions was interlinked. It was not letting me trace the beginning or the end of the things.

As usual, master had sensed my state of mind. He asked sensitively, "Tell me my son, what has happened?"

His affectionate voice snatched me from my aloofness. I struggled in consolidating my thoughts before putting across him.

"Nowadays master", I started speaking my pain, "I am undergoing huge pressure of losing my work; and to the worse, my continued efforts for finding new work elsewhere are not fructifying either."

"Hmm..." Master didn't respond more than that. Finding me waiting for his more words, he merely asked, "And...?"

I hesitated but replied, "I haven't yet owned a house. Having lived in a rented house for years it leaves me worried for the future. What will I really do?"

"Hmm...And?" He asked again.

I felt awkward. Instead of answering any, master was asking about more troubles with me.

But impulsively I added on, "The household ordeals are also growing very expensive nowadays. There seems no end to the aspirations of dear ones at home; and I don't want to stop them either. But this all has made me worried about the coming times."

"And...?" Master asked again.

I thought it was better if master had vocally declared that today he was interested only in ridiculing me. Embarrassed and infuriated, I turned back to him accidently.

Oh! He was right there and smiling at me in motherly love. "Don't look back my son!" he forbade me at once, "else the people will not stop making fun of you. Just look ahead and keep walking. Don't worry, I am with you."

I resumed walking.

"What else, my son? Has there anything left?" Master insisted again.

I turned baffled. I was not finding an end to my list of miseries; but at the same time, it was coming difficult for me to drape those in the suitable words for letting master know.

"There could be many more, master," I replied, "but it's getting difficult for me to explain all. Days and nights I am haunted by those."

"Hmm..." then said the master, "Let us say I ask you to make a list of your all worries so that you won't miss a single one, will that be possible?"

I didn't know what he was up to today. "List?" I uttered in surprise.

"Yes why not? If you think you have more troubles than you can explain in a day, you can take your sweet time and make a list of all. When you are ready with it, we will discuss it at length", master said.

"Master, what is making you so funny today? You know it well that no such list can be made by the human beings", I almost complained to him.

He burst in mirth again. In a moment he began saying, "Else, what should I do in this moment for making you sure that all these problems cited by you are actually no problems. Those are merely fooling you and keeping the central problem obfuscated from your sight."

"I didn't get it, master", I asked.

He said, "Say, here and now if I give you a big boon and do such a miracle that will resolve your all problems including the ones you have not cited; then can you guarantee me a thing?"

Was something special about to happen? I didn't know. I was bedazzled. I had no idea of his plan. "Which thing to guarantee, master?" I asked.

"That ever in life, you will not become distressed again?" He continued.

I knew it; he always had a point to storm me. I didn't answer.

"Tell me", he forced, "Do you guarantee that? If you do, I will perform the miracles right away. But also remember, if you dishonor your guarantee later, you will have to see the punishment as well."

Hopelessly I said, "O master! Really something has happened to you today. You are in playful mood. I don't think any such guarantee can be committed ever."

"Why not? It should be very much possible." He asked again, "Let me give you more time, say, one week. You must prepare the entire list. Then, even if you come back with thousands of written problems, I will give you the suitable boons and will also perform the miracle as I have promised."

Foolishly though, but I had started getting lured. "But master, maybe I still miss out on few more."

"Then will it be fine if I give you the time of one month instead?" He asked.

"Yes, it's better. But master, maybe I still err the same", I said in the state of being double-minded.

"Then will one year be good?" He asked again.

"Hmm... Yeah, may be. But still I am not too sure, master", said I.

"Then tell me yourself how much time will be sufficient to write down your problems?" He asked.

Now I had an inkling of his playfulness. "Isn't it enough you've already derided me, master?" I complained.

Now he told me this, "Did you notice my son, that in past

two minutes you had forgotten your earlier problems and were concentrating upon the biggest one?"

"Oh, biggest? Which one, master?" I asked in riddling voice.

"It's that how much time it will suffice you to prepare the list of your miseries."

"I don't get it, master!" I wondered.

"Son, listen to this with great attention." His voice was getting intense now, "Actually the number of problems you have cited before me today; and even those which you might write in your big list later, are not your real problems. Those merely keep you distracted from knowing the central problem instead."

"And what is that master?"

"It's the imperfect state of your mind", he declared. "It's alone your mind which has been fooling your mind itself through the tricky delusive thoughts devised by no one else but your mind alone once again. Can you really grasp this stratagem?"

"Oh master! What you said! Please repeat it once", I requested.

"Hear it again, son! It is alone your mind which has been fooling your mind itself through the tricky delusive thoughts devised by no one else but your mind alone once again. It's the mind which oppresses; it's the mind which afflicts; and it's again only the mind which memorizes the sufferings", master elaborated.

"As per you master", I asked, "if it's alone the mind, then what is that which keeps me sad and depressed all the times?"

"You are neither sad nor depressed, son. You are merely reflecting your mind on your body, which you have momentarily found comforting."

"Comforting?" I wondered, "But am I not in big troubles really?"

He smiled and said, "You say that only until you've not known yourself enough. You are not an entity which can fall in trouble ever. Never forget that you are lot more than your mind, which is appearing to be troubling you in this moment. Your ignorance about your higher powers has to be banished right away. The very moment you establish your superior dominion over your mind, it will cease deceiving you. Establishing dominion over the mind means catching it in the very moment it starts tricking you."

"What you say is true master, but aren't the problems which I have been citing also real? Should I really ignore the hanging sword on my work and overlook the imminent financial insecurity at home?" I asked.

"Son! Let us sit on that bench now." Master pointed his finger in far left. While walking in the direction, he remarked, "Sparingly anybody would come there. I must help you on this."

Reaching the bench, as I turned back, I found him smiling for me as ever. I bowed and touched his feet in great love. He caressed my head and motioned about to sit beside him.

He began saying, "You've been talking about these things on and off. I must tell you the truth which you should not only accept but also gleefully appreciate in an invariable spirit. My son! You are not living the miseries nowadays, but you are living only a life. You will always have to live it; or can you ever escape?"

I continued looking to his face.

He said, "If not more, let us sit in absolute silence for five minutes. You must concentrate your mentation only upon one thing - Will you accept the defeat in despair or will you fight back in hope of victory? Sit here in silence. Make a decision and then I will help you seeing the way ahead. While doing this meditation here, you must sit steadily but comfortably. You may also close your eyes if you need to. Don't look here and there; just keep looking at any one point falling in your sight and concentrate between the two choices given."

Master's presence was already magical and vibratory. I could feel that. I had mounted on the bench and began to think about the two choices put up. In no time I had realized that there was no question of accepting the defeat. I thought about my presented challenges. Master had said that I was not living the miseries but I was living only a life. Surely he meant that if I cannot stop living, I won't escape miseries even after accepting the defeat.

I was sitting with closed eyes. I wondered what worst could happen to me. Could I challenge the problems? Did I want to face things? Had I become too worried about the households to see anything else? But as per master, it was merely a deception played upon me by my own mind. Even though I had not found a very convincing answer to the problem, I was atleast sure that running away was not the solution. I must have put up a courageous spirit instead. I was finding five minutes actually longer than needed for making the choice.

Without scoring my minutes, I opened the eyes. Master was still in his meditational spell. Or perhaps I had opened my eyes too early.

In few moments master also opened his eyes. His smile was appearing more divine now. He turned to me.

"Did you see the light, son!" He asked.

"Yes master. I have chosen for the victory", I answered in tenderness.

He nodded his head and said, "Maybe you get surprised about this. Actually for getting defeated, there are innumerable territories in human life; but on the other hand, for establishing victory in the same life, there is only one territory, and that is mind. If you lose it in your mind, you lose everywhere else; but if you win in the mind, you win everywhere."

I was ears alone.

He continued enlightening, "You have been worrying about your households and financial security, but now when you have decided to strive for the victory, I will reveal the secret of your future life."

Picturesquely, I was glued to his words.

"Those who become keenly curious about their secret world and also keenly dutiful in their apparent world do not ever get perished. Such privileged men cannot be destroyed by the worldly forces which are already infirm. Nobody can ever harm them and nor can anyone annihilate their existence. Those who are able to live in the secret world and apparent world alike are protected by God Himself. Such people do not ever require the worldly protections or assurances. For so long as the financial and household responsibilities of such men are concerned, never forget that by way of such peoples' enlightened and dutiful discharge of life, the things are already taken care of by the Divine Itself. Such people do not live the financial or household responsibilities, but they live only dutifully."

He looked my face again and said, "You must not let yourself down by your mind. The very moment your mind starts throwing dark clouds on you; you must recognize this instantly. You must catch and tame it then and there. Son, whenever you are shaken by the ruffles in the apparent world, you must reestablish yourself in truth. You must remind yourself your choice made for the victory. Your battle field of life is battle not because of so called miseries that you have to face, but it is so because of the ongoing battle between you and your mind. Your worldly responsibilities are not your challenge, but your challenge is your mind which attempts to trick you and stray you from living a dutiful contented life."

He stared in my eyes and asked, "Do you know what exactly your victory is?"

"No", I shook my head.

"Your victory is you. It's you because whenever you will become despondent; your victory will be nowhere. And about your protection in this battle, son, can you appreciate that you are protected by the Divine Itself?"

I nodded my head in affirmation.

"In the moments you are realizing this, you will live free; and conversely whenever you will forget or overlook this protection of dutifulness, you'll land in the ditch of fear. Trust yourself being in the divine protection but don't take it for granted. If you do not strive your life skillfully, you will stop being dutiful; and that will be a curse. Never brag your divine protection in front of others, for there is no need of it. Rest assured and be engaged in your duty always. What little you have been worrying about your financial and household securities, infact you will attain lot more than that. Can you trust my assurance, son? You will prosper not only in your secret world, but in the apparent world as well. Banish from your mind the miseries of all kinds and liven up your natural bliss at once."

Master had never shown himself so authoritative earlier. I had no doubt in his words. He was still infusing smiles in my frame.

Great speechlessness had occurred to me. He raised his hand and said, "Go my son! Choose your duty conscientiously and be engaged in your chosen battle of life."

He patted me on the back and motioned for leaving. As before in the hills, he came along some distance for seeing me off.

In departing moments, I asked him in deep love, "But master, what had you been meditating in those five minutes?"

He flashed his typical smile, "Oh! On the hills I catch upon similar moments too often. And in such numerous spells I do the same thing again and again."

"Which thing master?" My curiosity leaped.

"I tender my love to the feet of God. I start talking to Him and He instantly responds. We make several talks. Sometimes we both grow so affectionate towards each other that it becomes difficult to guess who loves whom more. Such ecstasy becomes ineffable. Since ages I have been feeling the same bliss, which I am trying to impart you. Trust me, it doesn't make any difference whether you are living in the cave or in a house."

I found myself being too small to reflect his kindness.

He laughed on and said, "Go now my son! Join your share of battle before it gets late."

Abruptly I glanced upon my wrist watch. He was correct. As I moved a couple of feet ahead, I turned back for thanking him again.

But there had remained no one. I squeezed my lips and smiled. I came back home. Later in the day I found myself braver, sensible and more open to accept the truth. I also noticed that how the things, which until now had been frightening me, had started changing their course after seeing me braving. I had decided at least one thing, that I will not let my mind accept the defeat beforehand. My duty was to fight and only fight on the battle.

In the evening when I returned home, everyone was quick in noticing my cheerful alacrity. My shuttling between sadness and happiness was not a new thing for them, but perhaps this time they were hoping my happiness to last long. Realizing their hope, I was also feeling more committed to the victory.

Before retiring to bed, I intuited as if master had left a message for me.

Yes, I was right. In the wooden box, master had sent the following:

"Son, I must bestow you a great mantra which has been taken from a holy scripture. It is God's message to His devotee, to say - Offer to Me your every deed. Devoid of egotism (your exaggerated opinion of your own importance) and also devoid of the desire (expectation for results), and thus being inwardly centered in your soul (inner freedom), and also remaining ever calm and free from the worries, be dutifully engaged in your battle of life. My son! Always keep this message around you."

Surely, I was swift about copying the same in my diary. Following day, I had made a cardboard photo frame with the said words printed in it. Now I could read master's message any time, without fearing anybody at home yet.

THIRTY SEVEN

Conversation amongst Three Leaves

ONCE IT HAPPENED THAT I came across a book which belonged to other religion than mine. Day after day as I was evolving in the company of master and also in his bestowings, many myths of my old perceptions in the apparent world were breaking. More than getting marveled or overwhelmed on my new discoveries, I would rather find those now confirming the eternal truth.

I couldn't resist turning the pages of this book. The script language was different, but fortunately the translation was given. As I advanced in reading, I strongly felt that whoever the other person would be reading the same book in its original language will also be influenced to the same path of goodness. I observed that language was not important at all. The only important thing was the thought, and also how marvelously it was established in the book. By the time I had completed the said book, I was inclining towards the other sects and religions even more.

However on the gray side, my growing interest in the books was turning a dissent in Annie. She would often complain that I was not giving her my proper time or attention. Without spurring an argument, I would humbly agree to her complaints. I would try to make her understand about my new findings and discoveries made in books, but we did not conciliate anyhow. Somehow, in due course, I would manage to appease her. Maina would picturesquely watch our sort of spats, but would become glad for the truce made later. Even though she was only a child, but she was growing. She had started taking notice of the things.

Sometimes whenever dragged too deep in these turbulences, I would discuss with master. He always found such matters only general and reacted in cold. Only in order to pacify my momentary anxiety, he would say the same thing again and again. Through various stories and analogies, he would establish time and again that it was my duty to not let any perturbation emerging in my apparent world because of my growing interest in the secret world. He would say that my deficiency in settling the conflicts between two worlds was actually my imperfection. He would alarm me and show the ways too. After listening to his enlightening words, I would feel more contented and would successfully balance out the things in due course every time.

Largely, things were going fine in life; and it included my curiosities and discoveries about religions. My general cognizance of the apparent world would always accentuate the differences in the religions; whereas the secret world would establish only unity.

In the days when I was going through varied similar experiences, one evening the TV news channels reported that severe communal riots had broken out in the same town again, about where we had advertised in the newspapers previously. I became too depressed. I felt as if apparent world was just futile and it couldn't ever give solutions to its own problems. I wondered about checking its truth in the secret world. In the bed at night, I successfully invoked my divine vision and tried seeing about. The discovery I had made was phenomenal.

In divine vision, I found myself standing alone in the dark and holding the same small mirror in my hands. When I looked into it, it didn't show anything except the dark, but as I started wiping on the other side, I had started seeing across.

In far, it was showing me a small blue ball. Just when I had started concentrating on it, I felt as if the mirror swung out of my hands and flew away in the horizon. But surprisingly, even though the mirror was gone, the strange ball the still in my sight.

Gradually the ball started becoming bigger. In no time it had quickened the pace of enhancing its size. Only in a moment, the ball had grown to the magnanimous proportions. It was looking beautiful. On its entire surface it had both; water and sand, perfectly segregated from each other. As I began to watch it even more carefully, I felt I had become merely a size of mosquito. I was staring upon the unfathomable oceans and also upon the landscapes made of sand.

Till this moment, since I was completely engrossed in the beauty and magnanimity of this large blue ball, I didn't know my own whereabouts. I lured about going near to the ball and find out a place suitable for my roaming on it. Sandy landscapes seemed better than the watery surface. As I continued moving towards the ball, it became so big that I couldn't comprehend its roundness. In front of my eye was only a plain flat surface which was all made of sand and nothing else. Within only few moments, I was standing at a strange place; completely unknown to me; and it was hazy dark all around.

Even before I could start perplexing about my whereabouts, the darkness started going away. Some kind of white illumination increased. I noticed that I was standing on a large forlorn piece of land. Curiously, I looked around. It was all barren and unkempt; though in its center there stood one singled-out tree.

It was no difficult to ascertain that the entire landscape had no other vegetation. Tree's trunks were as huge as a grown up elephant. Up there were myriads of branches, sub-branches and leaves of all sizes and age. Aground, I looked up and tried to fathom the vastness of tree. Indeed, it was the largest I had ever seen in my life.

I had now walked a circle around it. Looking down I saw a few scattered heaps of half-dried and dried leaves; though upside, the tree was only lush green. Bright sun was peeping through the dense leaves. I started wondering as to why I was here. Except this lonesome tree, there was nothing else on the landscape which deserved a mentioning. If I wanted to go away from this place, I didn't know in which direction at all! Again and again I was glancing upon the heaps of dry leaves but sparking no interest in those. Looking upside was also equally uninteresting, for I didn't know what to do with the things in front of me.

In aloofness, I came near to the trunk and put my hands on it. But lo! Just as I had touched it, I began to hear a din of voices from all around. Frightened, I looked in all directions but it was desertedness all over. I trailed the direction of voices.

Oh! Certainly those were coming from above. I fidgeted but didn't see anyone sitting up in the branches. I moved far from the trunk and started noticing the voices more carefully now.

Indeed those were the human voices. I wondered as to without human beings themselves, from where the voices could come? I turned more meticulous in hearing. Yes, those were surely the human voices, but since those were numerous, I could not perfectly understand what those spoke or meant.

Surprisingly the voices were coming even when my hands were not touching the trunk. I moved farther from the trunk and began to look above the green leaves once again. Merely few yards away there was a low hanging branch. I felt like pulling its leaves and therefore I came underneath it.

Now few leaves were just ahead of my shoulder. As I raised my hand to touch, I was taken aback. Few voices out of the din were clearly audible to me. I looked in daze and easily became sure that these few voices were coming from nowhere else but these leaves only. Leaves were talking to each other. Just when I had fixed my gaze upon two particular of those, I could raptly hear their conversation.

One smaller leaf, which was bright green in color, was asking from a bigger dark leaf next to it, "Are you frightened that soon you will also become one of those lying on the ground?"

The bigger leaf trembled and replied, "Yes, a little bit."

"Oh!" The former expressed grief.

"But you need not worry that for yourself", consoled the older leaf, "You are too young to get there any early. You can enjoy life longer."

"Hmm...", uttered the pensive younger leaf. It couldn't restrain adding, "But still the very thought of inevitable frightens me."

"There is no sense in fearing the inevitable," said the older leaf, "Just enjoy what you are living on."

"Hmm...", younger leaf uttered again. For a minute they both remained silent. I didn't hear those talking.

Suddenly again, the younger leaf asked its senior fellow, "After you will die and drop down like those already there, have you given a thought which group of those you will join?"

"Yes, after dying I will stick to the same group which I have been belonging to while living", replied the older leaf.

To this younger leaf said, "But I think those all dried leaves down there are not very sure about. All through the day I watch them changing the groups."

"Oh! Is that? Probably I missed to take a notice. Do you know why they would be doing so?" asked the dark leaf.

Younger leaf replied, "I think just when the wind blows fast, many dried leaves change their groups."

"Hmm..., maybe you are correct", the older leaf said again pensively. It asked, "But what else those can do? For so long as those were alive, those could stick to their branches and remain staunch to their groups. But after those are dead and have fallen down now, I think wind can overpower easily."

Sinking in numerous thoughts, the younger leaf remained only quiet.

Here the older leaf continued expressing its fright, "I wonder how those would feel in the moments of being carried away by the wind every now and then. The already dead leaves would certainly feel worse for being forced by the wind to join and change the other groups which never belonged to those."

"None of us would know their pain unless we ourselves reach there someday", as the younger leaf said this, it started mourning.

"Oh! Do not cry, do not cry. You are too young to weep. See! You have still left many seasons to enjoy. Do not lose in crying", the older leaf tried to comfort its young fellow.

"Yes, this is what all other leaves on this branch always tell me."

Then after both leaves stopped their conversation and I started hearing the old din again. In aloofness I moved little far from this low hanging branch. Not long after I witnessed that wind had started blowing hard. I smiled for the absolute unpredictability of the wind.

Just then there formed a small whirlpool of wind. In no time the whirlpool turned into a hurricane. One by one all dried leafs started swinging and rolling in the air. I was marveling the scene. From far, it would have surely looked like a giant floating tube, which was swollen from the middle and was made of innumerable dried leaves.

Now the ground was barely empty. All leaves had joined the whirlpool. All this was so spectacular to look at. I couldn't say whether the entire scene was beautiful or awkward, for it basically depended upon the personal viewpoint of the onlooker. Awhile this great commotion was continuing; I grew conscious about the two leaves, which I had heard conversing minutes before. I returned to the same spot where those were hanging.

The strong bluffs of wind had been pushing the both hard. I started hearing their conversation again.

"Oh look! What a great calamity has come!" The younger leaf was screaming.

"Yes! I don't know why sometimes the wind gets crazy like this", the older leaf added.

"It is shaking even the green leaves on the tree so badly that it will snap us all in a moment", exasperated the former.

Scornful, the older leaf remained only silent.

The younger leaf became desperate and asked, "But what do we do now?"

"What else! Try to keep hanging as long as you can. This is

the only fight we can put up against the foolish wind", replied the older leaf.

But the little leaf couldn't be pacified. In despair, it said again, "What do you think who from us will snap and drop down first?"

The older leaf was stunned with the question. It didn't answer.

"Oh! Forgive me. I think I've lost my mind", the younger leaf started crying. It added again, "Witnessing a life-taking cyclone here I am really not able to judge my words. I think it might be any of us."

"No! That's not true." Said the older leaf in deep pain, "All through the seasons I've lived I have noticed that crazy wind snaps the oldest leaf first."

"Oh! That is so cruel", the younger leaf nearly fainted.

The older leaf, which had now started turning pale as well, didn't add a word.

For few moments they both remained desperate and miserable. Here my absentminded gaze was fixed upon the whirlpool which was not slowing down yet.

"But do you have any idea", breaking the horrible silence younger leaf asked, "which group of the dead leaves we will join if we are snapped away now?"

"If it's me first, surely I crave for joining the same group which I have belonged to while living here. My group is my religion. I won't change it in whatsoever case."

"What is our religion, do you know?" asked the younger leaf.

"It's the same which all other leaves have belonged to on our branch. The other ones which belong to the different branches than ours, do not belong to our religion. I will not join their group after dying", replied the older leaf in a determined voice.

"Hmm...", uttered the younger leaf. It began to look around for the other branches in the tree. Indeed there were different kinds of groups, which this older leaf had just started calling as different religions. It wanted to count all but finding those innumerable it became confused and gave up. Its gaze had set upon the whirlpool once again.

"But Oh!" suddenly screamed the little leaf, "How at all will you know where your group is placed? Inside this whirlpool haven't all groups mixed already."

"Oh....!" Older leaf gasped, "How wind can be so foolish? It doesn't know what it's doing. It is so dumb that it has mixed all. Now no one can know which religion I will join after dying."

I also looked to the whirlpool. It was one and full of leaves, whereas the ground was only empty and bare. Even I started wondering which religion the older leaf will join after dying.

Just then the velocity of wind turned slower and the whirlpool started deforming. In no time, all dried leaves which were swinging round and round in the air until now, started dropping on the ground and formed one big heap. Not even a single leaf had scattered elsewhere, except a shrunk brown one which was being tossed high by the wind at last. On the way of its swinging and coming back to the ground, it had stuck above in the tree and was slowly coming down after hitting one branch or the other.

Coincidently for a while, this shrunk brown leaf remained stuck ahead of the two talking leaves.

Both turned surprised for the guest.

"Oh! How merciless is the wind. This dead brown leaf has strayed from its group", aggrieved the younger leaf.

But even before the older green leaf could add any, the brown one interrupted, "Hey, but I am not dead! Why did you say that?"

Both leaves were astonished. "What! Didn't you die after turning brown and dropping from the tree? Isn't it really strange to hear you speaking? We thought you were dead!" asked the older leaf in great amazement.

The brown leaf couldn't restrain laughter. It replied, "O, it's now I understand the matter well. Even I used to think similarly. Before dying I also couldn't know the truth after death."

"What's that truth?" asked the younger leaf in great deal of marveling.

"It's that we never die. After I had also become shrunk and turned brown on one of these branches, one day the strong wind came and snapped me away. Only after that I could know that I had not died."

The old green leaf shrieked, "I don't believe this. But when you are able to talk and behave like us, certainly you must be alive in some way."

The brown leaf laughed again. It said, "No! It's the same way only. Till the time we are alive, we accept the truth only suitable to our taste."

"Maybe you are right", said the older green leaf, "but I have a question. When a dropped leaf gets too much dried, doesn't it get crushed and broken into pieces by the wind? How can you say that leaves never die?"

Brown leaf laughed even loudly. It replied, "That's the point I had not understood myself anytime before. Do you know that, brown leafs do not die even after those are crushed. Those mix up in the soil and make friends with water. Soon they start sending the nourishment to the trunk of tree, which further supplies that nourishment to the branches; and then further by the branches to the leaves. Since when I have known this truth, I am resting in peace."

"Oh! Certainly you seem to have attained higher knowledge than we", said the older green leaf overwhelmingly. It asked again, "Can you tell me after dying and dropping from this tree, will I be able to join the same group of religion which I have been belonging to until now?"

"Why are you particularly worried about religions?" asked the brown leaf in wonderment.

"I think one's religion or group is as important while his living as it is after his dying", replied the older green leaf. It asked again, "Can you tell me which religion I will join after being snapped from this tree?"

The shrunk brown leaf was failing to find rationale of the

question. Still, unmistakably it said, "You will join the same group which you had belonged to while being on the tree."

"Oh that's very great! Can you tell me where is that group now?" It asked in merriment.

"Look down! It's right there only", guided the brown leaf.

Now the younger green leaf interrupted, "But the wind has unmade all into one, you see!"

"Not really! Infact the wind has made it into one. Wind always has to do it again and again. When the different brown leaves gradually end up into different scattered groups, the wind has to blow strong and form one single whirlpool of all. Then after all leaves get unified. Only this unification is the final truth and nothing else. Only because the leaves continue forgetting and weakening this unity again and again, the wind has to take its course repeatedly. You think of this activity as perturbation, whereas for us it's an awaited periodic celebration", thus explained the brown leaf.

To this the old green leaf objected, "But that's not the way we live when we are alive on the tree!"

"Oh! What makes you think that?" asked the surprised brown leaf.

"Why? Don't we always belong to the different branches of the tree? Isn't that very true?" asked the old green leaf.

"Perhaps you are short sighted in that case. You can see different branches but not the single trunk below?" The brown leaf continued rebuking, "Did you ever talk this matter with the trunk?"

The old green leaf had started getting the point. In embarrassment, it meekly replied, "No, I haven't talked to the trunk yet."

"If the group or religion belonging to your branch can become independent of the central trunk below, you must be right. But if that is not possible, you are terribly mistaken", the brown leaf warned.

The older green leaf had realized its fault, but it was not

completely free from the doubts. It slanted toward the trunk and saw it. In a moment it asked, "Why trunk is always silent and never talks to us."

"It's because trunk is so busy in sending you the nourishment to survive", replied the brown leaf.

"And it's also because neither do we give our due attention to it any time," added the younger green leaf.

The brown leaf replied, "It doesn't matter to the trunk ever. You all are its children and it is too busy in nourishing you all the time."

Both green leaves fell into contemplation.

Then brown leaf asked a question, "Have you ever wondered why the trunk is strongest amongst all of us?"

The both green leaves couldn't answer.

The brown leaf explained, "It's because it is too rigorous in discharging its constant duty. It never lets anything affect it while carrying out its operation. It's only the duty which has made it strongest and nothing else. It never becomes desperate about groups, religions or even death or life. Can you see that wind has been shaking everything here but not the trunk ever?"

Both leaves now had understood the truth well. The brown leaf finally said, "Your religion and group are unimportant because those are made and unmade faster than the whirlpools of wind. Sooner you understand and accept this, stronger you will become in yourself. Then various kinds of wonderments will stop perturbing you. It's alone your unification with the truth which is important; and nothing else."

Standing on the ground here, this entire experience was captivating for me. Soon I saw that the brown leaf had slipped to fall on the ground. It was alone and away from the new heap of leaves. Certainly it must have requested the wind, when all of a sudden it flew up and joined back the heap. I could feel the joy of both leaves up there, for those had stopped mourning and crying now.

I came back to the trunk and touched it again. As I did this, my divine vision started vanishing. The small round mirror came back flying from the horizon and dropped in my hands. As I looked in, it showed me the blue ball becoming smaller every moment. In no time, the ball became smallest and finally disappeared. Now the mirror also had not remained transparent. It was showing my face. I was looking enraptured and in bliss. After all this time I had seen another dimension of truth.

Soon, even the mirror disappeared from my hands and I fell asleep.

Following early morning, I curiously tapped the wooden box in expectation of something. This time master had written only fewer words for me. I read and copied those in my diary before moving out for the morning walk. His message was as poignant as always. It read:

"God is faith and not reason. Whenever 'reason' is pushed around God, religions take place. Only oneness of 'faith' can nourish the oneness of God and nothing else. Religions are merely paths whereas God is the destination. Wind will not stop blowing; and neither will stop the branches from looking distinctive. Only leaves are supposed to grow stronger in the truth."

PART V

AND THUS CONTINUED THE JOURNEY

It went on, that master never stopped turning up for my rescue and enlightenment. Either through his splendid presence in the central orchard, or via his messages in the wooden box, or even by way of my divine visions, he was always dutiful towards my discipleship vesting in him. On different occasions and in manners he was guiding my path. Following in this book is merely a collection of important extracts, without much elaborations being given to the situations around my life. Master always said that situations were not important, but only the functioning of man's mind towards them was.

THIRTY EIGHT

The Biggest Need of Human Mind

ONCE MASTER WROTE IN the wooden box:

"The biggest need of human mind is the need of Freedom. This freedom doesn't come from anything else but from living fearlessly in your days. Fear robs you of your discernment; and once devoid of discernment, you are not able to comprehend the divine protection around your life. You instantly become insecure and therefore, fearful as well. Do not forget that the entire aforementioned stratagem runs nowhere else but in your mind. Whenever chocked by your fear from situations, you are allowed to take pause and reflect, but what you are not allowed is to prolong your reveling in that pause. The most effective way of taming your fear is to face it affront."

Reflecting upon the above message of master and weighing it against some horrendous situation presented in my life, I consolidated my scattering thoughts and meditated over the problem as a whole. It not only gave me new insights, but also a new zeal to tame the fear which was vainly imposed by the world upon me.

THIRTY NINE

Silent Correspondence of Hate

IT SO HAPPENED ONCE, that I indulged in a terrible error. I have had some bitter experiences with few people in my professional life, and I began to hate them in worst way I could. In my own reasoning those people were treacherous, immoral and hostile. My error was not in judging them, but it was in hating them constantly. Despite my displeasure, my professional duties couldn't refrain me from having their sight. I didn't want to see their faces, but situations often warranted me to come across them. It went to an extent that I wanted to erase their names from my life, but my destiny was only unlikely for this. Day after day, I was seething in agony; and of course harming myself most in this way.

One day during morning walk when I discussed this matter with master, he made me understand a unique proposition about it.

He said, "I've touched upon this matter earlier as well. Son, only your own position towards people is important and not the people's position towards you. About latter you may never come to know it perfectly, for it would change very fast and secretly. Considering your own position however, it matters a lot that how your mind functions in the moments when the people or things that you've badly hated suddenly appear in your way; and even stay for a while. More than it matters to them it matters to you, for it affects you the most. Also do not forget that contrary to your persisting belief, in core of their individual causations, actually people and things should never deserve your hatred."

To this I asked master, "Then master, how to deal with the pangs of hate, which attack my bosom terribly?"

"It's no deal at all to hate", he replied only succinct.

"But what to do with the hostility and treachery such people or things cause upon me?" I asked.

"Well, make your own position lot broader than the position of erring people and things. This you can do only by way of forgiving them", master replied and added wonderfully, "Forgivingness is not a weapon to fight with, but it's the flag of victory."

"But I doubt master, will this really make an impact with those errands", I asked again.

He smiled and replied, "I have already said that it is only your position towards them which is important; and not the other way round. If you are burning in agony and prejudice all days and nights, you'll demerit your position; but if you are able to recompose yourself in the forgivingness, you only merit it. After all, your life is all about you alone and no one else."

"But master, what happens when those threaten me too harshly?" I asked relentlessly.

"It's again up to you get threatened or not! I repeat; it's alone your position which is important. Think about your position in long life and nothing else. Work for you to make yourself immune from the threats. And you can do so only by strengthening your own scrupulous position by way of forgiving your offenders."

Perhaps not completely convinced, I remained silent.

Master sensed it and said, "Son! Tell me what compels you taking revenge?"

"It's their offence only, master", I replied.

"No, you're judging it wrong. The thing which compels you revenging is rather your imagination of weaker strength of your offender. If your offender is mightier than you, you only burn your heart and do nothing else. Isn't that right?" Master asked and struck laughter.

Oops! He was right. I nodded.

"And on the other hand even if you find your offender weak and therefore are able to take revenge successfully, your satisfaction becomes only short lived again. Only in next moment you start worrying, lest your defeated opponent may soon grow mightier than you. Revenge after all, is merely a part in the chain. Or isn't it?" Master asked.

Very thoughtfully I nodded again.

"Let me conclude this for you", master said, "Whenever you're stuck in the web of hate, you must identify your error of revenging at soonest. At once you must stop taking part in the silent correspondence of hate. There is no better medium of communication of hate than the silent correspondence of it."

Just having said this, master disappeared. For me the lesson was hard but subtle.

FORTY

Moral of All Childhood Stories

ONE SUNDAY NOON WHEN I was at home, Maina approached me showing one of her school text books.

"Papa, see this is my new book. It's got hundred stories you see!"

I resonated her wonderment, "Oh really, let me see." I took the book and started flipping the pages.

"But papa", she asked while skewing her eyes, "How come that every time I finish a story, I have to learn its moral lesson. Stories are always interesting but their lessons are never. Tell me papa, why do people always end up the interesting stories with the boring lessons?"

Perhaps I was able to understand the quandary of little child. I knew the answer but didn't know how to make her understand that. Nevertheless she was merely a child for all this. I laughed on her anxiety but she remained only unappeased.

"Papa! Don't laugh but tell me the answer", she began insisting.

"O my Chichi! I find you too small to understand the real answer."

"But anyways tell me that. I want to hear from you", Maina said.

"Yes, yes, Mr. Wise", Annie bugged in while just coming around. "Only I had sent Maina to you for this. After all where else we would have found a pundit like you?" She laughed a taunt.

I too mocked at Annie. Seeing this Maina began laughing. I

asked the child to bring me a piece of paper and pen. She rushed in and brought me the same instantly.

"Papa! What are you doing?" Maina had started peeping from above my shoulder.

"I am writing the answer you wanted."

"Ok", Maina said and watched me writing.

After I had written, I read it to her. Then I asked did she understand it.

She refused.

No fault of hers. But I knew what I was supposed to do about now. I folded the paper many times and made it a size of coin.

"Bring your piggy bank, Maina!" As I said, she rushed and brought it to me.

"Now listen carefully. I am dropping it in your piggy bank, right?" I said.

She cocked her head animatingly.

"Promise me whenever you will fetch your full piggy bank, you will read this paper. And unless you understand the meaning of my writing, you will put it in your next piggy bank every time. I am sure someday you will be amazed." I smiled and pinched her cheeks.

Maina thought we were playing some game, but she obediently followed. Later, when she was watching her favorite TV cartoon show, I took out my diary and wrote the same message again. It was:

"Moral of all childhood stories is one and the same – That how will you become able to cope the adversities of life when you will be risked to growing up."

FORTY ONE

God Connects Through Shadows

ONE NIGHT DURING MY divine vision, the small transparent mirror began to show me the strange things.

In my sight had arrived many sky-high mountains with only narrowed waists. Each of those was standing tall and appearing to look in opposite directions from each other. Those were of different colors and were made of different types of rocks. I intuited as if all those were completely unconcerned to each other, for there was no similarity at all, except their nearly equal height.

Although it was night time but I was able to view those vaguely. Feeling like seeing those closely, I came in the middle of all.

Now surrounded by mountains, I was taken aback by the strange voices being exchanged amongst those. I estimated that the mountains were quarrelling with each other. I didn't know their language, but for identifying a quarrel, language could never become an obstacle. Indeed this was nothing else but the din of bickering amongst mountains.

To my great wonderment, not long after as the sun had started rising, the tall mountains began taking shapes of human statues. And now, even as the Sun was growing higher in the sky, things started turning even more awe-striking.

Now even the sky-high statues of men were changing. Caused by the hot sunrays, whenever the shadow of one statue would stretch and fall upon the other, the latter would instantly turn into a live man. As Sun continued to become stronger in the morning, there had now remained not a single mountain or statue. There were only live human beings; all tremendously high.

Now pleasantly surprised about seeing themselves alive, they started talking about the shadows. Looking from bottom like a mosquito, I was perfectly able to grasp their language this time. They were dancing in the joy of getting life. They all remembered being statues and mountains in the past. They also remembered their bickering, which they never wanted to repeat. They talked that life had become possible for them only because of the shadows. They started believing that only shadows were their God. Soon, one of them came out and began writing on the ground:

"God always loves to give us life by way of connecting our shadows. Whether or not we ourselves connect ever, our shadows always do. Whether or not we move, our shadows always do. Such is the height of God's love for us."

As they all read the lines, they started singing too. Though I presumed that they would already know about turning into statues in the evening, and also into mountains at night, I was delighted for witnessing their happiness in the moment.

Just then, as my divine vision broke, I wondered that I had not thought about shadows in this way ever before. In human worlds, shadows existed not because of men, but those existed because of the sunlight. And invariably, this was also true; whether or not people would connect with each other willingly, their shadows would always do that.

FORTY TWO

When Beginner's Luck Fails

MY LIFE, ON ITS part, couldn't ever stop being an admixture of favors and adversities; though by grace of master, my own reaction towards these occurrences was seeing the radical changes.

On and off, I continued experimenting with several things in my apparent world. These experiments, however, did not always occur from my side deliberately, for these were also warranted by my ever changing scenarios. Such experiments were mostly about my work, career, colleagues, understanding with friends, my relationship with Annie, and also about my own competing mind sometimes.

Awhile all this was taking place I had started taking notice of another strange thing in my behavior. Often it happened that, on way of my any new experiment, I would get excessively enthused over the initial success. My mind would easily get carried away. But alas! At number of times I discovered that my initial success would not convert into a lasting one also. Many dreams, which were planned by me on the spur of initial success, would eventually tumble down. I would be left surprised, shocked and sometimes outraged too.

On each failure, it wasn't easy to stop wondering about 'whats' and 'whys'. Although it was not that I had to face only failure every time, but whenever I had to, my whole industriousness, which had gone into it, shattered into pieces.

Once, I sought to know about this from master. His reply came by way of wooden box. The message inscribed on the leaf was below:

"Son! You may name your ongoing quandary as 'beginner's luck'. If eventually this luck stops, do not consider it anybody's fault, not even your own. Isn't it the higher truth that luck, whether it's in the beginning or in the end, is nothing at all? It is merely the individual interpretation of the circumstances by man, which are taking place in the higher realm of spontaneity. Whatever has happened, is happening or will happen in your apparent world is guided through the spontaneity of life. You cannot change it, but certainly you can change the way you happen towards it. Beginner's luck must not sway you, because on this planet, no one can ever say that when and what is the actual beginning and when and what is the actual end of things. Therefore, seek perfection not in your luck, but in your interpretation of the spontaneity."

Truly, every time I came across master's words, I was spellbound.

FORTY THREE

One's Own Chosen Moral Duty

ONCE UPON A TIME, though humorous but quite a stirring incidence occurred with me. It had been more than a year that I had found an amazing friend in Mr. Johnson. He used to live in another city and I would pay him visits often. He was around twice of my age and had lately been a cardiac patient. In terms of experience and knowledge of life, he was quite impressive. By vocation he was an eminent businessman and was popular for his generosity and kindness towards all. Having a person like him in my life was no small privilege. Instantly we grew committed in the friendship and started sharing between us whatever true friends should. I was finding many great things to learn in his thoughts and deeds. For several reasons he would always seem to me a noble and ideal person.

But, as it should have been in a democratic relationship, there were also certain differences between our ideologies. For instance, I used to reprehend alcohol and non-vegetarianism whereas he was fond of both. On certain other matters as well we had different mindsets, but neither of us would ever force upon each other. Things were going well, unless a strange thing happened one night.

For past one week John (for 'John' was his favorite nick name) had been insisting me to join his secret birthday party. Partying a birthday was certainly not a troublesome event, but perhaps the way of celebrating he had chosen was. He phoned me to inform that on the appointed day I was supposed to reach at some place, where his other friends would also join in. The hatched plan was to have an all-gents party, wherein lots of booze and non-vegetarian foods were to be enjoyed. It was strictly amongst friends and not even family members of anyone were allowed. Sensing my hesitation during the phone call, although he assured me that nobody will force on me to have alcohol or meat, but I couldn't get rid of my apprehension completely. I hoped I was most sincere in wishing him the birthday, but it was an awkward place for me to be present late night. I pleaded for being excused but John didn't mend.

Exactly in the morning of appointed day, he phoned me to say that I was supposed to pick his other friend on the way, Kevin. Kevin, as a matter of coincidence, happened to live in the same city with me. Now on any possible pretext, I had remained no chance to escape or abscond from the booze party.

For me it was first time to meet Kevin. John had already texted me his friend's phone number so that I would connect the latter conveniently on the way. Driving my car, as I was nearing Kevin's place, my anxiety increased. About Kevin that day, whatever happened since afternoon till night was an astonishing experience for me.

Minutes after my last mile phone call with Kevin, I found him waiting for me outside the marketplace. On first sight I found him a young handsome man in his early forties. Wearing a strange red cloak, similar to that of eastern monks, he was standing over the footpath of a crowded lane. Indeed, he was astonishingly new to me. I waved my hands and his response to the same made it easy for both of us to recognize. I invited him in the car and offered a shake-hand. He responded to it very lively. As we began to talk, Kevin asked me to drift the car to his nearby home. He wanted to change his dress. I drove to his directions and reached his house soon. Tenderly, he took me on the first floor and introduced me with his mother and wife. He seemed quite nice in etiquettes. Seeking excused for a minute, he went inside a room and promptly came out in the changed dress. Now he was wearing a blue jeans and a bright T-shirt. Probably sensing my slight wonderment, he laughed and remarked that his previous dress was not for attending the parties.

As we came down the stairs, he showed me a secluded floor in which he used to run a mediation center. It was a big hall in basement. On its walls were hanging many life-size photos of renowned seers and religious exponents. The floor was carpeted for disciples' sitting. On the other end of the hall, there was also a raised altar, on which, I assumed, he himself would sit and preach.

While showing me the basement hall, Kevin had suddenly drifted to a corner and began to unplug some wires from a big box. He asked me to help him so that we could quickly put this box in the car outside. Awhile this he kept on boasting and taking pride in possessing such a wonderful music system for the meditation classes run by him. He said that this box was too excellent in playing the music and therefore he had planned to rock the party tonight with it. He had already informed Mr. Johnson about it. The anticipation of excitement came easy upon me.

Finally together we put the box into the car and started the journey. On way, we shared about each other's life. He told me about his high ideals for some particular saint or the other. He started giving accounts of many theological aspects and his knowledge into the same. During his talk in the car, several times it occurred to me that he was trying to justify the conflict about his clothing and mindsets. He bragged about his vow to keep from flesh and other bad habits continued till date. He also said that as per his religious staunch, he would never take wine or meat; but for sake of appeasement of his fastest friend John, he would make an exception with wine today. However about meat, he swore it several times to not take it in whatsoever case. He also appeared to keep the trait of friendship above all. Though I wondered it, but didn't offend to. It was bad to argue with a friend of friend.

Finally we arrived at the secret place of John's birthday. The charming host had already booked a two-bedroom suite in a private inn. All friends met in great zeal and instantly the party had taken off. Kevin was quick in assembling his musical boxes. In no time our place had started filling with vulgar music, boozy exhales and cigarettes' smoke. The series of so called fun and enjoyments went on and on. I was nothing more than a witness, for I didn't take wine, nor the chicken and nor the cigarettes. John, given that, was very loving and caring towards me. He ordered some snacks and beverages which I could've taken comfortably.

The party boomed. A couple of more friends had joined and soon it became a gathering of twenty people. Kevin had already grabbed the seat of music-jockey. He was changing all kinds of tunes for people's dance. Everyone was making one another drink and dance. Just then several new colors and shapes of wine-bottles had arrived. People's eyes brimmed even wider. They were joyful for the party and I was joyful for their joy. For once or twice, even if somebody tried insisting me for the wine, John forbade it carefully.

As grew the night, the flairs of intoxication mounted on people's head. After several continued hours of boozing and dancing, John cut the cake and all friends showered him with cheering carols and gifts.

However, after the cake and before late night dinner, a strange thing happened. Swaying in tipsiness, right in front of my eyes, John handpicked a plate of chicken-balls and approached Kevin to eat. So far in the party, though having taken lots of wine, Kevin had actually refrained from meat. Dancing on the musical tunes, John began to pour a chicken-ball into Kevin's mouth, who was sitting on the sofa. Latter asked, what was that?

John insisted that it was merely a piece of fried chicken and was superbly tasty. Kevin resisted.

"For me, please. Just one", very earnestly John requested. He was hanging his face very near to Kevin's.

"Oh! Is it so my friend? Then let your wish become my wish."

Having said this Kevin opened his mouth and took in the same.

I was watching all this animatingly, though unsurprised. Kevin, in the day, had already agreed to break his vow about wines. And now he had broken it about meat as well.

In some time the dinner arrived. Fortunately it was all vegetarian. I had a perfect fill for myself. After dinner, all friends thanked John for the amazing party and bade adieu to each other before returning to their homes. I also dropped Kevin on the way and drove to my home with loads of experiences in my mind.

Merely two days after, when it was Sunday, Kevin called me on the phone and started talking about that wonderful night. I couldn't sound anything except being courteous to his tales.

During the same phone call he now told me the most astonishing thing. He said that on the following day of party he had phoned John and asked why at all did the latter insist on him to eat the chicken balls? John, on the other side of phone call, was literally surprised that whether he had really done this? The host had prayed to be excused, for he didn't really remember anything. He said that he was so badly inebriated other night that he didn't know what he was doing.

While telling me all this now, Kevin was sounding submissive. He had lost his two vows; one for the wines by his own choice; and another for meat by the choice of a forgetful friend. After the phone call was over, I grew curious. How it happened? Whose fault was it? Whom to blame?

Next day while walking in the central orchard, master began laughing upon this. To my question, he said it was not much useful for me to worry about so many things happening in the world. He repeated that it was only my position towards others which was important; and not the position of others towards me.

When I asked that how should I perceive things for myself if I am caught in similar situation some time, he merely said that I must stick to my 'chosen moral duty'. Upon my insisting, he explained in detail.

Talking about the broken vow of any person like Kevin,

Master said:

"Man has been bestowed the fundamental freedom of choosing his moral duty. Later he can even change such choice when allowed by his discernment and conscience. However given the worldly allures often, one's own moral duty must remain to be a guide-map for him. Neither must he compare his own moral duty with that of other; nor should he forsake his own for the sake of someone else's. In both the cases it amounts to error, wherein the former gets bereft of his equanimity, and the latter lands only in fear."

FORTY FOUR

Childhood Returns Easily

ONE DAY AN EXPERIENCE came small but in a subtle way. I was standing in a neighborhood chemist shop and inquiring about some medicine for mother. Just casually my gaze had fallen on the long shelves which were displaying the baby diaper pads for sale. There were numerous identical packets in a row, and printed on the covers of each was picture of a laughing toddler. Sight of laughing babies always made me smile, even when those were merely the printed images. Particularly in that moment, I didn't know what happened to me, but my eyes had glued with those identical pictures. Maybe I have had seen those pictures in the same shop earlier as well, but this time I was finding those more striking than ever. I continued seeing the laughing babies until the attendant was ready with my bill. I paid it and before checking out, I glanced upon the laughter once again.

While walking towards home, still having that baby in mind, I compared, whether I was also similarly beautiful in my toddling days? Even to this day, mother couldn't stop talking about what a darling baby I was in my days. But now I wondered, after so many years, how could I see my childhood laughter once again?

Just in a moment when I turned to the lane of my house, one of my neighbors came across. It was late evening time and he had come for taking a walk outside. As usual he was holding his grandson in his lap. The young naughty baby, whose name was Shaurya, was already a darling to many in our society. I would never miss a chance to tickle its belly. I'd always loved to watch it laughing and pushing my hands away from tickling.

I repeated the act of tickling this time as well. As soon as it laughed, it jumped to me from its grandfather's lap.

Oh! Can somebody really know unless he himself experiences it, that what a great privilege it feels? A small baby leaving his grandfather's lap and coming to you for a moment! I made lisping talks with little darling. Although it was too young to speak or respond to my words, but it gestured about all. To amuse it, as I sounded a whistle from my mouth, it also rounded its lips and tried imitating. Now, more than the baby, it was I and its grandfather laughing. Thinking that we'd enjoyed its faint trial of whistling, the baby started clapping and cocking its head.

Then suddenly baby started staring into my eyes and raising its both hands upwards. I instantly knew what it wanted. It was not the first time. As I carefully moved the baby away from the chest and held up in the air, it brimmed in excitement. Though it was too young to speak a word, it already knew what I was about to do. I tossed it little in the air. The joyous childish shrieks spread in the air. As I did it more, the baby's laughter grew louder.

Just in this moment I felt as if the laughing picture of baby had printed in my heart. As I stopped, it wanted me to do the same again. I did too, but for fewer numbers of times. I had some idea that too much swinging in the air might cause the baby slight dysentery.

When I didn't follow baby's upwards gestures again, it jumped back to its grandfather's lap. After exchanging a quip with my neighbor, I shook baby's chin and waived my hands to say goodbye. As all children always do, it responded quickly. While coming towards the stairs to my apartment, I imagined the laughing baby once again. I also thought about the printed photos seen by me in the chemist shop. Weren't these all smiles really the same?

Indeed those were. After all, when the children are too small, they look mostly similar; and even their smiles seem identical. In the moments of climbing the stairs I easily knew how I myself would have looked smiling, when I was too young in good old days. Surely, I also would have laughed in the same way whenever somebody had tossed me in the air.

As I rang the doorbell of my apartment, it was Annie opening the door. I couldn't know how she did, but she had read my eyes accurately.

She asked animatingly, "Mr. Rube! Was it Shaurya again?"

Oops! Whenever it came about reading my mind, Annie was the smartest one. Noddingly, my smile became even wider.

Later, on the dining table, I narrated to all what I had seen in the chemist shop and also about my kidding with Shaurya downstairs. To this, mother smiled and remarked that one's childhood easily comes back while playing with children.

Having listened to the story, Maina also started insisting for tossing herself too. I broke my laughter. I said perhaps she had grown more than I could hold in the air. But she didn't relent and continued insisting.

For once, even I thought giving it a try. As I picked her little high, I could do that twice before giving up finally. To save myself and make the girl laugh, I pretended to drop away my tongue like a dog. It was all mirth in the air.

Instinctively, I was watching the smiles of everyone here. Smiles, of all kinds and in all ages, were always the same.

It was certainly a good evening; all about smiles; that too the childish ones.

FORTY FIVE

Austerity is the Key to a Fulfilled Life

ONCE I HAD AN opportunity of attending a lecture upon the subject of austerity. Somehow I couldn't interpret the speaker's words perfectly and started evaluating the perceived thoughts in my own life. My error of fallible interpretation actually led me to a chaotic state of mind. I was wrongly assuming that stinginess in my ways of life was supposed to be my austerity.

But thankfully, before I could have erred any big, master saved me. I was merely on the brink of introducing some harshest measures in my life ways, when master, in order to recalibrate my perception, had sent a wooden box message. As always, he had given a gem insight for me. He wrote:

"Son! I am not surprised for your error. Sometimes one cannot implement a doctrine without adequate guidance. You must clearly know that austerity is a self chosen penance, hence empowering; whereas stinginess is a self imposed curb, therefore bringing misery. Former is perfection of mind but latter is a continued fault. Austerity is about disciplining the needs of your physical life that you live in your outer ways; but stinginess, on the other hand, is a harsh regulation of same. Self-discipline always works better than harsh-regulation. No wonder that discipline bestows contentment; whereas conversely, regulation creates revolt."

FORTY SIX

Pain and Relief: Where are Both?

ONE DAY, ACCIDENTLY, A small pin goaded deep into my finger. Few drops of blood poured out and I felt the necessary momentary pain. I believed such a little matter it was that it won't require my attention. To an extent, my presumption came true as well, but not entirely however.

Later in the day I realized that whenever the said finger would accidently hit any object, a new short spell of pain would start. Though interestingly, instead of focusing on my slight injury or pain, I had started noticing my behavior towards it. Every time it hit, a tinge of blood would show and I would grow extra careful; though eventually my mind would be lost in other things and forget the finger. In such moments, if however it hit back, it would snatch my attention again.

Was I finding it up to intolerable pain? Certainly not! But the pin goading in my finger was doubtlessly successful in snatching my attention again and again. The hurt was equally painful every time. I wondered why my mind's momentary carelessness about finger couldn't be refrained completely. And if this was to continue, won't the pain stop ever?

Since only one finger was paining, I had now changed the way of operating my hands. I would try to keep this finger away and work with the rest ones. To a considerable extent it went successfully. I was no longer hitting it by accidents, and therefore no more painful chance occurred. It had been few hours now of my careful painlessness and I believed it was the end of my small infliction cycle.

But perhaps, knowing the real start and end of cycles was far from my grasp; so what if the matter was as small as a pin hurt. More accidental hurts, actually, couldn't be refrained completely. However careful I was trying to go about it, I would err and face the music. By the end of the day, I became sure that it was not the pin hurt paining me, but it was something else. But what?

Now, the very moment I thought this, the funny part of the whole matter emerged. What was it focusing and diverting my mind on the cyclic pain or relief again and again? Who was it giving me the repeating experiences? Who was it afraid of the pain and also assured of the impending permanent relief in some time? Although I had known that the instance of pin hurt was only insignificant, but still, who was it drawing and reinstating my attention into the same again and again?

Momentarily I thought that I had good questions to ask from master, but I stopped. What a foolish idea it was to bother my great master for a trivial matter of pin-hurt!

After taking my dinner as followed by relaxed ambling downstairs, I returned and settled on my study table. I started gathering my questions. Having opened my diary at first, I wrote all the questions perfectly. I imagined, what, if master was here, would have answered.

Oh! What a magnificent moment it was! I felt as if the answers of master himself had started emerging in my own thoughts. These answers were unbiased and as authentic. I glanced and smiled upon the diary and penned down below:

"Pin-hurt in man's finger is nothing but a coincidence taking place in the operation of nature; however man's reaction to it is an event taking place in the operation of mind. Pain occurs nowhere else but in mind, and similarly, relief also occurs therein only. The sense of protecting finger from hurt also arises in the mind. And what say more! Even the need of comparing between the two states of pain and relief also takes place in alone the mind. Indeed, it's entirely about mind and nothing else."

I read my words again and wondered, would have master approved those. Though my language couldn't be as perfect as it were if dictated by master himself, but I thought I was able to express what I wanted to.

Instantly, in the same moment, I felt as if master's smiling face had flashed across my eyes. I brimmed in joy. I knew it, he was happy for the way I was able to meditate without him this time. A trivial matter was only a suitable start for me. In my continued joy, I moved into the bedroom and slept. Later at night, I didn't know what time it was, but my mind was striking another great idea. It was merely one sentence, which perhaps I had forgotten to add in my diary. Following morning, the first thing I did was to complete my paragraph. It was:

"And various experiences after pin goading into finger are merely in the token of functioning of the life."

FORTY SEVEN

Escaping Big Accidents
but Hurting by Smalls

THERE WAS A TIME when my casual attitude towards the trivial matters of life became exposed to master. Though I had been uncompromisingly sincere, careful and industrious towards the significant matters of life, but towards the ones which I assumed only insignificant, my attitude was just reverse. I would give my cent percent attention to the ninety percent things of life, whereas would undermine the rest ten percent. For example, in office I would prepare the large part of a project report astoundingly wonderful; but would not give my best to the later small part of it. Neither at home my approach was different.

One morning, during a conversation being made in the orchard, master came to know about this matter. He mystically said, "Son! I will give you a small experience tonight."

For I was already anticipating it, the divine vision occurred to me that night. Holding the mirror in my hands I was intrigued.

I saw that I was ambling on the footpaths of a familiar highway. In evening hours the road was raging with zipping past vehicles. Not long after I felt like crossing the highway and reaching on the other side. I looked around but didn't find any foot-over bridge in vicinity. Wondering about crossing on foot, I glanced upon the rushing vehicles. There were cars, trams and all other kinds of. It seemed quite a tricky business to cross, but nevertheless I wanted to.

I anticipated the possible chance for me. Standing on the

brink of road I waited and judged my exact moment of rushing. I thought, however difficult it could appear, it won't be difficult for me. Crossing a road is nonetheless a trivial challenge. The very moment I found a suitable gap amongst the rushing vehicles, I jumpstarted my running.

My guessing about the closing-in vehicles was alright as usual. Smartly and safely I was able to evade the cars and trams. I had almost made it, though just about when I was reaching the opposite side's footpath, I didn't know from where under the high heavens, a rushing bicycle had landed in my way. Even though I had successfully evaded many heavy vehicles, but sick to my habit, I was undermining anything less dangerous. Just evading a car and rushing ahead, I banged into this bicycle. I slipped and dropped on my wrists. In the moment of tumbling I tried seeing the face of the culprit cyclist, but he fled. Lying down on the dangerous road, as I wanted to stand up, I found that my right hand wrist was not moving as per my wish. Perhaps it was broken. My knees were also bruised against the concrete.

Aah! How terrible the pain grew! It became an impossible wrist. Something was broken; either muscles or the bones inside. Just then I felt some liquid flowing behind my ear. I touched it with my left hand and saw. I was hot blood. I started losing my consciousness. Hoping to be only on the safer side of the road, I fell down. I didn't know for how long I had been unconscious there.

In that horrifying moment, I came back to my nerves about sleeping in the bedroom. My divine vision broke and I reminisced the forewarning of master. Indeed he had given me an experience along with a lesson. I had cared about the big things like cars and trams; and therefore escaped those successfully. But I had slighted the trivial things such as a bicycle, and it brought me no less amount of trauma.

I realized that master's concern over my casual attitude was actually well grounded. Instead of giving me a lesson in real life, he had done the same through divine vision. He had shown me my lackluster and also warned beforehand.

Following early morning when I turned to the wooden box, it showed me a new message:

"Son! Your living in the apparent world, no doubt, must come through your dutiful karma; but you do not bring greatness to it unless you make it skillful karma as well. You must not abandon your pursuit for perfection in the middle, not even while nearing the end. You must take it forward, not only till the end of job, but even further. For human beings, I repeat, it is indescribably difficult to know the real beginning or the end of the things. All they must do is only to continue the perfection."

Nodding my head again and again, I became reflective.

FORTY EIGHT

Apparent World is only a Muckle of Conditioned Harmonies

"DO YOU KNOW SON, when and how the human mind starts conditioning itself?"

Other day in the center of orchard, an interesting discussion had started. It happened, that I had asked master why my mind would usually think different from others, and not even that, sometimes different from myself too at two different occasions. I was arguing my wonderment basically on the contention that when I had already known enough about the secret world and apparent world, why at all the illusions of several kinds were still swaying my head.

Master continued humorously, "Understanding the subject of conditioning of human mind is quite an interesting deal. And the wonderment is that unless a man attains quite-some perfection in the secret world, the conditioning of his mind in the apparent world doesn't stop. Intermittently however, due to his efforts and establishing position in the secret world, his conditioning of mind may halt; but largely his situation remains back and forth only."

"What exactly the conditioning of human mind is, master?" I asked.

He started revealing, "For man, participation in an activity causes a particular kind of experience; and consequently such experience causes the conditioning of his mind in such a way, that mind starts reconciling its past and future experiences as well with the experience had by it in present. No wonder, this all functions in an endless cyclic chain. More the mind participates, more it experiences, and therefore more it participates again."

"But master, is such conditioning of mind always bad?" My curiosity was increasing.

He breathed deep and replied, "For so long as this cycle of participation and experience continues taking place bereft of the eternal truth established in secret world, the answer to your question is - yes."

Hearing this, I wanted to evaluate my own perfection in the eternal truth gained so far, but master just added, "But remember, once a human mind gets settled in the eternal truth, it rises beyond the question of conditioning itself."

"But master, won't such utmost perfection be very difficult?" I apprehended.

"No, it depends upon one's own will. Nothing is difficult in this eternity except what has been accepted by your mind to be so", he said and laughed.

I began wondering in my heart. For master, I thought, it was easy to assert because he himself had already attained the perfection. But for me, it was perhaps not yet.

"Oh master! But how this imperfection be overcome?" I asked in guise for myself.

"Supreme knowledge is the way to begin, but again, it's not alone sufficient. After 'JnanaYoga', 'KarmaYoga' has to follow. In other words, after attaining the supreme knowledge, it is the supreme experience which is necessary for establishing oneself in the perfection forever. Though both are necessary, but it is only latter which fructifies your efforts."

"Master, you already know my perplexing! Perhaps I haven't perfected. What's the word for me?" I asked.

"It's the same, son! Know more. Not that you need to know new things every time, but you only need to know better. Do not halt your quest for supreme knowledge; for your supreme experience is only the result of the former. You don't finish taking bath unless you soak your body in water completely."

"Oh!" I exclaimed and pleaded, "I think the root cause of my perturbation is in the conditioning of my mind. Impart therefore O master, the supreme knowledge to banish this conditioning."

To this master replied, "Let me give you an analogy. Then after you can meditate and expand its meaning for you."

This time I was more careful about the precept than analogy.

He guided while pointing his finger in far, "Look at that tall standing board and tell me what color it is?"

"It's red, master", I replied.

"You see it as red because you have been knowing the same color as red since your beginning, is that true?" He asked.

I nodded my head.

"But can you believe this? Maybe I am seeing that as yellow, but still calling it red because I have been knowing the name of whatever color seen by me there as red only. We both call it same, but see differently. And this phenomenon is merely an example. Similar wonderments about tastes, sounds, smells and touches are constantly taking place in myriads."

"But master", I interrupted, "between yellow and red, how it is possible?"

He laughed and replied, "Seeing upon a color, like we are doing in this moment, is one of the kinds of our experiences in the apparent world; and speaking the name of it is of another kind. Both these experiences may be true in our respective understandings, but not necessarily those will actually reconcile always. Take a careful note of this. Since your cradle days maybe you have been seeing this color as blue, but calling it red; and since my childhood maybe I have been seeing it as yellow but calling it red again. We both do this because although we are seeing differently, but from the days of our beginnings we both have been taught to call it as red only. This matter's another dimension is following. You say, for example, your favorite color is blue and I say my one is yellow; but we both do not actually know which color we are talking about. When for the first time an infant baby starts recognizing colors, it never knows or calls red as red or yellow as yellow. But it's its parents who teach it all about names. And no parents can teach their children more than what they have themselves known or been calling the things as. After all, haven't they also been living in the apparent world, which is nothing but a bundle of conditioned harmonies? Colors as expounded by me here, is merely one of the facets."

He indeed knew supreme, I was sure.

"For another example", master continued, "maybe you are finding the air cool in this moment but it is warm in my experience. What will you say when air is just the same for both of us? Will you try to prove either of us wrong or right? Will you say that my experience is false and your one is correct?"

"No master, I don't think it will make any sense", I submitted to his rationale.

"Therefore", he said, "you and me both are calling that board red, whereas we might be seeing it differently at present. The colors we see are different but merely the names given to it by both of us is common. Now the crux is here. It's nothing else but our individual conditionings of mind which is fortunately agreeing in the actual environment of disagreements. No wonder that sometimes it may also disagree in the environment of agreement, especially when two human cultures have been starkly aloof from each other. Son, if this analogy is to be trusted, aren't both of us living in illusion? In this way haven't we really conditioned our minds in the apparent world?"

I nodded in silent submission.

"You must meditate on this, and then you will acquaint more dimensions of the eternal truth. As I once spoke on the hills, this entire exercise will take you to the common destination, which is none but the oneness amongst all. Now listen carefully, only this oneness is called the eternal truth which has to be known and experienced by you."

While walking in the park master shared few more of his experiences. Then after he asked me to leave and join my apparent world. Reluctantly, I came back.

FORTY NINE

Curing the Spoilt Body and Mind

"YOU ARE NOT YOUR body or mind; you are above both."

One day when asked about how to cure if body and mind go spoilt and do not heed the calls of reformation, master stared replying.

He said, "If you practice and meditate, it will become your very nature to stand firm in the faith, that your real existence is much wider than your physical existence. Body and mind are only the instruments of your physical existence. They both get spoilt when you stray from the higher principle. And the only way to reform the two is to reestablish them in the same higher principle again and again."

"But master! What if both become too hostile to heed any?" I asked.

He took a pause and began smiling. He said, "Although one's body and mind may drag him to the ditch of desire born misery, yet he is not supposed to revenge the two any offensively. Just like a father who never stops trying to reform his spoilt child, man also must never stop trying to reform the two. He must constantly allure the both towards the beatific excellence on the greater path."

FIFTY

Changing Destiny is Possible

IN THE WOODEN BOX, once master wrote about destiny:

"It is only one's natural right to change his destiny by way of changing his karma. For instance, even though someone has cursed you from his heart, you can overcome the cursed ill-wish by way of repenting your earlier bad karma and performing the reformed karma now. The role which divinity plays in the course of human life is never rigid. Instead it actively responds to the quality of your Karma. This divinity sees your karma and turns it out into your destiny accordingly. And son! You must grasp this matter also. Such divinity does not reside somewhere else in the cosmos, but it ambles around the man himself always."

FIFTY ONE

The Evidence of Sub-conscious Mind

SOMETIMES I FELT AS if master couldn't stop being in funny moods. He became childish. He would tell me a story or two, and then in turn, would ask me to do the same. When I refused to know any story up to his stature, he would insist to know the stories from my own life. Though rare, but these moments were awkward for me. After all, didn't I already know that there was nothing unknown to him about my life?

Ignoring his wish for the stories, even if I tried asking my complicated questions again and again, he would reprimand me by saying, "Why do you have so many questions always!" And even then if I continued insisting the questions, he would give only half answers and leave the rest to my own meditation.

Once in the similar moments I was trying to know from him whether the sub-conscious mind really existed or not.

Before making a face and informing that he was going away to count all the trees in the orchard, he replied merely this, "Doesn't your mind sometimes notices that, just like a motion picture, exactly the same moment has happened with you previously as well? How do you think it is made?"

FIFTY TWO

Any Creative Expression is Art

ONE DAY WHILE READING newspaper, I came across a news that a painting made of nude woman was successfully auctioned for two million dollars. As my curiosity unfolded, I found that there were similar other examples as well.

Following day during morning walk, master commented on the matter in this way.

"Do not mistake art to be useful for creating astonishments only. Creative expression in any form is art. It shouldn't matter to you how somebody else, either being a creator or spectator, is operating; instead you must take care of your own creative expression of life. Set your own good examples of creative expression, and contribute in this way to your environment and societies."

After taking a brief pause, master laughingly added, "And son, appearing in newspaper has nothing to do with the creative expression of life. Life is much bigger than the bigness projected in news."

FIFTY THREE

When Poison Mixes with another Poison

ON ONE HAND WHEN I was growing better in personal life with the help of master, in professional life things were not improving at all. Mark Dallisi, my employer, was becoming more whimsical by every passing day. The known handful flatterers were constantly fueling him against me and my small team. Though I was aware of it since long, but I couldn't know the way of coping with. One day, all of a sudden, Mark summoned me in his chamber and informed that he had decided to dismantle my team and fire a handful of people. This news traumatized me. Mark was trying to explain the reasons which appeared only the vehement excuses in my opinion. Though he had retained my own services at least, but he had lost any good place in my heart. I knew very well that it was concocted by those cunning flatterers in the office. Mark had been heeding to them in an undue spirit. In the evening, I couldn't face my team members who had just been handed over their pink slips.

I couldn't sleep that night.

And the next day it was worse. News was in the air that Mark had decided to not only promote that bunch of flatterers, but also to reward them in various ways. He was going to allot them a slight part of equity, in ESOPs, so as to share the ownership of company with those crooks.

I was not able to contain it. How a foolish man like Mark could decide the fates of people. Those who had been working hard and sincerely in my team were robbed of their jobs only yesterday; whereas the evil-minded ones were being showered with rewards and promotions.

I couldn't comprehend God's justice in this. I simply couldn't contain. I myself wanted to resign, but the financial insecurity at home didn't let me. The entire day was havoc. After returning to home in evening, I left a note in my diary:

"When one kind of poison mixes with another kind, it may interest only those who are proud manufacturers in poisons. Only such people will be keen to innovate, and even be ready to invest in the facilities for creating even fatal admixture of poisons."

That night, desperately, I tapped the wooden box again and again, but it didn't open. I felt too lonely.

Following morning in the park, master appeared and walked with me. He knew that I was silently mourning. He didn't speak a word.

I didn't know what and how to ask him about the matter. We continued walking in silence. After about an hour when it was the time to go back home, I somehow gathered my broken self and asked,

"Why this injustice, master?"

"Son! You must not grieve over this. The spontaneous operations of nature are too complex to be explained by a reason every time. Human mind is too frail to comprehend the true distinction between justice and injustice; and also between beginning and the end of the things. On your part, remain content in yourself and remain empathetic towards both - the victims and the oppressors. I say, both, because man will never get to know that who indeed is the victim and who indeed is the oppressor in this great grind of time."

"But master", I asked in unfathomable pain, "isn't this all a fierce bias? How will I contain it?"

"Do not wail over it. Concentrate solely upon your dutiful karma and nothing else. Even though others' biases have nothing to do with your dutiful karma, but since you have wished to know, I will expound this matter for you. Biases are of two kinds.

Natural biases are those which occur due to the spontaneity in the operations of nature. Imposed biases, on the other hand, are all about human influences. Latter is the kind, which you have been facing these days. In natural biases man has no role at all, for he can only participate in their operation. Similarly in the case of imposed biases, again man has only a little to do. Always remember that man can either participate in or influence upon the biases, but he can never create those. It's alone the flow of spontaneity which can create or cease the biases. Man has never been an entity in doing that."

I had started understanding master's philosophy.

FIFTY FOUR

What to do with
Past, Present and Future?

ONE DAY ON SOME matter, master rebuked me, "Why you always seem appreciating your past more than your present? If you say that Dwapara-yuga was better than the present Kali-yuga, soon you will say that Treta-yuga was even better than Dwapar-yuga. And you might not hesitate in even saying that Sata-yuga was even better than Treta-yuga. Isn't it really worthless to figure the times in this way? By doing this, do you get any relief from discharging your duties in your present age?"

I tried reasoning and said, "But master, weren't the old ages indeed better than present?"

He replied, "We have already discussed this matter once. You are getting it wrong. If you continue thinking in this way, I won't be surprised if someday you will say that January is always better than February; March better than February; and so on."

I contended, "But weren't the people living in Dwapara-age and before more wise and reformed?"

"How can this be true but?" Master reprimanded me and asked, "What's the use at all, of talking about other people? Let us talk here about you alone, for this is what matters to you most."

Though not fully convinced, I didn't stretch the discussion. Later in the day, master concluded his answer through the wooden box. He wrote on the leaf:

"Past has only one utility, that you can take lessons from it.

Present is all what you have and you must appreciate it with a positive outlook. And also that, future should never be anticipated bereft of hope. Do not forget that even ancient ages like Sata-yuga, Treta-yuga and Dwapara-yuga had demons and satanic spirits, or didn't they? Getting to see demons and evil spirits in your present age again, is no sufficient reason to disregard the goodness existing in it at the same time."

FIFTY FIVE

Make Your Wishes Wise

NO WONDER THAT WHATEVER good thought could spring in my mind ever, it was due to the grace of master. Life had never been immune of varied experiences. One day I got engrossed in a new thought and contemplated upon it. I ended up writing the following conclusion in my diary:

"Man nevertheless achieves whatever is persistently wanted by him. It cannot happen that one ends up achieving what he has not been wanting consciously or subconsciously. Strong repulsion towards a thing or person is also a kind of negative want, which eventually turns into man's actions of hatred or hostility. The creation of an individual's apparent world is nothing but amassing of one's own persistent wants. To make one's world wise, first his wishes must become wise. Gross human life is all about the human wants; and its perfection is vested into making these wants wise."

FIFTY SIX

Why doesn't Vice Die Forever?

ONCE I HAPPENED ASKING this from master, "If vice is the negative energy amidst creation, why doesn't it get perished at once? You have been saying that vice never persists for long, but if it's so, why at all sometimes it takes too long to perish?"

He laughed. Perhaps amused by my curiosity, he replied, "Son, if you sift your question carefully, you will find the answer therein itself."

Sometimes I simply didn't understand his ways.

Finding me aloof he clarified, "Who you think must perish? Is it vice or the instrument of vice?"

Still I didn't understand much. "What is instrument of vice, master?" I asked.

"It's simple, son! Vice is an attribute, whereas instrument of vice is its career. For example violence is an attribute, whereas a human body which indulges in the violence is its instrument or career. Now rethink about it. Whom you want to get perished, attribute or instrument?"

Instantly a powerful reflection occurred on me

Master laughed. He said, "That is why I said that your answer was lying in only your question. Can't you comprehend the answer now?"

"Oh master! Indeed I am able to do that now. But still, tell me why the attribute of vice hidden in man takes too long to perish?" I asked.

"That is an ongoing battle between the attribute and its instrument. Do you see it my son! It's easy to start a battle but to finish is not. This is the reason it takes longer sometimes", master replied.

"Can vice win as well?" I asked on height of curiosity.

"No, it cannot. The best it can do is merely to appear winning. Eventually it has to only lose out."

"After losing", I asked master again, "does vice die forever?"

He broke into laughter once again. He proclaimed in joy, "It's now that you have asked a question of substance."

I was all ears.

He replied, "Dies only that, which takes birth. Vice is as immortal as is the virtue. Neither of the two takes birth and therefore neither of those dies ever. They both co-exist, however dominating one over other from time to time. What eventually die are only the instruments and careers, such as the human bodies. On your part, being a human being, all you can do is to take part in this battle and choose one of the sides for yourself."

"Hmm..." I uttered.

"Nevertheless my son," he rolled his eyes and added, "You have only limited time on this planet. Choose wisely and promptly which side to take. Once you've started waging this battle, you can only play well from your side, for its finishing is not your jurisdiction."

I looked about his face when he added again, "And yes, if you think you have taken a wrong side by error, you are very much free to change it anytime."

I couldn't stop admiring him. He was indeed a master.

FIFTY SEVEN

What is Maya or Cosmic Illusion?

WHEN ASKED IN DETAIL about Maya or the cosmic illusion one day, master enlightened me with following words:

"Every moment in human life, people can't stop seeing and experiencing innumerable conflicts in the operations of apparent world. However these conflicts do not dwell somewhere outside but only inside the minds of people, who are reacting and acting upon those in accordance with their individual perceptions. Given that, whenever all these small conflicts are amassed, it is called the great dichotomy of existence. In every instance of human life, people have two or more conflicting options to choose from. They choose either of those and forget the others. Such choice, once made, takes them to another set of conflicting options to choose from. Once again they choose one and forget the others; and in this way the chain continues interminably. Son! Only such human tendency of choosing one conflict and forgetting the other actually helps building the Maya around him. I repeat, conflicts never dwell in people, materials or situations; but those dwell in the perception of man. Doing away with the conflicts of all kinds whatsoever, is doing away the Maya; whereas anything other than that is about embracing the Maya."

Hearing this from master I asked, "Is Maya too bad for mankind?"

To this master turned very thoughtful. Only in a moment he could give small but perfect reply. He said, "No. Maya is not bad, only human ignorance about it is."

"But doesn't Maya forfeit the beneficence of mankind?" I

asked.

To this master replied, "Yes, it appears doing so, but you cannot blame Maya for it. Maya and the eternal truth both exist in the nature. Man's choice for either of two is always his own. On one hand where Maya forfeits the beneficence of mankind; the eternal truth expands it on the other."

"Then master, what makes man choose Maya over the eternal truth?" I asked.

"It's the same." Master replied, "Man's exaggerated need for gratifying the sense pleasure makes him choose Maya over the eternal truth. Soon he gets entangled in the bigger web when he makes several similar choices one after another."

To this I asked further, "Then how can one get rid of Maya?"

"It's easy, son!" He replied, "If man chooses for eternal truth, he starts getting rid of Maya."

To this I protested, "Only theoretically it seems easy but once the man has fallen trapped in the bigger web of Maya, I know well, it becomes nearly impossible to get rid of?"

To this master smiled and said, "Then there is another way also."

I was all ears.

He continued, "Man must cause Maya to perish for him."

"Perish!" I wondered.

"Yes, the very moment man comes to know that it is Maya, it vanishes for him. And more consistently Maya remains vanished, it perishes as well. Actually ridding Maya lies in recognizing it. Even as the very moment you figure out smoke appearing to be cloud, the cloud disappears; similarly Maya disappears after knowing the truth."

Today master had revealed a great precept, for I was turning very reflective now.

Here he concluded the matter in brilliance. He said, "Man's own mind, only when righteously cultured, can play significant role in defying Maya in the every aspect of his life. Although Maya is more powerful than gravity, yet man can conquer it by flowing along in the awareness. Remember, only awareness, or also called awakeness is the key. Flowing against Maya is not needed; it is only awareness of it what is needed."

Now an esoteric smile had come across my face too. I didn't have words to express my gratitude to the master.

FIFTY EIGHT

Where is the Light Most Needed?

ANOTHER DAY, TALKING ABOUT reflection and introspection, master bestowed me one great insight.

He explained in terms of an analogy and said, "Being in a totally dark room, if you want to see your face in the mirror, you won't be able to. However if you are holding an electric torch in your hands, it won't do great if you throw light only on the mirror and not on your face. Light is not needed by the reflecting objects, but it is needed by what is being reflected. Darkness will prevail if man continues throwing light in the wrong direction. The right direction is the direction of Self only."

FIFTY NINE

The Biggest Insurance

"PEOPLE SOMETIMES USELESSLY HANKER upon the insecurities", one day master started saying.

I submitted my own position as well, "What to speak of others, master! Even I have not been an exception to this."

"Indeed, man's sense of insecurity is his greatest fear. Only this fear engages him into several nuisances upon himself and upon others", Master added.

"But here in the apparent world people also use to try organizing these insecurities by way of purchasing several kinds of insurance policies", I said.

Hearing this master began laughing. He said, "But the biggest insurance is somewhere else.

"What?" I asked.

"It's the protection by God Himself", he replied.

Now I felt something. I asked him again, "But master, aren't the people already protected by God always?"

He smiled and said. "Yes they are."

"Then why they still need to purchase the insurance policies of several kinds?" I asked.

At my comment master looked only indifferent. He replied, "There are several things that people do by their own choices. It has nothing to do with the ultimate protection by God. Though He provides this protection to everyone, yet only a few are able to avail its benefits."

"And who are those people, master?" I asked.

He laughed again and said, "It's those who pay the premium

of faith, that too, not monthly or quarterly, but in every moment of their lives."

I too laughed.

Master added, "Son! This entire creation won't exist in the next moment if God decides to not protecting it. The constant untiring operations of Sun, soil, water, air and other elements are protected by whom other than God?

"But I was talking at the much smaller scale of individual human life, master!" I tried reminding him.

"Neither human life is any different from the operations that I am talking about." He clarified and added, "There may be no harm in purchasing the insurance policies of various kinds, but at the same time, man must also remain awake in the biggest insurance by God. He must have faith in the biggest protection. And do you know, what is the finest expression of faith in relation to this matter?"

I set my curious gaze on master's face.

He replied, "It's abiding by the laws of nature and divine. It's living the righteous ways of life. God doesn't ask man to worship Him days and nights, but He asks the latter to live only righteously for his own beneficence. This is the premium one has to regularly pay to remain covered under the biggest insurance of God."

As I began nodding my head, he added, "Those who live under the protection of God, live far superior lives, or don't they?"

My nodding was more visible now.

SIXTY

Is Science Limited?

MASTER NEVER TURNED RELUCTANT about enlightening me. In due course of time, for me also it became irrelevant that whether his messages were reaching me via wooden box, the divine vision or from himself. His each word was soaked in ultimate wisdom and also in deep love for me. I couldn't ever know how to express my gratefulness towards him.

At one occasion, master talked about the scientific developments of modern age.

He said, "Many spiritual scholars disregard the modern science of your age, but it is inappropriate. The evolving science is a boon; for it takes you through the higher knowledge of nature and its operations."

"But master", I apprehended, "I still believe that modern science has failed to bring an ever-lasting bliss for man."

"That is because of the void between man's understanding of science and the science itself. Lacking is not in science, but it's in man's understanding about it", master said.

His words made me curious.

Master went on, "In opposite to general perception of people, science is not about creating, but it's about discovering what already exists. And even no less regard to it; for scientific development is inevitable for mankind's education about nature and its functions."

I was secretly appreciating master's modesty.

He continued, "Science will have no limitation in the present eon. It will go farthest till the discovery of eternal truth. Since the entity of eternal truth itself is unfathomable, scientific discoveries will able so illimitable."

"Then master", I asked, "How should one view today's science as?"

"Obviously he must view it as the means and not an end", He replied and added. "Finish line of scientific pursuit can't be anything but the eternal truth. And I must make it clear that discovery of eternal truth is nothing but the discovery of Self. Only this realization is the subtlest connection that you are supposed to establish between you and the nature, which you are made of. Alone this phenomenon is called self-realization, and there can be no bigger science than this."

Later in the day I tried expanding my own imagination about master's words. Surprisingly, I had started making few discoveries as well. Before going to bed at night, I penned the following in my diary.

"What is scientifically known today is what is perceived by human mind as existing today. Human perception rejects the existence of that which has remained unproven by the science yet. Given that, the very moment science proves the existence of what had remained unknown so far, the human mind accepts it. In this way, what we call as limitations of science today will become tomorrow the discoveries. It's alone the matter of time."

I further wrote that in current times science is only in its preliminary stage. It has entirely focused on the discoveries about gross matter. Once it will do the same sufficiently, it will start focusing on the subtler entities, such as existence. Eventually it will also expand its knowledge about the spirit. As of today, what is being rejected by science in the blind opposition to spiritualism, in due course of time, the very same doctrines will be propounded by it in the common interest. If spiritualism is all about spirit; science will also discover that spirit is nothing but all about self-realization only.

And I also wrote the newest thing that I had discovered myself. Writing in diary had also become a form of meditation for me.

SIXTY ONE

Deepest Unbiased Wish

WHENEVER PEOPLE ARE ASKED about their wellbeing, they reply only typically, "Yeah, it's alright."

Do they reply in this way only for getting rid of the questioner? But won't someone asking about their wellbeing be only a well-wisher to the latter? If yes, 'getting rid' shouldn't have been a question. Another facet of this conundrum was that, people would always reply the ditto words, even when they were not alright, and even when they were in rather terrible state.

When this wonderment started fancying me, I found that this jinx was common across the globe. Whatever community, religion or country people belonged to, but they would reply only the same. Languages could be different, but the reply was ditto same - "Yeah, it's alright."

What made it possible? What had brought this uniformity? Had earlier anybody taken notice of that?

One night, when all were in fit of sleep, I got up from the bed and came into study. I switched on the lamp and began to unfold the mufflers. I hoped the box would be kind upon me and would open. In a moment, I tapped, and yes, it opened.

Master's each word was a gem. This time, the leaf read:

"Some answers come so naturally that instead of expressing the state of reality, those start expressing the state of wish. The kind of answer you are wondering in this moment is also the same. To be 'alright' is the most common and strongest wish of the mankind. When people are replying in this way, they are actually confirming

their own wish upon them. Son, the bigger truth, which may however remain oblivious to one's understanding, is that, in the center of his heart, every man's strongest unbiased wish for himself is to meet the ever new joy. This 'ever new joy' is nothing else but God Himself. In higher realm, God is no one but Self. Being 'alright', that you've been wondering about, is actually the deep secret wish of man for finding his ever new joy. Summarily, only the realization of Self is the eternal joyful wish of every human being in this world."

SIXTY TWO

Sometimes Life Looks so much Painful

ONE MORNING I WOKE up to a slight fever and decided to stay at home. Although fever was not tormenting, I thought it was good chance for taking rest in my otherwise crushing life. As few hours passed, the fever brought me headache and dysentery as well. Before the noon time arrived, I was in a terrible state. However, resting in bed and being paid extra attention by Annie and mother were enough to comfort me.

In few hours Maina also returned from school. She was pleasantly surprised about finding me at home. When she had washed and taken her meals, Annie commanded her to sit quietly on the table and start reading the text books. In those days Annie had been going highly anxious about the school exams of Maina. She couldn't stop warning the child again and again, lest the latter might go careless in her studies. It was tremendously important to score good grades. As per Annie, last year also, it was only because of her efforts that Maina could score a position in her class.

Lying almost helpless in the bed, I certainly knew that Annie was screaming her claims only to make me hear and realize. Actually Annie had maintained a complaint that I would never take sufficient interest in Maina's school curriculum. However knowing today that I was not keeping well, Annie was hitting her taunts only passively. Already infighting with my stomach pain and headache, I couldn't protest her taunts.

Next to my bed, on the floor, Annie had now fixed a mini table for Maina. In a moment both had started the usual course.

Just as I was anticipating, Annie had started frowning over the slight mistakes made by child. Annie was scaring Maina that how would the latter score good grades in this way. Already fear ridden, Maina would make more mistakes; and this would increase Annie's heat even more.

I couldn't help but remain silent. For me it was no new thing. If at all I had tried intervening ever, Annie would only rebuke me for shunning this responsibility. Already burdened with myriad things in life, I would meekly withdraw from the argument. Bedridden as I was, today my standpoint could fall even terribly. For so long as I could, I continued ignoring the scene.

But not long after the things turned horrible. Despite repeated warnings, Maina couldn't stop incurring mistakes in her note book. Unbearably frowned, lo! Annie had just boxed upon the ear of child. Maina dropped her pencil and burst into tears. As she began crying, Annie tried to quiet her up; but no success. I got up from the bed and looked about. Annie already knew what I was about to say. Even though knowing that I had moved from the bed, she pretended avoiding an eye-contact. She fumed and showed like giving up. Almost crazily, she snapped and crushed the paper on which Maina was writing. She stood up and banged into the other room.

I looked at Maina. She was more terrified than inconsolable. I didn't know her solace but I asked her to come on for my caresses. She didn't move. I rushed into kitchen and fetched a glass of water for her. She took it but drank only little. I pulled her to my chest and comforted. I also looked for Annie, but found it dangerous to enter in her room.

Now I lifted up Maina in my arms and asked her to sleep in my bed. I also slipped in. Amidst sobbing she slept. Now I was alone and perplexed.

Not long after, Annie returned and asked whether I had taken my medicines. I nodded. She asked about milk for me. Now I craned my gaze for taking her notice. But oh! She had tied up a scarf around her forehead. I asked what had happened.

Making a long face, she replied that she had caught severe headache.

I didn't speak about Maina. When I inquired about mother, she replied that after her regular church visit, mother could come back in any moment.

Now Annie came down and sat on my bed. I asked, need I fetch her headache pills from the cabinet? She replied she had already taken two.

Very this moment, the door bell rang. Annie rushed to open. It was mother. As she came in from the door, she saw Annie's scarf.

"Rubert, you must see her doctor. Annie has started catching up this headache too often nowadays", mother said in worry.

I nodded.

"And how about you?" She came about me and asked.

"I am better. Only in this day I would be fine", I replied.

Now mother sat in the nearby chair. She began to detach her knee pads. Pain was visible in her gestures.

"I think even these pads have stopped working now. More often nowadays my arthritis pain has been going unbearable. Only God knows what plans He has left for me, but living in utter pain is no less than death." Mother's voice was very strained.

"Mother, maybe we can consult another doctor. I think your old medicines must be replaced", I said.

"There's no medicine to the old age, Rubert", she replied and began to move towards her room. Just then Annie had brought a cup of milk for Mother. Latter stopped and sat in the chair again. After taking the milk, mother suggested a quack treatment for Annie's headache and wished her well. While moving as she turned to the other side, she saw the topsy-turvy table of Maina and also the snapped folio of paper. She took no time in understanding all, but again, she kept quite. She came a roundabout my bed and saw Maina sleeping. She smeared her hand over child's forehead and moved into her room quietly.

Annie also said that she was going into bedroom for taking rest.

Now I was alone and struggling a mindful pessimism. Wasn't it such a terrible day? Everyone was looking dejected with life. In this moment I wondered as to what master would have said about the presented scenario. Surely he would not have paid much attention to it. He would have said that such times were merely cyclic. As per him, it was better to wait in silence than to act in distress.

A faint smile crossed my face. For past few months it had been coming easier upon me to intuit master's mind on various matters.

I turned a bit and saw Maina's face. In sleep, her face was not showing any pain. Perhaps that was how a sound sleep would cure everyone's pain on this planet. My smile became wider.

I checked myself as well. It was better. Once again I imagined about master and his living in the high altitudes. There he was having literally nothing to comfort himself. I prayed God for bestowing relief to mother and Annie as well.

SIXTY THREE

Splitting Mind into Two

ONE MORNING, MASTER PREACHED wonderfully in the orchard. It was a technique about regulating one's mind for his own beneficence. He advocated that human mind must be split in two parts and both parts must operate in such a way that those do not create ruckus in the ordeals of life.

He said, "For ordinary people, nevertheless mind will remain as unruly and ungovernable as the wind. Remedy is not in killing or suppressing the mind, for doing so will never become possible for the modern mortals. Wiser solution will be to split the same mind into two clear sides – the Worldly side and the Godly side. Instead of getting offended by the unruly operations of worldly mind, one must be determined to not throw his body merely at former's will. For commanding one's control on his human body, let only his Godly mind act upon as king. Worldly mind may be watchful but invariably must remain obedient to the king. About man himself, whenever he is caught in a dilemma between these two, decision must be left to the king Godly mind. Obedient execution must be left to the worldly mind."

Upon being asked, that how exactly to identify this Godly side of mind, he replied, "Let me explain this with a simple analogy. Think of the psychological admixture of worldly influences upon you as a large web of wires of different kinds and lengths. Although these wires are many, that too badly entangled, but for connecting between your source and your ultimate destination of life, there is only one existing in the web. Son, your great deal is to find out one particular wire which connects between the said two points. Rest of the wires will create only web of confusions and dilemmas around the kingly wire. Once you've found the king, you must not lose hold on it."

He continued, "Do not wonder that identifying such important one wire will be too difficult. Experiment the worldly transactions made with your mind as if you are testing those wires one by one in the web. Do not allow your mind to respond to the wires which do not connect between your source and your ultimate destination. Instead, wait and quickly respond as soon as you find the one that connects. While doing this, however, you must have acquainted your destination of life beforehand. This is the necessary condition. Once you've found the relevant wire, make it your king. Rest ones merely exist in the web and never deserve more importance than the king."

At last he said, "Success in this experimentation actually depends upon how clearly you have acquainted the destination of your life. Remember, this destination is not about the materialistic attainments that you may like to attain while living, but it's about what you will leave behind you after forsaking the world."

SIXTY FOUR

The Final Abode is God

ONE MORNING WHILE MEDITATING, I found a gem. I quickly wrote it in my diary as below:

"Reaching home of God is not about first dying and subsequently reaching there. God's home is not a physical construction of masonry; instead it is a mental construction by man, which is all about his familiarity with the actual 'relevance' of God. This familiarity cannot be contained in the theoretical scriptural knowledge alone, though it penetrates better in one's own experience of such 'relevance'. Why a man should reach God's home only after dying; he must rather live in such home every moment. God's home is not away, it is right here and approachable by us; in fact it's inviting. Certainly, different people have different walks of life, but their distinctive walks must meet at the same place in God's home. And most interestingly, while walking in the direction of God's home, the path is as enjoyable as is the destination."

SIXTY FIVE

The Parallel Existence of Ghost and God

AT SOME OTHER OCCASION, master talked about ghosts and compared the phenomena with the precept of God.

He said, "Ghosts, or some people calling it Satan, exist for only those who intuitively believe that they exist. Mere talking about ghosts cannot make one believe in them. Similarly, God, or say the wiser element, exists for only those who intuitively believe in His existence. You cannot establish one's faith in God merely by talking."

In this relation, while talking further about the human mind he said, "Mind always enjoys an absolute freedom of selecting between the two, though can choose only alternatively. Those who choose ghosts cannot choose God; and it is vice-versa as well. Neither God nor ghosts exist in the physical body; both are only subject matters of the intuitive beliefs of the human mind. Either of two can strongly exist in the mind which gives the shelter to it."

When I asked what should be the yardstick of staying away from the ghosts and choosing God, he replied, "Ghost or Satan leads to suspicion and fear; whereas God or the wiser element leads to only freedom and bliss."

SIXTY SIX

Ðark Tunnel of Superstition

TALKING ABOUT SUPERSTITION, ONE morning master spoke wonderfully.

He said, "The predicament in superstition is that, more the man fails because of it, more intensely he wants to try again the same. Superstition is a kind of dark tunnel, wherein man can't resist but going farther in the hope of finding light at last. Even though he eventually realizes the absence of light at all, yet he only chooses to gamble again and again. Instead of withdrawing himself back, he only delves into deeper."

Having said this, master asked me to carefully observe the people around my life. He said the chances were always bright that I would find a person or two, who, even after having lost much, are not yet ready to drive away from the shackles of superstition.

He also warned that, although certain superstitious omens and practices could be meaningful as well, but depending upon those excessively was no good display. He pointed out repeatedly that success of human life was in the righteous action alone. The 'karma', as per him, must supersede the beliefs of all kinds.

Basis master's words, I observed a handful people in my coming days. To the extent of my personal knowledge, those were extremely superstitious. In however big way they had undertaken various kinds of rites, but their lives hadn't been easy at all. Whichever way they had tried tricking their lives with the help of superstitious omens, tokens or performances; but it was alone the spontaneity of life which had invariably ruled over them.

SIXTY SEVEN

Dewdrops, Raindrops and Moisture

AT ONE INSTANCE MASTER briefly talked about the distinctions amongst various religions.

He said, "Faiths of different religions are distinctive merely in their appearance. Just the way dewdrops, raindrop and moisture are no different from each other; different religious faiths are also the same."

By the end of this discourse, he also warned me that I must not drift from the truth if certain people, however dear those are to me, happen to pollute these drops of different kinds. Man's authority in water is restricted to consume it for his body's survival and hygiene; it is never in polluting it for his individual whims.

SIXTY EIGHT

Emancipation is Mirage

ABOUT EMANCIPATION, ONCE MASTER wrote in the wooden box:

"Sometimes, scriptures appear to be suggesting that emancipation is the ultimate destination for human life. But see, if emancipation is to be understood in terms of ending the wheel of reincarnations, I do not hesitate in disagreeing with it. Look at yourself. When life is already so beautiful that you can engage in the service of mankind during your each incarnation, won't you seek coming to this earth again and again? After attaining your secret world on the other side of mind, haven't you also started enjoying your life in the deeper sense? Then why at all, you or somebody else will want to stop living such wonderful ways ever?"

Next day in the central orchard, he explained the reason, "If enlightened minds like you will not chose to return on this planet again, then who is going to show to the people the ways of bliss? Do not make terrible errors in interpreting the scriptures. The true perspectives of mysterious text may go over the head of even wisest. Grasp the intention and not the literal text alone."

"Then master", I asked, "please help me in knowing the truest meaning of emancipation. Although earlier I had some understanding of it, but your words are shaking my perception."

"You do not need fathomless commentaries over this matter. Just understand that your true emancipation comes when you are live. If you can yield yourself an amnesty from the different kinds of trials in your apparent world, know yourself to have already emancipated. Once you've become so, why see the end of life? Instead see the longevity!"

SIXTY NINE

Majority is no Yardstick

I NEVER SHIED FROM asking master even about foolish subjects, such as national politics. His replies, however, were always deep rooted in the fundamentals.

At one time, I greatly wondered about the electoral outcomes of the country. Being myself completely unbiased to any political party, I was skeptical about the verdict of people. I grew impelled to question the gravity behind 'majority'. Why talk about the electoral ballot after five years, I felt the electorates were changing their minds every minute. I wondered about democracy, autocracy and monarchy too; but found that none had served the human societies sufficiently.

Although it could be a foolish matter to discuss with master, still I craved his view. After all, as I believed, it was a matter concerning the people and their welfare.

One morning, I quietly wrote a paper note about this, and shut it inside the wooden box.

When I opened the box again at night, the master had sent the reply. It was almost a rebuke. He wrote:

"What makes you think that it will be somebody else to help oneself? In the countries, administrative mechanisms are put in place merely to keep the belongings of masses in order, and not the masses themselves. Such mechanisms are evolved by men, and in due course of time, are proved to be imperfect by men only. Do you know, what makes the man prove his own creation imperfect? It's the imperfection in his faith. Unless the mankind doesn't perfect its faith, it will continue overturning the same dice of life again and again."

SEVENTY

Master's Way of Helping Many

"MASTER, DON'T YOU THINK that the way you help me every time, a lot many people would also need the same?"

"What makes you think that those need me?" He asked.

"I think in this way they will also attain the happiness and eternal truth", I tried justifying my point.

"I am nobody to help anybody, or even to help you", he said mercilessly. He continued, "Don't you remember what I said to you once, that it's entirely your own keenness which expands your presence in the secret world."

"But master, isn't the stimulation also very necessary? Without your divine stimulation bestowed upon me, could I've ever met the truth?" I asked.

Now he laughed and said, "Stimulation is nothing but a tiny matchstick. As quickly it produces the fire, as quickly it cools down. Unless someone has prepared a lamp to permanently light with it, matchstick has only fickle use."

"But master", I tried insisting my point, "if there would be many matchsticks available, one can rest assured of lighting up his lamp sooner or later."

As I spoke this I sensed that this discourse was heading to become special.

Master asked, "But what will you do if someone is not interested even in the lamp?"

I retorted, "How can it be so? After all isn't the lamp very necessary to light up in everyone's life?" In this discussion, the metaphor of lamp was symbolizing the lamp of knowledge and enlightenment.

He laughed again and said, "Don't you remember the story of Kontal which I once narrated to you on the hills? Once people have settled in the dark, they won't need even the matchstick, and here you are talking about the lamp."

I began recalling the story. Yes, on the hilltop, master had narrated the story about how creation of the world takes place. I couldn't argue the point further. He was basically correct. Yet without giving up, I knew that it was only master who could have helped the case.

Submissively I said, "But master, still I wish you must do something for the people."

Esoteric smile crossed his face. He said, "If it's so, let us do the same thing, which I did to you."

I was alert.

He continued with the same metaphor and asked, "Do you know why people are generally indifferent towards the lamp?"

I looked on inquisitively.

"Because they have no idea of it at all! They do not know what the lamp means to them; and what it can do about? The only thing we can do here is we can make people aware of this lamp; so as to say, we will give them a matchstick for searching about lamp and eventually lighting it up as well."

"But, what if that matchstick finishes even before they get any near to the lamp? They might really give up in disappointment", I asked.

"Then it becomes a matter of their faith. Without faith, even if I give them a million matchsticks, and even if they find out the lamp as well, they will not value it. Whether I give them one or a million matchsticks, it's the same thing", master replied.

I began to wonder about it. Both of us remained silent for a moment.

On a spur I asked, "Then what was it, master, that kept me going in the secret world? I think I too had not valued the matchsticks that you had been giving me in the beginning."

He smiled and replied, "But there was one good thing you didn't fail at. Right from the first matchstick, you grew curious about the lamp."

"Then, master," I jumped to prove my point, "I pray, you should not assume that other people will not grow curious about the lamp when they will be given the first matchstick? You must help them the same way you did for me."

His following reply surprised me, "Very well. Then I appoint you doing the same."

"Appointing me?" I was awestruck.

"Yes, why not? It's the same thing after all", he said.

I didn't exactly understand him. He continued saying, "Job of the tree doesn't finish with leafs and flowers, but it finishes only when it is able to give the seeds. You have been growing in the secret world stupendously, but now the time has come when you allow me grow a seed in you."

"But master I doubt, people will not believe me if I start telling them about the secret world," I said apprehensively.

"Why?" He quipped, "Is it because you don't have a long white beard like me?"

I laughed on his remark and said, "But I have no magical wooden box to give them. Neither I have the other things to give, you see!"

"Son, you know very well that the box you are talking about is already useless. It's only the message inside which is worth", master repeated his old warning.

Nodding, but I kept quite.

Master continued, "And even the divine vision, as you are wondering about in this moment, is a kind of privilege which is already possessed by everyone. How you are supposed to give people a thing which is already theirs? You have only to remind them of their hidden privilege."

"But again master, how will I exactly do that?" I expressed my wavering wonderment.

"Look out which way the people will be most comfortable

with! Don't choose the ways as per your want, but choose as per their wants. It may be writing; and sometimes it may be anonymous writing as well. It may be speaking and it may be silence as well at some occasions. It may be showing them the examples of others; and sometimes it may be your own examples too. This may also work in form of silent heart-to-heart communication, when it is made very compassionately from your side. Trust me son, there is not even a single thing which I can do and you cannot."

Master's words were encouraging me in the light of possibility. The new work, which master was assigning to me, was both, a responsibility and a privilege as well.

"Once you start doing that", master took up the conversation again, "I will be glad that the seed I grew years before has sprouted now. It won't need me any longer. The seed will be growing at its own."

Whenever master talked or even hinted about going away from my life, I couldn't contain myself. In strained voice, I asked, "But master, why you think your going away from me is necessary?"

"Every seed has to leave the branch, or isn't it?" He asked.

"And then what will be you doing?" I asked in hope of taming his casual indifference towards me.

There was a poignant silence before he replied to my question. He merely said, "I will do my duty. I will grow more seeds."

I couldn't contest his argument. In this moment, for the first time in life, I understood that he was on a bigger mission than I had known.

This meeting lasted for another half an hour, but it was an exclusive silence between us. Not a speck of word was exchanged. My mind was busy about my coming up responsibility; and I think his mind was also doing the same.

Later while returning to home, another anxiety gripped me. I had forgotten to ask master whether it was my last day with him!

I hoped and even prayed it must not be. It was indescribably difficult to imagine myself without him. But truly he had also said that every seed was supposed to set apart from the tree; even though it was a painful process. Perhaps, I had started undergoing the same pain, even without exactly knowing, whether I had already parted or not fully yet.

During the day, I was thinking more about my new responsibility than the imminent bereavement from master. I knew it, even master would have preferred me doing the same.

At night, just before retiring to the bed, I was curious to see whether the wooden box had still existed with me or not. Master had nevertheless warned that it will disappear after its job was over.

Heart pounding, I opened the drawer. But thanks to master, the box was still clad in the mufflers.

I took it out and touched it in great love. Quite surprisingly, it opened even without my tapping.

Yes, it was a new leaf there, but mentioning only a single line on it:

"Son, make difference to other lives, much more than I did to you."

I nodded, and also wondered that it didn't talk about staying or disappearing of the box. However in the following moment I thought that it was alone the master to decide. Even if I worried, it had no use. I wrapped the box in mufflers again and placed it into the drawer. It was coming clear to me that master had decided to withdraw it now. His one liner message was signifying the same.

In coming days, as I was going more watchful about my apparent world, I came across many occasions where enlightenment of others could be made with the first 'matchstick'. I had taken two important decisions; one, to remain only anonymous in my work, and secondly, to work by way of writing letters to the people. I had a growing faith that, writing, that too anonymous, was quite an effective way of invoking sincere contemplations within people. To start master's work, it seemed appropriate in my capacity.

I ordered a local printing shop to get me enough green paper sheets cut in the shape of Pipal leaves. I had purchased a handful of beautiful envelops as well. Whenever I felt that by way of anonymous writing I could make difference to people's life, I did. In such letters, I would never customize the heading to suit the situation, but I would only write - *'From the Secret World'*. Perhaps, as I hoped, it was also necessary to save people from reading the letters in hostility. Certainly, they wouldn't have liked reading anything which was titled in their criticism.

Many cases I wrote to were from my acquaintances. I was reasonably careful in not bragging about bringing a difference in people's lives. I wrote in utmost humility. Also, I wrote only when I could have a say in the matter. Instead of getting over-excited about peeping into others' lives, I would wait for an appropriate occasion. I had faith, that whenever my services would be needed more, more opportunities would also appear.

In each such case, I would first try to get to the roots of the problem. In almost every case I would discover that the strain inside people's minds was man-made, and most likely a self-made one. Indeed, it was disconcerting to witness people crafting their own perturbations; but going by the same reason, those appeared to me easy to fix as well. While doing the letters, I was particularly conscious that alone being anonymous was not sufficient, for I was supposed to maintain my humility as well.

I can recall and cite here few of the instances wherein I had tried. Once it happened between a newly married couple in my acquaintances. Both were the educated professionals and earning handsomely, but having only insufficient bliss at home for some reason. Not even a year had completed after their marriage, they both had begun clashing their egos. Each had started wondering more about his or her own individual life than that of his or her spouse. Turbulences in the new castle were unprecedented for everyone. All kith and kin were perturbed over the matter, but not the couple itself as such. One day I learnt that, they both might fall out to divorce. I feared that the things were happening too fast for them. I imagined, what could have the master said in this matter. I wrote all in the secret letter, and posted it quickly. I didn't know, whether it was by reason of this letter or otherwise, but the marriage was saved.

Another occasion, which seems worth citing here, was about a father-in-law who had been going too adamant to heed his newly married daughter-in-law. What a pity it spilled upon all; particularly the innocent young husband! Father-in-law didn't want to even see the face of daughter-in-law; and at no cost he would allow her living in the same house. Nor was the young lady was ready to stay in the same home. In this tussle however, the young husband was in a fix. He didn't want to separate either from his parents or from his partner. Secretly, having gathered the sufficient information to the matter, I wondered what master could have said into it. Certainly, he would have first laughed on this inclusive foolishness, but upon my insisting, he would have replied too. I meditated for his reply and wrote it down in an anonymous letter to the father-in-law. I pleaded him, as though writing from the secret world, that for him the time had arrived to make sacrifices. I suggested in the letter, that the biggest thing he was supposed to sacrifice was only his enemy, his ego. I assured him that he must not grow insecurity complexioned about the presence of new generation people in the house. I wrote that as and when he would restore and express his deep love towards the young people, they will also reciprocate the same, rather in increased proportions. In the letter I also wrote that if he wanted to meet me, the anonymous writer of the strange leaf shaped letter, I will agree, provided he works out a wonder in the house. I also sufficiently extolled him, that given his vast experience of life, he was nonetheless able to create magic at home.

One more occasion came, when one of my senior friends was appearing too much upset with his growing wayward children. He doubted that, given the modern age times and trends, the children were growing infirm in morality as well. While talking to me once, he said that he had been trying all kinds of means, including warnings and threats; but nothing seemed working in between him and the young crusaders. Although he was disclosing to me such of his personal matters, yet I suspected that he will not consider my advice because of my young age. Two days after, I wrote a secret letter to him. I pleaded him to assure his children in great humility, that too one by one in way of displaying secrecy, that although he was pained to see new developments in their lives, yet by his fatherly duty, he would standby them in all kinds of scenarios.

But this friend was very smart. He somehow guessed that the letter writer was me, though he didn't get annoyed over this. Only a week after he told me that the very moment he followed my advice, the hearts of children were filled in extreme love for their father. After this successful experiment, my senior friend never stopped calling me on the phone and discuss about other things. Neither did I disappoint him anytime.

Another time when I was at my neighbor-friend's house, I got to know that only previous night, the elder brother of my said friend who used to live in a different city, had become a father of baby boy. It was first grandchild in the family. Contrary to my expectation of happy faces in the house, I confronted a strange silence. Apprehending that it would only be a personal matter for them, I didn't inquire much. However in some time, while taking leave from my friend and coming down from the stairs, the newly grandmother happened to cross my way. Quickly, without being given time to even hesitate I congratulated the lady for becoming a grandmother. I exclaimed, what a wonderful news it was.

Oh! What a cold response! I cannot forget that in life. She merely said, "Good news or no good news, it's the same thing." I looked about the face of my fellow. Slightly embarrassed, he quieted his mother and gave me a hint. He said that his mother and his brother's wife did not share any good rapport between them.

What rubbish, inwardly I thought. But I walked out in silence. Four days later, I wrote a secret letter to that grandmother. Primarily I had asked her to imagine only one thing, that come what may, what she thought it would take from her to give the unconditional love; and what she thought it might give her in return? Even if there had been some bad experiences with the necessary people around our lives, what better option we had than to only forgive them and bestow our generosity?

I hoped and prayed that the secret letter could add at least some goodness to the family.

There were several other occasions as well. I was not doing anything on myself; merely I was discharging the duty ordained by my master. Since the letters were always anonymous, I had no opportunity of taking pride of doing wonders to the people. This was the best part of my work. Master's plans were always flawless. Even while working through me for others, he was spreading enlightenment amongst many; that too without giving me or himself a single chance of taking credit. He was working through me; and for me also at the same time.

SEVENTY ONE

Idealistic Worldly Life

MY FREQUENCY OF MEETING with master had slowed down. Probably it was also a part of his plan. I was increasingly discovering the myriad sources of enlightenment which had existed in the apparent world itself.

One day, almost by accident, I met with an old age saint on the railway station. He was clad in the garbs of ascetics and for unprecedented reasons, had started taking interest in me. I was also hearing his words carefully. Intuiting his advancement in the supreme knowledge and wisdom, I quickly grew respect for him. He said he was pleased with my humility and just before his train would leave, he would give me a mantra of life.

I was pleased. He uttered in the Hindi language - *'Dhan Kam, Tan Madhyam, Aur Man Uttam.'*

Just he said this he rushed to his starting train and disappeared along with it.

I quickly translated the mantra. It had three parts, which meant, Money should be less, body should be average; and mind should be the best.

Later I contemplated the mantra in my heart. Its first part was this - Only having as much money as was necessary to fulfill one's requirements of life, was an ideal position to have. Its middle part - the Body was good only when it was healthy and free from diseases, but nowhere overly strong to overpower others. And the last part - Mind, of course must be the best; for it was alone the mind which would make and unmake the creations. Master had also been teaching the same. True ideologies never had a conflict.

Once again I looked in the direction of train. It had gone too far now. I came back with a great new thought in my mind and an esoteric smile on my face.

SEVENTY TWO

Whom to Worship?

ONE MORNING I WOKE up reading in newspaper that a renowned religious honcho of the country, who was a self-styled god, had been arrested by the local police for the alleged charges of rape. A teenage girl, merely sixteen years old, had filed a complaint with police against him. After the news of arrest spread, the whole country was in commotion.

Although I myself was not a follower of this self-styled god, but across the length and breadth of world there were innumerable people who were in a fix over the matter. My only contact with this man had been only once, that too impersonal. It was years before when I had read one of his spiritual quotes on a billboard. I was greatly moved with his thought. He had written that, *"Only remaining even-minded and ever-happy is the highest worship to God."* Indeed, what a marvelous thought it was!

Now on this day, after learning about the allegations of rape and also the following news of his police arrest, I was reminiscing his quote seen by me on the other day. Instantly I came out from the dilemma. I was doubtless. Even today the quote meant same. I asked myself, should I change my opinion towards that man now? My discernment replied, yes; if he has done wrong, there was no need to have personal obeisance in him. I asked myself again, should I change my opinion toward the quote as well? My conscience rebuked; No, why at all?

For following days, I continued reading news about him. Procrastination in the legal proceedings and also the treacherous propaganda undertaken by that alleged god-man through his hermitage establishments had actually lost my curiosity. Finally I stopped reading about him. That day, still having faith in that quote, I wrote the following words in my diary:

"Only the transforming thought must be worshiped; and not the mind of man from which it sprang. Mind may corrupt, but thought does never."

SEVENTY THREE

Trace Your Bible of Life Soonest

ONCE MASTER NARRATED A matter of great significance. Perhaps he was indicating towards my solace, after he would have left me.

He asked, "One may not retain the privilege of accompanying scrupulous sages, and nor is the physical presence of one's preceptor always possible; then what will constantly help him?"

I grasped his pretext instantly. I looked to his face. He was smiling in deep affection.

He continued, "Your refuge will be in books. Without incurring delay, son, you must choose a book and make it your Bible of life. It can be any book from any religion or sect, provided it doesn't criticize the other religions."

Grief occurred to me. As master waited for my response, I somberly asked, "Which book for me, master?"

"Any one! Now you are wise enough to decide yourself", he said.

"Which book is your Bible, master? Perhaps I can take refuge in the same", I asked.

He laughed and replied, "I have had many Bibles for that matter, but subsequently I've stopped needing the text. After attaining the enlightenment and constantly living in that, I have become free from the needs of all kinds."

I remained quiet, merely thinking his words.

He said, "Son, you must not perplex about the kind of enlightenment I am speaking for myself; for the enlightenment received from books, which you regard as holy as Bible, is no small in any sense. Start with any one book and give yourself to it. Enjoy your beginning, progressing and finishing alike. There are certain books in the world which cannot be finished even after repeated readings. Start with one of the kinds, at soonest."

But I had no way unless master had suggested the name.

Master sensed it and finally helped me. "Son", he beatifically said, "if you insist, adopt Bhagavad Gita. No matter which religion you or the chosen book belongs to, but give yourself to it for sufficient period of time. Do not stop reading and rereading it unless you've explored its deepest applicability in your both worlds - Apparent and Secret one. I am naming one book and not the others, but it doesn't mean you will respect the others less. On the path of enlightenment, you must banish the infectious inclination about comparisons."

Having said this, master took leave. I too returned making plans in my mind.

SEVENTY FOUR

Even the Evil Craves for Good

AS PER MASTER, IT was altogether an inadmissible idea if somebody believed that evil will forever remain evil.

He wanted me to first know the meaning of evil in detail. As per him, evil was not some distinct type of people or human communities who lived hostilities against others. Substance of evil, as per him, was quite an intriguing subject if looked into properly.

To know more about the substance of evil, he asked me to first know wherefrom the evil originated at all. Evil originated in the human mind. Evil never took birth in some religion or community of particular kind, but it immanently existed in each and every mind living on this planet. As per master, evil's existence in every human mind was eternal and inseparable too. Invariably it was the same case with goodness too. Although evil was inseparable, but it was not indomitable at all. Master often argued that evil could be subdued by focusing on the goodness side living in the same human mind. He warned that it worked vice-versa too.

"Do you know what is it that decides which one of the two will dominate the other?" Master asked.

I couldn't word my vague ideas.

He answered, "It's the timeliness of one's own discernment. Indeed it's alone this which makes the apparent world for him a good or worse place to live. Outcomes of discernment are quick and prompt, and therefore timeliness is critical. While observing the attributes of apparent world through his discernment, man chooses either goodness or the evil side dominating over the other side in his mind."

Yes, he was correct, as always.

Master added, "And son! Do you know, amidst this ongoing battle between evil and good within one's mind, what he waits for?"

I was more curious to know than to reply.

He commanded me, "For a moment, son, imagine one cruel person in your knowledge and I will tell you a secret."

Oh! He was experimenting again. I thought about daily newspaper. That was the best place to find. Whenever it came about choosing one amongst worst people, newspaper gave many choices. Many pictures of the heinous criminals began rushing in my imagination. Though here, as was asked by master, I chose only one in my mind.

He continued, "Now listen. Whether or not that person in your mind is consciously aware of this, but he is waiting for the final victory of goodness side of his mind. It can't happen ever that he would crave for the final victory of evil side. One may want to devastate the world, but never devastate himself. One may foolishly enjoy being deluded, but he cannot enjoy this state forever. Sometimes the deep desire for goodness side's victory emerges on people's death-bed. In other cases, this desire may take many incarnations to sprout. And it's also true that some people realize this desire well in time. Evil dwells nowhere but in the human mind; and mind always discovers the truth at last."

My thoughtful silence was unbroken yet.

Master concluded superbly well, "Therefore son, a man tussling between his two opposite sides of mind, actually waits for the timeliness in his discernment. For so long as he faults in this timeliness, his evil side dominates; but whenever his discernment occurs, he instantly meets his blissful end."

SEVENTY FIVE

Last Day with Master

"KNOW WELL AND ACCEPT it soonest that one has to live his life only alone always."

Imminent as it was, master's declaration about separation had bombarded upon me.

While I was avoiding his line of gaze, he added, "It's not because I have taught you enough, but for seeing my success with you, you must live now at your own."

Still I couldn't utter a word. My head was hanging low and I had no courage to question his decision. He was determined.

"Do you know, son", he asked, "how you must react when being informed that wooden box will be withdrawn from you?"

He had been talking about it previously as well. However matching his expectations in this moment, I didn't show my dismay with the news. I merely looked his face and nodded.

Then he added again, "And you may consider it as our last meeting in this orchard. Henceforward you will be strolling here alone, though never without my blessings and wishes."

This time I couldn't help but protest, "But Master, why not allow me the continued glimpse of your holy feet?"

He smiled and said, "No. Only in this way you will be able to make your own feet as holy as mine. I can foresee your future endeavors. You will extend your enlightenment to the countless others; and only in some time you will become most interested in making others' feet as holy as yours, just the way I am wishing in this moment."

I was still seesawing between his truthful wisdom and my

childish resistance for stopping him. For several minutes, neither of us broke the silence.

"Son, before I physically step out from your life, I must give you a key", breaking the lull, master said.

This day unusual to his practice of coming from behind, for the first time ever in orchard, master was walking ahead of me. I was full of obeisance to whatever he said.

"This key", he continued, "is necessary to save you from the colliding interpretations of the scriptural text. I can foresee that after losing my physical contact, you will heavily depend on the text only. That's beneficial, but still I give you this key so that you will never run a chance of blundering in interpreting."

I was alert to his each word.

"This foremost key", he began revealing, "is simple yet most accurate definition of God. Never forget that God is Self and only Self is God. Whenever you will concentrate in the Self, you will instantly regain your position in the God. Whenever you will meditate in Self, you will see Him abundantly. And whenever, at a certain point in life you will become Self, you will not remain anything but God only."

Though it was mystical, but the key given by master was so easy to memorize that I didn't feel like having to jot down in the diary. Master had also emphasized that it was simple.

"Whenever caught in a fix over interpretation of the text", he added, "or when caught in the dilemma over your spiritual duty, you must test this key. For so long as you will be able to see your Self clearly off your egotism in the body or mind, you will find yourself resolved in the spirit of God instantly."

Listening about his words, I continued following him in silence.

"On the hills when we met", master said while breaking my emotional muteness, "I didn't give you one last lesson. I will give that now."

I noticed that my curiosity in this moment was on the same height as it were on the hills.

"This matter is about the way in which great annihilation takes place", he started revealing. "Son, this entire stratagem of universes, as you are aware, is made of five elements - Earth, Water, Fire, Air and Ether."

I nodded.

"Now listen about this process carefully. In the moment when great annihilation starts, the first element, earth, starts getting invaded by the second element, which is water. Unfathomable oceanic waves and the unbroken lashes of cloudbursts make the oceans forget their shore-lines and shortly after, the entire earth gets submerged in the water. There remains no earth, but only water everywhere."

I was raptly listening to this great unfolding of secret. Master continued, "When it remains only water and nothing else, the third element of existence takes place in mega grandeur; and it's the fire. Son, it's no mystery that water can extinguish fire only when it is more than the latter. But in opposite case, water certainly can't help."

"But master!" I interrupted and asked, "When the land had already disappeared, wherefrom this mega fire comes?"

He faintly laughed on my question and replied, "When fire doesn't go anywhere at all, why it will need to come from somewhere? Fire is immanently present in the water. Infact, the former resides in the very atoms of latter. It is permanently there. Actually, no longer finding the company of atoms of the first element - earth, the atoms of water find nothing to do with their energy. These atoms start colliding amongst themselves and create the first atomic explosion. Multiplying one atomic explosion into innumerable, the element of fire burns the activity of energy in the each atom of water. As these spectacular explosions continue, fire transforms all water into the vapors of gigantic dimensions. One form of energy changes into another. Sometime after when there remains no single water atom to get exploded, fire also subsides. Now there remain only vapors lifting in the air. It's now, the fourth element of existence, which is Air, comes into action."

Here enthused with the astounding exposition by master, I couldn't resist but chipping in my remark, "Then vapors must have turned into rain as usual."

"No!" Master ruled out my guess. He said, "Rains do not mean anything if there has remained no land at all. Without surface, where would the raindrops fall? Even for eons if rains continue falling without having to land, those will remain only vapors and nothing more. Do you find it difficult to imagine, son?"

I found master's revelation very well grounded. I nodded.

Master continued saying, "Now the activity of fourth element, Air, becomes least spectacular but very subtle. Gradually and silently, given its vastness, air absorbs the entire vapor in itself. Now it remains only Air, that too invisible."

Listening to this great account, I was trying to imagine the scene. I looked up in sky. It was clear and not a single cloud was showing up. Master sensed my wonderment and laughingly said, "Yes, it's somehow the same, but in actual annihilation process, you will not remain anymore to check about the things with your physical eyes."

At master's remark, I quipped in my heart, "But maybe I would like to have at least one chance of witnessing the real annihilation?"

He always answered what ran in my head. He said, "Those who have mastered in watching the secret world through their divine vision can behold the process of annihilation any time."

I blushed. He still had to reiterate the answers which I already knew.

Here master charged up my last lesson. "Now, after air has absorbed the vapor completely, the fifth element, Ether, starts taking its course."

Understanding Ether to be the last element, my keenness grew higher.

He continued, "What follows next is the most subtle part of

the process. Ether is endless and it works only in silence. Not a slight of sound it ever makes. It is so vast, yet it is entirely about nothingness. All over there remains only great lull and nothing else. Ether gives shelter to the entire great colliding amongst Earth, Water, Fire and Air. It assimilates all in itself, that too, most silently. Son! Now comes the most critical part of it. Do you know that all these five elements also exist in you?"

Oh! Suddenly master had started showing me the relevance of entire story. I moved my head in submission of my ignorance to his question.

He answered, "Earth is your body. Water is your consciousness. Fire is your spark of wisdom. Air is your all permeating mind. And finally Ether is your Spirit. Can you see the big connection? You don't have to live only the Earth, Water, Fire or Air in you; but you have to live all of them together; and you have to live in this way only to become the Ether at last. Your ultimate destination is to become the Ether, because only that can contain the rest of all within you."

As I looked to master's face in great daze, he revealed the crux,

"Ether is Spirit. And your goal is to become as vast as Ether. After you've known your truth about the fifth element, the four lower elements will not trouble you ever. In your concentrated pursuit for the fifth, all other four will become your obedient. You will master them all. Son, this was the last lesson I wanted to give you."

Having said this, master halted his walking and turned to me. Looking straight into my eyes, he said, "No matter what man wants, but he anyways becomes the spirit at last. In your case, now it's you to meditate and decide whether you want to become the spirit now or you want to wait till the actual annihilation takes place."

Master's last lesson was sweeping, mind boggling, stirring, or I didn't find a suitable word yet.

He remarked, "If you do it now, you master it now. You do

not need me or anybody else for doing that. You have to do it alone; and that is the reason I have been insisting that you must walk your life alone only. My job was to merely invoke you in your own eternal truth. Now I am immensely satiated to have lived my duty."

In great affection he continued looking into my eyes, as if he was seeking my consent to leave.

Still finding me silent, he insisted again, "Son, only the unenlightened minds find the annihilation afar; however the truth is that whatever is existing in the physical form amidst this creation is already undergoing the process of completing its age. Everything has to go. It's inevitable."

I could see that master was in hurry once again. It reminded me my last day with him on the hilltop. I had no merit to stop him, that too for my own hollow wish. I knew he had no regards for the physical forms, neither that of mine and nor that of himself. He was not harsh, but only truthful.

He began telling me in humble voice. "I repeat son, I am your master and not the teacher. I try to enlighten you but not to teach you constantly. You can tell someone about our meetings only after making sure that he is more interested in my message than in myself. If you ever wonder about re-visiting the cave on hilltop, you must know that I do not live anywhere permanently. Whatever one can think of searching in those mountains, I have already given you all. I am hopeful that you will not be anxious for my physical presence. It's the thought which must be worshipped and not the body of person revealing it. Persons always change but thought does never."

I was still speechless. Master had always been at his own terms.

He said, "Although I will be withdrawing the wooden box in evening, the divine vision will stay with you. It already belongs to you and not me. I give you a boon that, since you have perfected in interpreting the secret world, you will no longer be required to sleep before experiencing the divine vision. Instead you will now become able to invoke the same even when you are awake, walking or performing your daily duties. After all, divine vision is all about eternal truth; it must occur to you at any time or place of your wish."

Highly obliged, but I was still continuing looking towards the ground.

"I am so happy with you my son that I will give you another boon. For you will be living a life of householder, you will have to face many inevitable embarrassments on that account. Many such embarrassments will take place in form of your marital temptations, which you will neither be able to completely renounce, and nor crown upon your head. But here I give you a boon that you will have a regulated appetite for such temptations. Those will occur to you only when those exhort you to indulge. You will never crave for those in their absence. In this way, for most part of your life, you will live free from the guilt consciousness of being under the darkness of warm quilts."

In ineffable love, he waited for grasping my absenting gaze. I knew, he was adamant, and to his own terms only.

I gave in. But just then a new kind of embarrassment occurred to me. I had no idea how to farewell. I didn't even know how to look about him in this moment.

"O master, grant me a last wish!" I swallowed a lump of pain in my throat and pleaded, "Don't go unless I come back in ten minutes."

Though surprised, he nodded.

I rushed out of the park. I suspected whether in such early morning, would I be able to find a single shop open? As I came out and trudged on the road, I craned in both directions. My predicament was true. It was too early to expect any shop open for me. In that hurried moment, I couldn't think of anything but buying some sweets for offering an oblation to the master's feet.

It was pointless to wait for long; else the master would have gone. Suddenly, God had mercy upon me. Under the kind heavens, an old man had appeared while pushing his cart. It was laden with variety of fruits. Oh! Fruits were even better, I became glad. Instead of waiting for him coming in my direction slowly, I ran up to and stopped him. Unusual to my habit, I didn't check the prices and asked the old man to fill a bag with different kinds of chosen fruits. Instantly he followed my command and only in a minute, a bagful of fruits was ready to be taken away.

But alas! My anxiety grew manifold. During the morning walks, I had never been in a habit of keeping my wallet in the pocket. The fruit bag was in my hands, but how would I pay this old chap?

"Did you miss your wallet, Sir?" Surprisingly, the fruit man had guessed.

Only my eyes replied silently. I managed to say, "You have already understood the matter. I will never forget your favor, if you may please collect the money from my home." I wrote down my address on one of the scrap papers he had.

"Alright! I'll come in the day", he said.

Even more surprised upon how easily the fruit man had agreed, I thanked him once again and rushed towards the park gate.

Having both, doubt as well as the assurance of master's staying, I entered the central orchard. He was quietly sitting on a bench behind a large tree. I flung and while putting the fruits aside, I clasped his feet. This was perhaps after long time that I have had a physical contact with him.

"I cannot stop you against your wish, master!" I managed to say in choking voice, "but this is all I could think for a farewell." Kneeling at ground I was holding the bag in my lap.

He smiled and took out barely two oranges. "That's enough for me. You must keep the rest and let other people have those as my blessings."

I looked down gleefully, for I was holding bagful of his grace.

"Look, what's here! Would you like to take these as well?" By saying and pointing to his right side on the bench, master had taken me aback.

I looked on. Aside to him lying on the bench were two taproots. Oh! Instantly I recognized, for these were the similar taproots which I had been eating on the hilltop when master was my host. Those were somewhat pink and their thickness was almost double the size of biggest radish that I might have ever seen. Every day when I was on the hilltop with master, he would ask me to carry the taproots along with me, but in the moments of leaving his place, I would forget his reminder.

"Look! These haven't staled yet", master said lovingly, "These were for you and have been waiting for you since then. Keep these also in your bag, son."

In boundless gratefulness, I followed his word.

But still, I didn't know how to complete the farewell. I touched his feet once again and just in the moment when I blinked to look up his face, he had disappeared.

Master didn't give me a chance to cry even a single tear. Probably he didn't want me in that way. But it was difficult for me to contain. I couldn't think of doing anything else but continue sitting in the same posture.

SEVENTY SIX

Starting My Both Worlds Alone Again

I DIDN'T SCORE MINUTES or hours that I went alone in the park. When reached home, I found it was too late to start for the office. I phoned and informed my absence to the colleagues.

When Annie's saw the big bag of fruits, she was surprised. Upon her asking that how did I pay without my wallet, I replied that fruit vendor will come in the afternoon and collect money. When she began inquiring more, as to why at all I had to purchase so many fruits, I merely replied that those were supposed to be distributed in the neighborhood as sacred oblation. Finding two taproots in the bag she was awestricken, but seeing me in no good mood, she stopped interrogating further.

Here my mind was startling around the wooden box. It was true that master had not given me enough time for his farewell, but with the box perhaps I had a chance.

In the meantime mother had returned from the sermon and was now pushing me for taking bath. Seeing fruit bag on the table, she was also surprised. As she offloaded the bag, she also asked about the taproots. I told her that those were some unique fruits with no name known to me. Upon her persisting inquiry I replied that the entire bag was a sacred oblation and was to be distributed in neighborhood. She felt good about it.

In about an hour I was free from bathing and the following breakfast. As I started reading newspaper, Annie and mother moved to the other room and switched on TV in a lowly volume. It was still two or three hours for Maina to return from the school.

Good chance for me, I wondered. I came around my table and opened the bottom drawer. It showed the bundle of mufflers. I took it out. Pores of my fingers suggested me that the wooden box was still inside. I heaved relief.

As I unfolded the mufflers, I knew that I was seeing the wooden box for the last time. In the otherwise assurance of divine vision still staying with me, I was trying to refrain from getting too emotional about the box.

I tapped it, but only to find another great surprise for the day! Instead of showing its usual green leaf, the box was flaunting a sparkling leaf made of silver. It had the last message of master engraved on it. In moist eyes, I started reading:

"O Son! I chose to write on a silver leaf instead, so that you can keep my promise and reminiscences forever with you. Hopefully this leaf will make up your sorrow about bereavement from me. Now take the last message from wooden box. For you have advanced in the secret world, you can follow the method of 'Kriya' which I am giving to you in this moment. Son, in all moments of your life, keep your consciousness as a separate entity from your body, which is ego. Then become skilled in disconnecting the former from the latter at any time of your wish. In your beatific moments of meditation, whether with closed or open eyes, place your separated consciousness far above your head such as a satellite. Place it suitably high so that it can keep a watch over your thoughts and activities. Now establish an uninterrupted communication between that satellite and your mind. Once you master in this Kriya, all kinds of secrets that you may want to acquaint in the eternity, will unfold before you. You will discover that your life, as lived through the vision of such satellite, has become a permanent bliss. Son, it's alone the bliss that I wish you ever."

I couldn't put down the silver leaf and box from my hands. Tears began flowing, but I was supposed to contain. It was inappropriate to create scene in front of Annie or mother, if they accidently caught me in tears. I put the silver leaf in the upper drawer of table. Glancing at the wooden box for the last time, I touched it to my chest and wrapped again in the mufflers. Now it was placed in the bottom drawer again.

I stood beside the window and looked on absent mindedly. I didn't know for how long I stood in this way. In some time the doorbell rang. I knew it was Maina returned from her school. Before rushing to the door, I wanted to appear only normal in front of child.

Maina was pleasantly surprised about finding me at home. She put down her schoolbag and shook my hands heavily. As Annie heard her shrilling, she also came out.

It was a nice day as usual.

That old fruit man didn't come till evening. For me it was a small inconvenient debt which I couldn't ever pay back. Finally I assumed that it was nothing but merely a miracle by master, for he wanted to save me from the embarrassment of returning empty handed in the orchard. Or maybe he preferred oranges over Rasagollas.

Nevertheless in evening, I suggested to mother that we will visit our entire neighborhood and distribute the fruits. Everybody, including Annie, was excited about it. We went and met our all neighbors. We greeted them wishes and bestowed the fruits. Many of them were surprised for our sudden visit. They insisted us for coming in and taking tea with them. We couldn't refuse all. It was a wonderful evening.

Having returned home, everyone was tired. After dinner and chat on the table, my mind was engrossed in the box once again. I certainly knew the probable, but just before accepting, I wanted to confirm. While others were still chatting on the dining table, I moved and washed my hands before opening the bottom drawer of my study.

Yes, the squeezed shape of mufflers didn't show any sign of wooden box inside. As I picked up, it came true. I unfolded the bundle somberly.

The wooden box was gone.

Holding alone the mufflers this time in my hands, I came about dining and showed those to Annie.

"Annie, I think these are free now. You can keep those in the cupboard for the following winters."

"Ah! Is that? And what about that strange box?" She asked staring into my eyes while biting her pickle flake.

I was unprepared for the question. I somehow managed by saying, "These mufflers are no longer needed. You can keep those."

Annie just gave a look on the mufflers and exclaimed, "Oh see! Here's the one also, which I had gifted you on our first anniversary!"

"Oh! That's very nice", I meekly added.

She continued sensing my long face. Maybe she thought I was always the same.

Coming around, I put the mufflers on sofa and moved back to my study table. Opening the upper drawer I looked for silver leaf. I smiled. It was still there. I thought I needed to protect it better this time. I tore a newspaper folio and wrapped the leaf before putting it back into the same drawer, at least for now. I picked my diary and settled in sofa, just next to where all were chatting about the food. In a moment Annie finished her meal and was approaching me inquisitively.

"But Rube! There are only two instead of three. Shouldn't have these been three?" She asked me while flaring two mufflers in her hands.

I didn't understand much of a point in her complaint. But she didn't relent and insisted on.

I replied, "Maybe you check in the bottom drawer as well. Even third must be around."

Annie rushed and opened the bottom drawer anxiously; though all she could trace was a small piece of paper.

"What is this?" Showing me a paper note, she inquired.

"What?" I took it from her hand. I already knew that she

would never run out of giving surprises.

I read the paper note. Oh! I knew this handwriting, though it was written with an ink-pen lookalike.

It said:

"In your sweet memory, I am keeping one of the mufflers with me on the hills."

Still looking at paper, I waited for Annie's reaction. I suspected she might have already read it before handing over to me.

"Hmm...! You had quite nice times on the hills! Isn't it" She was rolling her eyes and whispering to me suspiciously.

"Oh, don't say that Annie", I corrected and replied her whisperingly only, "He was a long beard man of double the age of your father."

"Oh!" She cooled down. She derided me by adding her usual remark, "Most of your friends, whom you call to be true, are older than you."

I flashed a smile and the moment grew lighter. As I put the paper note on my study table, mother asked me to sit beside her. She began talking about the people whom we had met during the evening. Instantly, everyone's attention drew into that.

Before getting up and moving to another room, Annie surprised me with her remark, "I'm sorry Rube. I would be glad if you invite your friend to home in case he ever comes to Mumbai."

I looked her eyes. I didn't know who between us was more curious to see the master. I sadly replied, "I tried but he enjoys being on the hills more than being anywhere else."

In a moment Annie started collecting the plates from the dining table. As she moved a step, she slightly skidded on the floor and the water jug tossed down from her hand. As if whatever happened next was merely a motion picture; while rebalancing herself Annie just slapped on my table and the paper note had fallen down because of it. Before my eyes winked, all water in the jug had spilled on the floor and made the paper note drenched. Before I could quickly kneel and save it, it was too late. The ink-pen handwriting was already washed out. Heart-pierced, just when I drew the paper out of water, it broke into pieces.

Annie was frightful. She feared I would go crazy for the loss of my friend's note?

But I was smiling. Nonetheless I had witnessed the newest miracle by master. Whether or not I had retained the privilege of seeing him physically, but he had not stopped playing tricks with me. He didn't want me to posses anything except the silver leaf that I had already safe-put in the upper drawer.

Nevertheless, I had picked up the soiled paper and put it back on the table for drying up.

THE END

Can you intuit your
next book?

Can you figure?

S Y G
e o o
e u d

Now imagine what will happen when
God crosses your way, all of a sudden?

Sudhir Mittal

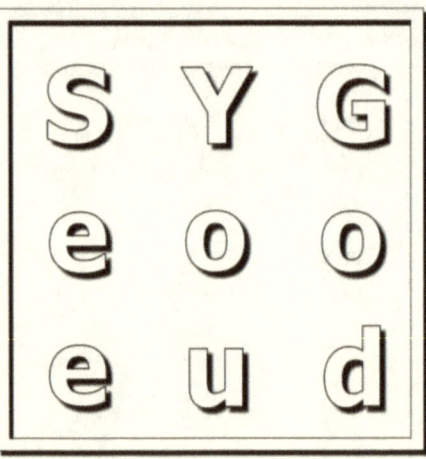

See You God

(from Chapter 11)

IT HAD BEEN A couple of minutes of our walk when little girl hadn't asked me any new question at all. Probably I was expecting one; and yes, I was right.

"Where were you going?" She asked all of a sudden as usual.

"Where!"

"In the car?"

"Oh. I was going to a holy place", I said.

"Holy place!" She wondered.

"Yes. By my staunch rule I use to go there every month."

"What is that holy place?" She asked.

I was sure now that her new questionnaire for me had started off. Nevertheless, till we reached the village, I didn't mind answering to her childish curiosity.

"Children always ask. Or don't they?" I was quipping in my mind.

"What is that holy place?" She asked again.

"Oh! There is a large mountain many miles away from here. I use to go there every month without fail", I said.

"What you do of mountain?"

I laughed. "No, No. I don't do anything of the mountain. It is generally believed that thousands of years ago God used to live there. So I go to see that."

"Oh really! Do you see God there every month?" Girl's

mouth was open in awe.

"No, No. I meant God used to live there thousands of years ago. He doesn't live there now."

"Then why do you go every month when you do not see God there any longer", asked she.

Was she trying to trap me again in her awkward questionnaire? I didn't know. Somehow I tried replying,

"There are so many people who go there every month and walk barefoot some twenty kilometers in the circle of mountain. They do so in way of worshiping God", I tried to answer even her coming up question.

"But you said God doesn't live there any more, then whom do the people worship?"

Thanks to the mercy of God that I knew the answer, "You see little girl! There is a very large temple made in the reminiscence of God. People go to the temple and light candles in the memory of Him."

"In the memory! Do people forget God when they come back home?" I knew her questions were getting intense.

"No! They never forget", I said as if I was replying to her challenge.

"Then why do they go again and again?"

"You won't understand this all. You are too small", I tried to hide my bewilderment behind a smile. She just stopped walking for her unanswered question.

"Ok." She said in a flash of confused smile.

While I was hoping that her questions had finished, I wondered in my heart, "Sometimes children ask big questions. Or don't they?" I was scratching my forehead again. "I do not know if God is really present everywhere or not. People say that He is. But when the millions of other people come every month for walking barefoot around that particular mountain, they also must not be wrong." I shrugged again, "Children sometimes ask only the hopeless questions."

∞ "WHAT WILL YOU DO if God comes in your sight all of a sudden?"

Although she had asked only innocently but, oh my God! Did she sweep me? I didn't know. I glanced again at the sight of village. We were still two-three minutes away. She was holding her stick in both hands and was waving it like the wings of an aeroplane. She was talking to me with rapt attention but her gaze was invariably fixed on the stick. Her question was awkward and I felt very reluctant to answer. Though I also knew that she would not let me go so easily.

"What will you do if God comes in your sight all of a sudden?" She repeated her question again.

"Oh! I know He will not come."

"Why?" She had stopped waving her stick.

"Because He never comes like this." I hoped I hadn't spoken this in a very chiding tone.

Suddenly, the stick fell from her hands when she turned her sad eyes upon me,

"Oh! Do you really think so?"

***

(from Chapter 19)

"Hey! Little girl! Tell me where we are going now?"

"We must reach there soon, well before the dusk."

"Where", I asked in curiosity.

"The Garden of Life."

"Garden of Life?"

"Yes. We must reach there soon, well before the dusk. That is your destination for the day."

∞ WAS THERE SOME KIND of heaviness in her voice?

Ever since I had met with little girl, her face didn't appear to me as somber. She was rarely smiling now and was no longer playful either. Her countenance was becoming grim and worried. Walking down the lane, she took my gaze while turning upon me in sudden.

Yes, she was although smiling, but it was similar to the way a mother would feel melting for her child. This was my most awestruck moment so far with her. She was looking straight in my eyes. Her stick was down and loosely held. Mild blows of the wind were cuddling with her white frock and curly hairs. Her face, as it appeared to me, was turning little pale. Perhaps she was afraid of something upcoming. I wanted to ask her about the matter, but before I could muster up my courage, she asked...
"Won't you like to see *The Garden of Life* in my village?"

I was already astonished by the name, *"Garden of Life!"*

***

(*from Chapter 20*)

Gathering my courage once again, I asked, "What is that *Garden of Life*?"

She didn't turn back nor did she stop. She was only a couple of steps ahead of me. I had been putting up a brave feet in keeping pace with hers. Without disrupting her walk, she replied.

"The Garden of Life is a garden."

"Garden? Is that any different garden?" I asked.

"Yes, it is the real garden."

"Real garden! Real in what sense?" I hoped my restless questions were not offending her.

"You will just see."

"I hope, not something dreadful is coming up in my way." Finally I had exposed my fear.

"Certainly it is not dreadful; especially to those, who have been waiting to see it", she replied.

***

(from Chapter 31)

Seeing such a hollow pit here, anyone could tell what it was. Being about nearly two feet in width, six or seven in length and five-six feet deep down, the pit was not looking a freshly dug one.

Although I had clearly understood it to be a grave-hole, yet before looking upwards to the board, I looked around for several times. I was in search of some otherwise reason in order of proving it to be anything else but not the grave-hole.

I couldn't find around anything except the vast barrenness alone.

Then very next moment, inexplicably although, a certain kind of courage began to fill in my heart. I had stopped fearing, if I started any. I said to myself,

"If it is so, let it be."

I lifted my gaze straight to the board. It said,

"WHEN WILL YOU DIE?"

***

(from Chapter 33)

WITHIN ONLY FEW MINUTES I was standing in face of a high mount cliff which was entirely made of the ground sand. On the side-walls of the downfall of it there were the countless of bird-holes. Those were indeed countless; and so were the playful birds flocking around them. Many birds would enter in some of the holes and then many others would come out from the others. Some time it would seem like all the birds were entering in the holes and none coming out; and some other time it would look like all were coming out, but without anyone getting in. There were many sparrows, besides the blue ones; and there were many birds, besides the sparrows.

"Certainly all these bird-holes must be interweaved from the inside", I thought. The playfulness of the little creatures was spectacularly unique in the garden. Enjoying their sport, I had also forgotten for a minute as to where I stood and for what purpose?

∞ "OH! THE SUN HAS started tilting to the other side of horizon. I must hurry up."

I gave a look at the birds, as if it was my last. But the very moment I turned my face, Lo! My sixth destination had fallen in my sight. It was right beside the other end of the cliff. It stood straight, just like the cliff itself. I kept looking at the birds until I had reached my sixth lamppost.

(from Chapter 37)

MY SEVENTH LAMPPOST LESSON was over. I didn't want to go. I wanted to stay in my *Garden of Life* for longer.

But I also knew that I had to go. It was little girl waiting outside for me. Only because of her I could have reached here. I clearly remembered when she had said, *"Not everybody gets the chance of being here"*.

As I began to move out from the in-fold corner, my gaze fell upon the lilies, jasmine and berries.

Smilingly, I took a few and put in my shirt's pocket.

But oh!

Before I could have made a mistake in the forgetfulness of the moment, I took out my phone.

I smiled on it as if I already knew it. Pressed a button... and Yes, the battery was live yet.

I came back a couple of feet, moved up my head, made a focus upon wooden board, and instantly...

"Click #7."

(from Chapter 40)

HOLD IT.

Without asking for my consent, little girl had now dropped the puppy in my lap. "Its name is Baby Puppy. And it is my best friend you see! Hold it."

In next moment, I was holding a puppy in my hands. My smiles were not stopping at all. For me it was not the first time.

I was willing to talk about the Garden, but little girl was once again up to her own terms only. She waved her stick in the air and started walking.

From some twenty steps ahead she turned back at me and commanded in her typical style,

"Come!"

(Grab your copy of 'See You God' today)

Book snippets from another fiction by
Sudhir Mittal

Nearing the Epilogue
of the book
'Life will Smile at You'

==== ==== ==== ====

Curious Seeker

ONCE UPON A TIME there was a curious seeker. For a very long time he had maintained an unresolved curiosity for attaining the supreme knowledge; more particularly, the knowledge of real substance of the world; and also the knowledge of the substance of himself in such world. In pursuit of his knowledge seeking, he had approached so far all the kinds of possible resorts. Yet he couldn't ever feel himself enlightened fully. He had met and talked to many great knowledge keepers, but he had largely remained confused. He had read many books, but remained unsatisfied. Many times he thought about finding for himself the most virtuous mentor somewhere, but soon he realized that it was the most difficult job on earth.

But yet, he couldn't stop being curious about his substantial and unresolved questions? He thought, if his questions remains unanswered, his entire life would go in vain.

God, who watched from above all about this curious man, thought, "Why such of my rare son, who at least rears the subtle questions about the existence, would think of his entire life going in vain?"

God appeared the very following night, in the dream of such curious man.

The Curious man had seen God for the first time here. Although he had a fair idea that sitting in front of him was none other than but God; but to become doubly sure, he asked, "Who are you?"

God smiled and replied, "I am your imagination."

"Oh! I thought you were God", said the man in a slight disappointment.

God smiled again and said in His esoteric voice, "But what difference does it make? Infact I am better to be your imagination than being distinct from that."

God's words were indeed mystic. The curious man intuited that he was indeed talking to God Himself. He had become very hopeful about his many unresolved curiosities. Glad in his heart, he continued a never heard before conversation with God.

"You said you are my imagination, but how?" The curious man asked.

God replied, "I am your imagination of goodness."

"But see!" the man enquired, "I always imagine many. Which one of those are you?"

God replied again, "I am your every imagination of goodness. Therefore, I am also many."

"Oh! I hadn't thought upon in this way", said the man in nodding.

God smiled, as always.

Then the curious man said, "I had many questions to ask."

"Yes, that's why I have come to your sight", confirmed God, "Ask, I will answer all."

"Tell me, what is happiness?" The man began asking.

"Happiness is you", replied God plainly.

"Me!" on the very first answer of God the curious man had become highly astonished, "How?" He asked.

"Because," answered God, "when you are sad; happiness will be nowhere."

"Oh!" the man said, "That was really simple. I never thought in this way."

God smiled again, as always.

"What life will be my best life?" asked the man.

"It's only the fearless life, what else?" replied God contentedly.

"Fearless life!" again wondered the man, "and how will I get it?"

God replied, "You will get it, when you will become intuitively sure that you are under protection of no one less but God Himself. Indeed there exists no bigger insurance than God."

"Will God Himself really protect me?" The man asked in surprise.

"He already protects all", replied God.

"So, if He The Almighty already protects all, then why I have to become especially sure that I am protected by God?" The man thought that he had made a very tricky question.

God smiled and replied, "Never fall by tricking yourself fool. It's always you and not God who needs the persistence in such eternal assurance of Him. The protected cannot ever take for granted the protection by protector. The very moment you feel protected, you become protected; and the very other moment you feel unprotected, you become unprotected."

"But what will make me feel unprotected when God already protects all?" the man asked thus another tricky question.

"Because whenever you will do a wrong, your thought of fear of wrong-doing will replace the thought of goodness in your heart. You will then be living a fearful life; and thence the protection of God will come off your mind. Once your mind will plunge into the fear, you will no longer feel yourself protected. Your mind is alone your territory of life. Hence the very need of feeling yourself protected, is of yours alone; and not of God."

"Oh!" highly enlightened with the answer, the curious man

began asking his another question,

"Tell me, what is illusion?"

"Oh! The illusion!" God began smiling. "Look up in the sky", commanded God upon man.

Man looked up.

God asked, "What do you see?"

"It's a blue sky today", replied the man.

God said, "What you are seeing upon at this moment is the blue sky, but in reality you already know that there is no sky at all. It is merely a big hollow. Yet you see something there and you call it a blue sky."

The man dropped into a brief contemplation.

God kept on telling, "And if you go only a few hundred miles up above the earth, the blueness of this hollowness, which you call as sky, will vanish; and then the sky will appear to you to be black or maybe of no color at all. But still, you will be seeing upon something there, which you will again call as sky or the space. Isn't that right?"

"Yes", replied the thoughtful man, "That's absolutely right."

God now answered the question of man, "Illusion is your perception of something to be real which is unreal; just the way as you said, it's a blue sky today."

The man continued swinging in the varied kinds of thoughts. Then he began evaluating the answer of God through his own knowledge-bank earlier collected in mind.

In a moment asked the man, "But can you really say what is the clear difference between real and unreal?"

"What remains there permanently is real and what doesn't, is unreal", replied God. His answers had always been succinct and straight.

"But how will I really come to know about that?" wondered the man.

"That will be always up to your individual choice only. If you will hold the impermanent things to be permanent, you will thus choose for yourself the illusion. And on the other hand if you will hold only the permanent things to be permanent, you will attain freedom from the illusion." God revealed.

"But", asked the man, "How will I really come to know that whether I've judged about the things correctly or not?"

"If you find, even for once, the casual pain of your inevitable life-sufferings to be intolerable, know yourself to have certainly misjudged about the things. And it is so because when you will become completely free from the illusion, you will never have to see again the casual pain of inevitable life-sufferings."

"Hmm...", hearing the words of God, the man became very thoughtful. Then he asked about his next curiosity, "What is the most permanent entity in your creation?"

God smiled big and said, "It's you."

"But I am human. Isn't it really human to die?" asked the man in a wondrous voice.

God replied, "That is only how you think. It means that you are not yet free from the great illusion of worldly existence."

"Why", the man wondered, "Don't I really die?"

God revealed here and now the higher truth to this curious man, "You do not die when you die, but you die when you die in the life of others. Even though you may have chosen to remain ignorant about your real entity, yet you cannot do away with this eternal rule of attaining immortality. The rule of your eternity is that – only physically you look to be a mortal; but in reality you can very much choose for you, the immortality. When you never stop living in the life of others, you do not die even after your physical death. The rule of attaining immortality is very much in your own hands. If however, you pretend to be not knowing this rule, it means that you have promoted for yourself nothing but the illusion only."

"Hmm..." lost in varied thoughts over the words of God, the curious man could utter only this.

After a moment, the man said again, "I had many other questions as well."

"Yes, ask. I said it, I will answer all", said God.

The man asked, "What is the test of a true friendship?"

"It's the *founding truth* of that reason of friendship which pulls the friends together. Whenever the foundation of this reason is realized to be untrue by the friends, the friendship remains no more", replied God.

"Hmm..." Then the man asked his next question, "How is it in the world that some are more fortunate than the others?"

Hearing this, God began laughing. He said, "No, no! It's not that. What you call as fortune is just about your own imagination and nothing else. You see a miser as miser and nothing more; and on the other hand, you see a privileged one as privileged one and nothing less. Defect of this discrimination lies in your seeing and not in the objects seen by you."

"But will not you agree at least on this", retorted the man, "that some people are fool and the others are witty. Isn't it really so?"

God replied, "In supremely liberated vision such as of mine, no one is fool and no one is witty. Only those are the wisest who have either already known or at least have begun knowing their own truest substance as equalized with the highest substance of mine."

"Hmm... What you say is indeed the supreme ray of light", said the enlightened seeker.

The man asked his other question, "Tell me this, when will I find my most virtuous mentor?"

God replied, "Maybe never."

The man was shocked. "Oh! How can you say that?"

God said, "Unless you develop a sincerest curiosity about your-own-Self first, you will not find your most virtuous mentor. Even if you will find one, you will always fail to recognize him. But once you become really able to develop a sincere curiosity about your-own-Self, you will enjoyably begin to find your most virtuous mentor, in yourself alone. Essentially in this way, your best mentor rests nowhere outside but he dwells inside your own

Self; maybe however you have not awakened it yet."

"Hmm...", said the man in very thoughtful nodding. He began asking another question then, "Why the man needs God every time?"

"Oh! That is utterly away from the truth. Every time the man needs God only because he thinks so. As long as he will think of God to be different from his own Self, neither will he attain God inside him nor will he find God outside ever. The man should thus continuously meditate upon the truth that God is nothing but man's own imagination of goodness only. To act upon God, he has to act upon goodness only. Once he begins performing in his actions the goodness side of him abundantly, his realization of supreme happiness realized in this way, makes him realize God Himself as well, that too, right within his very own Self."

"Hmm..." The curious man had never been enlightened better before. He asked another question, "If I want to know more about you, you God; what shall be the easiest way?"

God smiled and said, "No, there is no one way easier nor the other difficult. Infact there exists only one way. If you want to know more about me, you will have to know about yourself more."

"And when I would come to know", asked the man, "that I have known myself more?"

God flashed a *mystic* smile. He said, "Then you will stop having the numerous questions and you will become free from the anxiety arising around such questions. Listen here O my loving son, the paramount of one's knowledge. You will come to know the highest order of your entity when there will remain no you; but instead remaining in you will be your eternal oneness with your *Self* alone. And your *Self* is nothing but the part of God in you. This *union* will take place only when you can identify your *Self* with the *Self* of God, and not otherwise. God is no one, but He is the realization of your higher *Self*. Hence, always strive for attaining the higher you; and nothing less. When you will do that, you will become more about the answers and not the questions."

Highly satisfied by the answer of God, the man began searching his list of remaining questions now. Then he asked, "And, when shall I become liberated?"

"You already are", replied God.

"But I don't think so," the man apprehended.

"It is only why you are not. If you become truly sincere in your want of liberation, you will become liberated *at once*. But for so long as you will think of your liberation lying remote from you; you will remain at distance only."

"And what will make me believe that I am at a distance from my liberation yet?" asked the man.
God replied, "It can't be anything else but your own persistent fear, that you haven't deserved your liberation fully yet."

"Hmm..." Sunk in unfathomable ocean of thoughts, the curious man could say that only.

Then on a spur of thought, he said, "Oh! I think I am merely seeing a dream, as if reading merely a preaching book and nothing else. How can I rest assured that what I have been talking to you here and now is real, and not unreal?"

God smiled again and said, "The way you think, is the way you always become. Else, what around you is not a dream? Not only what you think as dream is a dream; but what you think as of the real world is also a dream. Indeed everything is unreal, except the eternity of the oneness of goodness between you and me."

Listening to the great revelation here, the curious man had fallen into a deep contemplation. However awakened in a moment, he asked God again, "Sometimes I wonder, do I really happen to have more questions than ideally I should have? Whether I am more curious than ideally I should become? And even that, whether having only the questions and questions always, isn't itself also a big trouble?"

God looked upon this man with a fatherly smile this time. He said, "But your all wonderings here have happened to be substantial only. See! If you raise a question only with the purpose of raising more number of questions consequently, indeed such tendency of mind is a trouble. But if you can sincerely meditate upon at least a few answers found, you will begin in this way helping yourself to resolve even your upcoming questions by the wisdom source of yourself alone. Once you attain this state, you will be asking more questions from yourself than asking those from the others. In my creation, there can arrive no bigger teacher of you than yourself alone."

Lost in numerous thoughts once again, the man could utter only, "Hmm..."

God continued further, "Only those questions must be thought to be important which belong to the eternity of mankind; and always remember that the eternity of mankind is no different from the eternity of my own. Infact, there remains no you and no me, but there remains only the oneness between both of us. Only the questions about this eternity of oneness are worth to be asked and searched for. Else, all the tumultuous questions about your world and also about your relative existence in such world, are subdued only. Dare always to ask yourself only the subtle questions and not subdued ones."

By this time, the curious man had already begun to become less curious now.

Now God confirmed the liberated state of this man by saying, "In this way, you will not only have fewer questions to perplex about, but you will also be able to intuit the answers within yourself alone. Not only you will have only the subtle questions to search for, but also soon you will attain your supreme peace by getting rid of anxiety generating from the all kinds of questions at all."

Seeing the man here beginning to get too much engrossed in contemplation, God concluded His talk well, "I repeat. Having important questions is a merit, but check, having unnecessary anxiety over those is a trouble. Anxiety should be avoided. When anxiety ceases in your heart, you will attain peace; and when you will attain peace, you will begin finding the answers in yourself alone. And also remember that you always learn those answers more, which intuitively come from within you. Only you are the supreme master and only you are the supreme mentor of yourself."

Then God beheld the man slipping into deep sleep, as if just after a long pleasant dream.

God had now moved about in the air, to reach somewhere else, far in the horizon.

(Read Full Book- Life will Smile at You)

Journey of Books with Sudhir Mittal

See You God

See You God is a one day story of a cute girl of 4 years and a man of 34 years. Both strangers meet each other in mysterious circumstances. As the hours pass by, the talks between them turn in to roaming around the mustard fields, a village and then after around The Garden of Life. Later in the story, the man comes to know about the seven lampposts of his life and also the truth of little girl.

Invoking The Self

Sudhir Mittal's elucidating book 'Invoking The Self' is not a translation or a 'verse-to-verse' commentary of Bhagavad Gita, but it is entirely about the practical need and application of such mystic holy science in our very day to day modern life. 'Invoking The Self' is not about 'Hinduism', but it's about 'The Humanism'.

Invoking *The Self*

The Treasure
of Modern Life
in
Bhagavad Gita

Sudhir Mittal

The Life You Choose

'The world is beautiful, and it starts from you.'
This is the heart of book - The Life You
Choose. This book brings you the wonderful
sixty-four insights around your life. It inspires you
to invoke your own supreme understanding
about many of your important and real life
scenarios. Reading this book, as is widely
acclaimed, is such an enjoyable journey.

365 Gold Coins

Do gold coins interest you? Of course those do, just as in case of anyone else. But do the great inspiring thoughts also interest you as much? Umm... I know you are smiling. Actually the 'relevance' of great inspiring thoughts is much bigger than that of gold coins. Gold coins only attract you, but those do not stay with you.

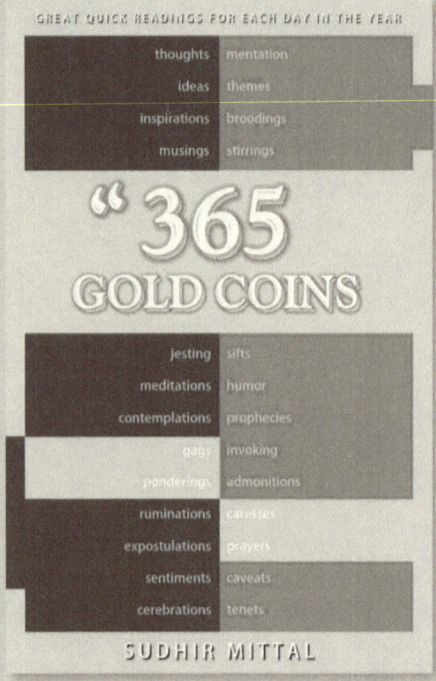

Lead Like A Master

'Lead Like A Master' is a book written for the evolving leaders. It contains not only one hundred insights to illuminate your personality and charisma, but also five hundred different ways of getting you the five star rating at your work-place and life. This book is an ocean for all those minds who are curious for the leadership genesis in them.

Appetizers of The Secret World

You can't wonderfully dominate in a game unless you've known its all tricks beforehand. Least to say, but 'life' is the biggest game that you continue playing in this world; though you might not play it 'superbly' because of your lacking knowledge about the necessary 'tricks' of it. APPETIZERS OF THE SECRET WORLD is a small astonishing book which gives you to learn the best of the worldly tricks.

Sud & Me

The Stories within...
What happens when you talk to someone more
authentic than God?

Life Again

The Story of Your Success
A powerful way to author your life yourself. Write
your journal in this book.

Connect with
SUDHIR MITTAL

Write your feedback at:
booksfeedback@sudhirmittal.in

Write a personal mail at:
sudhirmittal@sudhirmittal.in

FACEBOOK: sudhir.mittal.author
TWITTER: AuthorSudhirM
BLOGS: authorsudhirmittal.blogspot.in/
WORDPRESS: authorsudhirmittal.wordpress.com

Or Visit:
www.sudhirmittal.in